All that Glows

RYAN GRAUDIN

An Imprint of HarperCollins*Publishers*

HarperTeen is an imprint of HarperCollins Publishers.

All That Glows
Copyright © 2014 by Ryan Graudin
www.epicreads.com

Library of Congress Cataloging-in-Publication Data
Graudin, Ryan.
  All that glows / Ryan Graudin.
    pages cm
  Summary: "As Emrys, one of the faery bodyguards of the British monarchy,
is trying not to fall in love with her latest charge, the rowdy bad boy Prince
Richard, an ancient darkness starts preying on the rest of the monarchy"
— Provided by publisher.
  ISBN 978-0-06-218741-3 (pbk.)
  [1. Magic—Fiction. 2. Fairies—Fiction. 3. Bodyguards—Fiction.
4. Princes—Fiction. 5. Kings, queens, rulers, etc.—Fiction. 6. London
(England)—Fiction. 7. England—Fiction.] I. Title.
PZ7.G7724All 2014   2013037285
[Fic]—dc23   CIP
                                                          AC

Typography by Alison Klapthor
14 15 16 17 18 LP/RRDH 10 9 8 7 6 5 4 3 2 1

First Edition

To my mom and dad,
who showed me that true love is possible,
if you fight for it

Love's not Time's fool, though rosy lips and cheeks
Within his bending sickle's compass come;
Love alters not with his brief hours and weeks,
But bears it out even to the edge of doom.
—William Shakespeare, Sonnet 116

All that Glows

One

The sickness hits even before I reach the outskirts of London. A slow-burning nausea descends on my gut and claws through the intestines of my human form. I kneel by the side of the road and wrap my arms around my stomach. The first wave is always the worst. It will pass. It always does.

A light breeze hits my face as the cars whip past in filed lines, like single-minded ants. None of them will stop, I know, because none of them know I'm here. None of them notice the young redheaded woman crouched on the edge of the asphalt. With the remains of an hours-old veiling spell, the mortals' attention slips right off, like beads of water on fish scales.

Minutes pass and the agony of my nausea ebbs back into a dull ache. I straighten and continue down the road into London.

London. The city is different every time I step foot in it. Always, it is growing. More glass, more steel, more subways, more souls. Bricks stacking on bricks to house an empire of electric cables and grinding gears. My magic is weaker here. Some spells I can't even form. It's the same for all of us. Even the ill-willed spirits can't draw upon their full powers in the metropolis. The oldest among us aren't even able to come close to the city; its machines and electricity unravel their stiff spirits.

So the Guard is made of younger Fae, the ones who can withstand the forces of technology. Yet there's always that part of us that longs for the fresh earth: the minty shade of trees and grass, the aroma of rich, crumbling soil—better to us than wine. This is why, during our off hours, many of us haunt the grounds of Saint James's Park.

It's almost dawn by the time I reach the royals' stretch of green. The city has already begun to stir amidst its blanket of violet fog. Black cabs roam up and down the streets and the distant thrum of the Underground resumes beneath my feet. A woman sits by the edge of a lake. She's wearing tawny, high-laced boots, the same those well-pieced soldiers wore when they left for the Great War. There's a pouch of crumbs in the lap of her cotton dress, and purple-headed pigeons cluster at her feet.

I walk to her bench and finally sit, not bothering to hide my smile. "Good morning, Breena."

The bird woman looks up, her wrinkled face drawn back with surprise. Crumbs pour down like a small avalanche as she jumps up. "Emrys! What are you doing here? I thought you were stationed in the Highlands."

I accept the old woman's embrace with open arms. "I was—but Queen Mab reassigned me."

Breena draws back and brushes a stray silver hair from her face. "You look good!" Her eyebrows fly up. "That reminds me . . . you're not supposed to see me like this!"

In an instant, a very different person stands before me. Like me, she looks young—sixteen or seventeen perhaps. Her figure is as slim as a birch trunk and her skin flawless. Her yellow hair sits in a short, curled bob, which she begins meticulously picking through.

"Don't be vain. You can look however you want around me," I tell her. Throughout the long years of our friendship, I've seen Breena in almost every form imaginable: women both youthful and withered, slinking animals, and soaring birds. But these days she's fallen into the habit of the blonde girl, as I now never change my redheaded form.

She ignores my comment. "So you're with the Guard now? Who's your assignment?"

"Prince Richard." The sickness stirs again, tightening around my stomach like a hangman's noose. I fill my lungs with dewy air—as if breathing in the electric hues of morning will make me forget I'm in the epicenter of over two centuries' worth of machinery.

Breena's powder-blue eyes grow wide again. "Richard? Oh no . . . What did you do?"

"I might have managed to lose a Kelpie in a loch. Mab wasn't too happy about it." I laugh; a short, barking sound that echoes across the lake and sends a pair of swans flying. Their wings slice the mist like shears through a curtain—showing the weeping willow on the opposite shore. And beyond that: Buckingham Palace. "Although I can't say the incident was a complete accident. . . ."

My friend shoots me a knowing stare.

"What?" I defend myself. "I got bored shuffling the Kelpies around to the same pastures every day. I thought a change of scenery might be good for them."

"So you took them to a loch and lost one? It's a good thing you're so talented or else Mab would have shipped you off to the Isle of Man instead. You always were one of her favorites."

"Some might consider London an even worse punishment." I shrug off my friend's comment. It's true that I've advanced ranks in Mab's court much more quickly than others of my generation, but it isn't something I enjoy emphasizing.

"She must be mad if she assigned you to the prince." Breena sighs at the riotous pigeons that cover her feet, squabbling over the promise of crumbs. "There's no more, you've eaten it all. Now shoo!"

They fly away in swirling tempest of dust and feathers. I whip the cloud of dirt out of my face. "He can't be *that* bad."

"He's a challenge. No one volunteers to guard him anymore. He takes too much energy. When's your first shift?"

"Tonight."

"Friday night? You'll see." Breena retrieves the leathery shell of her seed pouch and folds it over her fingers, like she's binding a wound. "He's just returned from his graduation at Eton. There's bound to be some . . . *celebrating.*"

I roll my eyes. No prince could possibly be that bad, even if he is seventeen. No one, not even Henry VIII, had pushed the Fae to abandon our oath to the crown.

The last time I saw my least favorite monarch, he was covered in boils, grease dribbling down his chin as he tore into the leg of a goose. The ghosts of his wives— disturbed, unrested souls— clustered around, haunting him in all of their vehemence. But still, he kept eating. He never stopped cramming his gullet with the flesh of beasts.

Perhaps our magic is getting even weaker than I thought.

"I think I can handle him," I say in a voice even tarter than lemons. "I've guarded the royals before this, you know."

The acid behind my tongue only grows, rises like a beast coming out of a long winter sleep. I can't ignore it anymore. It's too present. All over. The edges of my mouth grow heavy with spit as whatever's inside my stomach begins its inevitable escape.

"The world's changed," Breena warns. "You haven't been in the Guard for a long time. My guess is you've gone soft."

My palm, flat as a board, presses into my lips. But it doesn't matter. The sick rises and I bend double. Gravel digs sharp into my hands, coating them in a layer of soft white dust. The sourness in my mouth gets worse—spills out. My knees shake and the bile sticks to my lips.

"You'll see," Breena says, bending slightly to give my shoulder a pat. "Welcome back."

It's been long years since my last shift—years spent tending to Mab's Faery court in the Highlands. It was an existence I quite enjoyed, soaking up the power of the hills for endless days and joining the scouts: Fae of old, too ancient to enter the cities. We scoured the land for wild, errant magic—spirits who sought to break that strict barrier between the realms of magic and mortal. Spirits whose chaos might tear the thinly stretched veil we maintain. I'd considered my days in the grimy modernity of London long behind me. But Mab had other plans.

Despite this gap, the necessary spells come like a reflex. I cover myself in all of the cursory enchantments before I head to Kensington Palace for my first shift. Helene, the youngling I'm relieving, exudes both gratitude and pity as she leaves me instructions.

"Don't ever let him see you, and if he does by chance, erase that memory. You must cloak yourself or take the guise of a stranger at all times."

I nod, barely suppressing my impatience. Helene is only telling me what every Fae in the Guard already knows. But Helene's younger than me; from the tinge of her aura, she's no more than two hundred years old. If we were outside of the city, spinning across the moors and lochs or feasting in the subterranean chambers of Mab's court, she wouldn't dare speak to me first, much less instruct me. Age is superior among the Fae. Everywhere, it seems, but here. In London, everything is messy.

"Oh, and don't *ever* let him leave your sight." The young Fae wags a finger in the air to make her words feel bigger, more important. "There've been . . . incidents over the past few weeks. Green Women and the like. Richard attracts them like moths to a bonfire. Tonight's bound to be a wild one, with his just finishing Eton and all. Good luck."

"Thanks. I've got it," I say curtly. I try not to think of how my mouth holds just a hint of bile.

Some breeze throws strands of flaming hair in my face. I don't have to turn to know that Helene has left.

Through the crack in the door, I see the corner of a large bed filled with rumpled cloud-white sheets. One of Richard's lanky arms drapes over the side, his fingertips brushing the ornamental rug.

Like the rest of London, the prince's bedroom is a living collage of the passage of time. Richard's bedside table—a decadent, nineteenth-century piece crafted out of wolf-gray marble and mahogany—is covered with the unnatural blinking lights of electronics. A digital clock. A mobile phone that shivers and glows at odd moments. His chrome-colored laptop is tucked in the back of the same antique desk Queen Victoria once wrote her letters on. Chubby, meticulously painted cherubs born in George I's era gaze down from their ceiling frescos at stereo speakers. They smile on, as they always have.

It's almost seamless, the way the past is entombed with the present here.

"Why are you sleeping?" I slip into the room and approach the bed. The light filtering through the curtains is quickly dropping into the bruised plum color of night. No normal mortal is asleep at this hour.

As I draw closer to the prince I can feel the magic pulse more strongly through my limbs. Something in the royal blood excites our magic, strengthens it. It's that source of strange, untapped power we call "blood magic."

The first time I saw Prince Richard, he was bareheaded and swaddled against his mother's breast. My second, most recent glimpse of His Majesty was during a visit to Breena over a decade ago, when he made his younger sister cry at Wimbledon by giving her an inappropriate and painful wedgie beneath her tennis dress. Through the tangle of sheets, I catch my first sight of teenage Richard. His teeth are no longer too large for his lips. The round, fat face of his childhood has sharpened—strong, freckle-dusted cheekbones rise to set off a nice pair of finely lined eyes. These, along with his sleek dirty-blond hair, are enough to make any girl aware of his presence, even without his royal title.

Richard gives a very un-regal snore; the noise makes me twitch. Was I leaning in too close? Even with all of the magical precautions, mortals sometimes feel our presence. I take a step away from his bed. Perhaps there are some things I've forgotten over the years.

His eyes open, and for the briefest second I feel their hazel irises on me. Something inside me clenches. I jump and check the veiling spells—the delicate magic that keeps me hidden from all mortals' view. They're perfectly in place.

Richard crawls out of bed, and when the sheets fall away his bare body comes into view. To my surprise, my cheeks grow hot and I find myself staring at the Persian rug: studying the story of warriors on horseback and blooming fruit orchards some artist wove into its jewel-toned threads. I know they're from a different time and place, yet they don't look so different from the Knights of the Round Table: waving their spears and swords, digging their heels into the stallions' flanks.

When the flush falls from my face, I get the courage to look up again. This is hardly the first time I've seen a monarch naked. Guarding royalty often requires front-row seats. Despite this, I keep Richard on the edge of my vision as he saunters to his vast walk-in wardrobe.

He emerges fully dressed, fumbling with the buttons of his shirt as he approaches the mirror on the wall. His eyes dip low and make the steady climb up his own reflection, taking all of it in. It's not until the prince sees his hair that he pauses to make an adjustment. He rakes his fingers through it, spilling it over his forehead in a boyish tousle.

"Just a few hours. Can't drink too much tonight." His fist moves down to rub the barely-there stubble edging his face. After a few strokes against his chin, he straightens and reaches for the velvet blazer on the chair in front of him.

"I hope you're right." I sigh and follow him out the door.

Two

Of course I find myself sitting at a bar. The prince's nightly play has led me to the Darkroom, a club nestled in the heart of London. My fingers tap against the lacquered wood as I stare absently at the cocktail menu. I should be watching the dance floor, watching Richard. But the movement of so many heads whipping to the music makes mine throb.

"Up to no good, that one." The bartender nods over at the prince and grunts as he wipes the counter down. "They let him in here because he's good for business. All the girls buy him drinks, and he gets drunker than a jilted woman on her wedding anniversary. Mark my words, he's gonna get us shut down for all that underage drinking. Him and all his kid friends. Can I getcha anything, love?"

I jump a little when I realize he's addressing me. In crowds as large as the one at this club, I don't bother wasting energy on veiling spells. There are so many pretty faces, Richard will glaze over mine without a thought.

I rub my temple and glance at the rainbow row of liquor bottles against the back wall. The brutal nausea brought on by the club's pulsing lights and stereos won't let me keep down anything more substantial than tonic.

"Just a sparkling water," I tell him, my smile apologetic.

The bartender's mouth pinches to the side, forehead scrolling tight with wrinkles. "Why's a pretty girl like you getting dressed up and hitting the clubs for water?"

I pretend I don't hear him as he slides the drink into my hands, creating fresh streaks on his bartop. It's easier than coming up with a lie in this storm of color and sound. "Could I get a lemon with that?"

"Sure, sure," he mutters, and retreats to the end of the bar. He doesn't even make it to the lemon tub before he's distracted by another order.

I take my drink to the edge the dance floor. There's a long booth in a corner made of shadows, where I can get a full view of the crowd.

The prince is still dancing. Amber liquid sloshes from the top of his beer bottle as he moves from side to side. Although several of his classmates from Eton are also on the floor, the dancing girls have eyes only for

Richard. They jostle one another, swarm around him as thick as ants on a piece of picnic bread. I can barely see the prince through the piles of hair and wiggling bodies. Thankfully none of them look dangerous. None of them are dressed in green.

The sparkling water does wonders for my stomach. I'm halfway through the glass when Breena arrives. The sight of her, with her tight silver dress and stilettos, doesn't startle me. I felt her aura approaching long before this.

"What are you doing here?" I ask as she slides into the booth beside me. She looks perfectly pieced together, as if the sickness isn't touching her at all—which would be impossible. Any Fae within a mile would feel the intense thrash of the Darkroom's electrical equipment.

"Just trying to look out for you." Breena shrugs. "I thought you could use an extra pair of eyes. Richard's not the easiest first shift ever. Plus I'm sure this is doing wonders for your stomach."

"I'll get over it." I take another bubbling sip and look over at the prince, who's taken a break from his dancing to get another beer. I've lost count of how many he's had.

"Of course you will." Breena pulls some bright lipstick out of her clutch and swathes her lips scarlet. I wonder how much pain this technology is shooting through her body. She shows no signs of it. "Seen any Green Women yet?"

"No. I don't think they'll try anything tonight." The last statement is more of a hope than a certainty. Encounters with Green Women are never pleasant. Especially when they're hunting.

"Oh, they'll come," Breena says. "It's Friday night. They're hungry."

"Then it's a good thing you're here," I tell her. It's assuring to have Breena's magic, about a century more seasoned than mine, as a backup.

"Yep." Her brilliant red lips curve into a smile as she glances over the dance floor. "How's Richard doing?"

I follow her stare. The prince is stumbling off to a table, half dragged by an eager, skimpy brunette. "He's certainly the life of the party."

The hair on the back of my neck suddenly bristles. Another immortal is here. Breena feels it too.

"See anything?" I ask Breena, unwilling to look away from Richard.

"Two of them," she says. "Front entrance."

For just one second I break eye contact to view the new threat. Two women, tall, blonde, and breathtaking, break through the crowd. Men and women, everyone they pass, stare at their lithe, supple bodies. More than a few mouths drop open.

The one in the pale green dress scouts the room for suitable prey. I can tell by the way her dark eyes widen that she's caught Richard's aura. She starts walking; each stride brings her closer to the prince.

"Move," I grunt, and push Breena out of the booth. My head spins, at the mercy of the club's stacked subwoofers. I push past the pain, the dizziness. There's no time for it.

The Green Woman has eyes only for her victim. She doesn't notice as I slip through the crowd and stop directly in her path. It isn't until we're inches apart that she suddenly registers my aura. She stops, her beautiful face wrinkles with disappointment.

"Back off," I warn in my most threatening tone. My fists are clenched. It's doubtful she'll try anything in a room full of mortals. Yet sometimes, if a Green Woman is desperate enough . . .

Her pale pink lips protrude. "Just a taste . . . I promise I won't kill him."

My eyes narrow. "There are plenty of other men here. Go seduce one of them."

When the Green Woman realizes her opportunity at

the prince is lost, she bares her teeth. They're flawlessly white and sharp. Fury clouds her eyes and I get a glimpse of her true form: the dead, gray thing that lurks behind such saccharine beauty. A shudder creeps down my spine, but my face doesn't flinch. I refuse to show fear.

She saunters off to resume her scouting. A rain shower of relief breaks over me—for a moment the world becomes steady again. The feeling is short-lived, however, when I turn to find that the prince is gone.

Curses form under my breath. I reach out and search for him with my mind. His aura is strong—he's still in the club. Pins and needles of worry bite into every surface of my body when I realize who else is missing: the other Green Woman.

"Bree!" My friend is closer than I expect. Just a few steps behind me. There's a wildness in her face. She's ready to fight. "Did you see where Richard went?"

"He ran off to the bathroom." The sequins of her dress slink and glow like a wet serpent as she turns, those wintery eyes tearing the room apart. "Go! I'll take care of the other one."

I run, faster than I should through a crowd of mortals, in the direction of the bathrooms. Two men in black suits—the prince's human security—stand outside the men's room. The Green Woman must have spelled them to stay away. I mutter a short spell and ghost past them, unseen.

The restroom is empty, with one obvious exception. A pair of forest-green stilettos peeks out from the bottom of the final stall. My heart flutters at the sight. I practically fly the distance and wrench the door open.

The prince leans against the side of the stall, head wreathed in obscene graffiti and eyes half closed with the weight of his evening drinks. The second Green Woman lurks close; her pale hair spills across his chest as she leans in. Her head jerks around when the door opens, eyes lit dark with rage. When she sees me, all the beauty of her flesh melts away. Her pink skin withers to a sickly greenish gray, like some corpse frozen in the depths of a peat bog. The teeth beneath her mottled lips grow ragged, meant for tearing tendon from bone. She hisses and grips her prey with long, ratty fingernails.

Although I've fought Green Women before, this one's ghoulish grin is unnerving. I have to look at Richard and see the smooth, unblemished skin of his throat to remember why I'm here.

I launch myself between her and the prince. At the same moment she lunges, grungy teeth aimed for

Richard's throat. I catch the bite with my shoulder, gasping with shock as the pain lances my bone. The force of my body throws the prince onto the toilet, far from the Green Woman's reach. He blinks slowly; his jaw grows slack at what he sees.

The Green Woman shrieks with frustration as she pulls away from me. Dark blood coats her teeth and stains her lips. Her feral eyes wheel to where the prince is slouched over the toilet. There's intense, desperate hunger behind her gaze. She'll do anything to have him.

"He's under Queen Mab's protection," I tell her, once more positioning myself between the pair.

"And what are you going to do to stop me, little woodling?" the Green Woman rasps. Her eyes focus past my wounded shoulder.

I ignore her name-calling and invoke the old magic: *"Blodes geweald."*

The familiar rush of power surges through my veins, seizes my body till I feel only barely in control. Every piece of me buzzes with the pure energy of it. The Green Woman jumps forward again and I hold out my hands. When the edges of my fingers brush her dead skin, a massive shock rattles through me. The world grows white with savage magic. It throws the Green Woman back with such force that the stall door crumples around her body. I watch the wreckage. Nothing moves. Small wisps of smoke rise from the Green Woman's body, but I know she's not dead. It takes more than a little flash of light to unmake them.

"Stay away from the prince," I warn the crisp, blackened body, "or it'll be worse next time."

There's a long, low hiss and the room fills with black smoke. She's gone.

A sharp cough draws my attention back into the stall. The prince is trying to stand, bracing himself with unsteady hands.

"Who—who are you? W-what the hell just happened?" The alcohol has messed with his balance. He slips and falls back against the toilet.

I sigh and walk through the clearing smoke to where the door lies. The Green Woman's outline is clear in the wrinkled metal. At my touch it smoothes back to its original casting. I direct the door back through the air to the frame, where it comes to rest on its hinges.

"I'm Emrys, your Frithemaeg. Your Faery guardian," I say, and turn to face him again.

He stares at me, his mouth gaping. When I kneel down close, he stays perfectly still. Our eyes meet, this time for real. My body hums with the same strange current that caught me on my first sight of him. Half of me expects it. I push past the feeling, forcing myself to focus on erasing Richard's memory.

"Bloody hell!" the prince exclaims, and breaks our eye connection to stare at his hands. They're soft, unworked. Only the fingertips are calloused, relics of practiced guitar chords. "Did you feel that?"

I fall still, uncertain of what to do next. Richard felt it too? What was it? I check the air for traces of a spell, but there's none outside of the banishing magic I used on the Green Woman.

The squeal of the restroom door breaks my concentration. Another mortal is here, in the room. I should get rid of him before he witnesses any magic. He'll have less of a headache if I use a banishment spell instead of a memory wipe.

This man is even drunker than the prince. That much is obvious as he swaggers across the dark tile floor. His eyes are oddly detached as they fall on me, on my body. A sick grin plasters his face.

"Well, well. What do we have here?" He lurches forward. The movement highlights just how arched and beaky his nose is. Like some bird of prey. "A pretty girl, all by herself in the loo. That's l-lucky."

Disgust overwhelms me. If I were mortal, truly powerless, there's no telling what this man might do to me.
He moves forward with awkward, wide steps—like a
puppet being worked by a five-year-old. He's less than
an arm's length away when he reaches out, his fingers
twitching and eager.

The magic isn't even on my lips when the man falls
to the ground. I blink. Richard is by my side, standing over the howling drunk as he writhes on the floor
clutching his face and his awful, running nose.

"Don't touch her." His words are deep, forceful. The
slur of his drinks has vanished in the adrenaline of the
moment.

Hands fall from the drunk's face, revealing a nasty,
crimson split above his lip. It melds perfectly with the
blood from his nostrils. He snarls and tries to get up
again. Tries to grab for me.

Richard's fist descends on its target with sobering
precision. This time the man doesn't move. He's a loose
marionette, all angles, out cold on the tile.

"Are you okay?" Richard asks as he shakes out his
fist, wincing.

The prince came to my rescue. He protected me. This

is so shocking, so unprecedented, that I can't think of anything to say.

I can't let him remember what happened.

"Forgiete." I face him, murmur my enchantment in the old tongue.

The magic is gentler this time. His face grows blank as the spell takes him, wiping away the past few minutes. I guide him toward the door before his senses clear up enough to see his passed-out victim. Dazed and disoriented, Richard wanders through the crowd back to the bar top.

Breena is there, lounging on a bar stool. I grab the empty seat next to her and try to ignore the sickness that's once again worming its way through my stomach.

"The other one?" I search the dance floor for a glimpse of the pale green dress.

"She's gone," Breena assures me. "Nice work in there. I see you haven't lost your touch. Need another sparkling water?"

I'm about to answer when there's a commotion at the other end of the bar, where Richard is sitting. I look down to find him pointing at me. For a moment, I doubt my spell's effectiveness.

"Get that pretty redhead a drink on me!" he shouts

at the bartender, and slings his arm over an ecstatic, big-breasted blonde.

I start to breathe again. He's forgotten all about the Green Woman. And that moment between us. Whatever it was.

Three

The prince's Monday morning starts early. An anxious rap on his bedroom door from one of the butlers wakes him only an hour after sunrise.

"Your Highness?" the staff calls through the crack in the door. "Your father's here. He wishes to speak with you in the dining room."

Richard's curses get caught up in the goose down of his pillow. To my amazement, he manages to twist out of bed and change into a freshly pressed shirt. The only evidence of his eventful weekend are fly-aways in his tawny hair and swollen knuckles. My own head still swims, hungover from the electrical buzz of subwoofers.

"Yes, thank you. I'll be there in a moment," Richard says to the door. He's thrown on his royal demeanor like a well-worn dinner jacket.

His father is in the dining room, just as the butler promised. Even surrounded by gold mirrors and turquoise walls, the king manages to stand out. He sits at the head of the table, owning the seven chair lengths of mahogany stretched in front of him. There's no food, only a steaming cup by his interlaced hands. I glance over at the king's guardian. She looks disinterested in Prince Richard's arrival and barely acknowledges mine with a nod. I have a feeling she's witnessed this scene before.

King Edward in his anger is an intimidating sight. The dead weight of his stare disrobes me, the invisible witness. Richard, however, seems unaffected. He stands at the side of the table with his arms behind his back and his jaw set.

Slowly, deliberately, King Edward spreads a crumpled magazine out on the polished wood. The front-page photograph reveals Richard, drink in hand, dancing. PRINCE RICHARD UNCENSORED: THE ROYAL'S TRUE COLORS looms above it in bold, blocky letters.

"'Prince Richard punched me in the face without provocation,' one insider reports. His face is deeply bruised from the encounter with the underage royal's fist. 'He knocked me out cold in the restroom.'"

Partway through the reading, Richard tucks his hands behind his back, the healthy one covering its damaged partner. I curse myself for not thinking to wipe my attacker's memory.

King Edward looks up. "Did you attack this man?"

Richard barely glances down at the page. His face remains stiff, unreadable.

"Did you attack him?" his father asks again. There's a dangerous edge to his voice.

"I—I don't remember," the prince says finally. He's not looking at his father or the magazine. His eyes dance around a nearby vase of flowers: all purple, green, and white, popping beneath the paradise-blue walls. Some of the petals hold crystal-domed dewdrops, fresh from the florist.

For a moment his father is silent. "You don't remember?"

Almost imperceptibly Richard gives a small flinch.

"You're making a fool of yourself, a fool of the crown!" The king's fist thunders down. His teacup of Earl Grey tips and bleeds its contents across the table. "You aren't even a week out of Eton and you're already getting so bloody plastered you can't remember if you attacked this man or not!"

The prince is a statue, still taking in every minute detail of those flowers.

"You're a strong spirit—I know that, Richard. Stop wasting what you have and get your arse in gear. How are you ever going to amount to anything if all you do is drink and punch people in the face?" The king's lip curls with disgust. "Some people think the monarchy is a relic of the past—that it should be done away with. But the nation still needs us, Richard. They need an heir they can depend on. Someone they can relate to. When I was your age, I was planning to travel the world for my gap year—to get an idea of what's out there. To culture myself! And you? You haven't even planned one! I'll go to hell and back before I let you spend twelve months pissing in the corner of some pub."

King Edward's streamlined face, so much like his son's, flushes from pink to crimson with the effort of his speech. The rage in his aura builds with the power of an oncoming wave. The room grows hot with it.

"Do you have anything to say?" He relents, once the breath wheezes out of him. "Anything at all."

Without a word, Richard turns and walks out the door. I have no choice but to follow, leaving the king to his crumpled magazine and spilled cup of morning tea.

It isn't until Richard is far from his father that the emotions begin to bubble up, a scalding boil. He walks quickly, furiously, like a sentinel ordered to march double-time. He wanders the same corridors twice, making

anxious loops past the paintings of long-dead men suspended along Kensington Palace's grand hallways. By his
third circuit, he escapes to the gardens. It's here beside an
orangey sea of marigolds that he kneels down.

"I'm sorry." I sit next to the prince. "I should've erased
his memory too."

The words don't make me feel any better. They can't
take back the red of his father's rage or those sharp,
flinty words.

The prince straightens; air, crackling and static, fills
his lungs. Bright pink lines his eyes. Part of me wilts at
the sight.

Richard's head turns slowly, clearly in my direction.
For a moment, I forget he cannot see.

"You sense me, don't you?" My whisper grows even
quieter as I double-check the veiling spell. It's as strong
as it's always been, keeping our worlds an unknowable
distance apart.

He shifts and I start, realizing exactly how close I'd
sat next to him. Closer than a watching Fae should.

The crunching of gravel causes both of us to look
up. It's Princess Anabelle, Richard's younger sister. Her
straw-colored curls, round and soft like a china doll's,
almost fall apart from the briskness of her march. The

rest of her is just as preened. Penciled eyes and lips. A dash of powder to bring life to her cheeks. At sixteen, the princess looks as pieced together as the portraits of her forebears.

Helene trails her at an acceptable distance. The distance a Fae should keep from her royal. I swallow, trying to ignore the guilt that's joined the rumblings of my still-tender insides.

"Hey." Anabelle kneels beside her brother, still managing to look all grace in her heels and pencil skirt. "Are you okay?"

Richard clears his throat. "Yeah. Yeah, I'm fine."

But his sister presses. "I heard the yelling. What happened?"

The prince, so rigid in the face of his father's fury, breaks beneath her question. "I don't know. That's the problem."

"Another blackout?" A frown lurks on the edge of Anabelle's pearly-rose lips, but she has enough control to hide it.

"I didn't drink that much. I swear . . ." Richard sighs. "Some guy told the tabloids I attacked him."

"And you believed it? Richard, it's a bloody *tabloid!*" The princess pats her brother's back and I notice even her nails are white-tipped and perfect. "I'm sure nothing happened."

"I woke up with this." Richard holds out his hand, so swollen I can no longer make out the bony ridges and valleys of his knuckles.

A look close to admiration crosses his sister's face as she inspects the injury. "Well, you must have had one hell of a good reason to hit him."

The prince laughs. There's no humor in the sound. "I'm a mess, aren't I, Belle?"

Anabelle places his injured hand back on his knee. "We all are. You just have a special knack for showing it."

"It's not like you could do anything wrong. Not in Dad's eyes anyway. You could run naked through the streets and he'd still think you were blooming perfect."

"Probably an exaggeration," his sister points out. "You know, the only reason he's so hard on you is because he loves you. He's worried about you.

"Dad does have a point though." The princess's voice plummets into a whisper, even though everything around them—the paths, the flower beds—is empty. "People are watching us, Richard. You and me. We're a symbol of something, whether we want to be or not. Sooner or later you're going to have to start living up to that."

Richard's only response is a long, leaden sigh. Like the sound of a sleeping bear poked into drowsiness.

"I think you should apologize to Dad."

"What?" The prince starts. "Belle, I didn't *do* anything! I told you, it was a blackout!"

"Maybe not, but you still put yourself in that position. The only way Dad is ever going to trust you is if you take the first step and show some initiative."

"I didn't do anything wrong!" Richard's cheeks mottle red and peach. "I was just having some fun with my friends like anyone else!"

"But we *aren't* just anyone else," the princess insists. "We have responsibilities."

Richard breaks in. "Who made you such a guiding light anyway? You don't have to pretend to be Mum. She does her own job well enough."

"I—I'm just trying to help," Anabelle says, the hurt clear in her earth-shaded eyes.

"I don't need your help right now, Belle. I need to be alone. I have to work this out myself." The prince rakes his hands through his hair and tugs at the back of his neck. As if the motions will rid him of his sister's words. "Go. Please."

"Fine," she says, all terseness. "But don't say I didn't warn you. Things have to change soon, Richard. You can't keep doing this to Dad and Mum."

Richard stares at the gravel. His eyes stay locked on the small, sharp rocks. When his sister is completely out of sight he kicks at the path, sending a rattling spray of stones into the opposite flower bed. They rain on innocent petals, fast and spitting, like shrapnel.

"What's wrong with me?" He looks down at his knuckles, at the hand he bruised protecting me. The edges of his dark lashes glisten, brimming with too much emotion.

I should be sitting by the flower bed, dodging those pebbles. I should just accept my blame in this and move on. I should wait for the next Fae to relieve my shift, so I can go ride the Underground and clear my head.

Instead I touch him.

It's nothing significant, just the barest trace of my finger on his shoulder. The act is so sudden, so impulsive and not me, that I don't realize what I've done until the prince reacts. He jerks back like a man burned, eyes darting faster than a spooked horse until they focus on where I'm sitting.

"Who—who are you?" he asks, his stare vague. "How'd you get in here?"

He sees me. It's not possible. The veiling spell . . . somehow, my magic has failed.

I'm like a hare, frozen by the headlamps of an approaching vehicle. My mind dashes in hundreds of directions, but I can't seem to make myself actually move.

"Where did you come from?" Richard's eyebrows dive together. His thoughts are churning, playing out on every corner of his face, trying their best to reconcile my sudden appearance.

I should wipe his memory, cause another blackout. The spell is simple, one I've formed thousands of times. It should be little more than a reflex to take the past minute out of his head.

But I can't make myself say the word.

"I—I have to go," I mutter as I stand.

"What? Wait!" The prince reaches out his hand. His fingers brush mine—warm, tingling.

I turn and run.

High Street Kensington station swarms with humanity. Women whose arms are loaded with shopping bags, hooded teenagers talking into their mobiles, and men with briefcases all rush past. They're unaware of the world around them, focused on getting home.

I get on the first train that rushes to the platform. The car is nearly full—I fight to wedge myself through the steel doors. More than a few times I feel like gagging. The train is all metal, sweat, and body heat. Grinding wheels on a track. . . . Everything the magic inside me hates. Writhes against.

But the train is underground, a grace that is more than saving. The countless meters of earth above and around us feed my spirit. It doesn't matter that I'm sitting in a metal tube, barreling through the tunnels. As long as I'm here, my magic will replenish.

I don't remember which Fae first thought to ride the trains. More than likely it was one of the younglings— the ones whose stomachs were closer to steel themselves. The ones who weren't horrified when engineers started carving out tunnels in our precious earth for the trains to burrow through. We all use it now.

The train is far from central London by the time I finally get a seat. I pay little attention to the names of each stop as we plow farther into the city's outskirts. I let my head rest against the rattling window. Wind through the cracks and the lullaby hush of the tracks help calm my stomach.

But the thought, the full weight of what I've just done, still makes me want to retch.

I revealed myself to a mortal—to Britain's prince—and instead of wiping his memory, I ran. I broke the barrier between magic and mortal. And I didn't fix it.

Richard isn't what I'd expected. Not at all. I went into my first shift ready to wrangle an uncontrollable party animal. Instead I found a young man who, despite his better judgment, was brave enough to defend me. Someone who wasn't afraid of me or the power I displayed.

Something about Richard is different from the others I've guarded. Something connects us: something dangerous and electric.

And I don't know why.

Urgent needles dig into the back of my neck, and all of these baffling thoughts flee my mind's center stage. The aura is both unsettling and hard to find. The train car is still crammed tight with bodies, wedged side by side in their seats or clutching the bright blue hand poles. All of the mortals are swallowed in their own little electronic worlds: music players, screens with words and moving pictures, conversations with people who are miles away. Not one of them sees the huntress.

Like me, the Green Woman is very visible—we have to be in such cramped, crowded places or we'd be stampeded. She creeps as slowly as she can down the train's wobbling aisle. Her dress clings to her like emerald plastic wrap, flaunting a bursting bosom and sculpted thighs. Those lips are quirked into a permanent coy grin as she goes down the line, eyeing men like baskets of fish and chips.

She's hungry. She has to be if she's being so obvious about her prowl: during daylight hours, in a crowded area, alone. Her aura is weaker than most, which explains why it took me so long to notice her presence. It also explains why none of the men are looking up. Her powers of persuasion are as watered-down as her magic.

Looking at the way she skirts down the car, so desperate for more power, so starving, I almost feel sorry for her. But she chose this life. She chose to prey on mortals just as I chose to protect them.

The lurch in my stomach reminds me that I'm not much better off.

The Green Woman is so focused on catching

someone's, anyone's attention, that she almost passes me by. Her smile, false as it is, can't stand my presence. Up close it's easier to tell that she hasn't killed in a very long time. There are cracks in the magic of her face, patches where her beauty isn't so dazzling.

"Sister," she says after we first lock eyes.

The way this word leaves her makes me wonder if I know this spirit, if our paths have crossed before. Long ago, in the days before King Arthur's alliance, the Green Women, Banshees, Black Dogs, and all of the other soul feeders weren't so different from us Frithemaeg. In the beginning of things, we're all the same substance: pure spirit, power drawn up from the earth. It's only when our lives become physical—when bodies are selected, choices made, and oaths sworn—that we diverge.

I look at this huntress long and hard. Behind the hollow sheen of her eyes, I see the lives of all the men she's devoured. All the souls she's fed on to make her own stronger.

And I'm sure we've never met.

"You should be moving on now," I tell her.

The huntress keeps walking; her stilettos stamp hard on the faux tile. Every step is a gunshot to my ears.

* * *

By the time the train pulls into Tower Hill, my entire car is abandoned. The feminine voice from the loudspeakers informs me that the train will terminate here. I stand, noting how much steadier my legs are after hours underground.

The streets outside are heavy with dark; only a few flickering streetlamps fight the shadows. Most of London is safely nestled behind locked doors, unaware that Black Dogs and other soul feeders are prowling, searching for easy prey in poor drunk souls.

Something twinges inside me. There's another immortal nearby. I tense, my stare roving across sidewalks cast star-set blue by streetlamps.

"It's just me." I turn at the familiar voice to find her outline, lean and unmistakable: Breena.

Dread joins my ever-present nausea. I know why she's tracked me down. She wants an account for what I've done: why I abandoned Richard so suddenly without requesting a replacement.

"Is there something you'd like to explain to me?" Breena approaches with selective steps, the same way a cat uses grass and slowness to snag a songbird. And as much as I want to, I can't fly away. The older Fae would only follow.

There was a time when I would've told Breena everything. We've endured much together: the fall of Camelot; watching the Black Death wash over the king-dom, luring soul feeders to every doorway in Britain. Those three days when London was alight, a living hell of fire and ash. Handling monarchs like John Lackland and Mary I with tendencies bloodier than uncooked beef. And wars: the Wars of the Roses, the Hundred Years' War, the War to End all Wars . . . so many wars.

Throughout all of this and against all the customs of our kind, Breena has treated me as an equal. Despite her one hundred years of seniority, she both advises and respects me. I trust her with my life and beyond.

"Let's go for a walk," she suggests. "I haven't been to the Tower of London in a while."

Breena's energy seems boundless as she strides ahead. There's no rust or corrosion in her aura. No weariness to her magic. As if all these modern metals and electric currents swirling around us don't exist.

"How do you do it?" I strive to keep up the pace, hoping that my question will distract her from the rep-rimand I know is coming.

"What?" She looks back, and seeing my distance, immediately slows.

"London. The sickness. All of it. You haven't been to the Highlands in twenty years. How do you keep going for so long?"

We approach the dreary, aging prison. I brush my hand against its cool lichen-covered stones, and a chill shoots through me. Death and pain lie in these walls, stained with so much royal blood.

"Love, I think," Breena says as we pass through the iron portcullis.

I blink, allowing the word to simmer for a moment. *Love.* A word most Fae never even think to utter. There was duty, magic, power, honor—but never love. That was for humans, to fill the gaps in their lives. To make the shortness of their years bearable.

"A man?" I choke out the possibility. Only a few of our kind got tangled up in the emotions of mortal men—we never spoke of them again.

"Oh no." She shakes her head, blonde curls bouncing. "No man. I mean all of them, the mortals. Their songs, their emotions, their creations, their stories. If you embrace this city and crawl under its skin . . . there's something here. Much of the Guard has seen that. That's why the younger ones have stayed here so long. Most of the older Fae are just too aloof to find it. They stay in the Highlands and dictate things from afar."

"But the sickness. It's been eating away at me for days." I wrap my arms around my stomach, where the nausea burns always, like acid.

"I don't even notice it anymore. For the most part," Breena admits. "It balances out after a few years."

"Will you ever go back to the Highlands?"

"Nothing but Mab's direct order can drag me away from here."

We walk into the center of the old fortress, coming to one of the few benches scattered across the Tower of London's grassy squares. Breena sighs as she rests against the hard wooden slats.

"Now, you must have an excellent explanation for what happened this morning, because, try as I might, I can't think of a reason why you would abandon your post like that."

I stare at the patch of lush, manicured grass. Beyond us, in the shadows of cannons and trees, sets of beady eyes stare back. They belong to the Tower ravens, gifted with speech and intelligence—prophets clad in black feathers. To call them "birds" would be an insult.

Though the Tower ravens can form words with their sharp tongues, it's only after receiving their visions that they use this gift. The last time they spoke to our kind was many decades ago, when a blitz of fire and smoke nearly razed the entire city. Their vision foretold that doom.

For now, they're silent. They lurk in the shadows, watching as I struggle for an excuse Breena might accept.

"It—it was too much. I got tired. I needed to go underground," I say.

"Why not call for a replacement? One of the young-lings would have been there in minutes."

"I wasn't thinking straight. I haven't been in London for over a decade, Breena! Don't you remember how intense the sickness is at first? I could barely cast a summoning spell. I needed to get underground."

The older Fae's eyes narrow, their arctic blue refusing to leave my face. "We both know that you're stronger than that," she says. "The prince got to you, didn't he?"

I look over at my friend, trying to quell my panic. Does she know about the failed veiling spell? About how, instead of murmuring the spell to steal Richard's memory, I turned and ran? I don't see how—none but the prince and I were there to witness it.

"He's different. . . ." I don't know how to go on. Many things, like the strange jolts that seized me when our eyes met and my careless touch, should be kept secret.

"Richard's made all of us emotional. There's not one Fae in the Guard who hasn't been frustrated after a few shifts with him," Breena assures me. "It's nothing to worry about. You just have to push past it."

Frustrated. Breena thinks I'm frustrated. She doesn't know what happened in the garden.

But what about the draw between us? The connection? Had any of the other Fae felt that?

"Why, though?" I ask. "What makes him so different? None of the other royals have ever caused such trouble. . . ."

Something of a smile plays across Breena's face. It's times like these—all blonde and knowing—that she reminds me of the angels in the illuminations which monks used to paint into their scriptures. They spent hours bent over their manuscripts, brushes poised at just the right angle to capture the etherealness of their scenes.

"I can't tell you how many times I've heard and asked that very question. I think," she pauses, allowing her thoughts to fall in order, "some mortals have spirits that are stronger than others. Souls they haven't yet grown into. They have potential, great potential . . . but until they learn how to harness it, they're all chaos. Richard is one of those: a strong spirit who doesn't yet know his place."

Strong spirit. Just the words King Edward used to describe his son. Perhaps Breena's on to something.

"I don't feel like I'm in control," I tell her. "I can't guard him like this."

"Emrys, you're one of the best Fae in my Guard." Breena is all severity. "You just need to deal with it. I know you can."

There's a loud, nail-biting screech and a flurry of black feathers bursts from the shadows. Everything inside me starts dropping, torn down and down by untold weight. The bird has come to speak to us.

The raven lands close to our feet, its head cocked just so. Minuscule versions of Breena and me glare out of its sharp, bright eyes as it studies us. A razor beak opens; hoarse, rough words roll off its tongue.

"Trouble. Trouble, we see. Shadows grow in Albion. Danger to the blood."

Breena's body is all rigid, poured full of molten iron. My own lungs are frozen; the chilled night air refuses to enter my flaring nostrils.

"Trouble we see," the bird croaks. "Fae must be ready."

After almost a minute of gaping at the feathery messenger, Breena finds her voice. "What—what's going to happen?"

The bird gives another mournful cry and stretches its flightless wings. "Only shadows we see, not shapes. Be on your guard, sisters."

The raven's stringy black feet carry him back into the darkness, leaving Breena and me in silence. We sit, staring at the dewdrops forming on the yard's immaculate grass.

"So the ravens have seen something. . . ." My voice is jagged after so much quiet.

Breena stands; her heather-gray dress falls like water over her knees.

"What are you doing?"

"The only thing I can," she says. All the weariness I couldn't see before is soaked into those five words. "I'm going to send a sparrow to Mab. Then I'm going to go back and check on the royals."

She's right. Against the vagueness of such words, there's little more we can do except tell Queen Mab and wait.

"And you, you will go back and finish your shift with Richard. The Guard needs you, Emrys. I need you."

Back to the prince. Back to that failed spell, that connection. Back to those things I can't explain.

I don't argue. Instead I follow Breena out of the Tower's walls, casting one more anxious glance back at the courtyards. The moon's skeleton glow calls out the ravens' huddled shapes. Several are gathered at the base of an acacia tree. Another pair lurks beneath a cannon. All of them stare after us, their tiny black eyes glued to our every step.

And I remember how they're never wrong.

A shiver coils around my bones as I retreat through the Tower gate.

Four

The prince is just getting back from a night out with his Eton chums when I return to the palace. The youngling I replace is all odd looks and cold shoulders in my direction before she leaves. My abrupt departure from the garden must be common knowledge among the Guard. In any other circumstances, this knowledge would press me down, give root to several years' worth of embarrassment. But there's no room for this feeling with the raven's words threading through all corners of my mind.

Shadows. Trouble. Danger to the blood.

Richard's blood.

I stay at the far end of the living area and watch as the prince shucks off his jacket. It crumples like a dead animal on the rug, the only thing in this grand room that's ruffled, out of place. Richard, in his once-crisp white button-up with the sleeves rolled to his elbows, still blends into the grandeur. His cut jaw and tall frame were meant for these rooms of gold crown molding and furniture that hasn't been upholstered since the Victorian Age.

I feel the veiling spell slipping again, sifting like sand through my grasp. It shouldn't be this hard. I shouldn't have to grit my teeth and weave new magic every few minutes to hide myself from Richard's gaze.

Something's wrong with me. My magic.

Has the venom of the machines finally settled inside me? Is the city starting to tear me apart, like it's done to so many of the older Fae? These thoughts call up panic, stuttering my heart and electrifying my chest at the same time.

No. It's not the machines or the sickness they bring. I'm too young. And, if that were the case, Breena would be falling to pieces too.

The revelation doesn't bring me much peace. The veiling spell is still fighting, wriggling out of my control like an eel caught by its tail.

I'm at the doorway, bracing against its frame. My invisibility, my absence from Prince Richard's senses, won't last long. In minutes, maybe even seconds, the spell will yank out of my control. He'll see me.

I could call the youngling back. I could explain

everything to Breena. She'd send me back to the High-lands, back to those snowcapped peaks that slope down to the tea-stained water of the lochs. The place where I'm whole, where I can fly without limit.

But it won't be the same . . . not if I'm sent back with this failure, this black mark on my record. The queen might think I've lost my talent. Or that I never had any to begin with. My position in the court would slide back so far it might take me hundreds of years to reclaim it. Maybe even thousands.

And Breena—she needs me, veiling spell or no. She has enough to deal with, running the Guard and shoul-dering the weight of the raven's prophecy. I can't make her burden heavier.

So my choice isn't really even a choice. I have to stay here. I have to guard Richard. Even if this means I have to let him see.

Would it really be so wrong for the prince to know of my existence? The other Fae don't have to know. . . . Maybe it would even be *better* if Richard knew about us, the secret world so thickly entangled with his own. If he's aware of the threats, he might be more careful.

These excuses rattle inside me, flimsy, shattering to pieces under the laws I've followed for years upon years.

Every shard is sharp, goading me toward the foolish. The inevitable.

They rain down, fleck harder and harder, like glassy hail, until I can no longer bear it.

By the time Richard finally turns to the door, my decision has been made. I let go of the frantically pieced spells, breaking into his reality before I can change my mind.

"Bloody hell!" he yells, and steps back into one of the chairs. He falls in a tangle of long limbs, stubbing his pinky toe on the lion's foot at the base.

I keep still, afraid that if I move or step forward, the prince will start yelling again. Richard stays sprawled, all knots, in his chair, watching me with narrowed, appraising eyes. I stare back.

"You—you're the girl from the garden," he says a few seconds into our gaze. "Who are you? How'd you get in here?"

It's best to just be honest with him. To let everything out. If things go wrong, I can always wipe his memory.

"My name is Emrys Léoflic. I'm the Fae who guards you." I say the words slowly, carefully—gauging his reaction.

At first, it's bewilderment that soils Richard's sharp features. Then he straightens up and stands. His eyes turn snakelike, slit and suspicious. "Edmund put you up to this, didn't he? How much did the bugger pay you?"

"It's not a joke," I tell him.

"Right." He laughs. The sound carries all the way up to the vaulted ceiling, where the Greek god Jupiter hovers over his human lover—the pair is as bright as they were when William Kent first painted them. "Look, I don't know how you managed to get in here, but you should leave. Security's a bit tight around here. If they catch you, you'll be in heaps of trouble."

If only he knew how true his statement really was.

"No, really. I'm your Frithemaeg. . . . Your . . ." I scour my brain for an interpretation, a term he might be able to fully understand. "Your Faery godmother."

Richard eyes me. Wariness has settled behind his stare, as if he's having second thoughts about my mental state. "Right. And I'm Father Christmas. Look, I'll give you one more chance, but I've got to call security if you don't leave."

Words aren't enough. I'll have to show him. I push myself away from the door frame and begin to weave a spell. It's a small cast, so insignificant that none of the other Fae will be able to sense it. *"Inlíhte."*

A Faery light appears, pulsing an otherworldly blue

above our heads. Part of me is all relief. There's no hitch to this spell. It seems that the rest of my magic still functions fine.

So what's wrong with my veiling spell?

The prince watches the aqua light only a few seconds before he looks away. His face is pale, whited out like a window looking into a blizzard. His shoulders give the barest of shakes.

I let the spell unravel.

"I won't hurt you," I begin. "It's my job to protect you, to keep you safe."

Richard blinks and his face starts to thaw. "That— that was magic you used? Real magic?"

"Yes," I say slowly.

"Shit. I've gone crazy," he mutters, and rakes his hands through his hair. A slightly maniacal laugh escapes him as he turns away from me, hands still gripping the top of his head.

"You're not. Crazy, I mean. I'm quite real."

Richard stands motionless for a long minute, his back still to me. Without the veiling spell or a crowd between us, I feel naked. Exposed.

"You're a *Faery*? But where did you *come* from?" He finally turns and lets his arms fall. "I mean, aren't you supposed to have a wand and wings or something? And aren't you supposed to be an old lady?" Richard pauses, looking me up and down, like he's really seeing me for the first time. "You're quite beautiful."

I know I'm attractive—most Fae are—but to hear Richard say it feels strange, off-key. "One of us is always here with you. You just can't see us."

"Always? So, like, an invisible stalker?"

I clear my throat. The process does sound a bit creepy when I explain it out loud. "It's for your protection."

"Protection? Protection against *what*?" The prince looks around the room, eyeing the maroon drapes as though some mysterious predator might leap out of their rich folds.

"Soul feeders. Green Women, Banshees, Black Dogs . . ." I stop the list short. Best to keep the explanation simple, so Richard doesn't become more confused than he already is. "Basically any immortal that feeds off of death. They get their strength from hunting down mortals."

"This has to be a joke." There's panic in his voice, in his aura. The prince starts moving closer to me, in the direction of the door.

"Where are you going?"

He doesn't stop at my question, only calls over his shoulder as he enters the hallway. "Well, I suppose if you actually have to follow me everywhere then you'll find out."

I have to walk twice as fast to keep up with the prince as he jets down the corridor. He strides furiously, blindly—tearing past rich oil paintings and priceless ornamental statues. I scan the halls anxiously as I keep up, looking out for any other Fae. It wouldn't do for them to see Richard speaking to me.

But we don't cross paths with any other immortals. Much of the palace is empty at this hour. The only other soul we pass is a maid, her feather duster dancing over one of the many marble busts.

Richard doesn't slow until he's wheeled his way into the kitchen. The room is empty and dark. The prince doesn't bother switching on a light as he starts opening cabinets.

"Where is it?" I hear him muttering through the clash of stainless-steel pots.

In contrast to most of the palace, the kitchen is all modernity. Gleaming metal appliances and black tile floors. The only evidence of the Old World lies in its Italian marble countertops. I lean against one of these and fold my arms to watch the show. Did I expect anything less of a mortal so far removed from Camelot? In their minds, my kind is a thing found only in movies and children's tales. It will take more than my word and a bobbing light to convince him otherwise.

The cacophony of pots and pans only grows louder as Richard moves to the next cabinet. He's almost waist deep when the room's lights suddenly flicker on.

"Can I help you find something, Your Highness?" The maid we passed in the hallway stands in the doorway, feather duster planted in her hand.

There's a curse and another loud crash as Richard pulls himself out of the storage space. He wipes his hair out of his face and pulls off a charming smile—the kind reserved for press and paparazzi. "Oh—er—hello, Marie. I was looking for some refreshments for me and my friend here."

"For who?" The maid looks around the kitchen, not bothering to hide her frown. Her eyes glaze right over me.

Strange. I have no trouble staying out of her senses. It's not my veiling spell that's the trouble. It's my veiling spell for the prince.

But why him?

Richard freezes. "You can't see her? She's right there!"

The creases of the maid's chin multiply as her frown deepens. "Your Highness, I don't know what you're talking about."

The horrible silence lasts a few seconds before Richard's grin reappears. He laughs, a sound that, if I didn't know otherwise, would be entirely convincing. "I'm just fooling around, Marie. I know there's no one there. I was, however, serious about the refreshments. Do you know where they are?"

The old lady shakes her head. "I'm sorry, sir, I can't help you. You know what your father would do if he knew."

"Right. Well. I hereby absolve you of all responsibility. I'll find it myself. Have a good night." Richard waves and stands up from the cabinets. A clear dismissal.

The maid edges out of the door, giving the prince one last strange look before she vanishes into the hallway.

"Why can't she see you?" His question is a hiss, so low even I have trouble hearing it.

I uncross my arms. "I already told you. I'm a Fae. The only reason you can see me is because I'm letting you." The back of my throat goes dry at this half-truth. What am I doing? I should have reported this minutes ago. . . . But I can't leave Breena alone here. I can't return to Mab's court with this failure under my belt.

"Or I'm seeing you because I've gone delusional. Dementia has sprung up on Mum's side of the family before." Richard rolls his sleeve even farther over his elbow and starts pinching his smooth forearm. "Maybe I've just fallen asleep. That's it. I'm dreaming."

"Carry on then," I tell him. "I'll be here when you're finally ready to talk."

Nearly a dozen tiny red welts appear on the prince's skin before he gives up. They stand in a neat row, like notches chalked onto the wall of a prison cell. He sighs and looks at me. This time his gaze is earnest, calm, taking all of me in.

"So—you're my Faery godmother?"

"Your Frithemaeg," I correct him, wishing I hadn't used the first term. "I don't turn pumpkins into carriages. And I'm not that frumpy."

"I noticed." There's a smirk, short and sweet, before the prince becomes all seriousness again. "But you're my guardian?"

"One of many. We're Fae who've sworn to protect the crown. One of my kind is always near you—we always have been, ever since you were born. We're watching you, keeping you safe."

Richard tries a third cabinet. This time he emerges with what he's hunting for—a bottle of whiskey and a weighty crystal glass. "What do these other immortals want with me? Why are they trying to kill me?"

I watch as he unscrews the lid and pours the liquid in a twisting amber stream. It smells of many things—aged wood, faint fruits, buttery caramel—but mostly alcohol. The fumes sting my nostrils and the back of my throat, even from this distance. "Some immortals feed off death. A long time ago, before I existed, all of us gained our powers from the earth. But when the men came—some spirits found power in their deaths. These are the soul feeders. The carnivores. Their magic is different. It lasts longer and it's less susceptible to the machines."

"Machines?"

"Technology hurts our magic. I'm far less powerful here than I would be in the wilderness. Only younger spirits can enter the cities without going insane." I cringe as I think of all the old Faery nobility who unraveled and disappeared at the dawn of the Indus- trial Revolution. Sometimes the machines weren't enough to destroy them—teams of youngling scouts had to put them down in order to preserve both man and immortals from their terrible, unstable strength. Sometimes they were even without bodies: all spirit, raw power. A maelstrom of magic destroying all in its path.

"There are spirits whose powers are strengthened by a mortal's death. These are the soul feeders. They like to hunt in the cities, usually at night. Nowadays they lie low, but in older times they were a huge problem. The humans were terrified of them—people could hardly leave their houses without coming across some kind of immortal." I pause for breath.

Richard sips his whiskey, and the fire of the drink cuts across his face. "Sounds petrifying."

I go on, ignoring both the drink and his comment. "King Arthur the Pendragon was the one who finally came up with a solution. I was very young then, but I still remember much of it. . . . Back then, magic ranged freely in the land. Even some mortals learned how to wield it. The crown of Camelot held some sort of higher power, one that we immortals held in great curiosity and envy. Arthur offered the Fae access to his magic, his blood right, as long as we swore to keep the soul feeders in check and to guard those who wear Albion's crown. Many of us forged an alliance, sealed with unbreakable magic. We've been Frithemaeg ever since. King Arthur was the one who gave us the name. Every king and queen since his rule has been under our protection, whether they knew it or not."

"Wait—" The prince sets his glass down on the swirled, smoky marble. "King Arthur was *real*?"

My thoughts trail back to those long-faded days, when I was only a few decades old. I can still see the grime on the monarch's face and smell the stale sweat beneath the armor he wore to seek out our queen's favor. He knelt at her feet, his hair mussed and golden like some wild mane. If he was a lion, then Mab was a gazelle—all slender grace and marked beauty as she looked down on him, her eyes shifting through every color in existence. I remember the bright flare of magic which bound Arthur's and Mab's oaths together, sealing the fates of the royals and the Frithemaeg until the crown would fall. An oath we could never break.

"As real as you and me."

"I'm still debating that point," he says, and lets out a deep breath. Air hisses out of a tiny hole in his lips like from a deflating car tire. "So you're saying that I have, like, special powers? Or something?"

"Your blood has magic in it, yes, though I doubt you could learn how to use it. Mortals stopped practicing magic several centuries ago. But your blood and the blood of your family is a huge asset to the Fae. That's why we guard you—to protect one of the more reliable sources of magic we have left. The machines are spreading so fast. . . . I don't know how much longer my kind will survive on the old ways. We need you. And you need us to protect you. It's symbiosis."

"If my blood's so valuable, then why are these other Faeries trying to kill me?" He picks up his drink again, swirling it around.

"Let's just say it makes you even more appetizing to soul feeders. They don't need your blood magic anyway. They survive well enough off of death." With fingers of lightning, I snatch the prince's glass from his hands before he can protest. It's still mostly full. "You shouldn't be drinking this stuff. It dulls your senses. Makes you an easier target, which makes my job harder."

I dump the rest of the whiskey into the sink. Richard's lips screw tight, almost frown, as he watches the nut-brown liquid whirlpool down the drain.

"So, now what?" he asks when I place the empty glass on the counter.

Yes. Now what? How long should I keep up this ruse? If Breena finds out what I've done. The taboo I've broken. . . .

But no one's been hurt. In fact, I might even be able to protect the prince better. Point out Green Women and Banshees. It's that or report my failing magic, and the thought of that is even more terrifying than the possibility of getting caught.

"You keep living and I'll keep guarding," I tell him.

Richard stares with a length and intensity that makes even me uncomfortable. I don't think he's realized how much time has passed between us in silence. "You're going to follow me everywhere? You never leave?"

"Not unless you want to be Banshee bait," I say, grim. "You just do whatever you normally do. Pretend I'm not here."

"Right." He bites his bottom lip. It goes lopsided, a half-done pink bow tie. "You'll have to be a bit less gorgeous if you want me to do that."

Gorgeous. I fight the urge to smile at his compliment. "Sorry, it's part of the deal."

"Shame," he says. Something in the depths of his voice tells me he's suppressing a smile too. "Guess I'll just have to bear it."

He walks out of the kitchen, leaving the lights on and the open whiskey bottle on the counter. I follow a few steps behind, trailing him into the hallway. Richard doesn't get ten paces before he glances over his shoulder to make sure I'm still there.

The prince's bedroom feels different now that I'm unveiled. Like I'm more aware of the humanness of it. The mess. No maids are allowed to clean here and it shows. T-shirts, both dirty and not, carpet the floor. A vintage turntable sits in one corner, the shelf beneath it piled with stacks of vinyl records. Their covers match the posters of classic rock bands which deck the walls alongside original oil paintings. One corner of the room even houses an electric guitar. Its surface is a shiny candy-apple red, made irreplaceably valuable by some guitarist's silver Sharpie signature.

"Sorry," the prince apologizes as he wades through the chaos of cotton, cashmere, and wool. "I wasn't expecting company."

"I'm not company." I step through the piles of dirty laundry to get to the window ledge and the armchair placed so conveniently beneath it. "Don't clean on my account."

"Right." Richard drops the pile of T-shirts he's been collecting and undoes the final row of buttons on his shirt. "I'm going to, uh, clean myself up a bit."

I wave him forward. "Go on then. I won't go into the bathroom. Just leave the door open so I can hear."

"I sing in the shower," he calls back as he disappears behind the door. "You might not like it."

Lulling sounds of water hitting marble rise into the air. I close my eyes and listen—my mind drifts back to the moors and the light patter of raindrops against clumps of grass.

It's all out. My name, my existence, everything. This thought is enough to bring back the nausea I'd almost forgotten about while I spoke with Richard. What am I doing? Just a few days ago I was telling Breena how much I wanted to go back to the Highlands . . . but I know if this failure to hold a simple veiling spell gets out, then all the progress I've made in Mab's court will vanish.

But if any Fae found out about what I've done tonight, of the taboo I've broken . . . I swallow and my heart rattles like hail against a tin roof. If anyone became suspicious—if word managed to get back to Breena—or even worse, Mab—then my career in the Guard would be finished. I could be banished to the Isle of Man, or worse, exiled altogether. To be cut off from Mab's court meant a life alone, unprotected by alliances and order.

Not many outcasts last long in the world of free magic and scavengers.

I'll keep it to myself for now. Wait until the threat the raven warned us about passes. Whatever it is. Then I'll tell Breena.

It's a thin line I'm walking, here with Richard. I just have to make sure I don't fall.

But why him? After so many years in the Guard, after so many different kings, queens, princes, and princesses . . . why is Richard the one who makes my veiling spell fail?

I don't know, and this fact scares me.

Richard emerges like some mythical figure from a billowing steam cloud, a towel hanging from his waist. I divert my eyes as he changes and yawns.

"Good night, Richard," I murmur, and settle deeper into the armchair. Although I'm comfortable, I'm far from relaxed. My mind and senses are on high alert for the dangers night brings.

"Good night, Embers."

"It's Emrys," I correct him.

"I know." His words grow weak under another yawn and he collapses onto his bed. "But your hair, it looks like embers."

I tug a strand flat between two fingers. *Embers.* I'd never thought of that before. I wind it around my knuckles, tighter and tighter until no more blood can reach my nails.

It's only when I'm certain he's asleep that I smile.

Five

Sunlight is just barely cracking through the curtains, bathing small sections of the room in blazing light, when Richard's eyes finally open. I sit as I have much of the night, the frozen watcher. He rises slowly, peeling the fabric off of his bare chest and sliding his feet onto the lavish rug of Persian warriors and orchards.

He catches sight of me mid-step. He stops, limbs suspended and pupils grown wide: black holes preparing to swallow the infinite.

"You're still here," he says finally.

I nod, my first movement since he woke.

The prince wipes his eyes. His knuckles dig deep into the softness of his lids, like he's trying to fling off the remainders of a dream. When I don't disappear, he blinks. "So, I didn't imagine you. . . ."

"You're awake," I reply. "And I'm here."

"So all that stuff about soul feeders is still true?"

"More than ever."

He cocks his head, those honey-warm eyes still glazed over with the otherness of sleep. "And you're here to stay?"

As I nod, I feel something freeze inside my chest. I'd spent all the moonlit hours thinking, debating, stretching the facts. There's too much swirling through my head: the words of the Tower raven, the great taboo Mab put in place so long ago that forbids any interaction with mortalkind, my fizzled spell, and the prince's role in it all. This path I've chosen isn't the best or the easiest, but it's the only one left to me.

For now I have to let Richard see.

"Good," he mumbles.

The word hangs in my mind like an unsaid spell. *Good? What does that mean?* But Richard offers no clarification. Instead he moves across the room and collects some clothes from an overflowing drawer.

Once he's dressed, he turns and looks at me. "Since you're stuck with me all day, I thought maybe we could have some fun with it. Do you eat food?"

"Sometimes. I don't really need it."

"Why don't we have breakfast in the gardens?" Richard squints out the window. The sky between the drapes is a clear and cloudless blue, the kind used in china patterns. "Have a little get-to-know-you chat."

"I thought that's what happened last night." The idea of breakfast with Richard isn't so bad. As much as I don't like to admit it, it's nice having someone looking at me. Talking to me.

But there are eyes everywhere, of younglings and mortals alike. It would be easy, so easy, for us to get caught.

"Are you kidding? There's no end to my questions." Richard makes a vain, mirrorless attempt at flattening his bedhead. "What do you say? Is it a date?"

My breath catches. "I don't know if it's a good idea. . . ."

"Why not?"

"The other Fae don't know I've shown myself to you." Guilt writhes in my stomach, like a bundle of earthworms struggling to find soil. "It would be a bad thing if they found out."

"Really?" It takes the prince a moment to register the information. "I won't tell if you won't."

"Fine." A small sigh escapes me, marking my relief. I'd been waiting for Richard to pursue the matter.

"Great. I'll tell the staff to set up."

I remain in my chair as Richard calls a maid and makes arrangements. The rational, Fae part of me is numbed, amazed that I've allowed the situation to go this far. At this point, any memory spell I'd have to use on the prince to cover up the past day would be incredibly potent. Noticeable. Breena would know exactly what I've done. I can't back out now.

A petite linen-cloaked table waits for us on the lawn, covered with plates of freshly sliced fruits, eggs, sausage, and toast. An elegant china teapot sits to one side, steam rising from its spout like the breath of a sleeping dragon. Hundreds of roses, in every hue, seduce me with their scent.

Richard jumps a few steps ahead of me and pulls out one of the quaint wooden chairs. "I asked them to set the table for two. . . . I hope that's okay for your secret keeping."

"Your staff is quick." I admire the setup and take a seat.

"They're used to my last-minute requests," Richard admits. "The food always seems to be top-notch anyway."

He's right of course. For the first time in a long time, the sight of human food is making my mouth water. The sickness seems lighter this morning, almost forgettable. It lets me pick at the fruit, which is as good as I remember from my last banquet at Kensington—back when Queen Victoria lived here with her widowed mother.

"Where did you come from?" Richard asks as he cuts into a well-cooked sausage link. Its scent, spicy and savory, rolls over the table.

I pluck the leaves off a strawberry, watching them drift down onto the lawn. "In what sense?"

"How were you born? Where do Faeries come from?"

"Do you remember the day you were born?" I ask with a slight smirk. Richard's birthday stands out in my mind with perfect clarity. I'd been visiting Breena the day his mother's water broke.

"Of course not."

"Well, neither can I. My earliest memories are of flying. Over the hills, drinking in the sky, the plains. We don't look like this when we first appear." I run a hand down my side to demonstrate. Richard's eyes follow, tracing every curve. "We're nothing. Pure spirit form. The older ones find us and teach us how to look like you. Inhibiting, but much more practical."

The prince leans forward in his chair, meal temporarily forgotten. "How old are you exactly?"

"I appeared a few decades before the treaty of Camelot," I say, even though I know the date means nothing to him. It feels wrong to cram my age into a number. "But I'm really not so old in the terms of the

Fae—I'm not a child, but I'm not old either . . . I'm in between, like you and Anabelle. It'll be at least another millennia before Mab and her courtiers consider me an adult. But that's nothing. . . . Some of the oldest Fae took form back when the very roots of the earth were knit."

Richard stares at me, his fork turning over and over in his hands. There's still a bit of sausage speared on its tines. "You've seen a lot, haven't you?"

"I suppose. It doesn't feel like that to me."

"And magic—you can do it all the time?"

I nod, slow. The garden, everything around us, is so green and full of life, so perfect in this moment. The cool morning light spilling over the prince's silhouette onto the table. The blue willow teacup at Richard's wrist. The pair of scarlet-breasted robins rooting for food through the rose bed's tangled thorns and mulch.

And I realize, for the first time in a long time, that I'm content. Not fighting. Not striving. Not worried. Just content.

"I like you, Embers. You're . . . how do I put this? I feel like I've known you a long time. Like we were meant to meet."

I look down at my half-eaten strawberry. Some of its tangy, irresistible juice has stained ruby on my fingertips. Something about the way he says "Embers" causes my stomach to seize.

"Maybe we were . . ." The prince trails off, a crooked half smile colors his face.

Before I can answer, I feel another non-magical presence edge into my conscience. I throw a sloppy veiling spell over myself and my plate just in time. A sharply dressed man rounds the nearest flower bed, holding some sort of glowing electronic device.

The assistant taps the hand computer; his fingers dart around at the same frenzied pace as his voice. "Prince Richard, your polo match is in half an hour. The car's waiting out front."

"Blast. I'd forgotten all about that. Thanks, Lawton."

Richard jumps up, his eyes flicker over my seat. From the pinched creases of his brow, I know he can't see me. It seems that this sudden spell is enough to keep the prince in the dark, though it shouldn't last long. My piles of skirts, flaming hair, and jade eyes—all of them are hidden.

"You're still here, aren't you?" he whispers in my direction.

"What was that, Prince Richard?" Lawton glances

up from the glowing screen, his pupils constricted to the size of pinheads.

Richard straightens. "Oh, nothing. Just talking to myself."

Once Lawton is turned away from us, I reach out and pinch Richard's arm. He jerks away, squealing like a ten-year-old schoolgirl.

Spells are malleable things, like clay on the bottom of a riverbed. It takes only a few words to alter my veiling spell. Richard sucks in his breath when I reappear.

"Try not to talk to me when we're around others," I say. "People will think you're crazy."

"Can you blame them?" Richard mutters before he takes my advice to heart. He doesn't say another word to me as he follows Lawton to the car. This doesn't stop him from glancing. He looks over his shoulder every few seconds and catches my eyes.

He sits close in the car, only inches from me. Heat from his body fringes into mine, making it hard to ignore his presence. I watch out the window for soul feeders and Fae alike, my shoulders tense as we turn onto London's knot of busy streets.

Richard's long fingers brush against my hand—

a sudden, unexpected touch. Their warmth and the magic of his blood rush up my arm, sending an eerie tingle across my scalp. When I look over I find his hand splayed across the leather, invading the no-man's-land of the middle seat. His fingers show no sign of movement. No sign that only seconds before they'd hovered over mine.

I cross my arms and wait for the prickle beneath my skin to die. It stays much longer than I'd like, all linger and burn, reminding me of that empty space between us.

Six

The day is hot, with the promise of rain swelling the air. It's not long before beads of sweat gather on spectators' faces, dripping past designer sunglasses despite the constant waving of programs. The Ham Polo Club is crowded, its bleachers spilling over with girls clad in the runway's finest. Most of them giggle when Richard rides onto the field on a striking, all-muscled bay. Their whispers slither and curl to the sidelines, where I'm standing guard.

I keep them at my back, leaning against the white picket fence that lines parts of the field. The air tastes of freshly mown grass and horse—scents that remind me of the countryside. I take them in slowly, allowing the smells to soothe the sickness in my gut, and watch the prince's game play out.

Richard is a gifted rider and player. His horse bears him well. They flow across the field as a single, fused creature, weaving in and out of the other players with effortless grace. In the hour-long game, the prince scores several goals—summoning large bursts of applause from the female spectators. Some of these mortal girls are quite pretty, revealing even more leg and bigger smiles every time Richard looks toward the crowd.

But his eyes find me every time.

The game ends without interference—both mortal and not. I follow Richard and his team to the stables. They're flushed with sweat and smiles as they hand their horses off. I hang back at the entrance, half hidden by the door while Richard dismounts and unclips his helmet. His eyes rove through the swarm of glistening horses and busy grooms, searching.

"That game was bloody brilliant, mate!" One of Richard's teammates—a pale young man with sharp shoe-polish black hair—claps the prince on the back. "Definitely worthy of a celebration. Eh?"

The hit seems to jolt Richard out of his private world. "What was that, Edmund?"

His friend frowns. "I was saying we need to round up some of the gang and celebrate. You know, get a few pints. And a few girls." Edmund winks and jabs his elbow into Richard's arm. "The old game. I know London's not as fun as Eton—but we'll make do."

The prince wipes the sweat off of his brow, adding another stain to the sleeve of his polo uniform.

"The old game?" The words fumble in his mouth, sludgy and slow, like he's saying them for the first time.

"Yeah," Edmund goes on. His thick charcoal eyebrows rise almost to his hairline. "Did you take a mallet to the head? You're acting a bit slow."

"I'm fine. Just thinking." Richard isn't looking at his teammate. He's still searching, eyes wandering the smooth concrete floors of the stables, where flecks of hay and dirt clods wait to be swept by the grooms. "Mind if I bring a friend along?"

"S'long as it's not that prat McCrady." Edmund's nose scrunches into the rest of his painfully white face. "God, I can't stand him."

"Not McCrady." He finds me. It was only a matter of time before Richard rooted out my hiding place, tearing back the shadows by the door. I don't know if he's relieved or terrified at the sight. "Someone . . . else."

"You can bring whoever the hell you want, Mr. Four Goals. Nine o'clock. The Blind Tiger." Edmund's hand falls on the prince's back with another smack. "Be there."

I stay still by the door, waiting for the prince to make his way to me.

"I guess you heard all of that." Richard's long arm waves to where the scene played out. Edmund is on to the next cluster of teammates. His cursing and jostling echoes off the arched ceiling, making every soul in the stable acutely aware of his presence.

"It was a bit hard to miss," I admit. It's all I can do to keep the dread out of my face, my sentence. Another night out. More drinks, more dancing, more soul feeders. More awful, pounding machines.

But I can't say no. Whether I'm visible or not, this is still Richard's life. I'm just an accessory, part of the backdrop. Where he goes, I go. That's the way it works.

"You can come," he offers as if there was some possible scenario in which I might leave him behind. "As your real self, I mean. So Edmund and the others can see you. It would be nice to have a little more solid proof for my sanity."

My real self. These words slide a knowing smirk across my lips. My real self, my core. The Emrys before mortals. The Emrys without body, without name. She's a feral thing. All power, magic, and fierceness. Richard and his friends don't want to see her. They can't. The creature I used to be—that deep, deep down inside I still am—might kill them.

No, they want what the prince can see now. The thing of fire and grace stitched into the form of a girl: speaking mortal languages, holding human memories. They want the diluted, pretty face I've been for a long time now. It's the only side of me they might be able to understand. The side meant solely for their world.

"Don't worry," I say, checking my voice against its weariness. "I'll be there."

The night starts early. The molten sun is just diving behind the skyline, creating blackened silhouettes of Saint Paul's Cathedral and the looming skyscrapers. Despite this, the pub is crowded. Tightly dressed women wobble like newborn colts in their stilettos as they make a path through the bodies, holding their glasses high above their heads. The men eye them with appreciation, taking long draws from their own pints and yelling across the room in booming, flustering syllables.

As soon as Richard steps in, his button-down Oxford shirt casually paired with jeans, a lull falls over the pub. He ignores the hushed attention, pulling me back through throngs of people. I feel their stares on me, following as close and relentless as Richard's security guards. Every woman at the bar is picking me apart: each orange strand of hair, my oval face, my flowy turquoise dress. The attention is petrifying. I try not to think of how many people are looking at me. How many possible ways this appearance could get back to Breena or the others.

I want to pull my hand away, to sever the connection between us, but I can't. Richard's fingers are an anchor, the only thing to keep me going straight in this collection of machinery and tight bodies. As soon as we walked through the door, the sickness lurched back into a vengeful status—the same as it had during my first day in London. It's all I can do not to double over onto the pub's beer-stained floor. All of my energy, my entire concentration, goes into following the steady tug of the prince's hand.

We go all the way to the back, where Edmund and several other guys sit at one of the few round tables. Some of the boys I recognize from the polo team. There's the lad with the corkscrew brown curls and an extra lump on the bridge of his nose. And the redhead whose chin is so square it looks like you could whet a blade on it. I've never seen the other two boys before—but Richard knows them well enough. They leap up before he reaches the table, clapping hands and bumping chests with primal grunts.

Edmund stays in his chair, jaw tilted back in the most casual of greetings. It isn't until his shined brown eyes fall on me that he comes to life.

"Damn, Rich. When you said you were bringing a friend, I thought . . ." He doesn't bother finishing his sentence. I hate the way he's looking at me, all slow and squinty, like he wants nothing more than to get his fingers on the zipper of my dress. "What runway did you get her off of? And where can I get one?"

Britain's heir is a mess of emotions: his aura flickers between the relief of having my existence confirmed and a sudden bristling at his friend. Richard stiffens, shifting his body ever so slightly to come between me and Edmund. "Her name is Emrys. And you should treat her with a bit of respect."

"Whoa, mate, take it easy. I'm just playing around." Edmund winks it off, like it's all a big joke. But the leer in his eyes—fed by the three drained pint glasses at his elbow and an ego the size of London Bridge—says otherwise.

He stands, balancing his weight on the table, and makes his way over to me. His hand is a dead thing, all cool and clammy as he picks up mine. There's no spark or zap of nerves at his touch. Only an intense desire to pull away. "A pleasure to meet you, Emrys. I'm Edmund Williams the Fifth."

I snatch my hand from his just before he can bring it to his lips. "Likewise, Edmund Williams the Fifth."

The corner of Edmund's mouth twitches up. Annoyance I think, from the soured curdle of his aura. Disguised as impishness.

"Another round then," he says, and returns to his seat. "You're late, Rich. Had to get started without you."

I'm not the only female at the table. Corkscrew Curls has his arm around a girl with pin-straight, mousy hair cut in a rather severe bob. A wispy blonde sits evenly between Edmund and the ginger-haired polo player. Her chunky black eyeliner becomes almost a solid blob as she peers in my direction.

I try a faint smile at both of them as I take a seat on the far side of the table. Only Mousy Hair's lips flicker in response. Eyeliner turns her attentions to Edmund, nudging in close to his shoulder and saying something I can't hear over the muffled roar of the pub's other patrons and the music that's starting to pump through the sound system's speakers.

Pain starts its inevitable rise. In my stomach. Everywhere. My teeth grind together like millstones.

When Edmund doesn't respond, Eyeliner aims her focus across the table, where Richard is sliding into the seat next to mine. "You were so good at the match today. So . . . fast." The last word leaves her in a breathless giggle, so clearly rehearsed.

"Thanks." Richard's response is vague, unrooted. He scoots his chair a little closer to mine.

"So what's the plan, mate?" Edmund asks. "A few more drinks here? Maybe we can meet up with Brick and his mates at The Green Fairy."

The word sets Richard on the edge of his chair. He nearly knocks over the fresh round of pints the server is trying to balance close to his head.

The stench of so much alcohol and malty wheat swirls up and into my head. The smell of food and drink, the smell of anything at this point is enough to wake the deeper sickness in my bowels. I clutch the bottom of my chair, my fingers digging, digging into its wood. This helps takes some of the edge off.

"Whatever sounds good," the prince says, recovering his composure.

The waiter sets a drink in front of me. Some kind of soft drink mixed with a sappy sweet liquor. I try my best to shove it away without anyone noticing.

The pub swarms around us like a hive, drones and worker bees shuffling and mingling on what soon becomes the dance floor. Drinks keep flowing. Somewhere between his third and fourth pint, Richard slides his arm around my chair. I don't have the heart to push it away. Eyeliner shoots daggers from the other side of the table.

The rounds ordered to our table soon evolve from pints to straight whiskey. The prince's breathing is already heavier and his movements a bit freer as he reaches for the glass.

Something magical, something other, smothers the air around us. The buzz of electronics in my head goes flat, dampened by whatever has walked into this pub. It's a soul feeder.

My fingers close around Richard's wrist just as the first douse of whiskey wets his lips.

"I think you've had enough," I yell above the music, and pry the glass out of his hands. I scan the crowd, searching every designer dress and every inch of skin for signs of my enemy.

"Hey, now," the prince starts to protest, groping for his lost drink.

I shove it far out of his reach.

"Buzzkill!" Edmund hollers across the table at me,

and claims the condemned drink as his own. He finishes the entire thing in one swallow. "You've got to learn to loosen up, love! Live a little!"

"Careful, Ed! Emrys can blow your brain into bloody bits!" the prince bellows back, his words slurred and slightly sloppy.

There she is. A vision of raven hair and skin of porcelain white, ebbing and flowing through the crowd, searching for flesh. A dress of gray gauze floats around her—making her look ghastly and otherworldly even to mortal eyes.

A Banshee. Strange that she should be here, picking through such thriving nightlife. Their main draw is death: funerals, deathbeds, fresh graves. Someone must have died very recently in this pub, or somewhere nearby. Otherwise she wouldn't be interested.

"We should go—" I try to tug Richard's arm, but he isn't paying attention. Like every other man at the table, he's staring at the hauntingly beautiful, dark-haired woman approaching our table.

The woman who's staring straight at me.

The Banshee presses her slim hips up against the table's edge, cutting through the space between Edmund and a very flushed Eyeliner. "Hello, gentlemen. Ladies.

Sister." She says the last word very clearly and carefully at me. "Care if I take a seat?"

"This is your sister?" Edmund blinks at me, trying to reconcile our very different appearances.

"Don't talk to her. She'll eat you!" I snap, and then turn the bulk of my fury at the deadly spirit. "You. Leave. Now. We wouldn't want things to get ugly."

"Eat me?" Edmund looks back up at the Banshee, his eyebrow cocked in his signature fashion. "I like the sound of that."

"Don't worry, woodling. I'm not here for your precious prince. His friends are meaty enough." Her fingers slide, thin and frail as spider legs, over Edmund's shoulder. "You're under no obligation there."

"Oh no. Oh no, oh no, oh no." Fear becomes everything on Richard's face as he realizes exactly what's unfolding in front of him. "Ed, you *really* don't want to get involved with that . . ."

"Too proud to share, Your Majesty?" Edmund is all sneer in the pub's dim lights. He takes hold of the Banshee's hand and pulls her down to him. "Take a seat, doll."

I keep my attention focused entirely on the Banshee. She's hungry but not starving: average strength. As long as it's just her, I think I can manage. "Back off, Bean-shìdh."

The soul feeder assesses me as well, picking apart my strengths and weaknesses as I sit in the chair, gripping the arm of a tipsy monarch. His muscles are all hardness under my fingers, sculpted by adrenaline and fear.

The Banshee is right. I don't have a responsibility to protect Edmund. The oath I swore under Queen Mab on the day of the treaty was to guard those with royal blood. I can leave now with Richard and pretend this never happened. The Banshee will slip away with Edmund into some dark corner, take him by the collar, pull him down, get her lips to his ear. Then she'll scream. Tomorrow Edmund Williams V will be just another listing in the obituaries. Death by alcohol poisoning, his soul mortared and pestled to sate the Banshee's hunger.

But, no matter how slimy and base he might be, Edmund is still a friend of Richard's. His life has value. I should try my hardest to save it.

The soul feeder smiles at me, stepping back behind Edmund. Her hand is on his other shoulder now, prepared to fling him forward in case I aim any harmful spell her way.

"I'm serious, Ed." The prince finds his voice again.

"She's a soul eater. . . . I mean, feeder. Thing!"

The Banshee's blackened eyes spark with understanding. "He knows? You broke the Frithemaeg taboo?"

Now there's no question. I have to take care of her.

Edmund is squirming out of her grasp, trying to get a closer look at the creature behind him. It's in this moment, when she's busy tightening her fingers into the socialite's shoulders, that I strike.

Since she's placed Edmund in front of her as a shield, I have to go up. I lunge to the top of the table in a single movement, ignoring the stress on my humanoid muscles and how much I want to vomit. My mind is bent on magic—only dimly aware of the scattering remains of beer glasses and sloshed whiskey.

My first spell misses, grazing only centimeters above Edmund's hairline and ending in an explosion of light on the wood paneling behind him. Seeing that her human shield has no effect, the Banshee lets out a long, heart-crushing wail. It's not a death scream . . . that fatal blow she administers to each of her victims. The empty pints at my feet shatter with the sound, carpeting the table in glass. The magic in her scream fills my eyes with sparks. My ears feel like they've been stuffed full of cotton, heavy and useless.

But that doesn't mean I can't speak. I braid the spell together with my tongue, sending it out into the bright, speckled dark of my vision. *"Átemian!"*

The wailing stops and my senses resurrect to their old, keen selves. The mortals are hunched over at my feet, their hands crumpled over their ears in agonized angles. Only Edmund and Richard are looking up, taking in the events with dazed eyes.

The Banshee clutches her throat, trying to coax back the voice I stole.

I leap again, over Edmund's head and onto my opponent. We fall to the floor, a tangle of turquoise, red, and black. Up this close, her face looks like death—so white and chilled, like a body tucked away in a crypt. I see the knowledge playing out in her eyes. The realization that I'm stronger. That she's lost.

My hands envelope hers, crush over her larynx. My energies are fading fast, sapped between the tangled electronics of the pub and our fight. I have to choose my next few spells carefully. Her silence is more important than her banishment. And I'll have to take care of the humans' memories as well.

"You'll leave this pub," I hiss. "You will speak of this to no one."

Her eyes become little more than black lines. My fingers tighten.

"*Cyspe.*" The binding spell twists out of me, sliding through her tightly shut lips and dissolving on her tongue. She won't breathe a word of what she's seen here. She can't.

Before I can let go of her throat, the Banshee shrinks into a taut, furry thing that slips and slides through my fingers. I crouch, my hands still curled, as I watch the weasel slink in and out of the grove of feet. In a flash, she's gone.

Richard and his friends are recovering, along with the rest of the pub's stunned patrons. Groans and curses rise behind me like a tidal wave, swelling and growing into full-blown panic. I have to take care of it fast.

"*Forgietap.*" My magic mists over the pub like rain, snatching memories of the last few minutes into irretrievable nothingness. Only Richard's head is immune. He needs to remember this, to know the danger he's in every time he hits the pubs.

I have no more fight left in me. Not with the sickness battering my gut. At least I don't have to worry about Green Women. They give the Banshees a wide berth, out of mutual dislike. It's the other Banshees and the Black Dogs I have to worry about. Their voices can reach so many dark places in the night.

I return to the table slowly, trying to reconcile the reeling in my head, my stomach. It wasn't this bad last time, at the Darkroom. I thought Breena said it would get better. . . . This—the lightning lancing through my gut, tearing blades through my veins—this is agony.

I have to get out of here.

It's as if Richard already knows. He's out of his chair, waiting for me. The tabletop is all chaos in front of him, dripping alcohol and broken glass. His friends are taking it in—this loose end I don't have the energy to fix.

"What the bloody hell happened?" Corkscrew Curls is the first to recover. His hands shake as he reaches out to pick up the largest piece of glass. It's no bigger than his thumbnail.

The prince looks at his friends, their explicit surprise. The rest of the pub dances on to the same song that was rattling the speakers before the Banshee arrived.

"They don't know?" he asks as soon as I get close to him.

I shake my head and almost fall into the chair.

Richard reaches out, bracing my shoulders with his hands. The touch steadies me, keeps my head from swirling like a leaf caught in crosswinds. "Are you . . . are you okay?"

I shake my head again. "Too much," I manage, before the threat of vomiting forces me to close my lips.

He understands. The pub, the drinks, the mortals and their machines. All pressing down on me, threatening to crush.

"Let's get out of here," he says.

The tree is the first thing I see when I lurch out of the pub. It sits on the other side of the street, past a barricade of beetle-black cabs and Mini Coopers. From the gnarled lengths of its branches and the way it sits alone, I see it's quite old. The city has grown around it, the sidewalk and curb parting to give it a rare patch of earth to feed from.

I only get halfway across the road before the sickness gets the better of me. Sparkling water and bile coat the asphalt under my feet. There's the squeal of brakes and headlamps bright in my face. Someone yells, their anger punctuated by a car horn.

"Lay off it!" I hear the prince yelling, somewhere above me.

An arm loops around my shoulders, lifting and

guiding me out of the vehicle's path. We're on the sidewalk again, only this time there's something for me to cling to. The tree's bark is rugged and rust red: relief under my fingers. I lean into it.

The change is instant. Energy, slow and hearty, pumps into my body. I no longer feel drained, beyond helpless, but I'm still a far cry from what I could be.

Richard stands close, hands shoved into his pockets. The way he looks at me now is different—it's not fear, but close to it. Reverence maybe.

I close my eyes and breathe. Diesel and dust cling to the air in my nostrils. I focus on the tree, on its roots and the soil far beneath them.

For several minutes, it's only the distant sounds of music and the cabs pulling in and out of their parking spaces. My breathing grows stronger, steadier. I no longer feel like I'm about to break.

"You just saved Edmund's life, didn't you?" the prince says when I open my eyes.

"Yeah." I cough out the word. "Guess he owes me."

"What was that thing? A soul feeder?" There's just an edge of shakiness in his voice.

"A Banshee. They'll suck out your soul with a scream. Not quite as painful as getting eaten alive by a Green

Woman." I think back to my shoulder and the long-gone bite of fire.

"But—but it turned into a ferret."

"Weasel. She shifted into a weasel," I correct him. "They like turning into stoats too. And hares. And hooded crows. Keep an eye out for those."

Richard looks over his shoulder. Across the street I see his security guards, watching. They haven't moved from their posts by the pub door. Richard must have asked them to stay.

"Don't worry, she's gone." There's nothing nearby either. No Black Dogs or fellow Banshees. This one was hunting alone.

The prince looks back at the tree, where my hands touch the bark. "What are you doing?"

"Recharging. The pubs are hard on me. . . . Too much technology, I guess. I was already strained before the Banshee appeared."

"That's why you threw up?" Richard glances over at the oily patch in the road. It winks back at us, reflecting the headlamps of a passing cab.

Is it getting worse? I swallow the decay from my mouth. Hard to tell.

"This . . . attack. This isn't the first time it's happened, is it?" The prince appears very grounded and clear-eyed as he thinks this out, all drink evaporated from his system.

"There've been a few other incidents," I admit. "It's hard to avoid them in the pubs."

"The blackouts I had . . . that was you?" He examines his hand. The swelling is mostly gone now.

"I do what I must to keep you alive." I push myself away from the tree. "Period."

Richard looks like he wants to say something, but the words get caught in his throat. There's a commotion on the other side of the street. Men with cameras moving down the sidewalk. Seems like the paparazzi finally got tipped off on Richard's whereabouts. That's the last thing I need: my photo gracing the front page of *The Sun* for every Fae to see.

The prince sees them too. "Great," he mutters, shoving his hands deeper into his pockets.

"I think it's time to go home," I tell him.

"I think you're right," he says, and waves across the street to his bodyguards. "Enough for one night."

My legs are still shaky, ready to collapse. I reach up toward a tree branch, tangle my fingers into its leaves. A few of them break off into my palm—a piece of nature to take with me into the car that's now wheeling around, ready for Richard's quick escape from the paparazzi.

The night feels full of eyes as Richard opens the car door for me. Tonight was too close. If there'd been even one more soul feeder on the prowl, I would have failed. Richard would be dead.

And I don't even have the choice of backup. Not if I want to keep walking this thin line, this only path.

The leaves fold over and over in my palm, my only comfort as Richard comes in on the other side and shuts the door. The car pulls away, back toward the curling iron gates of Kensington.

Seven

Your presence is requested at Queen Mab's court.
You must leave immediately.

Paleness invades my face as I stare at the words I just unrolled from the sparrow's leg. The messenger appeared in the last minutes of my shift with Richard, forcing me to rush out of Kensington with little more than a hasty good-bye.

Being called back to the Highlands this early in my detail could mean only two things. There could be a briefing about the ravens. Or it could mean that she knows.

A sickness beyond the machines stirs in my gut. I'd known the risk of staying and showing myself to Richard, but I'd gone through with it anyway. I'd clung to the glimpsing hope I could get away with it.

"What have I done?" The brittle paper collapses to dust in my hand.

The bird's head turns sideways. A dull black eye blinks at me twice before it swoops down to the gravel drive and starts picking for food.

When Mab summons, I have to go. I'm bound by the oath I gave her so long ago, after she found me roaming the Highlands in all my newborn wildness and gave me a choice. A choice to follow her, to hone my power and contain it, or to continue, raw and aimless, over the moors.

Because I chose her, chose tiers of nobility and order, I now have to face the consequences of what I've done. The rule I've broken.

There's still a chance the queen doesn't know. This request for my presence might have nothing to do with the veiling spell. Helene acted perfectly normal when I handed the prince off to her just a few moments before. But this prospect, a meeting about the prophecy, isn't much better. The raven's words spoke of something monumental, something that could change us all.

I swallow my fear and close my eyes, concentrating on that very essential part of me—magic. It seems that I have enough energy to carry me out of the city, which is all I need. Once I'm back in the realms of true nature, the magic will take care of itself.

I take to the skies. London becomes little more than a strange sequence of slanting roofs cut through with a snaking river. I weave in and out of the wispy cirrus clouds, fast and graceful. The city falls behind; the ground below becomes a patchwork of green, yellow, and brown farmland, bordered with hedges and fences.

Minutes become hours and the land grows wilder. Rolling hills with dustings of snow and black-watered lochs replace the towns and their tamed pockets of earth. There's something in this raw wilderness, tangible and pure, that lifts me up, tugs me to greater heights. I feel as though I could keep flying for years.

Here, in this tangle of mountains and narrow lakes, Mab holds her court. I manage an unpracticed landing on the highest peak, half tumbling through remains of snow, now melting with the summer's creeping heat. The mountaintop appears empty, but I know better. I stare at the sheer rock face only a few feet away. To the lone, mortal climber, it seems like many of the other mountainsides in the area. Only a Fae can sense otherwise.

The gateway to Mab's court lies between two discreet boulders—as it always has. Its hidden door swings wide as soon as the opening spell leaves my lips. I step into the heart of the mountain and pause.

"Lady Emrys."

A woman with hair of glistening sterling, all svelte and towering, waits at the tunnel entrance. It's Duchess Titania, one of the older Fae whose essence can't stand the presence of technology. As far back as my memories go, she's held a high position in the ranks of Mab's court, directing scouts and spearheading hunting parties. She's also one of the few Fae who openly resents the promotions and favors Mab has often granted me. Under her eyes I feel inspected, torn apart—treated like a child for my age and ignored for my experience.

I must smile and bear it, because that's the way of our kind. She is older. Therefore I must respect her.

Titania's lips are pulled tight in obvious displeasure. "Come with me, youngling." This term digs, makes me tense. "Queen Mab wishes to see you immediately."

She waves me on and starts down through the tunnel. Mab's court is deep in the mountain's core—crouching under many layers of dirt and stone. Our path winds down through the hill, as if it's been drilled through with a corkscrew. Faery lights shine faint from pockets in the tunnel wall, giving the earth a ghastly, underwater glow. Their shadows lick the space between Titania and me.

I've walked this path hundreds, if not thousands, of times. Returning from scouting expeditions off the plunging coast of the North Sea or the craggy peaks of Aviemore, reporting on the latest uprising or disease that rocked the mortals' primitive world, sloping down,

down, down these halls to give Mab the worst news of all: how Mordred's blade found the smallest crack in Arthur Pendragon's armor. How the very first king under our protection fell victim to death.

This time the walk feels different. I don't know what it is. There's a tension in the air, clinging to everything: the walls, the duchess, the morning glories which coat the ceilings.

Titania doesn't look back. She charges down, spurred by this anxiety. I struggle not to think of what's waiting below, but Titania's agitation gives me hope. She wouldn't be so irritated in the face of my demise.

Despite being underground, Mab's court—like everything else our queen prizes—is a thing of beauty. Roots drop like chandeliers from the cavern ceiling; pastel Faery lights smolder on their ends. Walls burst, full of bluebells, rhododendrons, and wild heather, their sapphire and violet petals fed by magic instead of sunlight. Messenger birds dive in and out of the vine-draped walls.

The queen and all of her highest officials are waiting. Duchesses, countesses, and ladies, all the loftiest titles in the ranks of our world, line a long oaken table still rough with bark. Like everything else, they are stunning beneath the moon-washed light, hardly a flaw in their polished faces. Worlds apart from the pretty, wearied visages of the Guard. The wildness of this place glows just under their skin. It's a wonder they even bother keeping human form at all. The reason, of course, is Mab. It was her love of the humans' tamed form, her desire to perfect it, which led us to take up these bodies in the first place. The older ones tell me she was the first. (All of this was long before me. Back when humans caught their earliest glimpse of Britain's white cliffs, standing at the bows of their crude wooden boats.) Other Fae followed.

Stepping close to these nobility, I feel lesser. More like the humans I've spent the past few days with than these older, power-filled Fae.

The council stares, faces void of emotion, as I gather my tattered skirts and take a seat. Queen Mab is seated far from me, at the very head of the table.

The Faery queen. She is power and more than a hint of ruthlessness. She has to be, to lead so many creatures with magic of their own. No spirits ever feel completely at ease in her presence.

The queen's face is as immovable as stone, just like the others, but something in her shifting opal eyes speaks of worry.

"I need everyone's full attention," she says firmly. "I've summoned you all here to inform you of some alarming developments our scouts uncovered in the north."

Stale breath, some of it held for hours, leaks from my lips. Mab knows nothing of my liberties with Richard after all. I'm safe from judgment, from the condemnation of so many aged Fae. For now. Looking at their row of profiles, so severe and marble-carved, I wonder if any of them ever had trouble holding up a veiling spell.

Probably not.

"As many of you are aware, the ravens have received a rather troubling vision. As soon as I received the Guard's message, I deployed scouts to investigate. Over the past few days, these scouts have detected traces of abnormal spells throughout the kingdom. All of them point to a single, malevolent source—a quite powerful one. If it's a Fae, then she's old, possibly even older than me."

Murmurs erupt along the table, surprise stirring to life.

"That's not possible." Duchess Titania's voice soars above the others. "All of the Old Ones are unmade. We were more than thorough."

"It's possible we overlooked one or two of them," Mab offers, although her words harbor the same incredulous doubt that the others in her court feel.

"How could they stay undetected for so long? It's been over a century since we had to put the last one down. They were so sick they could barely control their magic for a day, much less one hundred years." Grim lines carve trenches in Titania's face. She, like the rest of us, prefers not to dwell on the memory of the deluded ancient sisters we had to destroy. That very dark period in our ever-evolving history.

"I don't have any answers for you," the Faery queen says, "but according to the ravens, this force poses a threat to the crown and the royal blood, which is our utmost concern. Therefore I propose heightened security measures for the Guard and an increase in scouting patrols. We need to glean all the information we can." Mab's fingers lace together, seamless, as she looks over the council. "Are there any thoughts?"

The table is silent. Mab's new intelligence falls heavy on the room. And it should—the revelation that our enemy is ancient is hardly comforting. Magic, like wine, ripens with age. A spirit older than Mab would be potent, powerful, and extremely dangerous.

"If I may, Your Majesty." I raise my hand slightly

and try to keep the shake out of my voice. Addressing so many older Fae at once sets my nerves alight. Mab nods for me to continue. "The Guard isn't prepared to deal with this. We're all young—but a lot of the Frithemaeg are only a few hundred years old. They'd have no chance against one of the Old Ones."

Every face around the table spoils with grimace. Compared to their thousands of years, Breena and I are hardly more than children. The other London-based Fae are nothing but babes.

"And yet we have no choice in the matter. Breena is the oldest Frithemaeg who can handle the city. . . . The rest of us are too old. If only all of our younglings could be as gifted as you, Lady Emrys." The queen sighs and her brow furrows. "If it's an Old One we're dealing with, then she's survived this long by not approaching civilization. The royals and the Guard should be safe from her powers as long as they remain inside the city."

A whirring noise pulls everyone's attention away from the table. There, winging though the colorful subterranean flowers, is a sparrow. It's a London bird, I can tell from the dinginess of its feathers. The flighty creature must have left only minutes after me; I can feel a special spell meant for speed woven into its stubby wing feathers. Its message must be urgent.

All is silent when the tiny bird tumbles onto the table. It steadies itself and ruffles its feathers, oblivious to the many piercing eyes of the Fae around it. I know, even without seeing the script, that its message is grave.

Mab is unflinching as she winds the parchment back into a tight coil. She looks straight at me as she speaks her next, unthinkable words.

"Emrys, you must return to London immediately. The king is dead."

Eight

By the time I reach London, the city is hardly recognizable. Sirens and flashing blue lights appear every few blocks. Tearful citizens wander the streets, their many shuffling feet gathering at the same place: Buckingham. The palace's gilt gates are crowded by thousands of frantic mourners. Compared to the pressing crowd, the palace courtyard is eerily still; the only movement over its gravel is the occasional group of policemen and their bright sapphire lights.

Breena is shaking when I find her on the borders of Saint James's Park, where nature bleeds back into ordered city blocks.

"What happened?" I crouch close to the earth. My fingertips dig into the mulch beneath the oak Breena is slouched against.

"He's dead. I don't know when—Ferrin summoned me as soon as she discovered him. She went to relieve Muriel and found him slouched over his desk. It was just after you left for Mab's court. The mortals think he had a stroke. That's what it looks like anyway."

I've never seen Breena quite like this: every part of her body filled with shiver and tremors. Everything except her eyes. Those are dead still, set straight ahead at the palace.

"Muriel . . . Muriel's gone." It takes a very long time for my friend to say this. "We can't find her."

The same dreadful stupor which has seized Breena begins washing over me. This was no accidental death, no oversight of the king's health. King Edward was murdered. Death by magic.

I let my body fall the rest of the way to the ground. "What happened to Muriel? Was she unmade?"

Breena shakes her head. "None of the traces are there. Either she was taken, or she fled on her own. There are signs of a fight . . . but it's very possible they were staged. No way of knowing."

"Treason or kidnapping," I mutter, and stare back at Buckingham Palace. The mortals keep pressing against its iron fence, their rows of heads growing thicker. Their arms curling around the bars and stretching toward the palace. Red-coated guards stand beyond the clamoring crowd, their bodies stiff and their stares as unyielding as Breena's.

"I never thought an assassination would actually happen." Tears roll clear down Breena's cheeks. "Not on my watch. I should have put the Guard on double duty as soon as the raven warned us. If there'd been another Fae with Muriel, then—"

"Then she would be missing too," I interrupt. "This isn't your fault, Breena. Whoever's behind this is smart and resourceful. Mab and the council think it's an Old One."

Breena's eyes widen. For the first time in a long while, I see fear behind them. "An Old One? How?"

I shake my head. "I don't know, but that's what the leftover spells point to."

Stray wind rips through the park, tearing leaves from their branches. They swirl down, ballerinas in a full pirouette, joining the carpet of vegetation and decay at our feet. Breena keeps trembling. Her hand slips over, touches mine.

"We have to protect Richard and Anabelle. You know that, right? We can't leave them alone with the younglings. Not with an Old One out for their blood. We're the most experienced—it has to be you and me. We'll put the younglings on perimeter patrol."

I open my mouth to protest. I should tell her about

the breach in my veiling spell. I should confess how I've let Richard see. How I'm not fit to be a Frithemaeg any longer.

But I see the look, the nearness of failure and death in her expression, and I can't. She needs me. My years of experience, the idea of my magic behind her. I can't fail her now.

"We'll keep them safe," I say.

I find Richard with the rest of his family in Buckingham Palace's private apartments. The family sits in a tight ring by the fireplace. The room feels too bright, too full of towering mirrors and gold moldings to have any room for sorrow. But it's here. Heads are buried in their hands, shreds of tissues pressed to damp faces. Anabelle sits only an inch or two away from her brother, smearing tears across her cheek with a curled fist. Her other hand has found Richard's—their fingers locked and bloodless.

On the other side of the circle, untouched, sits their mother. Her hands are folded over her coral-pink skirt, no tissue crumpled between them. In some ways she reminds me of Mab: her shoulders and back are rigid from years of posture training, lips drawn thin, like a cobweb ready to snap. Only by reading her aura, the deepest feelings of her soul, do I know that she is really, truly devastated.

Richard stares straight past his mother, into nothing. The shock is setting in, glazing his eyes and sapping his skin. He looks almost like a corpse himself.

Though I'm sure he won't notice me, I keep the veiling spell strong and solid between us. As long as other Fae are in the room, I'll try my hardest to keep up the charade, even if it means refreshing my enchantments every ten minutes.

Hurt echoes deep in my chest as I watch him. I don't like the way this stillness has settled over him. I shield him from bites and Banshee screams. But this . . . pain, loss, death. I can't protect Richard from this.

Five Frithemaeg watch the scene unfold in silence. They strike me as awkward, huddled together at the fringe of the mourning humans. The presence of death unnerves them.

"How long have they been like this?" I ask.

The younglings all turn at once, necks snapping to attention like a herd of startled deer. All of them are wide-eyed with their own shock. I stare hard at Helene, huddled in the rear of the group.

"How long?" I ask again.

Helene blinks those doe eyes and clears her throat. "Two—three hours maybe. It took the mortals a little longer to find the king's body. . . ."

"Has anyone checked the perimeter?"

Blank-slate stares and gapes are my only answer.

"There's an assassin on the loose and no one bothered to check the room?" Irritation heats my veins, my voice. I fling my hands toward the row of vulnerable, high-lit windows. "What are you waiting for? Go!"

Helene and another youngling dash off to secure all of the room's openings with spells.

"Attend to your details," I tell the three remaining Frithemaeg. "You can't protect them if you're hiding in this corner."

They scatter like roaches caught in the light.

"Helene," I call to the Fae who's still busy sealing the window. She looks up, brushing dark hair from her face. "I'm taking Prince Richard off your hands. Breena will give you your next assignment."

Richard shifts on the love seat, breaking his long, void stare at the branching light fixtures on the far wall. A subconscious response to his name. As I look back at the prince, a sudden realization sinks in and claws my throat.

Richard will become king. Not immediately. He's still seventeen. A regency, with his uncle, the Duke of Edinburgh, as its head, will be set up in his place. But only a few short weeks now lie between him and the crown.

Something just behind his dead expression tells me he knows. None of the family has spoken a word since I entered the room. Despite their togetherness, they are each alone. Their thoughts are far from the throne and who will fill it. Only Richard remembers, and I can tell the thought petrifies him.

As it should.

I walk back to the love seat, just a few inches from the prince. Tears are finally starting to surface on his breaking face, clumping like dewdrops against his lashes. I mutter under my breath, words unheard, "It's okay, Richard. We're in this together."

It's well into evening when Richard finds himself alone. He shuts his bedroom door in a daze and stares into the unlit room. Every muscle in his body is rigid, unyielding. Just like his mother's.

Death—the aftermath of it—is a strange thing to watch from the pedestal of immortality. I've seen death in every way: as a thief in the night, as the heat of fever, as the lust of a warrior. Yet I've never really understood grief, or what it does to those left behind.

But seeing Richard alone in the dark. It breaks away pieces of me. I'm a glacier, plunging, falling apart against the sea.

The spell between us dies, becomes dust on the fibers of the rug. Richard doesn't start when I appear. His head turns, slow, in my direction. He blinks, taking me in.

"Where were you?" His question is just splinters, barely containing his tears.

The dam breaks and Richard's aura floods the room. Becoming everything. I gasp at this pain. At the sheer aching magnitude of it.

Shadows gather in the corners, lurking beneath the chairs and growing behind doors. I stare into them, trying to ground myself against the grief in the air. So much has changed in the course of a day, both beyond these walls and within. Thoughts of the Old One and Richard's pending kingship fight for space in my clouded mind, but I push them away.

This isn't the first time I've seen a monarch cry. But the others had friends, spouses, to soak in the sorrow. To help carry the burden. For now, all Richard has is me.

What should I do? Say something? Words feel so tapped out, empty.

I do the only thing that feels right. What I've seen so many times before in the privacy of grieving halls. I reach out to him.

At first he stares, examining my fingers and their neat, rounded nails, like he's seeing a hand for the first time. Then his eyes slide up, up. Past my arm, my throat, my mouth. His gaze latches into mine.

We stand like this for a long time. My arm aches, its muscles become lead, but I keep it stretched out. I don't know what else to do.

At last he takes it. My fingers slip smooth around his, holding them together.

I don't let go.

I don't want to.

Westminster Abbey is where they lay King Edward to rest. Misting rain creeps through the great open doors of the church. The floor is so crowded with people that I'm forced to leave Richard's side and observe him from the Abbey's towering stone vaults. The aisle is lined with all of the kingdom's distinguished men and women, turned respectfully toward the casket as it glides past. A bright flag of the family crest covers the coffin from view; a cluster of lilies spills over its sharp edges. The pall-bearers set it down at the head of the sanctuary, only a few paces from Richard and the rest of the royal family.

The air hangs gray, sodden with mourning, but it doesn't make the Abbey any less breathtaking. Soaring stone, echoes of color and fragmented light, visages of carved marble saints. I take all of these in as the scriptures are read—a reminder that beauty still exists in the humans' cluttered lives. There's a peace here too, traces of the Greater Spirit linger in the etched grave markers and polished choir pews.

Richard stands straight, without wavering. His prominent jaw is set as he stares at his father's coffin. I wonder if he hears any of the priest's words as they leap from the leather-bound book into the officiant's vocal cords.

"When the perishable has been clothed with the imperishable, and the mortal with immortality, then the saying that is written will come true: 'Death has been swallowed up in victory. Where, O death, is your victory? Where, O death, is your sting?'"

I hear Breena rustling next to me. She's restless, her eyes picking apart the crowd. Other members of the

Guard crouch like angelic gargoyles in the open arches of the Abbey's upper levels. All of them are alert, and like Breena, they're waiting. The death of a king is something very few soul feeders would fail to observe.

"Look there." Breena nudges me and points into the mass of mourners. "See her?"

I follow the trajectory of her finger into the rear of the crowd. A woman stands in the back, leaning against a thick stone pillar. Her sleek hair is especially black against skin that looks as if it's never seen the sun. A familiar twinge breaks my calm as I stare at her.

"Banshee," I hiss through gritted teeth.

Breena's curls bob as she jerks her head toward where the creature stands. "She's not alone."

Beside the woman, clinging against her skirts, is a huge, shaggy Black Dog. Only its long yellow canines are clearly visible against its matted fur. The outlines of its body are fuzzy, bleeding into the shadows around it.

Every soul in this sanctuary is in danger.

"We'll go together." Breena's face sets into a determined grimace. "I'll get the rear. You try to talk them away. They might go peacefully."

I hold back words of doubt as we coast over the crowd.

The Banshee sees me coming. Her rosy lips curl into

sickly white cheeks as she grabs the Black Dog's ruff. It's growling; I hear its rumbles of discontent over the service's swelling organ music.

"Good day, sister," she addresses me just as the others did—in the tradition of the days before we were divided, pitted against one another as Frithemaeg and soul feeders.

"You're not welcome here," I tell her. "Leave the dead in peace."

"It's not our way." She smiles down at the dog. Its black lips slide back, exposing sharp, flashing enamel.

I ignore the dog's threats. "You need to leave."

"Tell me, sister, why do you bother? They're weak. They're frail. They're nothing but fodder. Albion belongs to our kind. If you try to protect them, you'll fall as well." The Banshee's unnerving smile retreats into the stunning, harsh angles of her face.

"Is that a threat?" Every muscle in my body is taut, ready. The fight is coming. I feel it.

The Black Dog snarls; a long drop of saliva reels out of its mouth and pools onto the flagstones.

"It's the future," the Banshee says. "Tell the Guard that unless they disperse, they will be treated as mortals."

"You know we can't. That choice was made long ago." Back when Mab shook Arthur's hand. When Frithemaeg and soul feeders became entirely separate breeds: one existing to prey on humans, the other to save them.

"Ah yes. I see it's worked out well for your kind." The beautiful predator smirks. "How much longer will you survive off the blood magic? It's only a matter of time, sister. I'm offering an easy solution, a way out."

Fire knots and twists under my skin as I gather my magic together. This deadly woman isn't just some scavenging prowler. She's a messenger.

There's a flash of yellow in the shadows behind the pair. Breena creeps to their backs unnoticed.

"Who sent you?" I know she won't tell me, but the question buys the few seconds Breena needs.

The Banshee's pale arms spread toward the congregation and the bright, blooming coffin. Like she's presenting an offering. "The one who brought this to pass. There's more to come."

Breena's magic rushes hot through the air, singeing the inside of my nose, my throat.

All at once, the Black Dog lets off a terrible, skin-peeling howl. The organ's strained notes fall silent and several humans look around, eyes wide. They won't see anything when they look to our pillar, but the Black Dog's cries sends chills through even the deafest listeners.

The Banshee wheels about, lashing at Breena's magic with her own. I open my mouth to speak a spell, but a lunge from the shadowed beast cuts it short. The Black Dog's aged-yellow canines snag my many layers of skirts—it ends up with only a mouthful of taffeta and cotton. I aim a powerful kick at my attacker's side. Half yelp, half snarl, the beast turns for its second assault. This time I'm ready.

"Áfeorse." The spell ripples from my fingertips and meets the dog head-on. Blazing white tendrils of magic cling to the beast's torso like Kraken tentacles, dragging it down, tighter and tighter. The Black Dog rips and snaps at my spell with magic and curved daggers of teeth. But my magic is stronger still, even in the city. The dog's stocky legs tremble as it tries to resist the banishing spell, but they buckle beneath the curse's weight. Sulfurous light envelops the animal spirit, banishing it far from the cities into the moors of its birth.

At the loss of her companion, the Banshee abandons the fight. She dresses herself in the silver and black feathers of a hooded crow, and wings through the church doors, becoming just a speck against the heavy slate sky. Breena and I stand for a few seconds, staring at the scuffed stones where our opponents just stood.

Pieces of their magic linger. I wrinkle my nose at its taste, tangy and foreign. Like metal.

"They were messengers," I say, recalling the Banshee's words. "They came to warn us. There's more to come. She said if we protect them, we'll fall too. Whoever's behind this wants to take out the entire crown."

Breena's eyes are ice. They glaze across the congregation, taking in the hundreds of bowed heads and folded hands. "They want a clean slate . . . no more mortals."

"And no more machines." I murmur a reminder of how drained we are, how far from our prime. It's better than last time, this aftermath. The Abbey's Portland stone, thick with memories of its long ages beneath the earth, helps keep my energy up.

Organ music surges from brass pipes, chasing all remains of the Black Dog's howl out into the narthex. It's the final hymn, one I've heard many times before: "Amazing Grace."

"We'll send Mab a message," Breena says, mostly to herself. "Ask her to send the scouts to the edge of London. That way we'll have a good warning when the attack comes."

I shake my head. "There won't be a full-on attack. They'll do it with assassins, just like King Edward."

Through the crowd, I glimpse Richard's tall, sandy head. Even with the herd of black suits and dresses around him, Britain's prince looks painfully vulnerable. The distance between us seems wider from my anxiety. It isn't safe to stay away from him.

"It's like you told me in the park. The best we can do is stay with them until Mab and the scouts figure this whole thing out," I say. "We'll try to keep them in the city."

Breena's face is a mess of frown and doubt. "They'll get them, Emrys. Sooner or later, we'll make a mistake."

I try to absorb her words, move past them. But, like so many other noises in this place, they echo.

The casket's mound of lilies quivers as the pallbearers lift it up. A lone white petal slips out of the bouquet, tumbles to the floor. The coffin glides through the broken crowd, commanding the attention of everyone present. I bite my lip as King Edward's shell floats past, trying to ignore the sick lurch in my gut.

It won't be Richard in the coffin.

Nine

It doesn't take long for things to change. Not two days after the funeral, Richard is walking around his room, tearing rock-band posters from the walls and rolling them into tight tubes. Faded shades of men walking across Abbey Road and swirling neon colors that bubble into words like *who* and *doors* join the growing pile of boxes by the doorway.

The oil paintings stay, but the walls seem lesser, mined of meaning. Richard moves on to his record collection. He picks through each individual album, inspecting its sleeve before nesting it away into a box. He does all of this sorting with strangely attentive detail.

I sit on the bed and bear this process. Everything is silence. The turntable was the first thing to be packed away.

Since that night of fresh loss, when our hands locked and I held him there, I've said nothing. I don't know what to tell him. Richard hasn't eaten and his night hours are more pace than sleep. He's retreated into himself—to some inner sanctum I cannot reach. I know that when the time is right he'll emerge back into some semblance of his old self.

For now, all I can do is be here. Watch and wait.

The box of exquisitely organized records is almost full when the door swings open. Richard starts. A copy of *The White Album* drops between his legs.

The woman who walks in is the image of pristine— a mirror of Anabelle in future years. Her silvering hair is swept up flawlessly with unseen clips. Her skirt and blouse are immaculately pressed and her heels tread with the confidence and grace of someone two decades younger. They leave a trail of camouflaged indents all over the rug. Holes where no one can see.

"Mum." Richard speaks his first word of the day, his voice hoarse, rusted from hours of disuse.

"What are you doing?" His mother's question is sharp. She glares at the boxes by her feet.

Richard retrieves the fallen record and tucks it gently into the rest of his collection. "Packing."

"The maids can do it for you." She flips her wrist, catching a flash of her silver watch face. "We've got to go."

The prince selects another album from his slimming

pile. His fingers brush over it with tender familiarity, wiping away dust and memories as he prepares it for its journey.

His mother's eyes train in on him like a stalking tiger's. There's nothing close to Richard's grief behind her gaze. It's all hardness. She's like a diamond—all the pressures of her life, her lover's death, have crushed her into something terrifying, unforgiving.

"Didn't you hear me? We have a meeting with the prime minister and your uncle today to discuss your preparations for the crown." She stops, just now catching sight of Richard's garb—jeans and a white V-neck. "You're not even *dressed*?!"

"Sorry. I forgot." Something in Richard's sullen words makes it obvious that he's lying. That and the fact that Lawton reminded him of the meeting at breakfast this morning.

"They're expecting us in fifteen minutes, Richard!" His mother grits her teeth. "This meeting is of the utmost importance. You can't be late."

"Tell them to reschedule. I'm busy."

"Reschedule! Don't you get it? There is no rescheduling! This is the prime minister, Richard, not one of your Eton chums. You're going to become king in one month! You can't just ignore it or pretend it's not going to happen! You have to grow up!" With every word, her voice pitches into a shriek. It's amazing how, with so much brokenness inside her, she still resembles a perfect, slightly aged porcelain doll.

"I don't want to go, Mum." Richard's words are all the same tone, robotic despite his mother's awakening temper. "I'm not ready yet. I just need a few days. I thought you'd understand."

"You see. This. This is what did it—" She stops short. "You can't keep acting like this. It's time to grow up."

But the prince doesn't let her previous statement go. "This is what did what?"

His mother's cheeks pale, her mouth pinches with regret. I can tell by watching the curve of her chin that she's shaking. "Nothing. Forget it. I'll reschedule the meeting for tomorrow."

Richard stands. The album he's sorting tumbles onto the rug. "What did you mean, Mum?"

"I told you to forget it," she says, eyes flashing. "Tomorrow at noon. Don't be late."

She strides out almost as quickly as she exploded in. The door slams behind her, startling and final. Richard stares at it, deadpan.

He turns to me after several seconds. The look behind his eyes is devastated. Smoking ruins. "She thinks I killed him."

I swallow, not knowing what to say. I want to tell him she didn't mean it. But it doesn't take magic to read the thoughts that ran through his mother's mind.

"I didn't——" Richard catches his breath. "I never got a chance to apologize. I never got to make things right."

I slide off the bed, closer to him.

"It's not your fault he died." As soon as I say this, I see the danger in my words. Looking at Richard now, his hair dull and shoulders slumped, I know he isn't ready to know about the Old One. There will be a time to reveal the truth, to inform him of the assassins out for his life. For now, he needs to focus on living itself.

But the prince is so swallowed in his mother's inference, so drenched in his own guilt, that he doesn't realize the significance behind my statement. That I know why King Edward died.

"The doctors were always telling him he was putting himself under too much stress. At least, that's what Anabelle used to tell me. She was always better at talking to him. . . ." His laugh has no joy in it. It's a breathless thing, blowing stale in the air between us.

"The last time I talked to Dad . . . I probably upped his blood pressure by ten points."

"You didn't do this," I say, firmer now.

But he's not listening. He's not even here really. He's back in the turquoise dining room, staring at flower arrangements and fighting off his father's anger.

My hand finds his. It's surer this time. The soft of my touch breaks him out of his daydream.

"They want me to take his place, Embers. They want me to be king." His grip twists and writhes, becomes deathly in mine. So hard my fingers turn numb. "I can't, I can't be him."

"You don't have to be him," I tell him, trying to ignore the twinges in my crushed knuckles. He's stronger than I thought. "You'll become the king you're written to be."

"I can't—" He stops short, looking all around the room. At the landslide of boxes, the four-poster bed covered in shirts still buttoned on their hangers, the tumbleweeds of hair and dust hovering on the rug's borderlands. Everything, even the angels on the ceiling, with the paint of their smiles breaking into hairline cracks, feels in shambles. "I have to get out of here."

Visions of the Darkroom and The Blind Tiger lurch

through my head. Light, sweat, nausea, hungry soul feeders.

And now assassins.

No. I have to put my foot down. No more bars. No more watching Richard lose himself to drink.

Before I can tell the prince this, he's tugging my hand. Pulling me through his piles of unpacked possessions, toward the door.

"Let's go for a walk. Get some fresh air."

A walk. Feeling his frantic pull, the way my joints stretch and strain to keep up, I suspect it's more of a run. Tearing for any chance he has to get away.

Ten

"Hyde Park," Richard tells his driver.

I swallow back the stirring in my stomach and slide against the car's leather seats. They hold the shine and smell of polish, awfully pungent in such a cramped space. *Just a short ride,* I tell myself, *then trees and the Serpentine.* A chance to strengthen my magic.

The chauffeur, an older man, peeks into the mirror from beneath his dark cap. "At this hour, sir?"

The driver is right. The afternoon is late, shifting fast into evening. Prowling hours. Even though we're avoiding the pubs, I'll have to be wary.

Richard shuts his eyes and rests his head against the window as the driver weaves us in and out of London traffic. I look out of the glass, watching for watchers. Richard's fingers are still around mine, curling infinitesimal distances, the way ivy slowly invades a wall: crawling, inch by inch, until there's nothing but leaves to see.

The perimeter, woven tight with wards and spells, is still. The younglings aren't paying attention to what's leaving. Only what might come in. I'm glad for it. It would be hard—no, impossible—to explain why my hand is folded into the prince's.

The whole action, this touch, is against everything I've practiced since the day Queen Mab learned of Guinevere's betrayal and the Pendragon's death. Though we took on their form and speech, gave up so much of what we were to be close to them, to protect them, we faded into the realm of lore and legend. For entire lifetimes, we were only inches away, always watching, always taking care, and they never knew.

Until now.

I look at our hands. At the gravity of meaning between them, and I feel fear.

The car ride lasts only a few blocks. The air is cool and soothing, cut by the lingering traces of the last few days' rain. I step out of the car into the borders of Hyde Park and breathe deep. Good green things surround me—keep the nausea at bay. There's a fresh, minty rush—like wind—threading through my veins. Colors seem brighter, leaves shine almost neon in the reflections of leftover puddles.

Here, out of all the places in London, I feel alive.

Richard catches my eye and glances at his body-guards. "Do you think you can make them forget? Distract them?" he whispers, words barely formed. His hand clenches tight in mine. "I need for us to be alone."

I nod and cast the magic. They wander over to a path-side bench and sit.

"They'll be all right, won't they?" Richard looks over at the pair. Their heads slump over their shoulders as they drift into a complete, dreamless sleep.

"That spell isn't harmful." I feel out into the sur-rounding hedges. There's nothing there other than birds, but I can't ignore the possibility of other immor-tals in the park. Though Green Women prefer crowded bars and subways, and Banshees haunt wakes, Black Dogs hunt in fringed public places. Alleyways; lonely underpasses; dead, tangled underbrush. Places like Hyde Park.

Richard isn't thinking about any of this. He's walk-ing down the path, through puddles, getting as far away as he can from the car. I have no choice but to follow, watching perfect pictures of the sky ripple apart under our feet.

I'm just getting used to the silence, this invisible beat

to our stride, when Richard finally speaks. "Who was your favorite king?"

This question feels rambling, desperate. Like a grappling hook violently flung by some plummeting climber.

He sees the way I'm looking at him, trying to dissect and diagnose his hurt. "I have to talk about something. It's too quiet."

Partly my fault: my not knowing what to say, how to approach his grief. "My favorite king?"

"Sure." He shrugs and his walk slows. "Besides Arthur."

It takes me a moment to adjust my own pace. Our fingers strain against one another. Almost break. "Why do you think Arthur was my favorite?"

"The Pendragon? I mean, c'mon. The man could do no wrong. He's one step down from a god!"

"Arthur had his faults." I think of how the Pendragon married off his own sister to a vicious warlord. How pale and shaking she was when she stepped onto that boat with her new husband, began her exile across the sea. I'd always thought ill of Arthur for it. "They all did." Out of all the names and faces of the royalty I've guarded only a few stand out—many terrible and a few exceptionally noble. So many centuries of mortals easily turns into a blur. "My favorite monarch was a queen actually. Elizabeth I. She's the reason I turned my hair red." I brush the ends of my hair with my free hand.

"Why her?"

The path splits. Richard chooses the way. To the right. Away from the sinking sun.

"She knew who she was and what she wanted. She was a survivor. And she held excellent dances." I sigh at the memory of so many beautiful silk gowns and powdered ladies, spinning endlessly to harpsichords and lutes beneath the candlelight. Such things of beauty have died off under the harshness of stereos and electric bulbs.

"Your father was a good king." As soon as I say this I wish I hadn't. It's all I can do not to use a memory wipe and reel those six words out of Richard's past.

The prince's face glows gold in the evening light—giving him a surreal, beyond-human appearance. I watch as the window to his pain flicks past, like the light of a train car at full speed. There and gone.

"I guess he was," he says after five long steps. Then nothing.

I clear my throat. "You'll be a good king too."

He stops walking. His hand falls out of mine. In the

far reaches of my chest, beneath flesh, veins, and aorta, there's a pang.

"It shouldn't be now. . . ." His Adam's apple jags across his throat, flatlining after the swallow. "There was supposed to be more time. . . ."

A cloud passes over, low enough to break apart the sun. Richard's halo is gone.

"I'm not ready," he says.

"You will be." I don't know this for sure, but I say it anyway. It's what he has to hear.

He shuts his eyes. "How?"

"One step at a time. That's all it takes."

"I don't even know how to begin."

"Well. You can begin by going to the meeting tomorrow." I place my hand on his chest, feeling the light cotton fabric of his shirt. It's a familiar touch. More familiar than it should be. . . . "And by wearing a suit."

He laughs. The sound rumbles his body, buzzing through my fingers. "Basically catering to Mum, you mean."

"She means well." And suddenly this conversation, these words, remind me very much of Anabelle's civil lecture in the garden. "We don't have to talk about this anymore, if you don't want to."

His eyes open, all tawny and flecked. I see the thanks in them.

"Should we keep walking? Or do you want to go back?"

Richard looks up the path, memorizing its winds and bends. Gently he peels my hand off of his chest. For a moment the air is chill around it, but he doesn't let go. "Forward."

I wait until we're a comfortable distance, in both time and space, from the subject of his future and his father's death to speak again. "Who was *your* favorite king?"

"I've never really thought about it." He frowns. "Honestly—I fell asleep lots in history. Never got much out of it."

"Most of it's depressing." I catch myself and veer away from the topics of decay, death. "Is there any subject you did enjoy?"

"Polo." It takes me a moment to realize he's joking. Only his smile, a brief, faint twitch at the side of his mouth, betrays it. "I dunno. Maths maybe. I was good at it, at least."

"What about music?" I ask, thinking back to all the coiled, rubber-banded posters wedged between the packing boxes.

There's the key. The grin is real this time. "Yeah. Mum tried to make me learn piano—I detested it. But guitar . . . God, I loved that thing. I even tried to start a band a few times in fifth form. They never lasted long."

"Why not?"

"The other guys weren't so used to the . . ." The prince pauses. His tongue runs quick over his lips as he searches for the perfect word. "*Exposure* . . . that comes with being me. The tabloids picked at them a bit too hard."

"You could've performed on your own."

"Have you heard me sing?"

I think back to the wailing excuses of lyrics that rose along with the steam through the prince's bathroom door the first night I revealed myself to him. Before the world around him became too serious for song. "It's not *so* bad. . . ."

"Are you kidding me?" Richard laughs. "I'm bloody awful!"

The trees crowding along the ribbon of gravel give way to open spaces. The path grows wide under our feet, making room for a series of benches. Richard nudges me toward the closest one, an aged, wooden thing with armrests of intricate metalwork.

"Let's sit."

The slats, coated in lichen and splinters, groan as I come to rest on them.

Richard settles next to me. His leg presses lightly against mine as he throws his arm on the bench behind me. I'm closer to him than I've ever been.

I don't pull away. Instead I stare at the sky. Deep purple has seized the horizon, bleeding out all of the pastels of daytime. The colors are like souls being swallowed back into the depths of the earth. Quick and fleeting. Soon gone.

I'm not cold, but when Richard's hand curls around my shoulder, I shiver.

Notes—music—carry through the falling night. It sounds like the soft chords of a piano.

"What's that?" I ask. Richard cocks his head to the side, drinking in the sound.

"Must be a concert. They have them out here sometimes." He flicks his wrist up and looks at his watch. Movement made of habit. "Lucky timing, I guess."

I think back to the candy-apple shine of his Stratocaster, how he hates piano. "This doesn't sound like your kind of music."

"You'd be surprised. I like a lot of things." I feel him

looking down at me. His breath tickles the side of my neck, causing all my finer hairs to prick awake.

I close my eyes and try to listen through this intense, unmovable feeling. The melody is there, woven with harmonies into intricate chords, flowing across the fields and through the tree branches. I soak it in, along with the goodness of nature and Richard's touch— heavy, always on my shoulder, sending notes of its own under my skin.

It's frightening, this song of his fingers. This thrill of his touch. Unknown and new. I should pull away from it.

I should, but I don't.

We sit like this for over an hour beneath the music and the rising moon. Every few minutes the melody changes as a new musician commandeers the keys, but our bodies stay the same. Eventually the music fades and the noises of night take over. Somewhere in the distance is the ever-present hum of traffic.

Sooner or later, we have to return to that world of rot and endings.

The prince's fingers stroke up and down my shoulder as he traces invisible patterns against my skin, keeping time to music now silent.

I look up, suddenly very aware of how close Richard's lips are to mine. He draws nearer, pulling me toward him. His other arm wraps around me, strong and steady, pressing me to his chest. The magic of his blood thrums through me, causing each and every hair to stand on end.

I don't know how long the kiss lasts. I'm too distracted by the life pulsing through his lips, tender on mine. All I know, all I care to experience, is Richard.

Finally it's the prince who pulls away.

"Strawberries and spring," he murmurs. "That's what you taste like."

What Richard has just given me, my very first kiss—it's beyond anything I've ever experienced. Nothing in my existence compares to it. No magic, no adventure, no flight has ever awoken me with such great urgency as this meeting of lips.

All of my insides are alive, thrilling with light. I never knew it could feel this way.

He leans down again. And for the slightest moment, in another life, I let him.

But now, I turn my face to the side, catch his lips on the softness of my cheek. They linger against my skin; his breath ghosts out, down my neck. I hear the sadness in it.

"I'm sorry."

It's all I can say, because I don't trust myself to speak further. I don't trust myself to do anything. The past two weeks play back at me and I see everything I've done at a new, illumined angle. Dropping the veiling spell, showing and telling who I am, reaching out my hand . . . Had I done all of those things because I wanted to? Because I knew, in some unreached part of myself, that there was *this*—spark, flame, inferno—between us?

Suddenly I feel selfish. Undone. No self-respecting Fae would do what I just did. She wouldn't be so weak.

It doesn't matter how many soul feeders and sorcerers I've fought. How many missions I've completed at Mab's command. How many long-dead kings and queens I've guarded. In this, I've failed.

Richard pulls back. Says nothing.

I don't move, because I know that as soon as I look at him, as soon as I turn my head, I'll want more.

"I'm sorry, Embers," he offers finally, his voice rough and low.

"We—" I falter, not knowing what I was going to say. The flavor of him is still etched into my lips. Cinnamon and clove. Sun-soaked spice. My head spins with it.

"Should we walk back now?"

I nod. He's the first to stand; his arms fall away, release me. I hadn't realized how much warmth he held into me. The air creeps damp against my skin and blouse.

We walk back, slow and apart. The first half of our journey is silent, winding through silhouettes of bushes, bowing branches, and speared leaves. I'm very aware of my fingers—how they're holding nothing.

"You're right," Richard says after the fifty-sixth step. "I should go to the meeting."

"It would be for the best." These words feel foreign and false, because it's not really what I want to say. I want to ask about the kiss. What was it? An escape into a moment without pain? Something else?

But Richard, all tall and lank on the moonlit path, doesn't look like he knows the answer.

More unsaid words ache between us until the pressing noises of the city are broken by something else. Another melody, but one that's much more fragile and elegant than the ramblings of the piano. Birdsong. At first it's only a single tune. But then others join in: a duet, a trio. Their notes both clash and sound incredibly right together, as only birdsong does.

The prince hears them too. He looks up into the

near-invisible tangle of branches above us. "What's gotten into them? It's dark out."

"They're nightingales." I feel into the trees. There's an entire family of them, weaving in and out of twigs and leaves. Their chorus grows, swells with every passing moment.

"How can you tell? Maybe it's just some insomniac sparrows." Richard's voice is all smile and tease, and I know that, for now, everything is back to normal between us.

"They're my favorite birds," I say. We round the final bend. I see the sleeping bodyguards and, beyond them, the car. "They sing when no one else will. When it's darkest."

The girl in the bathroom mirror glares at me, eyes burning emerald, like Saint Elmo's fire. Copper hair sweeps elegant around her neck, like a foxtail, curling just past her shoulders. Her face is a contradiction: soft, murmuring angles, ready to become a snarl at a moment's notice.

The longer I stare at this reflection, the harder it is to see the difference between human and Fae. I look so very much like one of them.

And now I feel like one too.

He's in the room behind me. Asleep under a mound

of downy covers. I'm so aware of every breath that cycles through his body, the presence at my back.

I look hard at my lips. Both fragile and full, like the blooming, spidery letters of Edwardian script. A piece of him is still there, smoldering with memories of that kiss. The kiss that collapsed all the air from my lungs, took me up to the nest of the stars and down to the molten core of the earth. The kiss that changed everything.

I should have seen it coming, in the hand-holding, the occasional tingle of his touch. The laughter. Any human girl would have seen the signs, read them for what they were. But there was too much sickness, too much danger for me to even notice what's now undeniably obvious.

I've become attached. What I thought of as protection, as being a guardian companion, was all along something else entirely. . . .

I bite my bottom lip hard, teeth piercing rose-quartz skin.

It's not the kiss that scares me. It's the fact that I want more. I want to kiss him back.

My duty as a Frithemaeg, my existence, is to keep the blood magic safe. Nothing more, nothing less. That's who I am: this pledge I made at Mab's feet so long ago.

Anything beyond that is an affront to my magic, my essence.

And yet . . . I see the reflection of the door; the room beyond is a charcoal sketch, revealed in shades of gray. Through the dim shapes I can make out the lump in the bed that is Richard.

What if Mab was wrong about the taboo; staying hidden and apart? What if things are supposed to be different?

And maybe, probably, he didn't even mean the kiss. I've seen it so often, humans with heightened emotions, doing things they don't mean. Things they regret. It could be that Richard was drunk on grief. That our lips touching was nothing more than a way out, his escape.

It doesn't matter what he meant. Or how these feelings carve like a riptide through me. It doesn't matter because nothing else will happen. It can't.

Blood wells, staining the edge of my teeth, running red through the shallow crevices in my lip. I stand straight, dab the hollyberry stain from my mouth.

I'll keep guarding Richard. We won't kiss again—no matter how badly I might desire it.

Eleven

"We've arranged for a press conference at the end of the week. Your speech is being written as we speak, but you'll have to be prepared to answer the press without a teleprompter. Can you handle it?" the prime minister asks from his seat across the wide oak table.

The prince is ringed on every side with important figures of British politics. Parliament members, the prince regent, and his narrow-eyed mother all wait for an answer.

"I've given speeches before." Despite the steadiness in Richard's voice, his hands don't stop twisting under the table.

The past hour has been a painful session of details. What Richard has to wear, what he has to learn, who he has to learn it from. Letters, banquets, charity events. How to deal with Parliament. How to handle foreign diplomats. Richard has taken in all of the information with never-ending nods.

I've watched it all from the far side of the conference room, seated just out of the prince's view. This action is just as much for my sake as it is to keep Richard from glancing my way, being distracted. All morning I've caught him staring: those hazel irises darting away with intentional quickness.

I've done a good bit of staring myself. Richard's appearance is the same: sculpted cheekbones; tousled, wet-sand hair; eyes like almonds; phantom traces of freckles over the bridge of his nose. But something is very, very different.

It's like a gear inside me has shifted. I can't look in Richard's direction without thinking of the burn on my lips. And when that memory comes over me, the fire spreads, a flush comes to life over my arms, the top of my chest.

I've spent the whole day with my arms crossed and my hair fanned out, trying to hide it.

"It's different now." His mother breaks her tight-lipped grimace to speak for the first time. Her hands are in front of her, wrapped around a teacup. Her grip is so tense, with tendons and bone bulging through drawn skin, that I'm afraid the blue-willow china might shatter. "This speech is unlike any of the others you've given."

"You mean now that I have something to say?" Richard cuts her off. "Now that Dad's dead and I have to take his place?"

The regent, Richard's uncle, clears his throat. "I think what your mother is trying to say is that a lot of people will be watching you, Richard. You should keep that in mind while you prepare."

The prince's answer is short, tart. "I can handle it."

"Then that answers that," the prime minister says. "We'll send some trainers to Kensington to help coach you before Friday."

"Buckingham. I live in Buckingham now."

A cloud of confusion wisps through the old politician's eyes as he processes Richard's correction. "Ah yes. Forgive me. Things have changed so quickly."

I look over at the prince, letting the truth of the prime minister's words color my view. Yes. Things—and Richard—have changed quickly. The prince is morphing, in that strange stage between caterpillar and butterfly.

Only time will tell what he will truly become.

Richard spends much of the week getting trained, groomed for the public like a prime show dog. When Friday arrives, he's more than ready. He's rehearsed his speech so many times that he's memorized its eloquent, carefully penned words. He recites it with a convincing, earnest air. One that will make the kingdom fall in love with him.

But he looks sick as he stares into the gilded floor-length mirror. He fumbles with the top button of his collar. It slips through his fingers and a swearword escapes his lips, all syllable and punch.

"Need some help?"

He seeks out the echoes of my face in the glass, eyes weighed down with pleading. I walk up behind him and grab his arm. He doesn't protest as I turn him toward me and secure the button with one swift movement. This is the closest I've been to him since that evening in Hyde Park. In many ways I feel like a mouse dancing on the edge of a trap, trying to catch just a taste of cheese. Tempting fate.

Being this close, I can feel his terror. It pulses off of him in shocking, uneven strikes.

"Are you okay?" His face is unusually pale. Sallow, even. Before I really know what I'm doing, my fingers leave the buttons and move up to stroke his cheek.

He shakes his head. "I'm not ready. I can't do this. Don't make me do this."

"I'm not." It's so nice to be touching him again. I let my hand linger against his cheek, soaking in the warmth of his skin. The ghost of my reflection, the snarling, dutiful beast, is screaming. Reminding me of the promise I made, the blood on my lips. Reminding me that I'm a Fae, and Richard is mortal. That this is wrong.

You are a Frithemaeg, the Fae inside me growls. *You have to let go.*

I'll let go. I'll stop touching him. Just not yet.

"Let's go somewhere. Somewhere else."

I should tell him no. I should force him to walk out those doors and face the room full of cameras and report-ers. But I know, deep down, that this isn't what he needs. Bullying him to the edge of his fears won't make him any stronger. It won't mold him into the perfect king.

"Where?" I know, even as I voice the question, that it's wrong. I shouldn't be helping him.

There's a lot of things I shouldn't be doing. I look at my hand, so vivid and light against Richard's sun-kissed skin. My pulse starts to gallop. I feel it in my fingertips, beating against the tenderness of the prince's cheek.

"Anywhere. Just not here," he says.

Footsteps, faint in the hall, reach my ears. My hand

pulls away, lashing back like a bullwhip. My fingers become a fist, curling deep into the unworn skin of my palm. Nails dig, forming bright pink crescent moons in unseen flesh.

We both look over at the door, listening as the muted thuds in the rug grow closer, closer, closer. Finally they're here. And then the footsteps pass, their tempo fading, growing silent. My fist remains, a bundle of knuckles, joints, and guilt.

No more touching.

Richard looks back at me. Light from the window pulls a rare green-blue sheen into his eyes. They remind me of the ocean, how it looks just after a storm: weathered, eternal.

This is going to be hard.

Twelve

It takes a miracle and a little bit of magic to escape the palace unnoticed. We walk down London's streets, together but distinctly apart. My hands are tucked into my elbows, and Richard has his shoved into the pockets of his trousers. It took me a few minutes to decide where I should walk. In front of him? Behind? How close? I settle for two feet from his right side, farther from the steely cars that rip past the sidewalk, leaving behind the stench of peeling rubber and exhaust.

The afternoon is gray, overcast. The smell of almost rain swells through the air. Even so, Richard soon starts sweating in his dress shirt. He rolls up his carefully pressed sleeves and loosens his collar.

"I hate this bloody getup," he mutters, and undoes the button I just fastened. "It makes me feel like a mannequin."

"It used to be a lot worse," I tell him. "Fur cloaks and chain mail. You've got it good."

"I think I'd cut a rather dashing figure in chain mail, don't you?" He laughs. It's strange how quickly his mood has lightened, away from the palace. The storm clouds that dampened his spirits and lurked behind his eyes are gone. The weight of his father's death is only a shadow.

"You'd be dashing no matter what you wore."

"You think so?"

"Stop fishing for compliments. You know you're sickeningly handsome." I mean for these words to be teasing, but they betray me. Come out earnest.

"So you're saying I make you sick?" Richard pulls a wry face and teases back. I don't know what's behind his verbal parry. Unlike most humans, he isn't very easy to read. Even his aura is murky and muddled. It's difficult to pick out his feelings from my interpretations of them.

"You flatter yourself." I skirt the subject, like a mouse that's decided it's had enough cheese. "The machines do that well enough."

We turn off of the street, into an abundance of trees and grass. All of the breath abandons my body in a single gust when I realize where we are. Without meaning to, I've followed Richard back here: Hyde Park.

"You're okay, though, aren't you?" he asks.

"Yes, I'm not old enough to be seriously affected. For now." I can't help but shudder. Such talk only serves to remind me of the Old One. Of the threat that looms, far more heavy and devastating than a group of rain clouds.

"Does being here help?" He nods at the collage of trees, all bursting into the shades of early summer: mint, jade, emerald, olive, celadon.

So much green. It reminds me of the wilderness. Of the feelings of wholeness and health. It makes the constant nausea at the base of my throat all the more awful.

"As much as it can," I tell him. "I haven't thrown up since The Blind Tiger. I'm getting used to the city, I think."

"That's why I brought you here, you know. Last time. Figured it would be better than a pub."

"Much." All at once I see where this conversation is going. Just like our physical steps, crunching hard on beige gravel, getting closer and closer to that bench.

"Look, I just want to know." He stops and scuffs the ground, calling up clouds of chalky dust. "Why did you stop?"

"Stop what?"

"You know . . . our kiss."

I try to keep walking, but Richard stays anchored.

Soon there's a haze of gravel particles roiling through the distance between us. We're up to our knees in it.

He goes on, trying his hardest to kill the silence I've settled into. "There was something there. I know you felt it too. Why did you stop?"

There's an ache. An emptiness inside me I didn't really know about until now. Has it always been here, waiting for this one moment to show me how much I don't have? My mouth falls open, hoping to let it out.

But all that escapes me is more wordlessness.

Richard watches, relentless. "You're different from all the other girls. . . ."

"That's because I'm not a girl!" The words explode out of me like some triggered land mine. Hot and piercing. They rain on the prince like shrapnel. "I'm your Frithemaeg, Richard! My job is to protect you . . . nothing else!"

"But you felt it, didn't you?" He doesn't give up. Doesn't flinch. "Just tell me you felt it too!"

Those eyes, I feel them on me, staring through darkened lashes. And I'm sure he knows the truth, sees it rising in the blood just under my skin.

Stupid human face. Stupid, stupid, stupid.

"It doesn't matter what I felt," I say.

Richard looks on the verge of a smile, ready to chase

the matter with the complete dedication of a hound pursuing a fox. But his mouth stays straight, set. "Damn."

He's not talking to me. I know this because his gaze has shifted, its arrows no longer cracking my breastbone. "What?"

The prince nods over my shoulder, and I immediately understand. Just a few yards away, lurking by a wildly untrimmed hedge, are men with cameras. Their shutters click with bursts as rapid as machine-gun fire. I'd been so caught up in the heat of the moment, the tangle of emotions cocooning me in, that I hadn't felt them coming.

Richard stiffens. "They can't see you, can they?"

I check my veiling spells. They're altered so only Richard knows my presence. All the camera lenses see is the prince, walking through the trees, talking to himself.

"I'll take care of it." I face the paparazzi, trying to work out the spells I'll need to erase the memories in their minds and on their cameras.

Before I can weave the spells, every single photographer stands straight, turns, and jogs away.

"Nice work," Richard says. "Wish that would happen every time."

"I—I didn't do that—" The air thrums with magic: a banishing cast that isn't my own.

I don't fully sense the other immortal's presence until it's too late. The bushes at Richard's side shudder, and a long arm, pale as larvae, bursts through the leaves. A knife-edged cry leaves the prince's throat as the attacker drags him back into the towering hedge.

I waste no time. A wordless spell rips through my arm into the bushes. There's a shudder and a high, grating wail. The hand retreats into the flaming leaves. Richard stumbles forward, eyes wide.

The unearthly keen stops; the only sounds are the light snaps and hisses from the fire. The bush is a torch, blazing, its leaves curling into tiny black scrolls.

A Green Woman bursts out, gold-strung hair radiant with a halo of my fire. She lunges, a terrifying beauty wreathed in flame, fingers gnarled and teeth bared.

The rush of magic is magnificent when we collide. The Green Woman's power, so foreign, yet familiar at the same time, jolts through my bones. It buzzes between my joints and behind my teeth, leaving a slight burning taste on my tongue.

"*Blodes geweald!*" I manage to shout just before her hands find my throat.

The soul feeder's grip is strong, trapping air inside my windpipe—stopping any spells from being spoken.

The white burn of my own magic wraps around my neck, eating away at my skin. My failing arms rise to claw her face, only to be singed by the flames there. The Green Woman doesn't seem affected by the fire that swallows her. There's a shield between her and my spells—its magic tastes different from the Green Woman's. It's far older and richer, like a honey-gold mead poured over vinegar. It reams through my senses, brimming power and shock: the protection of the Old One.

A sharp kick loosens my opponent's grip, if only for the slightest second, and I scream a well-chosen word: *"Adwæsce!"*

The flames wither into nothing. My neck no longer feels like pins and needles are being jammed through my veins. I twist, thrash, flail. Try to get away from the Green Woman before she can speak again. Her face is clear now, unmarred by flames, her lips managing a grim smile.

"I see you did not take our warning, sister. I'm sorry!" As the words leave her lips, the mirage of supple flesh melts away. Beauty becomes a beast, peels back into vein-riddled, charred-parchment skin. Teeth like a shark's. Bared and ready to tear.

I feel the spell building up inside her. It's

powerful—not meant to hinder or disable but extinguish. She means to end me.

My mind scrambles to find an effective defensive spell. The words, treacherously hidden within the many layers of my memory, don't come. I'm going to die, and Richard with me.

Shouting, growling fury fills my fading ears. There's a flash of charcoal suit and human skin; the Green Woman's withered hands are wrenched from my throat. I cough, sit up. The Green Woman lays only an arm's length away, paralyzed by shock and the fact that a lanky-limbed man is on top of her. Richard has her pinned to the ground, his face a war mask. The prince just saved our lives.

"Hold her throat!" I scream at him, my voice hoarse under bruising skin. "Don't let her speak!"

He responds quickly; his long fingers wrap harsh around the creature's strung, knotty neck. She's effectively gagged.

I pick myself up off the ground, wasting no time with sore joints as I move over the helpless predator. A spell as horrible as the one locked up inside her cannot be released without a word, so it stays, corroding her soul instead of mine.

"You have violated the treaty of Camelot," I rasp. "You've committed treason against Queen Mab and the rest of our kind. For this, the consequence is death."

I bend down and study the shield clinging to her gray skin. It's older and more powerful than I first realized. I don't know if my magic alone can shatter it.

"What do I do?" Richard yells. His knuckles are tight, white as a winter moor.

"Just don't let go," I tell him, my mind scrambling for the right spell.

Slowly but surely, it comes to me. Word by word, the magic builds inside my body, taking the form of something dangerous and unwieldy. If I don't handle it right, Richard could end up dead.

"*Ábrece innan. Áfeorse!*" All of my energies pour out, raging against the shield.

For a terrible moment, the Old One's magic seems to hold. Then cracks, nearly invisible, race across the Green Woman's skin, splitting off one another like a quickly spun web.

"*Læte!*" I shriek the final word.

The huntress's eyes meet mine, solidly unrepentant. I watch, my jaw set, as the body in front of me starts to dissolve. It begins at the edges, pieces of her disappearing like sand sucked through an hourglass. Richard's gasp of horror reminds me that he's still straddling the dying creature. I put my hand out.

"Stay there. Don't let go of her throat."

He nods dumbly. His hands stay clenched until there's no longer any neck to choke. The Green Woman is gone. I stand and stare at the smoking ground, where her body lay seconds before.

Richard stands slowly, wiping loose crumbles of dirt and leaves from his irreversibly stained trousers. "What the hell was that?"

I ignore his question as I feel around the park. It seems the Green Woman was alone in this attempt. But her death is fresh in the air; it won't be long before other soul feeders arrive to investigate. There's only one safe place Richard and I can go. The place we never should have left.

"We've got to get back to Buckingham. Now."

But he doesn't move. "Embers, what just happened?"

"I'll tell you everything when we're back on the palace grounds. I promise." I look at his hand. It's trembling, fingertips blurry with movement. I don't reach out for it.

* * *

Richard's mother is waiting for him. Her face the definition of anger—colorless and winched tight, ready to snap—as she watches him stumble down the hall. Clods of earth are still wedged in the tread of his oxfords, leaving a distinct bread-crumb trail of dirt as he follows me. Although I know she can't see me, the queen's glare is enough to send chills down my spine and give me pause. Richard keeps walking. Past me, past the lifeless stone busts of his ancestors, past his mother.

"Where have you been?" she sputters once she realizes he isn't going to stop. "What happened to your clothes?"

He keeps walking.

"I asked you a question, Richard!" His mother marches after him, heels stamping over her son's filthy tracks. "You just stood up the prime minister and a room full of journalists! At least have the decency to answer me."

Richard reaches the door to his private apartments, rooms that were once his father's. It's here he pauses and looks his mother in the eye. "Not now, Mum."

She stares at him; her wiry lips slack into a perfect, speechless O.

I slip, fluid, through the door as soon as Richard opens it. Every single corner of the room is scoured clean by my magic. No soul feeders. I know now, after our hasty walk back through the gathering rain clouds, that this was my fault. Even though I knew there were assassins on the loose, I'd let myself get caught up in Richard, in these . . . feelings I can't seem to shake. I ignored my duties, skipped protocol. Richard almost ended up dead for it.

More angry words fly behind the door, all spark and heavy black smoke, before Richard finally enters and shuts it behind him. His back leans hard against the thick wood.

"My father didn't die of a stroke, did he?"

Rain is falling, beating against the window beside me. The sound should be soothing. Instead all I can feel is the blade of the Green Woman's magic, still slicing and paring my skin.

"No. He was assassinated. It seems that whoever, whatever killed King Edward is trying to kill you too."

Richard's lids close.

"I'm sorry. I should have told you before. But you had so much going on with your father's death. I didn't know if you'd be able to handle it." The excuse seems flimsy now, worthless.

"I'm not a child." The edge of his jaw bulges, the beginnings of anger knotting his muscles together.

"I never said you were."

"I'm stronger than you think I am."

I think of the way he risked his life, a mess of flesh and screams as he overpowered the Green Woman, pulling her off of me. How, again, he's the one protecting me. "I know."

This seems to take the fight out of Richard's voice. "What was that thing?"

"A Green Woman. They look like beautiful, green-clad blondes to bait men. It's not until they go in for the kill that you see what they really look like. . . ."

"If my blood is so helpful, then why was the Green Woman trying to kill me?"

I pause. The question is an obvious one, but it isn't so easy to answer. To get into the mind of the Green Woman and the Old One who sent her is a challenge even for me. The answer lies in the past.

"When royal blood is spilled by an immortal's hand, the blood magic doesn't just fade. It transfers somehow. The attacker grows stronger from that death. We don't know exactly how it works—such an outright attack on the crown has never happened before. Arthur and Merlin warned us something like this might happen. We'd begun to think it never would. . . . There'd never be a need for an immortal to kill the royals. Someone's just gotten desperate. Or greedy. They're trying to kill you to take the blood magic all for themselves. They'll go on down the line until they have enough power to accomplish their goal. Whatever it is."

Something the Green Woman said during the flurry of her attack hasn't left. It's been looping through my thoughts, spiraling into me ever since I first heard it: *our warning. Our* warning. She knew what the Banshee told me under the vaults of Westminster.

This shows me the power of the Old One's influence. She's taken two very different castes of spirits, the Green Women and Banshees, who despise each other, and pieced them into allies.

She's united the soul feeders. It's not just Richard's blood she wants, but all of mortalkind. She wants to take the island back as her own, and now she has the numbers to do it.

"What about Anabelle and Mum? Are they in danger too?"

"Everyone in your family who has royal blood in their veins is in danger. Although not quite as much as you. Blood magic is strongest in the crown's direct successor. That's why the Green Woman was going after you instead of the regent," I explain. "But Anabelle and the other royals have Fae guarding them as well."

Richard opens his eyes and walks around the plush velvet furniture of the ornate sitting room. He stares through the window, at the rain that's started slapping against glass.

"There are things you can do to make my job easier. The same goes for the rest of your family."

Richard stops pacing. "Like what?"

"Right now the city is our best defense. Whatever's after you appears to be quite an old spirit—she won't stand to come anywhere near London. That's why she's been sending assassins to do the job for her. Banshee and Green Women I can handle. An Old One is a different story. It would be best if you stayed within London's borders."

There is an unpleasant turning in my gut, as if to remind me of the city's true feelings for my kind. What it actually means for me to stay.

"Stay in London? For how long?"

"As long as it takes." I grit my teeth, waiting for the worst of the pain to pass.

The prince shakes his head. Weariness, just a flash

of it, crosses his face. "It's not possible! Once I accede the throne, they'll expect me to tour—to go overseas."

"Well, let's just do it for as long as we can. Until we figure out a better way to guard you outside of the city. Same goes for your sister," I add.

"And what am I supposed to tell Anabelle?"

"Tell her anything you'd like. Lie. Just don't let her leave."

I try to distract myself from the nausea by examining several small, recently acquired burn holes in the top layer of my skirts. The bright teal silk is peppered with charred spots. Ruined. I frown. The skirt, snatched from a duchess's closet two hundred years ago, was one of my favorites.

"Do you think there will be any more attacks?"

"Definitely." I nod. "Someone powerful wants you dead. I don't think the death of a single assassin will deter them."

Richard sighs. The sound deflates him. "I need some tea."

I watch as he picks up the phone and rings Lawton. He's calmed down considerably since we first entered the room. Color has returned to his face, and his voice is steady as he requests the hot tea. How had I thought he wouldn't be able to handle this?

"What made you attack the Green Woman?" I ask when he sets the phone back.

"What do you mean?" He collapses on the end of an embroidered love seat.

"I've never seen any man attack an immortal head-on like that. You had no chance against her. Why did you do it?"

"I don't know. I just did. You needed help, so I came. There wasn't too much time to think." He pauses. "Why do you ask?"

"It—it's happened before. You coming to my rescue."

Richard knows what I mean in an instant. "Then that man in the tabloids was telling the truth? You were there when I punched him? You erased my memory?"

"Yes. He was harassing me." I can tell by the look on his face where his thoughts are jumping. Back to that morning with Edward. I want to kick myself for dredging up the painful moment, for forcing him to dwell on that one scene he's worked so hard to move past.

"At least the punch was worth something then." But his wavering expression tells me it doesn't change anything his father said. It doesn't make things better.

A sharp tap from the other side of the door breaks apart any words I'm about to say. Richard looks warily at the door, as if he expects a pack of hellhounds to come barreling through it at any moment. Considering that his mother was the last person in the corridor, the possibility isn't all that remote.

But it's only Lawton with the tray of tea. The young assistant leaves as quickly as he comes, pausing only to pour a bit of the coppery liquid into the china cup.

"It's been hard, since Dad . . ." Richard falters. "I mean, just a few weeks ago I was at Eton and my biggest worry was whether or not the prefects would find my stash of booze. Now it seems as if everybody wants something from me. And I have nothing left to give. I don't know if I even had anything in the first place."

I can taste his sorrow; it pollutes the air around him.

"Tell me," he goes on after a moment of silence, "do you ever think about death?"

"What about it?" My question is cautious. This is a holy, sacred subject we're exploring. Especially in this company.

"I mean, do you ever think of what's on the other side? What's beyond it?"

"Not very often," I admit. Only now in the past week

has death been so present in my thoughts.

"I guess you don't have to. Must be nice, living forever," Richard says.

I say nothing.

"Sometimes I wonder if he's watching me. Dad, I mean." The prince swallows. The teacup in his hand rattles, spitting amber drops on his suit. "I wonder if he likes what he sees."

"He might've had a few words about what happened today. . . ." I could have said something false, comforting. But I know that no matter what, Richard will stay bound to his father's ghost. Best to just spill out the truth, quick and cutting. Hope it leaves its mark.

Richard groans. "I don't think I'm ever going to be able to live that one down. I'm sure the papers tomorrow are going to be fabulous. It's just—I dunno. I couldn't make myself do it. Seems silly now, doesn't it? That I should be afraid of something I was raised to do?"

"Every mortal has that problem. I believe you call it 'stage fright,'" I tell him. "What perplexes *me* is that you're not more worried that there's an ancient Fae out for your blood."

"I don't think there's room for any more fear. And, I have you."

I stare at the empty space next to Richard. I want, very much, to go sit with him.

My body—bones, tendons, and all—feels frail. Distinctly human. I'm sick of standing, and the prince's love seat is the closest piece of furniture. All it would take is three steps. Three steps and I could be next to him.

No. The ambush in the park happened because I got caught up in Richard. If I knew what was best for me, for him, I'd stay far, far away.

I want to tell him he should be scared. That he should be terrified. What he doesn't know, doesn't realize, is that he was the one who saved us.

Without him, I would be nothing now. Unraveled into ether and air.

Thirteen

Richard's sleep is still deep and dream-soaked when his sister arrives. In the nights he's slept since his father's death he's kicked the sheets, twisting them into inextricable knots with his long legs. The fight with the Green Woman drained this restlessness out of him. He's as still as a body laid out for a viewing, the sheets draped over him flat and unwrinkled.

"Richard! You're not still sleeping, are you?" Anabelle's knocks grow louder with each passing second.

I glance over at the bed, wondering if I should wake him. But Breena is on the other side of that door. If she catches sight of Richard and me, all is finished.

After another minute of pounding her fist against the wood, the princess finally shoves the door open. Everything—her hair, her makeup, and her wardrobe—is as coordinated and flawless as always. The princess is a jigsaw puzzle without the cracks. It's only when you look straight into her eyes, between mascara-coated lashes, that you can tell something's wrong.

Anabelle strides over to the bed, her high heels sinking into the plush rug. She makes a face at the mountain of laundry on the floor before she leans over and shakes her brother's shoulders.

"Wake up, Richard! It's almost noon!"

He starts at his sister's touch. The headboard—a piece of birch hand-carved by long-dead woodworkers—shudders from the movement. Beating against the rust-red walls like an incoming telegraph. I take a sharp breath when his gaze glimmers by me and shake my head as barely as I dare.

Fortunately Richard seems to receive my subtle message. He blinks up at his sister.

Anabelle puts one hand on her hip. No amount of powder or paste can hide the glower she's aiming at her older brother. "I take it, since you're still asleep, that you haven't read the papers today."

A copy of the morning post dangles from her free hand. A picture of Richard swallows the front page. My stomach turns to see it—he's walking down the gravel path, mouth open in what's clearly mid-word. I know that the empty space beside him is where my image is supposed to be.

"*Prince Richard Abandons Speech and Converses with Imaginary Beings: Has Britain's Future King Cracked?*" Anabelle doesn't even get halfway through reading the headline aloud before Richard falls back into the bed, his face completely engulfed in the goose-down pillow. "What is this?"

"Yes. What is that?" Breena glides up next to me. "What happened in the park yesterday, Emrys?"

My mouth dries as I stare at the paper. I'd forgotten all about the paparazzi and their intrusive cameras.

Richard rolls back over, bleary eyes inspecting the wad of paper and ink. "They're exaggerating, Belle. You know how they are."

"This isn't *The Sun*, Richard. This is a reputable news source. I can't help but worry about your sanity when you go AWOL from a press conference and have intricate conversations with the air in Hyde Park." Anabelle tosses the paper aside and looks down at her brother in earnest. "Are you okay? I mean, really?"

Richard pushes himself up. The sheets slide slowly down his chest, and I try my hardest not to stare. Seeing him half naked under the buttery slants of morning light, I can truly understand why Mab was so capti-vated by the human form. Why she wanted us to imitate it. The sculpt and dive of his muscles against summer-singed skin is like a masterpiece rendered by the Renaissance artists.

"Are you asking me if I've gone mental? Did Mum put you up to this?"

"Mum actually left for Bath this morning. She's checked herself into a spa." Anabelle sighs. "I'm asking out of the concern of my sisterly heart."

"Mum went to Bath? She left London?" A storm cloud of worry rises, builds behind Richard's face.

His sister scowls. "You're going off topic. Answer my question."

"No, Belle. I'm not crazy. I was talking to Edmund through an earpiece. The reporters took it out of con-text like they always do."

"Emrys!" Breena's fingers snap just by the slope of my nose, and I remember that I'm not supposed to be looking or listening to the royals' drama. Richard's on his own. "What happened in the park?"

My mind scrambles. Richard's excuse is better than any I could've dredged up. I decide to elaborate on it.

"He got cold feet and ran off to the park. He called

one of his Eton friends to talk. That's when the press found him."

In the fringes of my attention, I hear Richard speaking, low and serious. "Listen, sis. Promise me you won't leave London any time soon."

I grit my teeth. If anything would arouse Breena's suspicions it would be this. . . . If only there was a way to keep him silent without my friend catching wind of it.

Fortunately all of the other Fae's attentions are focused on me. She doesn't see Anabelle frown. She doesn't hear Richard's feeble explanation as to why the princess should stay in the confines of the city.

"There's something I should tell you. . . ." I begin, thinking of the best way to keep Breena's attention on me. "There was an attack last evening. Just after the press saw him."

My friend's face freezes at the news. Her expression tells me this incident was something I should have reported hours ago. "An attack? By whom?"

"It was a Green Woman. She had some sort of protection over her. I was barely able to break it. She almost finished me." And Richard. I glance over Breena's shoulder to see that the prince is out of bed now, throwing on a navy V-neck.

"But you unmade her? Why didn't you report it right away?"

"There was too much to deal with. I had to track down the press and wipe their memories. Then I had to handle the prince. The incident was rather traumatic, he didn't forget it that easily." I breathe in and out solely through my nose. The exercise keeps my voice and aura steady—makes it easier to lie.

The only thing it doesn't ease is my conscience. I didn't know what I expected when I first showed myself to the prince, but it certainly wasn't this. Not lying to my closest friend and jeopardizing all of our lives for the sake of secrecy.

But maybe, just maybe, the truth doesn't have to stay hidden.

This is bigger than me now. Bigger than my rank or Breena's worries. If I mess up again, if I keep letting these *feelings* get in the way, then Richard will be six feet beneath the earth, in a wooden box just like his father's.

My fingers fidget over the many different fabrics of my skirts. If I don't tell Breena now, I don't think I'll find the courage for it later.

"There's something else I want to talk to you about."

One of Breena's flawless eyebrows disappears under

her fringe of tangled curls. A question. "What's wrong?"

"Remember the night we walked to the Tower of London? The night of the ravens?"

"Of course."

"Do you remember what we discussed?" I ask.

Breena blinks, her eyes rolling back as she tries to remember.

"The emotions. They're not stopping, Bree. I tried to push past them like you said, but they've just gotten worse." My throat begins to swell under the pressure of my confession.

The other Fae's lips pull paper thin. "What exactly are you saying?"

"It's—" I take a deep breath. "It's not frustration or anger. I think . . . I think it's something else."

My friend stares, her blue eyes becoming hard, glacial. It's in moments like these I can feel the years that lie between us.

"I feel drawn to him. It's hard to explain. . . ." I falter. Breena's glare hasn't flinched. I know, just from this one look, that telling her the truth won't bring me freedom.

"You're playing with fire, Emrys," she says so softly even I have trouble hearing. "You know how this will end if you keep going. You know the sacrifice that must be made if you choose him. . . ."

I fail the courage to go on. I swallow Breena's words and steal another look at Richard. He's raking absent fingers through his hair as he talks to his sister. There's something about the way he looks when he first awakes—disheveled and wild—that makes my chest throb.

None of the other Frithemaeg can guard him any better. In the end, Richard is better off with me.

Isn't he?

"You're going to have to report this to Queen Mab."

"What?" My throat collapses into a choke.

"Mab needs to know about the attack," Breena says. "Perhaps she can spare more scouts to see if they can trace how the Old One is directing the assassins."

Relief tingles over me when I realize what Breena's referring to. "I'll send a sparrow this afternoon."

"Make it sooner." Breena glances back over her shoulder at the royals. "We might not have much time left."

We sit alone in the yard. Richard rolls up his sleeves and works beneath the harsh energy of the sun. There's a new speech in his hands—one thrust upon him as soon as he approached the prime minister and the regent with a half-mumbled apology. I stretch out in the grass as he memorizes his chance at redemption, savoring the time outdoors, yet never taking my eyes off Richard. It's not so bad, having a constant excuse to watch him.

But every time I watch him—take in his movement, smile, and sun-salting of freckles—I fight. Those feelings that started that night in Hyde Park as a slight powder of snow keep falling, sliding. A never-stopping avalanche. There's nothing between us except my rapidly fading common sense.

"Three weeks," Richard says, and lets the sheets of paper he's poring over drift into the grass.

"Hm?"

"In twenty-one days, I turn eighteen. I'll become king." The prince bites his lip and stares down at the scattered papers. He hasn't had them for more than four hours, but they're already worn through with numerous creases and folds.

"Yes. You will."

"I used to do my homework out here when I was in primary school. My tutors hated it. Too much sunburn and grass stains."

Try as I might, I can't imagine ever hating the sun. "And you still made them come out?"

He shrugs. "I was . . . strong willed as a child."

"Some things never change."

"I did my multiplication tables under that tree over there." He points, his finger arrow straight, to a distant sprawling Indian chestnut. "French conjugations I saved for the pond. I liked to shout them and scare the swans."

"Sounds like you were positively rotten." I say this with a smile, thinking of the pair of swans I'd startled so many weeks ago. How their feathers fanned, all cream and knifelike through the mist.

"It's funny, how cyclical life can be," he muses. "Though I much prefer you to any of those stuffy old tutors."

He flops back into the grass, arms and legs spread-eagled like he's about to create a snow angel in the lawn clippings. The flail of his limbs sends his right hand far. Tips of fingers, blunted and tough with callous, brush just against my arm.

Even after so many days apart, his touch, the barest pressure of his fingers, still sends a thrill across my skin. The desire, the lure to draw even closer to him, builds, rattling me. I try to shove it into the back of my thoughts. This time with Richard, lazing under noonday sun and clouds spread like lacework, should be enough. It has to be.

His hand doesn't move. I don't pull away. The place where our flesh meets feels frantically alive, like the glint and thrum of jeweled hummingbird wings.

He's looking at me. Really looking. Like a man who's stood in front of the same painting for hours, memorizing every hue and brushstroke. Richard is doing this with my face, my eyes . . . and what lies beneath it all.

"Emrys?" My name rolls off his lips with the syrupy grace of a foreign language. I barely recognize it.

I'm too scattered, too paralyzed by the war swirling black and white inside me, to answer.

"Why do you let me see you?"

"I—It makes my job easier if you're aware." There's a staleness to my words. They're translucent. I know Richard can see through them.

"I was wondering if there might be another reason," he says, careful and deliberate.

Was there another reason? Besides the failed magic and fear of Mab's retribution? Besides it being the only way out?

I open my mouth to speak when I feel it. Another

immortal presence in the air, rapidly approaching. I know, just from the briefest taste, that this aura belongs to another Frithemaeg.

"Don't talk to me," I hiss in Richard's direction, a fast jerk severing the connection between us. I throw up the veiling spell, vanish from his eyes.

Breena appears in the yard: a burst of golden curls and flight. The hasty flare of her magic tells me she rushed here.

"Emrys, you've been summoned to Mab's court. She wants you to leave immediately."

I frown and pick at some longer blades of grass, rubbing their fleshy lengths between my fingers.

"But I sent the sparrow. . . ." I begin weakly.

The older Fae shrugs. "The message she sent me seemed urgent—she's granted you a three-day leave from your duties. You should go now. I'll watch Richard until some younglings can relieve me."

A sudden fear digs its long ice claws into my shoulder blades. If Breena mentioned anything . . . If Mab has found out about my lenience with Richard—or worse, my emotions for him . . . I squirm in the plush layer of lawn, tossing the shredded grass away. It drifts to the earth like confetti.

There's no choice left to me. I can't drop the veiling spell; I can't explain to Richard why I've vanished. I can only leave things like this. . . . Unsettled.

I allow myself one last glance at the prince. His eyebrows are drawn together in a concerned V as he pretends to study the strewn papers. I can only hope he won't call for me. That he won't betray our secret to Breena or the younglings guarding him.

"Right. I'll be back soon," I say, more for Richard's unhearing ears than for Breena.

"You know Mab," she chides. "I wouldn't promise anything."

Fourteen

Mab sits alone in the throne room. Her hair, dream-white, like the dust of moth wings, spirals tight into a bun. This makes her profile calculated, clean like the edges of a shadow. Highlights the fierceness of her.

The first time I saw her, I remember, her hair was down. It streamed over her shoulders, colorless lengths catching the sun like a crystal. Iridescent. The beauty of it was overwhelming—light-dazzled mist at the base of a roaring falls—painting both power and peace. It was enough to make me, in all my spin and zephyr, stop and listen. To hear what she wanted to offer.

It had been simple enough. My loyalty for so many things. Protection. Order. Spells. A body like hers to anchor to the earth. To contain everything that was *me*.

I don't remember why I said yes. It's hard to remember what I was before this. There are times, out here, on the edge of stony-shored lochs, that I remember. The feralness stretches inside me, pinpricks of claws scratch against recollections of unbridled magic. The stench and tang of it. Wilderness and wildness, all at once within me.

Mab waves me forward; the many rings on her fingers click together, calling me back with their strange music. I look down to the ring on my own thumb. It's a silver, curling thing—a prize from a duchess's open jewelry box. So solid on my finger, it reminds me of the realness of this body. How much I've both given and gained.

"You've guarded Richard for several weeks now," Mab says when the last echo of my steps soaks into the chamber's moss-coated floors. "I've called you here to give a full report."

A report on Richard. I swallow. It's one thing to test Breena's tolerance of my emotions. But Mab . . . My memories drag me back to the Camelot days, when Guinevere, a Fae, declared her love for Arthur and relinquished her magic. Became mortal. The rage of our queen was unparalleled. Half of the court feared for their lives.

Time to be objective.

"Well, let's have it then. How's the prince coping? Drowning in the neck of a liquor bottle?"

"Actually he hasn't touched a drop since the funeral.

He wasn't eating either, but he's started taking care of himself in the past few days." I keep my face steady, an amazing feat considering the anger that flares out of nowhere. I've never felt such emotions toward the queen before. Not even when she ordered me back to London.

This mortal is ruining me.

Mab is very still. Her hands rest flat against the throne's gnarled, earthy wood. The gauzy sleeves of her gown, woven of web and fog, fall over them, hiding nothing. "He'll be back to the bottle soon. Give him a few weeks. If there's one thing I've learned through the years of our treaty, it's that mortals rarely change so simply. You have to stay objective. It's never good to let your charges get too . . . close. It never ends well."

Something about her final words sets me on edge. My scalp needles under the unflinching, ever-changing colors of Mab's stare. While the queen appears empty, unreadable, I know she's probing me with millennias' worth of magic. No matter how rigid I keep my face, how steady I thread my aura through the hoops of acceptable emotion . . . there's no way my guard will keep up under her scrutiny.

Sooner or later, she will know.

But if she suspects anything, catches a whiff of

longing under my piecemeal armor, she shows no signs of it. "And what of the Green Woman's attack? I understand you were the only one to witness it."

"Yes, Your Majesty. She attacked from the bushes. There was some kind of shield over her, made from someone else's magic. From its strength and style, I'd say an Old One made it."

"But you broke it?" Her bleached comma eyebrows twitch, the first sign of emotion since I curtsied my way through the door. Doubt.

"Barely," I offer. "It took everything I had. A strong spirit cast it, much stronger than any of the Guard."

Mab's fingers dance over the breathless lace of her dress, pausing against the empty spaces. "I've always known you had something special, some talent—but to break an Old One's shield is quite impressive indeed. Thank the Greater Spirit you managed it."

I don't bask long in the compliment. "The Old One has united them, Your Majesty. The Banshees and the Green Women. They're working together in this."

"The soul feeders?" She frowns. "Together?"

"I don't know how she did it. But whatever's going to happen . . . it's big enough for the Green Women and the Banshees to form a truce. They're allies now. I think . . . I think they mean to take the blood magic and wipe out the mortals with it."

Mab rises from the throne's ever-knotted roots and drifts toward the edge of the room, where a single rose-bush bursts into flower—stark white in a chamber of dusk-light lavenders and blues. She takes a half-open bud between her fingers, studying the frosty tendrils. For a moment it seems my queen will snap the flower from its stem. Instead she strokes a velvet petal and leaves the bush be.

"She's everywhere then. The Old One. Arms like snakes. Crawling through everything . . . getting it tangled . . ." Mab is muttering to herself, half the words whispered, unrestorable.

I fold my hands together. Even my own touch is startling in a place like this. Against every wish it makes me think of Richard.

"I believe we've been compromised." She turns to me. "I had my suspicions when Muriel disappeared after Edward's death. But now this new attack . . . It was too targeted. Too specific. The Old One's been informed by someone on the inside."

Betrayal beyond Muriel. It's . . . possible. I feel flighty, a complete fool for not thinking of it until now. Have I left Richard in a den of wolves? "Milady, it could all be simply coincidence."

"And how is it they didn't even begin to pick up traces of the magic until well after you should have been dead? Hyde Park isn't far from Buckingham. The perimeter guards should have sensed such a disturbance. Someone delayed it. Someone on the inside." Mab's sigh is wither and crumble, a strength diminished. She glides close; her hand rests against the tendons of my shoulder. I have to stop myself from gaping at the power behind her colorless, translucent skin. She's old—far older than I'm ever likely to become, with how swiftly technology is spreading.

"I hate to put this on you because you're so young, but you're the only one I trust. You had a chance to save the prince and you took it. I know where your loyalties lie. The rest . . ." My queen's words become gravelly before they fall into stillness.

"What about Breena? I know she's loyal."

"Whoever blocked your spells from reaching the other Fae had to use strong magic, more powerful than anything most of the, ahem, younglings, could have conjured. It's Breena who worries me the most."

Her words sink in. *Breena? A traitor?* There's no way on this earth my friend would betray the royals.

"Breena was nowhere near the attack!" I reason.

"That doesn't clear her." Mab's words aren't gentle. She has no room for it. "I've heard even in London magic can work at a distance."

I have no argument for this. I keep my mouth shut, waiting for my queen to continue.

"I want you to look into the matter—the Guard must be clean and loyal. Root out anyone you deem isn't. That includes Breena," she says. "I grant you permission to ignore her orders if you think that they will in any way endanger the prince."

"But, Majesty, what about Richard? I'm supposed to be guarding him. . . ."

"Leave two or three Frithemaeg with him if you're gone. I doubt a traitor would try anything with another Fae in the room. You have my permission to relieve your detail as often as you need. Just make sure you don't leave him with the younger ones for too long. I'll call you back in another month for a report, but if you uncover anything sooner, don't hesitate to message."

"Of course, Your Majesty."

Under her opal eyes I feel like quartz: brittle and translucent. "You reek of modernity. The city has been hard on you, I take it?"

"Not easy," I answer, honest.

"Stay here for an evening. It will do your spirit some good. Give you some luster." The way she says this is an order. Not an offer.

"Thank you, my queen."

"One more thing." The queen holds up her finger and digs through her hushed layers of gown and petticoats until she pulls out a slim caramel envelope labeled with curling letters. "I'd like you to deliver this message to Herne first thing in the morning."

The spells woven into the envelope's seal call out to me as I brush my finger over it. Mab will know when it's opened and who tore the paper. The queen's giving me this message means only one thing: it's too secret to send by sparrow.

My thoughts are swimming, full of mirage and possibilities as I tuck the letter into my skirts and bow out of the chamber. Breena . . . not one iota inside me clings to the belief that Breena betrayed the humans she so fiercely guards. But the younglings . . . any one of them could be privy to the plot to bring down the mortals. To end Richard's life.

Richard. The thought of him is a tattoo inked against my heart, pained and always there, even when I'm not looking. I wonder what he's doing right now, apart from me. What the younglings around him are doing. Protecting or plotting . . .

"Richard will be fine." I say the thought aloud, but it doesn't help. I'm strung tighter than a harp, ready to get back to him.

I don't stay under the earth. Unlike Queen Mab, I've never been a creature of closed, tight spaces. What feeds me, makes my soul sing, is wide plains. The soaring openness of the sky and the lunge of mountains rolling up to meet it. There's plenty of this spreading out from Mab's stronghold. Miles and miles of rugged land, cradled in mist and ribbons of mostly melted snow. In the full daylight, when the lochs and their streams echo the blueness of sky and the black of their depths, it's possible to see past the ruins of castles and defiant, layered hillsides, all the way to the sea.

It's in one of these far-forgotten fortresses that I claim sanctuary. I spend my evening among its bald relic stones, taking in the ever-clear song of the stars through a roof collapsed by long-melted blizzards. Just feet away, the tar-dark waters of a loch swish and hum with the movement of Kelpies and oh-so-shy Sprites coming up for air. There are mortal creatures too: deer and hare grazing the unkempt grass.

In such a place, I should feel whole, complete. Lacking nothing. It's where I was knit and made, where I am alive.

The sickness is gone. Nothing in my body feels the stabbing zing of current and gears. I'm at the height of my bound, incarnate power, ready to take on an army of soul feeders.

But something is unmistakably missing. A hole has been sawed through my chest. A piece of myself I lost without consent.

I can't *not* think of him. Even under such a dazzling sight as these silver-dusted heavens.

And I hate myself for being so weak—like so many of the other girls who bemused me over the years, the ones feverish with daydreams and first kisses, mooning over romanticized versions of men whose lips they touched. I'm a Fae. I'm supposed to be above all that.

But the thoughts spin regardless, over and over, picking apart Richard's every expression. All the words he's ever said to me. Especially the last ones: *I was wondering if there might be another reason.*

And all at once, I know.

There was nothing wrong with my magic. The fault

wasn't in the veiling spell or the sickness. I showed myself to Richard, dropped the enchantments, because, in the most mysterious, unreachable places of me, I wanted to. Some part of myself, the piece that's gone now, wouldn't let me hide from him.

At one time, I could count on the world. Winter's hard freeze, the bitter howls of gray wolves, the colors and laughter of May Day, and the bonfires of Samhain, the twines of magic holding me together . . . Things once constant, now suddenly not. Nothing, not even the immortal, is safe from decay.

How much of ourselves have we lost? I'm not the Fae who dwelled among these ghost-filled barrows and emerald hillsides so many years ago. I'm not the Fae who tumbled into Saint James's Park and watched Breena feed the pigeons. I don't know what—who—I am.

But I do know that Richard has something to do with it.

Fifteen

In the end, I can't stay the night. Whips of worry spur me south, under the moonrise, back toward Richard's London and all of its machines.

The heavens are still black as I wait for Herne on the borders of his forest, a nervous, unwilling messenger. I'm eager to be done with this particular errand— encounters with powerful free spirits like Herne aren't something I relish. Their magic is too unrestrained, above any law or crown.

A whistle leaves my lips, forlorn and low, infused with pieces of Herne's ancient name. Leaves rustle against the force of the summons, their edges curling in response to such close magic. The ground grows uncertain beneath my feet, trembling with the shake of horse's hooves. A magnificent stallion, its coat lusty with dark and starlight, bursts through the trees, a flash of rolling eyes and gaping teeth. Wild magic sears off its flank, although I don't need an aura to know that the creature isn't mortal. Its rider is proof enough for that. A being, perhaps as tall as the horse itself, sits proud in the saddle. Though most of him resembles a man, his flare for the dramatic emerges in the twin antlers wreathing out of his skull. They twist all the way into the shivering branches, their sharp points even impaling a few unfortunate leaves.

"Who summons me?" Herne halts on the border of the trees. His horse stamps the ground, ready to be off again.

"I bring a message from Queen Mab." I wave the envelope like a banner of surrender above my head.

Herne stays motionless in his saddle. Something of a flame flickers behind his shadowed gaze, sending sheaths of frost down my spine. I struggle not to shudder. It's better not to show fear around creatures like Herne.

"I will not cross the borders of my forest," the spirit finally says. "Bring the letter to me, youngling."

I step out, wary as prey, holding the envelope as an offering.

"Hurry up," Herne snaps. "I don't have all night. There are things to hunt."

My stride jolts to life with the fear of his words. I stop just before the borders of his forest. Only the envelope breaches the invisible boundary. Herne snatches it up like a magpie gleaning silver things. He tears—careless— into the seal and glances through the lines of Mab's spidery script.

"So—Mab wants me to allow large numbers of immortals into my forest. Wants Windsor to be a safe haven, I expect. Can't blame her, with what's stirring up north." He looks up, eyes boring full force into my body. Their effect is similar to nausea. "Does your queen require a response?"

"I'm on my way back to London. You should send a sparrow."

"One of the Guard, eh? Perhaps I'll see you here at Windsor—I always welcome the company of a pretty young Fae."

I back away, my smile weak. "Yes, perhaps."

The roar of Herne's laughter rattles the air even after he gallops away, far into the reaches of his forest.

Morning's early hours greet the world with an eerie, thistle-blossom glow as I land outside the palace gates. This time the sickness is only an aftershock, weak and secondary. I ignore it; push down the pain as I step past the bars of solid iron and pause for the two younglings who sidle up to me.

"State your name and rank!" The first of the new security is harsh, excited with her words.

"I'm Lady Emrys Léoflic—Prince Richard's Frithemaeg." Richard's Frithemaeg—these words feel sinful, their hidden meaning threatening to explode like fireworks in my aura, my face. Startling spark and neon. Showing all.

But the younglings aren't really listening. What I couldn't hide from Mab is easier to conjure out of their attentions.

"We need to see your signature," the other Fae says, her voice calmer.

I hold up my right hand. Magic seeps like nectar, sweet and gold, from my fingertips. Light stretches out, ebbing and molding into the form of a regal bird as it glides around the guards' heads. It's a mark of who I am, a piece of my essence no other can imitate. Satisfied that I'm no soul feeder in disguise, the younglings step back.

Although Mab's direct order was to spend these three days in surveillance, I have to visit Richard first. Worries of treason and assassins in corners shadowed and sharp have taken over me. Grown like mold, ruining everything. Only seeing Richard, taking him in with my own two eyes, will put this to rest.

I cross the courtyard's brick-red gravel in the calmest manner I can manage. The entire border Guard is watching me, fixed on my every move. I can't betray my true eagerness at seeing the prince, or my new distrust in his Guards. If the corruption's as widespread as Mab implies, then no one should even suspect an investigation.

I peer into Richard's window, but the glare of breaking morning beats off the glass—all yellow and amber—hindering my sight. It takes nearly a minute for me to make out the shapes of his bedroom. Ghastly wads of T-shirts and slacks flung upon chairs appear alongside the stretched, pale faces of some eclectic band on the opposite wall. A lamp lies sideways on a marble-topped table; a hairline crack snakes through one of the windowpanes. Signs of a struggle?

A sharp jolt twists my stomach as I study the bed's hovel of sheets and blankets. Richard isn't there.

Panic, pure and throaty, shatters all my years of disciplined training. I don't even bother opening the window, my hands burst through like hurled stones. Diamond glass rains across the outside sill, piercing my palms and knees as I push myself into the jagged hole.

"Lady Emrys? What are you doing?" It's Helene.

Her hair is askew, the edges of her eyes puffed pink. Something isn't right.

"Where is he? Where's Richard?"

There's a faint groan from the other side of the room. Richard's groan. My neck snaps back at the sound. He's slouched in a corner chair, wearing the same clothes I left him in. His shaggy head rests on a small writing table. On the desk's edge, nested in the papery carcasses of his new speech, is a decanter for whiskey. Clear and very empty.

Richard's moan grows louder; he begins to twitch. An eye, its specks of cool gray green and gold shot with crimson, cracks open before I can pull away.

"Embers?" My nickname is mumbled along with an incoherent string of vowels.

"*Slæpe*," I whisper at him. The spell slips, light and silvery, into his temple.

The sleepy gibberish fades from his lips as my magic drags him back into dreams. I study his rumpled features: the hot, tangled mess of his hair, that half-unbuttoned shirt, and the jarring sting of his breath. Alcohol.

I turn back and face the other Fae. Their faces are pale with confusion, as if they aren't certain whether or not to blame me for this mess of glass and spells.

"What happened last night?" I hear my voice rising,

but I can't stop it. My anger swells like dough riddled with too much yeast.

"Some of his Eton buddies came over for a couple of drinks. . . ."

Edmund. I should have known the drought of his calls and pub invites wouldn't last. He must consider Richard's mourning period over.

Helene's dark, liquid eyes don't flinch from mine. "I thought you weren't due back for three more days. What are you doing here?"

I buy time with my response by fixing the shattered window. Tiny shards of glass fly back into their puzzle parts, glinting rainbow light across the younglings' faces. They're both staring.

"I received a warning that there might be an attack. I came back to check, and when I didn't see the prince in his bed I broke the window," I explain, as if it had been the most rational reaction in the world. "Anything to keep Richard safe, yes?"

"Everything's been quiet," Gwyn tells me with a frown. "The soul feeders are lying low."

I clear my throat and gather what's left of my dignity. "Well, I guess there's no need for me to stay. I'll be back in three days."

This time I leave through the doorway. I try not to look back at Richard's crumpled slumber as I walk out of the room. A foot, angled and odd, pokes into my vision, igniting a new wave of anger.

After all the warnings . . . everything I've told him, showed him, Richard still decided to put himself in danger. He laid himself out like a lamb for slaughter, drunk and open throated. An assassin would barely have to try.

Something dangerous, lethal, writhes inside me. It's beyond anger, although there's plenty of that shooting through every vein. It's myself as I was in the beginning: spirit unsoiled by the sugarcoated trappings of humanity, unbound by Mab's laws. Snarling, carnivorous magic. Magic that, with the right trigger, is meant to destroy.

I stop walking, lean against the hallway's art-smothered wall. It takes more than a few drawn-out breaths to clear my head, silence the rage inside. With great will, I force the creature I once was back to where she's long slept, beneath years of civilization.

I shut my eyes, imagining Richard's face behind the darkness of my lids. My insides are a mess, puddles of anger and sorrow swirling together, making me sick. I hate that it hurts so much. That I let him get to me.

Sixteen

I spend the next three days in surveillance, watching the other Fae, noting their every move. But even after so much watching, I have nothing to report back to Mab. If the Old One has an agent, they're craftier than a few days of observation can uncover.

At twilight on the third day, I return to Richard.

He isn't in Buckingham Palace. The unmistakable gravity of his aura pulls me to a pub two blocks off of Regent Street. The prince is in a private back room, crouching eye level with the forest-green felt of a pool table.

The old crew is here, in this room of delicate smoke, dewy pints, and pool cues. Edmund tosses his stick back and forth between his hands as he crows about his last victory. Eyeliner leans against the edge of the table, her cleavage thrust unsubtly in Richard's direction. Mousy Hair and her boyfriend stand to the side, watching as the prince tries to sink the last of the colored balls.

Helene and Gwyn are eager to be off. Their report is

brief, made only of snippets before they vanish through the door's treated wood. I glower in the corner, burning hotter every second, like a coal fanned completely orange.

The other Fae are long gone when I snap, the agony of my anger sparking against dry tender. They don't feel my magic work. They have no idea when I drop the veiling spell.

Edmund is the first to see me. His hands grow stiff, forget to catch the pool stick that's sailing into them. It clatters to the floor, forgotten.

"Whoa. Hey, Ginge," he manages.

All at once the others find me, heads whipping about like a murmuration of starlings, perfectly synchronized. Eyeliner's face withers into a scowl.

"Embers!" Richard lays his pool stick on the table and straightens up.

Edmund, clearly more than a beer or two into the evening, takes my nickname in with a snicker.

"All of you leave. Now." The poison of my anger drives into Edmund's face with a single stare. I don't dare use magic to make them leave. There's too much emotion venting up; I'm a volcano on the verge of eruption.

"And just who do you think you are? Ordering us about." Eyeliner pushes off the pool table. "Where the hell did you come from?"

Richard swallows when I look at him—his Adam's apple bobbing with the sudden knowledge that I'm angry. That he messed up.

"Go," he tells his friends.

Edmund doesn't hesitate. Instead he's the leader of the pack, snatching his still-frosted pint from a nearby table before he heads toward the door. "Good luck with that, mate."

I have eyes only for Richard as the others shuffle past, though I can feel Eyeliner's snarky pout behind my back. It lasts long after the door closes.

I stare and stare and stare. Richard swallows twice more before he attempts to speak, "You're back."

"You thought I wouldn't be?" My voice is sharp, armed.

"You were gone, Emrys. Just gone." His eyes drop from mine, focus on the eight ball, so starkly black and white in the middle of the table. "No good-bye or anything. I thought you'd come back, but you didn't. Not that day or the next—I thought maybe you'd left for good. Then I—I began to think you might have been a dream. When I saw you in my sleep, I thought for sure you were inside my head."

"It wasn't a dream." My lips purse. Any effort to stay calm, too keep myself in check, slides back like a viper coiling to strike. There's too much emotion roiling through me, ready to be spit out like venom through fangs. "I broke through a window because I thought you'd been kidnapped. You were passed out in a corner."

My accusation needles and digs under Richard's skin, making him squirm.

"So as soon as I disappear you decide to get drunk?" I ask.

He shakes his head. "It's not like that."

I walk to the opposite end of the pool table and grab the closest ball. It's striped, one of Edmund's. My knuckles bleach white around it, the color of bone. "No?"

"Okay, so Ed called. He wanted to go out to the pubs, but I didn't think that would be a good idea."

"Right." I roll my eyes, wheeling them pointedly about the room. "Look where you ended up."

"I can't just hide for the rest of my life behind all that wallpaper and iron!" Richard's arm flails in the vague direction of the palace. "Anyway, that first night we didn't go out. I was going to say no, but I was worried about you and feeling lonely, and I hadn't seen them since Dad died. So I let them come over. We had a few drinks. . . ."

"It takes more than a *few* drinks to make a man pass out. Do you really not understand how much danger you're in? You bloated yourself with so much alcohol it would make a horse stumble! What if you'd been attacked? You'd be dead." I let the pool ball roll off my hand. It drops onto the table with a muffled crack, rolls over to the corner pouch, and disappears.

"Yeah?" The prince's eyes cloud dark with sudden anger. His voice swells. "Maybe that wouldn't be such a bad thing! Then you'll be free and you won't have to baby-sit me and wipe my ass every second of the damn day!"

My breath turns sharp. I hadn't expected Richard to fight back. My jaw clenches as I struggle to keep my frustration under control. One slip, one spell accidentally brought into being by my wrath, and the prince could die.

"Go on! Leave again! I know you want to! Why don't you just let them take me and be done with it? At least they'll put me out of my bloody misery!"

Richard's words are like punches in my gut. Pointed and perfectly aimed.

"It wasn't my choice to leave you! I was called away! It's no excuse for you to get wasted."

"That's just what I need. One more person in my life telling me what to do! Why can't everyone just leave me alone?" Richard aims a stern kick into the base of the pool table. The force of his foot causes the pool cue to shudder and fall to the carpet.

Silence, terrible and great, engulfs us both as we stare at the solitary stick.

"You didn't mean that." I can't keep the hurt out of my voice. It stains everything inside me. "You don't want me to leave . . . do you?"

For a terrible second, I think his answer will be yes. That Richard will banish me from his life. I hadn't realized, until now, just how much such a rejection might hurt.

"Would you leave me?" He turns the question back on me. Under the greenish light above the pool table, his eyes have no color. They're black as dead coal. "Wipe my mind clean so I never knew you?"

"If . . . if that's what you want." It feels like someone else is saying this. Someone who isn't unsteady. Ready to collapse.

"No," he says. The word is solid and sure. "I want you to stay."

Richard looks around the room, as if seeing it fully for the first time. An ashtray of half-finished cigars smolders in the corner, spitting out secret, smoky messages. Hollowed pints, scattered on every available surface, seem so many they could make an army of blunted glass. Most of them are congregated in Edmund's corner of the room.

"You're right. This is stupid. It's always been stupid, just like Dad said." Richard avoids my eyes. "It's just another way to get lost. It's easy to hide in here.

"I'm trying. I really am." He goes on, trying to swim his way out of this reeking, ash-filled cave. "But it's too much. It's all just been too much. Dad's death. The expectations. Everyone wanting something. I didn't ask to be the oldest! I didn't ask to be made king!"

No king does. I want to tell him this, but my lips stay shut.

"And I don't want to think about it. I don't. All I want is to run and be somewhere else. But it doesn't help. Even when I'm here doing all this . . . something's still missing."

Richard's words wrap tight around me, carry me elsewhere. And I'm back in the castle ruins, face to the stars, wondering how I'll ever be whole again.

"It's just that, the only thing that's been keeping me sane since Dad's death is having you around. And when you were just gone . . . I—I don't know. I just kind of lost it. I made an arse of myself."

Something behind his words causes me to flinch. I know it's the memory: the last exchange between father and son, the challenge that he'll never be good enough. My accusations can only remind him of that awful, last morning with Edward.

Yet as terrible as he surely feels, I feel worse. There's a sickness inside me separate from the machines. It writhes with a life of its own. I want, more than anything, to get rid of it.

"We have something." My words are uncontainable, like vomit. "Do you know what I've risked showing myself to you? To get close to you? If Mab knew about you, about us . . ." I'm unable to finish. My chest feels raw and bleeding, as if someone has battered it with a mallet.

"I'm sorry," Richard says softly. "Please believe that I'm sorry."

Just like that, the fight is gone, drained out of me. Richard takes slow steps around the pool table, draws closer, until he's only inches from me. I feel the heat rolling off his body, carrying spices of cologne and that faint earthiness. I close my eyes, but the darkness only makes his scent stronger. My heart claws hard against my ribs.

I know where this is going. How it will end. Lips will touch, carrying me away from the wildness of hill and moor, stitching my fate so much closer to the mortals. If things go wrong I can always erase it, say the simple spell that will make the prince's memory of me fuzzy at best. The one thing I won't be able to fix is myself.

"I couldn't stop thinking about you, Embers. Your being gone was . . . agony. I never stopped seeing your face. That's my truth."

Richard's fingers brush a strand of hair from my face. I open my eyes to find him staring down at me. "You're like no one I've ever known. When you left—I felt it."

My heart becomes a lion, roaring and beating against its fibrous, fleshy cage. Yearning to be free.

"You're right. There's some connection—something between us. I felt it that first time I saw you, your eyes."

Richard leans down, closing the gap between us, drawing me into him. Our lips meet, smooth and seamless. There's a nameless desire in the way he kisses me.

I feel it rising in me as well, swelling like clear, triumphant notes. He pulls me close, his kiss growing deeper, a never-ending crescendo.

This—this is something else. It reaches deep inside me. Sparks my soul.

We come up for air. Faces flushed, hair disheveled. He's looking at me, his mouth quirked into a crooked, bass-clef smile. I'm alight under his eyes. Someone breathtaking.

Want surges through me, searing static, burning away all thoughts of Mab and the taboo and who I was before.

I stand on tiptoes and pull his feather-boned cheeks to mine. Freckles press into white-board skin, becoming one. This time our kiss is even fiercer, desperate—raw energy fuels our lips. My fingers tangle, swim wrist deep through Richard's damp straw hair as I tug him closer. Something inside me rises, builds. Wanting to consume.

His breath is a razor, cutting and quick as he pulls away.

My thoughts are everywhere, a herd of deer startled by gunshot. They take several seconds to gather as Richard steps back. His fingers are close to his mouth; they come away with a tinge of red. Blood.

Dread, heavy and sick, floods my stomach as dozens of memories return. Memories of Fae who'd fallen in love with mortals: of the choice, the sacrifice they had to make to be with their beloveds. Memories I didn't need, didn't want, until now. Because Richard was never an option.

Was. My lips still prickle with magic and something else entirely. Does that mean I think he *is* an option now?

No. Magic and mortals don't mix. Breena's right. I'm playing with fire.

But the hole is there, howling. Begging to be filled. Calling out for more of Richard's touch.

"What the hell was that?" Richard pulls a small handkerchief out of his pocket, cleans his fingers.

"It's my magic." My voice trembles under this earthquake of emotions. They rock me back and forth, thrashing between elation and sorrow. "I'm sorry."

"Your magic?" He looks at me with an eyebrow raised. The handkerchief is crumpled in his right hand; crimson splashes peek through gaps in his fingers.

"I think I got too excited. . . . I don't know. I've never lost control of my magic before." I cast him a second glance. "Are you okay?"

"You still taste like strawberries." Pure joy lights his face, melting away all lines of weariness and grief. He leans back into me, warm breath diving down into mine. Our lips connect before I can stop them. His mouth is soft, like down and velvet. It makes all of me unwind.

It isn't long before my magic strikes again. I feel its wicked, wanting rush and pull away. But not quickly enough.

Richard swears and grabs his mouth.

I back away, hit the edge of the pool table.

When Richard's hand falls down, I gasp. His bottom lip is fat and shining, as though someone punched it. There's a thin split down the middle, filled with blood. He pokes it with a tentative finger.

"Don't." I hold up my hand. "It's bleeding."

"So I take it that wasn't a one-time thing?" He winces and his finger drops away.

The memories are clearer now, coming into harsh, unmistakable focus. Before the taboo, it wasn't uncommon for Fae to fall in love with men of flesh and bone. One by one they came to Mab, handing over their magic for the sake of being with a mortal. I never understood why they joined the ranks of such helpless, short-lived beings. Why they handed their bodies over to the rot of the grave, all for the sake of someone else.

"No," I tell him. "It's not."

"Why didn't it happen the first time we kissed?"

"The magic escalates with the excitement. I guess a single kiss isn't enough to trigger it...."

"So... we can't..." He looks down at the floor. It's hardwood, polished. My feet are over a board's length from his.

"If a Fae wants to be with a mortal, she has to become human."

Magic and my immortality are what I would have to pay in order to really be with Richard. A single, happy lifetime against all the ages and power of the world. The choice should be obvious to any Fae. It should be easy to make.

But it isn't. Which is why I'm still here.

Richard walks over to the edge of the room and sits on a padded bench. I stay against the pool table, my thoughts consumed by what I've just said.

"So if you wanted to be with me, you—you'd have to become human for good?" Richard asks.

"Yes. I would die." I would pass on into the unknown, just as the other love-stricken spirits gave themselves over to death. Guinevere, Alene, Isidore, Kaelee . . . all faded into the growing sea of mortals, becoming as transient as spring's first flowers. One burst of glory and then gone.

"That's not much of a choice, is it?" The prince tries to laugh, but the sound comes out wrong, more like a choke. Sad, gray shadow dampens his face. It hoods his lashes and glazes his eyes.

And I wonder what he's mourning. *Me? The kiss? Being scared and running, always running, away from it?*

No, it's not much of a choice. I shouldn't have to think twice about it. There's so much to lose.

Staring at Richard now—curled over himself like a question mark, fist digging into his chin, all of him pensive and full of promise—I can't help but wonder what's on the other side. What it would look like to rest and really be in his arms. Wanting nothing.

Just thinking about it makes the jagged missingness inside me echo. It feels wide and forever, like the empty space between stars.

I try to shake off the moment by bringing up another, less tender subject. "I'm sorry I left without saying anything. I didn't have a choice. I was called away by other Frithemaeg."

"Where did you go?"

"North. To Queen Mab's court. When she summons me, I have to leave. Don't worry, there are other Fae protecting you when I'm gone," I assure him.

"Will you have to leave again?"

"Probably." Definitely. "But I'll return to you as long as it's in my power."

Richard walks over to the table and grabs the abandoned stick. He knows that conversation is over. "Are you any good at pool?"

"I'm good at everything," I tell him.

"Excellent." He smiles, tosses me an extra pool cue. "I've been searching everywhere for some decent competition."

"Here I am," I say.

Seventeen

Every word of his new speech is memorized. It rolls off of his tongue, sometimes even in his sleep. But he keeps reading it. Over and over. I'm always close. Listening as the words bore into me, weaving and slow like a river carving through bedrock. I too know them by heart.

"Don't you think you've studied enough?" I ask, looking at the paper in his hands. There are holes, minuscule tears, where the speech has been folded too many times.

"I don't want to mess it up." His eyes dart across the neat type, manic.

I reach for the sheet. Its paper is supple and worn, almost leatherlike. I can feel it about to tear under my fingertips. "You won't."

"How do you know that?" Richard holds his end of the paper with equal strength.

"It's not the words that are the problem," I say, and

give the paper a sharp tug. Richard doesn't yield. It seems that neither of us is letting go.

He looks across the crowd of letters and blank white at me, mouth tight with things unsaid. So many times he's stared at me like this, since the poolroom. It's a gaze that makes me want to put up the veiling spell, become invisible to his eyes.

There's a shiver and buzz somewhere in the prince's clothing. Mobile phone. The bubble of burn in my throat tells me this before Richard fishes it out of his pocket. I let go of the paper, edge far enough away so the nausea isn't so sharp.

"Sorry," Richard says when he realizes what the phone has done. He holds it far in the opposite direction. With the screen facing me I can make out a wan, pixilated version of Edmund.

Richard stares at the picture as it shudders, electric in his palm. It's not hard to guess what the call is for. Past the yawning windows of the study, the sun is beginning its long dive into darkness. The time when pubs spring to life.

His thumb hovers, then lands decidedly on the crimson button. The screen goes black.

"No more of that then?" I ask, watching carefully as Richard shoves the machine back into his pocket.

"He's a prat. Always has been. Just took you for me to realize how much of one he is."

"Really?"

"Well, maybe I always knew. But it's not the easiest thing making friends when you're born with a pedigree. When I first went to school, it seemed like I had heaps of pals. But so many of them were just looking for a way in. Muckraking stuff for the tabloids. Every single time. Eventually you just give up looking for real connections . . . because just when you think you've made one, a new story appears in the front of *The Sun* and you get hurt. It's easier not to care. To get pissed in the corner of a pub." He echoes his father's words. "The only person I could ever trust in my life was my sister."

I try and imagine what life would be like without Breena. Without anyone to talk to or trust. Being the only island in a sea of your own kind. How lonely the waters are when you're surrounded by them, trapped.

"But now I have you."

"You trust me?" I ask.

"I used to have a nanny, her name was Louisa. Back

223

when I was very young. I was in her charge. She was supposed to watch every single thing I did. Louisa was usually very good at her job—kept me out of lots of trouble. But there were a few times when she failed." He holds out his left thumb, where a pearly scar arches just over the knuckle. Then he pulls up the leg of his jeans to show a shiny patch of old hurt on his shin. "The first one was a little thing. I was trying to open a can of Coke and sliced up my finger. I think Louisa was even more upset than I was. She even started crying. Begged me not to tell Mum and Dad about it because she'd lose her job. I still don't think they know about it."

"What about the other one?" I look at the mess of scar on his leg, hairless and raised. The remains of awful pain.

"After the Coke can, Louisa watched me like a hawk. I was getting older, nine, and I started really hating it. Mum was having a garden party one night and she let us kids come. I managed to run away from Louisa and get off on my own. It was great fun for a while, until the dog came." Richard gives the scar a slight prod. "Mum used to have a sheepdog. A big thing, all silver and white. Something got into it that night. Maybe it thought I was about to kick it. I don't know. . . . Whatever happened, it got hold of my leg and didn't want to let go. It was bad."

"What happened?"

"I had fifteen stitches. Louisa got fired and then she went to the media and did some huge tell-all. I never saw her after that."

"That's . . ." I try and think of what to say. "Not a happy story."

"You're not like Louisa, Embers. You've saved me every time." Richard lets his trouser leg drop. "That's why I trust you."

"How do I look?" Richard stands in front of the mirror again, tall and ramrod straight, like all those portraits of his predecessors.

I take in the picture of him, immaculate in his Turnbull & Asser suit. "Very mature. Very pre-kingly."

"That's what I'm going for." He tugs down the front of his suit, fixing it just so on his shoulders. His stare slips to the door, eyes flooding with apprehension.

"You're not thinking of running, are you?"

"I can't." He shakes his head, his hair spilling over the edges of his face. "The crown's coming to me whether I want it or not. I've always known that—from the first day I went to Wetherby, and the other children treated me differently." He takes my hand. His palm feels so warm and right in mine. Reminding us both of the impossibilities, the worlds between us. "Stay close please. I need you close."

"I'll be with you the whole time. Someone has to block you from the exits," I tease.

"Ha-ha!" His fingers squeeze my hand. "The least you can do is give me a good-luck kiss."

The memory of blood on his lips and my awful, unlifting guilt flash back through my mind. I know that if I kiss him, if I allow myself to get caught up in the tenderness of his touch, the consequences could be even worse.

"Just one kiss," Richard urges. "For me."

"What . . . what if I get blood on your nice suit?" It's a stupid defense. The only one I can fumble up in such short, breathless seconds.

"So be it," he whispers, and bends down.

It's so easy to lose myself in the feel of him. His tongue just barely grazes the edge of my lips. My hands slide up around his neck, anchor in his shaggy hair, pull him closer. With a single finger he traces the ridged pathway of my spine all the way down to the small of my back.

The touch discovers shudders I cannot control.

It's like being in another universe, a time apart. Nothing else in the world matters but how he's touching me, making me move.

Just as it's Richard who begins the kiss, so he ends it. He pulls away and I gasp, fighting the intense need to bring him back to me. But I feel traces of magic stirring like a lioness at a zoo, pacing just behind the glass, waiting for it to shatter. This feeling is enough to bind me back, to keep me from consuming him whole.

"There." He smiles down at his spotless dress shirt. "Completely blood free."

I try to mirror his smile, but the thought of what almost happened, what would've happened if Richard hadn't pulled away corrodes my thoughts. I wouldn't have stopped. I couldn't do what Richard did.

"Right. Well, here goes." He squeezes my hand again and pulls us toward the door.

The pressroom we enter is brimming with journalists and machines. Digital cameras, bright, novalike flashes, the large bulging lenses of video cameras. There are too many of them. Nausea flares the lining of my gut with near-crippling pain. I suck in a sharp staccato of breath and follow Richard up to the podium.

The prince wears his charming, for-press smile, the one no onlooker (particularly female) is able to resist. He waves to the room of scrutinizing cameras and jotting pens as he settles at the podium. I stand to the side, invisible.

"There's a well-known saying: better late than never. I believe it serves me well in this scenario."

A faint echo of laughter rounds the room. The shoulders of the reporters in the front row begin to relax. Mine are the opposite, tense and bursting as I look at Richard. What he's saying wasn't on the paper. It's not some contrived speech written by people on the opposite side of London. These words are his own.

"Most, if not all, of you know of my rather infamous no-show on our last scheduled meeting. I'm here today to officially apologize for my infraction. The truth is, if I must be blunt, I wasn't ready. To be in the public eye—to have your every move watched and judged—is trying even in the best of times. But in the midst of grief and loss it's unbearable. What happened in Hyde Park is an example of that. I ran because I wasn't ready to face the world. I wasn't ready to talk about my father's death, but the cameras found me anyway."

A few of the photographers shift their weight. I wonder if they'd been present for Richard's escape to Hyde Park.

"All I needed was time and support. I needed to find who I was in the face of all this."

Cameras flash, blindly sickening as they spot my vision. I look at Richard instead. He stares straight into the bursts of light without flinching.

"I'm ready now."

Eighteen

Midsummer brings a small celebration for the royal family. Anabelle's birthday. Her party is a modest affair for family and friends, held under tents in the palace gardens. It's the first time since the funeral that the entire monarchy, along with their Frithemaeg, have all gathered together. This fact makes the Guard more than nervous. I stay unusually close to Richard's side, making it hard for him to feign ignorance.

"You've got to stop looking at me," I hiss as Richard's uncle, the prince regent, walks away. "People are starting to notice."

"Well, it's a bit hard when you're right here and looking so blooming perfect," he mumbles between clenched teeth.

I look down at the dress I concocted for the occasion. A mint-green, lace-trimmed piece of silk vanity. Perhaps a little overboard, considering only Richard and the other Fae can see it.

Richard's eyes snag a gleaming silver tray of champagne flutes as its waiter glides by, but he turns to the hors d'oeuvres instead. He's in the middle of picking prosciutto off an asparagus spear when a voice calls his name.

"Richard!"

We turn in unison to find Anabelle standing, one hand propped on her slim hip and the other clutching a tiny plate of finger foods. The morsels seem untouched, toted simply for show.

Breena seems relieved at the sight of me. She edges away from the princess's side and leans close. "How was your meeting with Mab? Is everything all right?"

I tighten my lips, hesitant to speak too loudly for fear it will distract Richard's conversation. My words are careful, selective. Even though I trust Breena, Mab would have my head if I shared what she considered confidential. "She just wanted to hear my report in person. How are things on your end?"

Richard grows rigid in my peripheral vision. He's having a difficult time ignoring me, but Breena doesn't seem to notice.

"This one's kept me busy." She nods at Anabelle. "She just keeps going and going. I haven't been able to take the days off yet. I'm afraid the younger ones won't be able to keep up with her. At least she doesn't drink, thank the Greater Spirit."

I nod, wanting to defend Richard, but afraid of distracting him even more. I wish I'd thought to modify the veiling spell *before* the party. If I try it now, Breena or one of the other Fae will certainly notice.

"How's he doing?" Breena scans Richard as she speaks. "How are *you* doing? Been able to sort through all of your emotions yet?"

"I'm working on them." I stay vague, feel like I'm tiptoeing over eggshells. "But yes, Richard's doing well."

"Really? Anabelle's still worried. I mean, she's always worried, but apparently he's spending an inordinate amount of time alone—" Breena chokes to a stop; her cheeks wash white. She isn't looking at me.

I turn my head, searching for the sight that stole the blood from her face. My body turns to bundled nerves when I find Richard's hazel eyes bearing into mine. He couldn't resist the temptation. He had to look when I said his name.

All three of us stand paralyzed for a second.

"Richard, what are you staring at?" Anabelle shakes her brother's arm. The action breaks our stare.

I look back to Breena. The rest of her has bleached pale; she looks like some tragic heroine floating dead in a lake.

"He—he can see you?" Her voice collapses into a whisper before the question is through.

"Yes." There's no point in fighting or breaking out into hysterics. Breena knows now and that's that. I can't stop what's coming. "He sees me."

My last sentence causes Richard to flinch, but he stays concentrated on his sister's conversation.

"Oh, Emrys." My friend's sob is dry and bony. "I didn't think you would be foolish enough to reveal yourself."

Foolish? I find myself bristling, even though I know the word makes perfect sense.

"Who else knows?" Breena asks.

"Just you and him." The coolness in my veins reaches my voice, reflecting the freeze in Breena's blue eyes.

"Then there's still time to fix it before word gets back to Mab. You can wipe his memories and carry on without her noticing. How long has he been able to see you?"

Wipe his memory. This phrase puts me instantly on the defensive. Of all the ways I thought I'd lose Richard, I'd never seriously considered this. "I'm not erasing his memory, Bree. I—I can't."

"What do you mean, you can't?" She looks at me, her expression tart.

I stare back, not knowing what to say. My friend, so perfectly pieced and whole, so unlost, could never understand.

"I thought you knew better. If I'd known you would let things go this far . . ." Breena stops short as the Duke and Duchess of Wellington saunter by, exchanging their greetings with Richard and Anabelle and clinking their champagne glasses together before wandering off again. Their Fae trail them, showing little interest in our conversation.

"Don't you remember the reason we began hiding in the first place?" Breena hisses in a low tone once the other Fae are far enough away. "Remember what happened to Guinevere? Do you remember the fall of Camelot and the death of Pendragon? Remember Mab's shame? We can't make that mistake again."

"I'm not Guinevere," I tell her. "I don't make my choices lightly."

"So what is your choice? Are you going to leave us?" Hurt colors Breena's words.

My choice. The thing that's stayed locked away, banished from all active thought. As if not mulling it over and exhausting it will make it go away. But it won't. Sooner or later, the truth will find its way back to Queen Mab and my choice will become absolute: leave Richard or be banished from the courts of the Fae forever.

"Maybe Mab was wrong to go into hiding," I think aloud. "Before Guinevere, there were intermarriages all the time. It would be so much easier to protect the crown if they knew what was going on. Now that Richard knows he can keep his family from leaving London, they can stay safe."

"Nothing good can come of this," Breena says. "The choice to go into hiding was necessary. Our races would've destroyed each other. . . . They would have sought after us for magic and immortality and we would have used them dry. Mab's always acted in our best interest. You know that."

But this time she might be wrong. I long to say these words, but I know they'll only incite Breena into further arguments.

"I ought to report this. I should demote you," Breena goes on.

But she can't. We both know this. It's not because of our friendship or her loyalty to me. It's not because she wants to spare me Queen Mab's wrath. It's because I'm Richard's best chance at survival. I could be the difference between his life and death.

We stand still for a minute, watching the royal siblings converse.

"You know . . ." Anabelle chews her lip; her mocha eyes drift toward the satay chicken skewers and cucumber sandwiches on her plate. "I think it would be good for us to have a family getaway. Get some fresh air. We could go to Windsor for a holiday. What do you think?"

I don't get to hear what Richard thinks because Breena speaks again. "I'll keep your secret, Emrys. Just please, be careful. And when you do make the choice—" She pauses to push past the slight choke in her throat. "If you choose him, please tell me so that I can say good-bye."

A lump grows hard in my own throat, a mere hint of the pain it would cost to give up this life. I close my eyes and wait for the emotion to pass.

When I open my eyes she's gone, following Anabelle off to another cluster of guests. I stand alone, fighting off a sudden chill and skin that turns to goose flesh under caressing silk. It's as if Breena knows which way I'll choose.

Perhaps she sees something I don't.

"What happened?" Richard asks as soon as his bedroom door clicks shut. It's the only place we're certain to be alone. I can tell he's been dying to ask the question all evening, fighting every temptation to speak with me.

I collapse onto the bed. "You looked! I told you not to look!"

"You said my name!" he protests. "I can't help my reflexes! It's like telling me not to swear when I stub my toe!"

The mattress gives a large squeal as Richard flops beside me. His added weight dips the bed, slides me closer to him.

"Well, now Breena knows."

"Breena?"

"Right." I forget how little he knows, how much I have to tell him. "She watches your sister. We've been friends for a long time. . . . She's the oldest of the Guard—the oldest who can handle the sickness without unraveling or going mad.

"She's my best friend. The closest thing I have to a sister," I add, thinking of everything Breena and I have been through. "She knows me well."

"What did she think?" Richard props his head up

onto his elbow and stares down at me. From this angle, I can see some imperfections—the little things that make him clearly and wonderfully human. One of his nostrils rounds larger than the other. There's a thin patch in his left eyebrow, making it look the slightest bit crooked.

"She doesn't approve. Not that I expected her to. But I think she'll keep the secret. She won't tell Queen Mab."

He reaches out and picks at a lock of my hair, curling it absently around his forefinger. "What would the queen do?"

"She'd send me away, most likely. I'd go back and do scouting patrols in the Highlands." Or she'd strip me of my magic. My teeth grind together at the very thought.

"And you'd have to go?"

"Her word is law. I can't fight it." Unless I gave up my magic altogether. Willingly. But this is something I don't want to bring up.

"Then I'm glad Breena won't tell her. I want you to stay."

I close my eyes and feel the cool evening breeze wash through the open window. It's this weather, this lazy, chilled twilight that I've loved since my younger years. Something about the wind soothes my nerves, makes it easier to breathe.

Richard lets the rest of my hair unravel from his finger before his hand moves even closer to my face. The very edge of his fingertip brushes my cheek. His barely-there touch shudders through me.

Being so close, yet so far from him, is agony. I feel danger lurking just beneath the surface of me, like a Kelpie under black waters, waiting for just the right moment to strike. I have to pull away, keep him safe. But Richard draws closer, enveloping me in the heated scent of his cologne.

Just one kiss. It's what we both want. I let his lips find mine. I savor the taste of him, rest in its warmth.

But this time Richard doesn't stop. He pulls me closer—our bodies fit together with skin-tingling perfection. Our kisses grow bolder, deeper. Forging new ground. Everything—the Old One, Breena's discovery, the choice—fades out of my mind. I lose myself in his kiss. In its perfect glowing feeling.

Unbidden spells rise, creeping up my veins with the same golden glare as my passion. They gather speed and strength. Pull me under with cutting Kelpie's teeth.

Richard's cry is awful, like something wounded. It snaps my senses back into place. I roll away, heartbeat scattered and sharp, like a broken mirror. The thin line of sheets between us is charred gray and brown. Smoke rises, creating an acrid screen between Richard and me.

Through the haze, I see that the prince is still, eyes closed. There's something wrong in the way he doesn't move.

"Richard!" I call to him, my voice hoarse, a shriek. I don't dare touch him. Not even to shake him to life again.

Eyelids flutter open and his lips mold a slow groan. He glances down at the smoking sheets, dazed, and pulls himself up in one sluggish movement.

"Holy hell, you pack a punch." His laugh quickly becomes a wince.

I want to get closer, to investigate any wounds, but I'm afraid the spells will leap out again. "Are you okay?"

"I'll live." Richard wheezes and lifts up his shirt to show clean, unmarked skin. "Feels like I just got struck by lightning."

"I'm sorry. I'm so sorry." It's all I can say as I edge away from Richard and the ruined sheets. I never should have let it go this far. I knew I would harm him and still I kept going.

"Don't." He reaches out and grabs my wrist. I flinch

under his touch, afraid that even the simplest stroke of skin will unleash me. "It was my fault too, Embers. I knew better."

I hold my breath and look at his hand on my wrist. Nothing happens. No sparks or white flash of magic. But this doesn't stop the terrible knowledge from settling over me. I hurt Richard. This . . . whatever we have . . . can't keep going.

Not as I am now.

"Your friend—Breena. You told her you couldn't erase my memory. Why?" He lets go of my wrist. It falls, limp against the rippling green of my dress.

"Because I'm selfish." I almost yell this at myself. "Because I want things to be different from what they are."

"Maybe—maybe it would be better if you just got it over with. If there's no chance of anything . . . of us . . . then there's no point in pretending like there is." He swallows, trying his hardest to make his face look unbreakable. It doesn't work. I know the sadness in him too well. "Erase my memory and get out before it hurts too bad."

I try to imagine what it would be like: leaving, but not really being gone. I could ask Breena to take over Richard's duties, but I would still see him. And I know, every time, I would wonder what it was I missed. "Is that what you want? To pretend this never happened? Go back to the way you were?"

"I might not remember if you wiped my memory, but I know I'd still feel you." His words are sulfurous, flaring like a comet's tail. "You've changed me too much."

I pull my knees up to my chest. Crème-de-menthe fabric falls luscious over my legs, pools into the whiteness of the bedspread. "I'm not wiping your memory, Richard."

His mouth is still as he looks at me, but his eyes say all.

So there's still a chance.

Still a chance.

A chance.

I bury my face in the bare cradle of my arms. As if I can hide from it.

Richard suddenly slides off the bed.

"Do you know what I haven't done in a long time?" he asks as he excavates a particularly large pile of laundry and books.

"What's that?" I lift my head and peer through the thin netting of auburn tangles.

"Danced!" He grunts, triumphant as he pulls an old record casing out of the pile. "Listened to much classic rock before?"

I shake my head and the hair spills away, back behind my shoulders.

"You'll like this, I think." Richard places the bumpy, black plastic circle on top of the turntable and eases the needle into its grooves.

"I thought no one used records anymore."

"True." Richard smiles as the opening guitar riffs flood the room. Though the vinyl and its player are old, the speakers are not. The room brims full with the rich, textured sound of chords. "But I think the music sounds more real on vinyl, and this baby's a classic." He gives the turntable a loving stroke. "Vintage 1948. I found it in a loft at one of the estates a few years back."

The catchy tattoo of drums joins the wailing melody, rattling the window frames. Richard skips into the middle of the room, his feet kicking through piles of debris like a kid destroying a sand castle.

"Come on!" He waves for me to join.

I push myself off the bed, watching the prince move this way and that. His dancing now is so different from the dancing at the clubs. He enjoys this music. It moves him.

The music *feels* different too. Maybe it's because the

technology is older, less abrasive. It doesn't seem to sap my essence like the pub's subwoofers.

Richard sees me standing still and sways over to my spot on the rug. "You have to dance!" he shouts above the music. "It's no fun unless you do it too!"

His arm latches in mine and pulls me to the middle of the rug. Plush fibers swallow my bare feet, help me stay awkwardly rooted against the dance. The dancing I've seen at Elizabethan balls and the Faery circles was nothing like this. That music was softer, more suited to twirls and wide, billowing skirts. This song is made of grunge and edge. I frown and try to wiggle my hips, but only succeed in looking absurd.

"Just feel the music. Let it go through you." Richard grabs my hands and pulls me into his own movements. It's so easy for him to move as the music writes, to feel out the notes and let them pull him where they will.

"Follow me." He guides my arm over my head, forcing me into a quick turn. The sudden movement breaks me out of my dancing stalemate. My feet glide across the rug on their own, my toes darting over patterns of peonies and paradise birds. Richard lets go with a smile, releasing me to dance to my own beat. I don't stop swaying, afraid that if I do, the dancing might not start again.

We dance through all of the songs on the album. Richard puts on another record. Its music is slower, the edgy hum of the guitar closer to beats I know well.

"Do you have any favorite dances?" He takes my hand and brings me close. His touch is so easy to feel against the sheerness of my dress. I can't help but stay rigid under his fingers, on guard against any more passionate magic. "Something slower maybe?"

"None you would know," I tell him.

"Try me."

"The galliard, the canary, the saraband, the volt." I couldn't forget if I tried the fine array of rainbow silks and corseted waists weaving in and out of men's doublets and ruffs in such elaborate patterns. For years it was all I did, watching the rich and privileged dance and dance to the pulse of harpsichords. The hum of lutes.

"You got me there. Will a waltz do?" Richard starts swaying to the three-step beat. We spin slow circles, the room becoming a blur around us. "Can't let all those years of dance lessons go to waste."

"A waltz is just fine." We weave a delicate path between mounds of books and laundry. Any faster and I would be dizzy.

"Were they any fun? Those balls?"

"For the people who were there, yes. I got bored after a few of them. You would've hated it."

"Oh?" He draws me around in a twirl so I can only see snippets of how his eyebrows quirk.

"It was all duty and tradition and masked feelings. A world of rules." As I say this, I realize how much of what I described could apply to Mab's court as well.

"How well you know me." Richard smirks.

"I'm getting there."

"Right, so now I know your favorite dances. How about your favorite food? Let me guess. . . ." His head cocks to the side, birdlike. "Strawberries."

"Delicious but a bit too simple." The same balls where they danced the volt also had tables and tables of food. Fresh fruit, roast beasts, caviar, and smoked fish . . . the combination of ingredients was deliciously endless. "Baked mushrooms stuffed with herbs."

"That was my next guess," he says with a wink.

"What's yours? Steak?" I venture.

"Close. Beef Wellington. Favorite color?"

"I—I don't know. . . ."

"You don't know your favorite color? Who *are* you?" Richard's arms grow stiff around me, his features a portrait of mock horror.

"Well, it's not like we Fae flit around asking one another these questions all day. We have very important work to do, you know." I feel the impish expression come to life on my face. "I suppose I've just never thought too hard about it."

The sparrow tilt of his head returns and his lids narrow as he studies me. "Hm . . . I'm going to say green."

"What?"

"Green." Richard nods at my dress. My eyes. "It's your favorite color."

I can't help but smile, because as soon as he says this, I know he's right. Green. It's the shade of envy and predators, but it's also the color of grass and leaves and life. It reminds me of the rolling hills of the high country.

As the steps go on, becoming looser and less formal, Richard hugs me closer. My head rests against the steady width of his shoulder.

Richard takes his hand off my hip and strokes my hair. "Anabelle has her heart set on spending some family time at Windsor Castle. I tried to make some excuse, since we're not supposed to leave the city, but I don't think she'll let it sit. I told her we'd have to wait until— until after my birthday."

There's tension in his words, and I remember that

the dreaded date is only a week away. A week. Seven days until Richard becomes king.

"You're going to be a great king," I whisper, and lift my head to look at him. "Honestly Windsor's the one place outside of London you would be safe. That's Herne's territory. I don't think any soul feeders would try to reach you there."

"Who's Herne?"

"Herne the Hunter. He's a very old spirit that guards the woods of Windsor. His magic is very wild and powerful, and he doesn't answer to anything. Not even Mab." My fingers press tighter into Richard's back as I remember my last encounter with the spirit. "But he won't harm the crown. He only cares about his woods, and since you technically own them, he doesn't forbid you to step foot in them. If you can make it to Windsor without being attacked, you should be safe."

"So he's not a soul feeder or a Fae?"

"No. He's free magic. There's a good deal more supernatural creatures than Fae and soul feeders. Kelpies, Will-O'-the-Wisps, Ad-hene, Brownies, Redcaps, Sprites, Dryads . . . far more than even I can keep track of. And then there are spirits like Herne, who have no category. Generally they stay out of the cities. They almost never bother humans."

"Good to know." The prince squeezes me closer. "Any more spirits who like to run around on my property? Perhaps there's a vampire in the loft? A ghoul in the kitchen?"

I laugh. "If I find one, I'll let you know."

A smile warms his lips and he pulls me into another, skirt-swirling turn. "Good. I'm glad I have you to count on for such things."

"Always." I freeze even as the word leaves my lips.

But if Richard hears it, if he wonders what the word might mean, he gives no sign. He wraps his arms back around me and continues swaying. We move together as one being, in sweet unison to the lingering guitar solo. We dance even after the last notes die, moving about in each other's arms to some unheard song. We dance until nothing is left.

Nineteen

Mab's sparrow soon arrives, a mess of mud-flecked feathers and parchment summoning me west, to the center of England.

After I tell Richard farewell, I ride high on the winds, taking hold of my new energy. The land passes flat beneath me, yellowed with long, waving grass. The plains of Albion. The heart of Britain, the place where many of my younger memories were formed.

Today the Faery queen's court presides at Stonehenge, one of the few wells of deeper magic left to the south. A long time ago, it was a place where spirits flew up from the ground, an overflow of magic. More than a few Fae came to life here. But, like all of the other sites, Stonehenge's womb now lies barren. There are no new spirits. Only us.

Mab and her attendants are planted in the middle of the aging circle, soaking in all the strength this jumble of stones offers. Their magic rattles through me as I land, careful to avoid the human's fragile security system.

"Look at them gawking," Mab says, pointing to the crowd of camera-toting mortals beyond the fence. "Nothing is sacred anymore."

"They forgot what this place was for, Your Majesty." I bow my greeting, hands folded in front of me. Out of the corner of my eye, I glimpse mercury hair, unbearably bright under so much daylight. It's Titania, leaning against one of the upright stones, staring and staring.

The queen's face stays solemn. "It's almost not worth the trip down here with all of their contraptions clouding the air. Sooner or later they're going to kill these stones. Then where will we be?"

"There's always the crown, Your Highness," I remind her gently. I focus my vision solely on Mab, as if blocking out the duchess's glare will make her disappear. Under the open, seamless blue sky, the queen I've followed for so long almost looks small. Swallowed in the icy iridescence of her gowns and hair.

"For now." Her mutter is so grim and quiet that at first I'm unsure of what I heard. I stand still. It's been ages since I've seen Mab in such a horrible mood.

It takes the queen a minute to break free of her foul thoughts and remember my presence. Her clear opal eyes refocus on me, startled. "Oh, Lady Emrys. Sit." She waves at one of the nearby collapsed rocks.

I sit on the lichen-laced stone, my smile weak and watery. A spell, one of Mab's, envelops us. Our conversation, the words between us, is now secret.

"It's my understanding that there have been no further incidents. Is this correct?"

"Yes, Your Majesty." I nod. "Everything has been quiet."

"And the prince? How's he?"

I concentrate on keeping my response normal and deliberate. "He's doing better than before. There's still sadness. But I think he'll be all right."

"The other Fae tell me he's been spending a good amount of time alone." I wait for Mab to say more, but she lets the sentence fade. Her eyes never leave me. They hardly even blink.

I clear my throat to dismiss what hangs unsaid in the air between us. It could be that Mab knows nothing. That she's just fishing for signs of guilt. I mustn't give her any. "It seems his grief is a very private thing. I'm sure a few more weeks will see him back to normal."

Mab flattens her palm against the rock she's sitting on, drinking in its ancient magic. It's strength she's saving. Strength for later. "And your investigations . . . have you found anything significant?"

"None of the Fae have shown any abnormal activity. If one of them is a traitor, they hide it well," I say.

"Then you aren't looking hard enough."

"My queen, with all due respect." My voice dips and breaks like a dolphin plunging for air. No matter how slowly I breathe, I can't keep it steady. "There might not even *be* a traitor in the Guard. I think it would be best if we simply continue to guard the royals like we always have. Keep the scouts searching. We'll find something eventually."

"You're too young, Emrys. Too trusting." A slight, wry smile plays at Mab's lips. "There's a traitor. I know it. If you used your magic more than your head, perhaps you'd feel it too."

My jaw clenches at the queen's little dig. "It's dangerous to waste magic in the city, milady. It's not so easy to recharge in London's streets."

"What's important is that you stay on task," she shoots back. "You haven't done everything you can to seek out our Judas. I expect you to use any means possible—magical or otherwise—to uncover the identity of the collaborator. Report back next month."

I blink, trying not to let my frustration breach any more than it already has. Emotions have no place in Mab's court—they're almost as despised as technology. "Yes, my queen."

"Perhaps there will be no need . . ." the queen muses. "We've caught a trail. It's faint, but a trail nonetheless. We've followed it here, down south."

"She was here?" Goose bumps prickle my skin. "This close to the cities? I thought an Old One couldn't be this far south."

"Her movements are a bit freer than we expected." Mab's tiny shoulders slope up in a shrug. "But we're closing in."

The tingle grows; my muscles burn with a cool, eerie premonition. The Old One isn't giving up without a fight.

"It would be a relief for this threat to be over," I admit.

"All the more reason to root out any traitors in our midst." Mab starts to stand. "If they find out their mistress has been defeated, they'll grow rash. It would be best to prevent such tragedies."

I nod, partly to camouflage my frown. The longer I've spied on my fellow Fae, the more I've come to realize

I won't find a traitor among them. There's a better way to find answers, one that doesn't require so much sitting and waiting.

It's time to go hunting.

"Still, it would be prudent for us to have a backup plan if London doesn't offer the protection Richard needs. Herne has agreed to let us use Windsor as a gathering point, in case a retreat is necessary. If the need arises, don't hesitate to—influence the prince to take a holiday."

"I'll keep that in mind." I fight back a shiver at the memory of Herne. Part of me is surprised that the jealous spirit granted Mab permission to gather on his land. Usually only a few brave Frithemaeg dare to accompany the royals on their holidays there.

"And tomorrow is Richard's birthday, is it not?" the queen asks.

I nod. This week passed with Richard anxiously eyeing the calendar. Slash by red slash we've arrived at the eve of his accession. Tomorrow, whether he wants to or not, Richard will officially become Britain's king.

"I expect then, that you'll be extra vigilant." The Faery queen is right. The moment Richard becomes king, he'll be made even more desirable in the Old One's eyes.

"Of course, milady. We'll be on our highest alert," I promise.

"Then may the Greater Spirit go with you, Lady Emrys."

"And with you, my queen." My many skirts rustle with my sudden curtsy. "I'll resume the surveillance straightaway."

"Good." Mab nods. "I'm counting on it."

I don't go back to the palace. Instead I fly to the heart of the city, on the edge of the churning, muddy river just across from Parliament. Darkness is falling just as my feet land against the paving stones. The moon is already high, casting its blush into the Thames.

The evening is pleasantly warm and the sidewalks swarm with people. Some are hooked together at the elbow, the girls resting their heads on their partners' shoulders as they saunter down the path. I stay still by the river's edge, watching them pass. It's too early. I must wait a while before I have a chance of snaring what I'm looking for.

Despite the bustle and life of the city—the street musician's cheery steel drums and the gold-brown scent of sautéed onions over hot dogs accenting the roar of red double-decker buses—all I feel is the shadow of what will come. There's no stopping it. The Old One has moved south—her fingers of assassins stretching into every corner of the city. Reaching always for Richard.

The possibility of losing him is thick, swallowing me whole with its terror. I can't let it happen. Not because of failing Mab or doing my duty. Not because it would put a black mark on my career as a Frithemaeg. I can't lose Richard for a single, undeniable reason.

I love him.

The truth is clear now. As clear as the evening sun spreading across the river waters. I love Richard. I always have. It's only now that the thought has been so sure, so utterly cemented in my mind.

"Love." I make myself say the word. Test it on the tip of my tongue. It tastes strange, but good. It makes the hole inside me shrink, the emptiness lessen.

But with it comes a fear that has nothing to do with the Old One or her minions. I've watched so many versions of the fairy tale. So much is uncertain, unmapped. Richard likes me . . . yes . . . but that means nothing when the stakes are this large. When immortality and death are tossed about like poker chips to the highest hand.

Is Richard willing to pay the price? Even if he does love me, if he says so, he's still so young. Seventeen years. The blink of an eye. How can he know, truly know, if he wants to spend the rest of his days with me?

And me—could I die for him?

In dusk's illuminating glow, the surface of the Thames looks less full of sewage and debris and more like the mighty brown god it once was. I stare down into the water, tracing all of its swirls and eddies as the current rips past. I let these thoughts drift off with it. I need all of my concentration set on the hunt.

The sky fades rapidly, its flashy neons diving into the melancholy blues of night. The city becomes an island of electric light; the rays of the streetlamps create a world of bone-white shapes and shadows. The places soul feeders, especially Black Dogs, love to skulk. It's in these dark nooks and crannies that I must start searching if I want to find any answers.

I don't expect to find anything so early, but when I approach the bridge I feel it. My fists curl into themselves as I edge closer to the beginnings of a tunnel under the bridge. Mortals avoid the dark underpass, choosing to hike up the steps and cross the street instead. That's wise, considering what's waiting there for them.

I duck into the walkway's shadows and pause, glancing up nervously as the roof rattles and shakes beneath every passing vehicle. Something in the far corner springs to life. The sharp *tap tap* of animal nails fills the tunnel.

"*Cyspe!*" My binding spell shoots out, wraps around the beast's char-black, barrel chest.

The Black Dog howls as the spell seizes its limbs, collapses it to the floor. Under the light of my magic I see just how large this scavenger has become. It's almost the size of a small pony, engorged on all of the innocent lives it sucked away.

I bend down and grab the beast by its haunches. It snarls and thrashes as I drag it closer to the white-tiled walls.

I look around to the dim entrances of the underpass and whisper a blocking spell. Any mortal with courage enough to enter the poorly lit tunnel won't be able to resist my repelling magic.

I kneel back down in front of the dog, far from its snapping teeth. I can't bind its mouth. To answer my questions, the Black Dog needs to be able to speak.

"What's your name?" I ask the spirit.

The dog growls; its custard-yellow canines glow beneath the scant light.

"Blæc." The name blends in perfectly with the rest of its rumbles, caught only by my sharp hearing.

"I won't hurt you, Blæc, unless you give me a reason," I add. "I just want to talk."

The snarls die. Poison-bright eyes roll back to look at me.

"You're a London soul feeder. You must be aware of what's going on at Buckingham. Tell me, who's doing all of this? Who has your kind allied with?"

The Black Dog shakes its head; a high keen of a whine leaves its muzzle. "I don't know. I don't bother with events beyond my territory."

I twitch my finger. The binds on the animal's legs clench tight, drawing out a yelp.

"You're lying," I say. "I know the howls that travel at night bring news between your kind. You *must* have picked up some tidbits from those."

Sounds of begging and pain become a mumble of gravelly words. "She doesn't come here, doesn't speak to us. We do not know her name!"

"Then how do you receive orders?" I feel the anger, my own monster, stirring. My teeth grit against it.

I need to keep the dog alive if I want answers.

"There are those she speaks with: messengers, leaders," Blæc pants. He's twitching, squirming under every cruel white lash of my spell.

"Who? What are their names?" Now I'm getting somewhere.

But the Black Dog's muzzle snaps shut—a row of zipper-tight teeth and twisted black lips. Its eyes paint over with a familiar sheen. Blæc is afraid.

The savageness inside me wants to pull, winch his bonds tighter and pour more pain into his haunches, but something else in the creature's eyes stops me.

"I'll erase your memory," I promise. "No one will find out what you've told me. You'll be safe."

Blæc whimpers, unsure of my proposal. The dog is walking a dangerous line, caught between immediate pain or the possibility of another spirit's wrath.

"I swear it," I hiss into his cathedral-arched ear. "I swear it by the Greater Spirit."

His uncertainty wavers, mists apart like windswept smoke. "There are two the Old One speaks with. Two that I know of—Jaida, a Green Woman, and Cari. She's a Banshee. All of the orders go through them."

I lean back on my heels, eyeing the animal as I

commit the names to memory. A Banshee and a Green Woman. Together. Though it's something unheard of, I know the dog's telling the truth. There's no deception curled around its grooved, tire-black lips.

"And where might I find them? Jaida and Cari?"

Blæc's head shakes, causing the rest of its body to shudder. "I don't know."

Another truth. This creature doesn't know much. It lies at the bottom of the totem pole, a hulking scavenger of souls in the lamp-flecked London night.

"Very well. That's all I need to know." My finger sinks deep into the clumped, matted fur of the creature's forehead. *"Forgiete."*

While the spell permeates layer after bewildered layer of the beast's mind, I sever its bonds and all but run for the closest entrance. Once the memory spell settles, the Black Dog will become its old, snarling self, ready to tear into any creature that steps foot in its territory. Sure enough, when I reach the end of the tunnel, the creature is howling. The sound curls the end of every hair, tugs at my heels. I drag through it, step decidedly through my blocking spells. If the dog wants food, it'll have to venture out of its miserable underpass, into the tangled city streets.

My mind races, but I keep walking down the river-front at a steady pace. Jaida and Cari. A Green Woman and a Banshee. Defending Richard against their powers is one thing, but being an aggressor is another thing entirely. It'll be much harder to wring information out of those two soul feeders than it was to subdue Blæc—a lone wolf of a spirit. I'll need help in my hunt. I'll need Breena.

Mab's warning forks like lightning through my thoughts: trust no one. Including Breena. I pick up my pace, nearly barreling through a slow couple in front of me. Breena isn't the traitor. I have to trust her. If I can't, then there's no one else for me to depend on to keep Richard safe.

And if there's one thing I know for sure, it's that I can't do this alone.

Twenty

My search for Breena doesn't take long. I feel her familiar aura even through the city's electrical haze. Anabelle's in a tiny, upscale restaurant: the type that needs a reservation months in advance. The type with polished hardwood, pure silver utensils, and antique furniture so aged it looks like it might fall apart under the slightest weight.

Being invisible in a restaurant is an interesting challenge. Servers and hosts zip past, balancing trays of well-dressed plates and cocktails. I cling close to the wall, following Breena's aura like a bat tracing echoes: up the crimped, narrow stairway and behind a door of lushly cobalt curtains. I find her in the princess's private dining room. The table is ringed with Anabelle's school friends: blondes, brunettes, diamonds, and pearls. I look down the row, remember the loneliness in Richard's voice as he spoke of friendship. It's rarity. How many of these girls would stand by Anabelle if they knew what was coming?

Breena stands by the window, taking in the same scene, face half masked by a potted-palm frond. "Emrys! What are you doing here? Where's Richard?"

"I left him with Ferrin and Helene. Listen, I need to talk to you." I edge close to the windowsill. Outside in the darkness someone passes on the far sidewalk. For the faintest second, I imagine it's a Banshee.

"I haven't told anyone, if that's what you're asking," Breena chips in. There's a new edge to her voice; it makes me uneasy.

"That's not it," I reply. "Not at all, actually."

I take a deep breath. Including Breena in my plans is risky. I have no guarantee she won't report back to Mab or try to use her age to order me into submission. But without Breena, the plan is even riskier. I could end up dead. Trusting our friendship is my only choice.

"I need your help."

She brushes the palm frond away, caressing its fan with her fingers. "With what?"

"I think I know how we can end this—get to the bottom of the threat. I tracked down a Black Dog. It gave me the names of soul feeders who are in contact with the Old One. We can hunt them down for information."

Breena's hand freezes, splayed in the exact silhouette

of the plant she's touching. "You went hunting? On whose orders?"

"It was my decision," I tell her. "I'm sick of waiting on Mab's scouts. The trail to the Old One is here, in the city. You know that."

"Does Mab know what you've done?" The dining room's light is warm, reflecting off rich wood and gold-threaded wallpaper. It falls on Breena's face, calls her out from the darkness like a figure in a Rembrandt painting.

"She encouraged me to investigate." My stomach twists under the half-truth. Mab would be appalled at my proactive methods: hunting down the enemy instead of waiting patiently for the evidence to surface on its own. So many weeks ago, when I was wholly hers, I would never have considered this.

"And what are their names? The ones you want to hunt?"

"Jaida and Cari. One is a Green Woman and the other a Banshee. That's all I know. Apparently they relay the Old One's instructions to the other soul feeders here in the city. They're the link, Bree. They can lead us to her." My speech gains speed. The thought of exposing the Old One is enough to make me giddy.

Across the room the princess laughs. The sound jolts,

cuts through the air like a battle-worn bagpipe. For the briefest second, I have the sensation that everyone in the room can see me. I glance over my shoulder, but none of the diners even look up from their watercress salads.

"I don't know. . . ." Breena begins. "It sounds awfully risky, not to mention impossible. Who knows how many Banshees and Green Women are crawling through this city? And if we do find them and manage to make them talk, then what? Do we kill them?"

"We'll figure something out. . . . Wipe their memories or gag them." I shrug, trying to dismiss these problems I hadn't thought all the way through.

"And if their magic is too strong for that?" Worry grays Breena's face. "We could both end up dead, Emrys. Then where would Richard be? I know you're eager to protect him, but we have to think of all the ramifications, all of the consequences. You haven't been thinking clearly—you're riding on your emotions."

I don't try to argue. I know better than anyone that emotion . . . love . . . is pushing me into this hunt. "We have the element of surprise. That gives us something."

"And I suppose if I say no, you're going to go off and do it yourself anyway?" Breena says with a roll of her eyes.

I nod.

"Of course," she mutters.

"Please, Bree. I need this."

"Well, it *has* been a while since I've gotten into a brawl. . . . Fine." She sighs, as if some heavy weight is sliding off her back. "I'll go with you. But only because I don't want you getting yourself unmade in some filthy, rat-strung alley."

"Oh! Thank you!" I throw my arms around her, an action she clearly isn't expecting. She stands awkward in my embrace, her own arms dangling at her sides like limp fish.

"We should do some reconnaissance first. I don't want to go plunging into a situation," Breena says once I let go. The stiffness of her voice reminds me of just how human my embrace was. "And we're out when I say so. Understand?"

I let the last statement glide over, try not to think about what could happen. "We'll go the night after Richard's birthday. That'll give you time to order a replacement Guard for Anabelle."

She nods, but I see the apprehension behind her tundra-washed eyes.

"We'll be careful," I tell her. "I promise."

Twenty-One

A chance. A chance. A chance. This is what the silence whispers when I return to Buckingham. I sit on the edge of Richard's bed, watching him swim deep through dreams. The music we danced to after Anabelle's birthday party is long gone, pushed back into its cardboard sleeve and shelved with all the other records.

I take in Richard's smell: a tangy mix of soap and his own natural musk. Earth and sea salt. I memorize every inch of exposed skin, noting the freckles and scars: the crescent-moon Coke-can sliver on his thumb, the knotted, pearly dog bite.

Love: a word that holds so much in four brief letters. What does it mean for me to love him? It's a thought so huge and foreign I can barely fit my brain around it.

One thing I do know: being so close to him helps me forget the gut-shredding sickness, the traitors, and the Old One. It would be so easy for me to just stay here, watch him forever.

But I don't know if that's enough.

Eventually he opens his eyes. He finds me there, watching. He doesn't flinch when our gazes meet. Instead he holds my eyes in a steady, unrelenting stare. Fear, yearning, love. All of these swirl up inside me, a pillar holding right now together, pulling my old self apart. I'm motionless on the edge of the mattress, scrambling to read what might be behind those irises of henna and green.

And though that draw is still, always, between us—a forte of feeling under my skin—Richard seems now, more than ever, unreadable.

"I don't think I can get out of bed," he says. His breath blows hot against my face.

The hairs on my arm rise, like tiny twists of fire, flickering for more breath, more touch. I try my best to ignore them. Right now is about Richard. About helping him face the day. "You start by sitting up."

He groans, buries his bristly jawline into the creampuff pillow.

"You're still afraid?" I ask after a while. Richard stays burrowed, as if some fabric and feathers can really shield him from the hours, days, years to come.

Finally he breathes deep and rolls onto his back, exposing all the tautness of his shoulders and chest. I focus hard on his stubble-coated, pillow-indented mess of a face. "I don't *feel* like a king. I have absolutely no bloody idea what I'm doing. . . ."

"None of the new monarchs did. Most of them felt the way you do now." I reach out and take his hand. It's cooler than mine, trembling like a discarded autumn leaf. "There's no reason you won't be a good king. All you can do is get out of bed and try to do best by what's been handed to you."

"They were scared too? My father was scared?" Slowly, surely, his grip steadies until I can't tell if I'm holding his hand or he's holding mine.

"Oh sure. Some more than others. They all had their fears. Henry the Third was a mess. Albeit, he was nine years old."

"I guess that puts things into a little perspective."

Right now, in this little heaven of cloudy sheets and amber dawn light, I long to graze my palms against his face, kiss him. More than that, I want to tell him everything, to pronounce, so loud and clear and eloquent, the word *love*. But fear spools out, painting so many different futures: Richard accepting my love, asking me to give up everything. Richard running, tearing me to pieces with his denial.

I don't know which would break me more.

So I swallow it back, for another time. "You're going to be an amazing king, Richard. You have Edward's steel. And more, I think."

The smile on his face is fresh, full of newness.

"I'll always believe in you. Now get out of bed, you lazy arse. We have a birthday party to go to."

Richard shoots me a look of bale and mock contempt. "That's no way to treat a king!"

"Even kings need a push every now and then." I slide off the bed. "Oh, and Richard?"

He grunts and starts sorting through his floor laundry for an acceptable outfit. From the look of the crumpled shirts and slacks, I doubt he'll find anything of worth in that pile.

"Happy birthday."

Richard pauses; the smile on his face blazes like the noon. I tuck the sight away in my mind. I know I'll need it, to remember, in the days to come. "Thanks, Embers."

The party is extravagant, a worldwide affair of friends, family, and unstoppably grinning diplomats. There's an elaborate five-course meal of fruit, pheasant, and every other expensive ingredient. A multi-tiered cake towers in one corner, waiting to be cut. There are more toasts than I care to count—explosions of corked tops fizzing gold into glasses every few minutes—pour after pour after pour in Richard's honor.

Under six pear-shaped chandeliers of blazing crystal, they dance, mingle, and drink until they glow. I feel as if I've stepped back in time, watching them. Silk-clad women glide around pomegranate carpet, cocktails in hand. Men in sharp tuxedos gather in groups. Their conversations of politics and art are as circular as they've been for centuries.

As the night goes on, the furrow in Richard's brow grows. He watches his mother flit in and out of the crowds—newly refreshed from her time in Bath. She hasn't said a word to her son. Not that she needs to. I can tell the occasion is too much for him. These scores of distinguished guests, the orchestra, the flower arrangements that resemble small jungles. There's not an eye in the room that hasn't pinned and examined him like some elaborate foreign insect.

It doesn't help that there's alcohol in the room. It flows abundantly, in champagne flutes and endless wine bottles. The crowd of faces grows increasingly flushed and the laughter grows volumes louder by the hour.

It's all too much. It doesn't take a Fae's sense to know he'll run.

Richard's gracious smile stays, faithful as a trained dog, when he heads for the door. He glances over his shoulder to make sure I'm following. I weave through the crowd, ducking beneath martinis and wild-slung elbows. Though it would be easier to fly over their coiled, braided heads, I prefer to preserve my magic. Tonight, with the confused crowd and newly anointed power of Richard's kingship, is the perfect opportunity for the Old One's assassins.

Richard doesn't stop at the door. He walks through the palace's grand, public rooms, roped off and dimmed. We pass through these silhouettes of grandeur like a night train, flying past the bruise-shaded darkness without braking. Although we're in the same building, it feels as though we're worlds away from the bright noise of the party. The silence of the halls is strange, invading after an evening of constant chatter.

"Where are we going?" I ask after we plow through the second room.

"You'll see." Richard pauses to let me catch up with him. Somewhere in his journey out of the ballroom he managed to snatch an unopened bottle of champagne. He grips its gold-papered neck with terrible tightness.

More questions rise, about the bottle, our path, but I bite them back. The last thing Richard needs right now is more pressure. I have to let him lead.

We continue to the far corner of the palace. To a place Richard's daily duties never take him. Out of all of Buckingham's many rooms, the one that holds the swimming pool is my favorite. Its walls are all windows, presenting a full view of the gardens beyond. Now, with the night, the light of the stars creeps through the panes, raining silver on the water. The pool is smooth and undisturbed, acting as a mirror.

Richard sits. The jungle-green bottle tinks hard against the tile as he sets it down. His fingers uncurl, fall away from it.

"Some birthday, huh?" His laugh, the hollowness of it, bounces off the windows, rounds us like a repeating canon.

"Your mother does know how to organize a party." I come to rest just inches from the pool ledge, inches from him.

"It was Belle, I think. If Mum had her way, she would hide me forever."

"You've done a good job today," I tell him.

The sudden tilt of his head, the slant of his eyes on me, speaks surprise. "You think?"

"Of course." I think back on the day, full of more press conferences, meetings, and paperwork. How Richard walked through it all with steadiness, poise. "Anyone would be tired after today."

Richard's agreement is a sigh, low and whistling like a cello note. He reaches for the bottle, his fingers working hard and quick to unwrap the paper and twist the wire that tamps down its cork. Even though I expect it, the blast of the cork stops my heart.

Richard watches the carbon-dioxide wisp out, his four fingers coiled, python-like, around the neck's ripped paper. I wait and wait for him to bring the glass to his lips. But he doesn't.

"Want any?" He holds it out so that the smell of flowers and apples and air fills my head.

I shake my head, fighting the sudden urge to knock it from his hands and watch it shatter against the poolside. It's *his* choice. His alone.

He squints a single eye down into that mass of bubble and fizz. Then looks back at me. He sets the bottle on the ground, at his other side, so there's nothing between us. I'm still breathless as Richard edges closer.

His lips are close and he's going to kiss me. I want him to. I want him to so badly. But I think of the champagne bottle and where we are and what's behind us and I can't let him.

"I—I don't want to be your excuse," I manage, pulling the fight from some subconscious part of myself. Because now I know what this means, our lips touching, making me love him more. And I want it to mean the same thing for him. Because if it doesn't . . .

The thought makes my heart raw-edged and bloated with its fullness.

Richard pauses. His nose is so close to mine that I can't tell if we're touching or not.

I go on. "You have to stop running."

"I'm not running." He pulls back, his manner a puzzle-work of confusion, restraint.

"Are you sure?" I think of every kiss, every touch, born at the height of emotions so strong they singed the air around us. I point to the bottle beyond his thigh. "That used to be your escape. What is it now? It can't be me. I'm not some high you can just keep going back to again and again to drown out the rest of the world."

"Embers, you aren't my escape," he says, solid and sure. "You're the reason I've stayed."

So I kiss him. The truth of it all is that he has become my escape. The way his skin melts into mine, how his fingers dance against my cheek. It sets every cell, every fiber of my being ablaze. In this moment I can forget the sickness and the loss. The decay of everything falls away into something healing, altogether beautiful.

But it's short. So short. We break before the room lanterns bright with my magic.

We both sit in darkness, full of hard breath and pulled into ourselves.

"You know," he begins, "I used to be terrified of swimming."

"Really?" I look down at the pool's shimmer and gleam. The sight of the two of us, sitting so close together, makes me ache.

"Yeah." Richard reaches out and dips his fingers into the water. Our images are instantly ruined, distorted by the ripples coursing through them. "I thought there were sea serpents in the water. I don't know why. . . . But I put up such a fight that the swim instructor gave up."

The image of a young Richard, kicking and screaming

to get away from the pool, is both humorous and saddening.

"Of course Anabelle, she jumped right in. She picked it up so fast you would've thought she was a mermaid." Richard's voice swells with admiration for his sister. "She's never been squeamish about stuff like that. When I was younger, I'd always had this idea that when Father passed on I'd abdicate in favor of Anabelle. It's just as well I didn't have the choice; I had to prove to myself, to *him* that I could be a good king."

I touch the water. It's tepid, soothing beneath my fingertips. "What changed? What made you decide to learn to swim?"

He shrugs. "I grew older. I realized there were no such things as sea serpents."

"I wouldn't be so sure about that," I tease. My insides feel less leaden, less torn in the moment's lightness.

Richard smirks. "Well, none in my swimming pool anyway."

He stands upright, looking very much like a young king. His dinner jacket slides off his shoulders, crumples onto the poolside tiles. He kicks off his shoes and holds his arms above him, hands clasped together as if he's praying.

Richard leaps, his swan dive close to perfect. He cuts effortlessly into the water. Small droplets of bleach and chlorine spray my face. My nose wrinkles its distaste as Richard surfaces, his hair plastered against his face like some strange war helmet. He treads the water well despite his soaking clothes.

"Come on!" He waves, flinging more beads of water through the air. "Don't be shy!"

I cast a dubious look into the water, so clear and laden with chemicals.

"It won't hurt! I promise!" Richard calls. "No sea serpents in here. I checked!"

"Oh. Well, in that case." I lunge into the air, taking advantage of my magic to perform a string of elaborate acrobatics before I sink into the pool's embrace.

Despite the pungent chemicals, the water slides like silk off my bare skin. I surface with a gasp, spitting the distasteful liquid from my lips.

"See. It's not so bad." Richard swims toward me. The force of his waves beat against me. Relentless.

"Richard! What the hell are you doing?"

Our heads whip at the sound of Anabelle's sharp voice. The princess is standing on the pool's edge, staring incredulously at the wrinkled dinner jacket, orphaned shoes, and brimming bottle of alcohol. Even in her annoyance, she's stunning. Her dress is a sleek midnight blue, hugging her enviously slender form. Her hair is set in its usual loose curls, the front half pinned up with a diamond tiara.

Richard gives his sister a blithe arc of a wave. "Just taking a dip! Care to join?"

"But—but the party! They'll expect you to give a speech. . . ." Anabelle falters.

He wipes his wet fringe from his face. "How'd you find me anyway?"

"Lawton said you headed this way," his sister says, her voice crisper than a harvest apple. "They need you to cut the cake in five minutes."

Richard stretches out to float on his back. "Everyone's too tipsy to notice by now. Jump in, Belle! It's refreshing!"

"I've been planning this party for *weeks*, Richard! God help me if you pull a stunt like this at your coronation. That's going to take a bloody six months to organize!" His sister frowns, taps the champagne bottle with her foot. It tumbles over, topaz liquid sheeting all the surrounding tiles. "What's gotten into you?"

"As your king," Richard continues, not even batting an eyelid at the wasted alcohol, "I order you to jump in."

"You—you can't do that." Anabelle's hand finds her hip to punctuate seriousness. It's her eyes that give her away. Laugh lines, barely formed, appear just beside her lashes.

"Sure I can." Her brother gives a great kick. A wall of water rains down on the princess—flattening hair and smearing makeup.

"That's it!" Anabelle flings her high heels to the side and lunges into the pool, evening gown and all.

It's then I get a good look at Breena. She's staring at me, jaw set to the side in clear disapproval at my soaking state. I paddle to the edge, grip the wet tiles.

"I see you're having fun," she says. Her tone holds something close to disdain.

"There's no harm in it."

Instead of looking at my friend, I choose to watch the king and his sister. Their laughter is so loud it rattles the many glass panes that surround us. The pool is now a mess of expensive fabric and well-aimed splashes.

When Breena finally speaks, her voice is robotic, stiff. "Just make sure you're ready for tomorrow night. I don't want any distractions."

"I'll be ready," I promise, never tearing my eyes off of Richard. I can't afford not to be.

It's long past midnight by the time Richard falls asleep. Once I'm sure he's deep in his dreams, I crawl onto the bed and fight my way through the ridiculous layers of comforter and sheets to be close to him.

I don't dare move for fear of waking him, so I lie still, just inches away from the harsh angles of his biceps. All my senses are lit with magic. I know everything that moves in this room: from the small family of mice beneath the floor to the nervous twitch of Richard's pinkie toe. I see and hear everything. The murmur of his heart, the jagged beat of mine. Full of wish and hope and *I love you*.

I almost told him. After our kiss at the poolside. I should have.

He's said so many things that make me think he wants to speak the word too. But I don't know this for sure. I don't know it at all.

Not knowing is like a blade just over my heart, with all the weight and death of a guillotine. Every day that passes it grows sharper, more present. Ready to drop.

Tomorrow. I'll tell him tomorrow.

Then I'll wait for the fall.

Twenty-Two

Although I can't see the sunrise, some deep part of me feels the sun's beams first kiss the earth. Outside the world is just beginning to take shape: a watercolor layered over and over with brighter shades. I stand by the window, greeting the pastel light as it washes through the curtains. When the rosy rays of the sun lap onto the bed, Richard squirms and tries to yank the covers over his head.

"Good morning." I smile in spite of the Old One. In spite of everything. "I think you should take the day off."

"What?" His voice is hoarse. "It's my first official day as king! I don't think it'll go over too well if I just disappear."

"That's the beauty of magic. I can clear your schedule. No one will notice." I lean against the bed, hoping he won't fight much more. If he does I might lose my courage, forget the words I'm so determined to say. "Take a day off. For me. We'll go out and see the city."

Richard rakes an absentminded hand through his wayward hair. Like some grandiose magician, he sweeps the sheets away. "You can do that? Clear my schedule? Why didn't you do that the last time?"

I fight back a grimace, decide to be honest. "I didn't think of it. But we won't make that mistake again. The paparazzi and the public won't recognize you today," I call as he shambles off to the bathroom. "Or me, for that matter."

"You?" He pokes his head back out of the doorway.

"It wouldn't be a very good date if I was invisible to everyone, would it? Now hurry up and get ready." My insides tremble, but I don't betray their nervousness. My grin is so tight it's almost painful as I shoo him back into the loo.

A good ten minutes passes with me alone in the bedroom. I try my hardest not to think of what I want to say. What I have to say. The thought turns my stomach over and over. Far more terrifying than the idea of hunting soul feeders with Breena tonight.

I'm almost to the point of talking myself out of it when Richard steps out of the bathroom. His hair is combed back, a few loose, wet strands hanging over his eyes. His jaw is clean, as smooth as his chest. The fresh scent of soap clings to his skin, the towel around his waist. It's all I can do to stay by the bed while he disappears into his wardrobe for a suitable outfit.

"Nothing too nice," I tell him. "Try jeans and a T-shirt."

His laugh echoes into the cavernous room. "I think I know how to blend in. You, however, are the last one I'd turn to for fashion tips."

"What's *that* supposed to mean?" I look down at my outfit. Layer after layer of colors. Sea-foam tulle peeking out from aqua and daffodil cotton. Silver-threaded plum fabric mixes steadily with champagne silk.

"That's not exactly street wear. Where did you get all of those skirts anyway?"

I spend a few seconds in steaming silence before I decide the anger isn't worth it. "They were my favorites. I've seen a lot of styles over the years. If I saw something I liked, I would snatch it after the queens and duchesses took them off."

"You stole them?" Richard emerges from the wardrobe fully dressed. I see he's taken my suggestion, with a simple red T-shirt to contrast his well-worn jeans.

"I suppose you could see it that way. I prefer to think

of it as payment for those many hours spent watching them." I roll my eyes at the memories of teatimes and garden parties crammed with endless, droning conversations about society.

"How morally ambiguous of you." He pauses and looks around the room. "God, this place is a mess."

"That's generally what happens when you don't clean for weeks on end." I nudge the nearest pile of shriveled button-ups with my toe. "Or when you lock your door so the maids can't come in."

"I just feel weird having them go through my stuff." Richard moves over to the other side of the bed, makes a feeble attempt at straightening the sheets. "Hey—do you think you could—"

"No."

His eyebrows arch up in mock plea as he lets go of the sheets and laces his hands together. "Please? It'd just take you a second. Like Mary Poppins."

"I'm not magicking your room clean," I tell him, resisting the temptation to ask who Mary Poppins is. "It's a waste of valuable energy."

"Oh well. It was worth a try." He shrugs. "Maybe next year. For my birthday."

My throat becomes a desert. Cracked and long dry. If we stay in the path of the Old One, this unyielding hurricane, there likely won't *be* a next year.

Richard is too blinded by the newness of morning and the wrinkles in his sheets to notice my pause. "Where do you keep all your skirts? Like when you wore that other dress. The green one."

"In an invisible closet."

"No, really." He flops forward on the mattress, rumpling the sheets he just pretended so hard to tidy.

"I . . . I dunno. I guess I just wish them away. It's like anything else. My hair, my skin, my eyes. I decide what I want and it just appears. The green dress was for a special occasion."

"I liked it. A lot." Richard is on his hands and knees, crawling forward at the speed of a garden snail.

"It's not really street wear either. Do you want me to change into something less bright?" I shut my eyes and picture myself in an outfit almost identical to Richard's. He gives a grunt of surprise and I look down to find myself in a scarlet shirt and jeans. The trousers are so tight, constricting.

"No. Keep the skirts. I like them. They're you."

He's close now. The gravity of him tugs, luring me

into his orbit. I want to be as close to him as possible. Even closer.

But the whiteness of the sheets glares back at me. A reminder of what happened the last time we kissed on the bed. How the wildness is still inside me. Ready to kill.

Richard reaches out, his hand grazing mine. The skin he touches becomes hot and biting, sparks of desire. I tighten my fingers around his.

"Skirts it is."

"So," he says, all grin and re-mussed hair, "how about that date?"

Twenty-Three

The midday sun beats down, glaring summer heat off the metal grating of our café table. The brightness, its diamond-scale pattern of light, forces me to squint. But that doesn't stop Richard from staring.

"What are you looking at?" I laugh, my finger circling endless laps around the rim of my mug. My latte is untouched despite the hours we've lounged at this sidewalk coffee shop talking and soaking up the morning. Always the *I love you* is on the edge of my throat, waiting to be said. But right now, even in this perfect afternoon of coffee and talk, I can't seem to find the courage.

"You." His smile stretches long, like a sun-drunk cat. "I was just thinking about how beautiful you are."

Dozens of men and women shift by our table, gripping packaged sushi and wrapped sandwiches as they plow their way down the sidewalk and back toward their offices. Normally, with my veiling spell down, I would feel naked, aware of every strange look. But here, across from Richard, watching him watching me, I feel like one of the only souls left in the world.

"The way the sun is playing through your hair—you look alight." Richard reaches out, strokes his fingers through my locks. "And your eyes. Always your eyes."

He leans in closer, so that I feel his breath grazing my cheek. Deliciously hot. Here (away from the bed's feathery sheets), I think it will be easier to stop. I let our lips collide, press soft into each other. He tastes like coffee and earth—something rich. I linger in it until I feel the magic buzzing, tearing up my throat like nausea.

For now, it is enough.

I lean back on my chair, its finely wrought iron etching hard into my spine, and try hard not to think about what will happen when it *isn't* enough. What I'll have to choose.

"So where do you want to go? Saint Paul's? The Tower of London?" Richard takes a long sip of his drink and pulls out some money for the check.

We've spent the day layered in magic. My energy is stretched, constantly feeding spells to shield the king's identity from the hundreds of people passing us. Much of my senses are dedicated to being alert. Although the city streets are sunlit and crowded, I shouldn't dismiss the possibility of an attack.

Richard senses that part of me is on edge. Once we get up from the table and start walking, he pulls me close. His touch brings me back into the moment, into the day I should be enjoying. I'm determined to enjoy these hours. To enjoy Richard before I face the guillotine.

"No, not the Tower." I shake my head, steer us toward the river. "I have an idea."

"This is nice." Richard sighs, contented, as we walk. "I've never been able to enjoy the city like this, outside of a car, away from the crowds and security guards."

A smile flutters, fragile, across my face. I scan the endless string of passersby, going breathless at any flash of green. "Well, you're not entirely free of guards. You never are."

"You don't count, Embers."

We reach the Thames. Under the full force of daylight, the river seems more disparaging than mystical. Its water is thick and brown, carrying bits of rubbish with every extra push of the current. Tourists and Londoners alike walk past without so much as a backward glance. But then, they never knew what the Thames once was. When the great stretch of water was surrounded by nothing but moorland. When every bend and curve of the great river spoke of strength.

Sickness kicks up in the pit of my stomach with a sudden vengeance. My steps falter and I bend, drawing quick, gritty breaths to keep the queasiness at bay. Richard halts with me.

"Are you all right?"

"It's nothing." The words leave me in a gasp. Although the pain has been latent over the past few weeks, its return is fiery and lancing. My knees nearly buckle under it.

"It doesn't look like nothing." Richard sets his coffee on the stone ledge and wraps his arms around me. His grip is steady, holding me up when I would have fallen.

In a single moment, I lose all of the sparse contents of my stomach. The sip of coffee I tried an hour earlier and half of a croissant paint the sidewalk all sorts of unappetizing colors. Bitterness curdles, stains my lips. I wipe them hard with my shirtsleeve.

Richard guides me gently away from the puddle of vomit, lets me lean against the stone wall that borders the river. "What set it off?"

"I . . . I don't know." My voice is weaker than I'd like. "I think . . . I've been using a lot of magic today. More than usual."

"For us to go on this date?" Richard frowns. "Do

you want to go back to the palace? We can sit in the gardens and you could get some rest."

I stay still for a moment, willing the pain in my stomach to go back to its usual, tolerable ache. Slowly, grudgingly, it retreats, leaves me be.

We should go back, considering what Breena and I are going to do tonight. I'll need as much energy and magic as I can muster. But I know that if I turn back now, my courage will crumble.

"No." I shake my head. "Not yet."

"Are you sure?" His fingers tangle into a coppery strand of my hair as he brushes it back behind my ears. "We could do this another time."

No. The time is now. It has to be. I swallow the tremble out of my voice and start walking, pulling Richard with me. "I'm sure."

The riverfront passes by our slow, together steps. An artist stands at the far side of the walk, squinting out at the Thames with a brush wedged between her lips, teal paint streaking her cheek. Couples, so much like us, walk with fingers linked, stopping at various points in the stone wall to point at the scene beyond the chocolate waters. A young man with gnarled, knotted hair sits on a bench, plucking a guitar.

*If you embrace this city and crawl under its skin . . . there's
something here.* I remember Breena's words. How, despite
the sickness, I'm not the only Fae who's lost herself to
these people, this place. Slowly and surely it's swallowing us all.

"Where are we going again?" Richard asks.

"It's not far. Just a few blocks down, actually."

"That doesn't leave too many options. Are we going to
go gape at Parliament? Or maybe Westminster Abbey?"
He lists the sights with a jaded tone, as though he's certain
nothing down the Thames will be new to him.

"No." I smile coyly, satisfied he hasn't guessed.
"We're going to look at your kingdom."

He frowns, perplexed by my comment. We continue
down the river at a solid stroll, our silence filled by the
hungry *bprrrs* of pigeons and the distant blare of horns.
Richard's face lights with understanding when I pull
him into the winding queue beneath the giant white
Ferris wheel.

"The Eye," he mutters under his breath. "You're
talking about the London Eye."

"You haven't been on it, have you?" I rise on tiptoes to see past the dozens of people in front of us.
The queue snakes slowly forward, passing a glassy ticket

booth before mounting the ramps to step into the clear, creeping capsules.

"You've brought me to the one thing in London I haven't experienced." He cranes his neck to take in the massiveness of the wheel. "Two, really. Queues and the Eye."

"I could magic us to the front." I frown. Are there always so many mortals clamoring for a taste of flight? The queue is so sluggish it makes my skin itch.

Richard laughs so loudly that the family in front of us turns and stares. "No need. I'm perfectly content to stay here and wait with you. It's not every day I get to stand in a queue. Besides"—his voice drops—"I don't want you to get sick again."

"I'm fine." But even as I say this, I don't know if I am. My insides are churning: *Tell him. Tell him. Tell him.*

So we wait, side by side, talking about things eavesdroppers will find useless. Though I don't use any spells to advance our way down the queue, I do cast a small charm when we finally step into the clear glass observatory. While the capsule has enough room for over twenty people, I secure a single car for just us. So we can be alone.

The wheel pulls us above the city in a lethargic rise.

I feel like the dawning sun, really seeing and discovering London—looking down on the tangled monuments and buildings, the milling ants of people.

Richard's nose presses against the glass, his breath creating steam spots on the capsule's curved walls. All of his attention has been pulled into the city and its endless string of details. The three spires of Saint Paul's pointing gold into a robin's-egg sky, summer-green trees lining the Thames, boats and barges sliding under bridges arched like a skipping stone. Parliament, so small it looks like some kind of sandstone Gothic cake.

"It looks different from the sky. I mean, I've seen it from airplanes and stuff, but never like this."

"Strangely beautiful, isn't it?" I come up next to him, place my palms against the glass.

"Beautiful . . ." Richard is both beside me and before me. Solid flesh and phantom reflection. Both versions of him smile. "Is this what it's like? Flying?"

"Not exactly." How do you describe flying to someone ground-bound? It's like trying to describe food to someone who's never eaten. Or air to a person who's never drawn breath.

And then I think of what it would be like, being always on the ground, forever tied to some surface.

I look at my own feet, how flat they are against the pod's metal-plated floor. Just at the tip of my toes is the edge where metal meets glass, what few inches keep us from a fall of meters upon meters. I see the ground, patched gray and brown below, and my head starts to spin.

"You're lucky. Being able to fly." Richard is still talking into the glass, looking out at the great heights he'll never be able to reach by himself. "Most people would kill for that."

I look back at him.

Richard or flying. Richard or everything I've known and been my entire life.

The human and the Fae writhe inside me, snapping and hissing dragon flame. One of them has to die.

"Richard?"

He looks when I say his name, his eyes boring into me as they always have, setting every piece of molecule and matter that is me alight.

I think of what I want to say, what I've been holding back for hours, days. If I let it out . . . There's so much more at stake than his denial. In fact, if he says no, if the blade lets down and my head and heart spill away, it might almost be a mercy. It will spare me the choice of tearing myself apart.

"What is it?" he asks. His eyebrows dive, become a pen-stroke V, the way a child draws a flying seagull.

They rise up: the old Emrys and the new. The desire against what-has-always-been.

Is he enough? they ask. *If he says yes, promises to be with you always and gives you everything you want, will he be enough? Will the hole be filled?*

"I don't know," I say aloud, hoping the words will silence the chaos in my head. Let me think.

He stares. Unyielding as a sphinx.

I turn away, walk to the bench in the middle of the capsule. I look through the clearness on the other side. There's no reflection from the curve of that glass, but I still see faces. I see Guinevere and Isidore. Alene and Kaelee. I see the men they loved. The ones they left us for. All gone, now dust and memory.

I remember them, everything they gave up, and I know that I can't promise Richard my love without everything else too. There's no point.

"I'm sorry. I don't know," I say again.

I hear Richard's steps behind me, light and metallic. "It's okay, Emrys."

He sits on the bench, slides his way down next to me so our shoulders are touching. Richard reaches over; his finger shaves up the side of my cheek. It pulls away, glistening, and I realize with a start that I've been crying.

"I *do* know. I've known for a while now . . . but the timing has never been right." His voice is deep and everything in this glass chamber. "And I've been scared. Scared of what you'll say and scared of what this means for you. For us."

I look into his face—the goodness of it. He's studying the clump of my tears shining against his knuckle. It catches the light, a tiny inverted mirror of our world rolling down Richard's skin, falling to the bench between us.

His eyes lock into mine. Steady, sure. "I love you, Emrys."

He loves me. *Me.* My heart stretches full with the joy of these words. For a fleeting moment I'm giddy, until I feel the strain of tendon and aorta. The fight that's still there, the tension of magic and mortal.

I want to respond, but what can I say? How can I profess a love I can't commit to? How can I say anything except yes?

Richard goes on. "I know it's impossible—us together. I know what you would have to give up, and I could never ask that of you. But I just need you to know how I feel."

The tears come back as I try to smile at him. I lose sight of his face.

"It's been a good day," he says softly. "Thank you for it."

His arms swallow my shoulders, so much comfort and togetherness. I rest my head against his chest—it seems unhindered by my weight, ready to carry anything. I lean on him and watch the world rise up to receive us. Parliament tower's owl-eye clock face winks against the sun as we draw level with it, start to descend.

"You know, I was thinking," Richard begins.

"Hm?"

"I want you to meet my sister. You've become such a big part of my life that it feels weird, her not knowing you." His words rumble through me, almost as if I'm a part of his body. "But only if you want to. And if it's okay with your Faery friends."

I shift, remolding myself into his chest. "I'd like that."

"I'll set up a lunch, then."

I rest against him a little longer, listening as his heartbeat drums me a personal lullaby. The capsule groans, creeping like a wandering feather toward the Thames and the crowds below. I look out on the endless threads of asphalt and cars weaving through buildings and wonder what tonight's hunt with Breena will bring.

"Want to go around again?" I ask as the platform and its endless queue of tourists draws closer.

Richard glances out the wide, curving glass. "We only paid for one round. It would be rather unkingly to steal a ride."

"We'll slip a little more money into the till on the way out," I promise.

Genuine concern lurks behind the lines of his face. Something about it touches me. There's a compassion in him that runs deep. It's what made men like Richard the Lionheart worthy of the crown—what made them true kings.

"All right," he says finally. "One more time."

"Good. I'm not ready to leave yet." I rest my head back against his chest, push away all thoughts of the hunt. Instead I let his confession linger in my mind. Three words, short but so vast, lifting me up and giving me new meaning.

For now, they are enough.

Twenty-Four

In the darkness, the city takes on a different personality. Lovers who strolled in the sunshine retreat to their hotels and flats, replaced by snappy, sparkly strangers who roam the sidewalks in herds.

I lean against a brick wall, taking it all in. Several flushed, swaying boys eye me as they pass. A few even catcall. I cross my arms, resisting the temptation to give them a zap. I must save all of the magic I can tonight, conserve all of the energy I managed not to spend on my date with Richard—I'll need it for the hunt. That's the reason the mortals can see me at all.

I spot Breena almost a block away. She's wearing her sequined dress, the one that shines like polished pewter. I glance down at my own wardrobe choice: a slim black dress touched up with lace. Without my skirts I feel close to naked.

The men see Breena too. They throw more yells and whistles her way, but she charges forward without a glance.

"Maybe being visible was a mistake," she mutters as she draws up next to me and digs through her clutch for her habitual lipstick.

"If we use veiling spells it will alert the soul feeders," I remind her. "Besides, it'll be slow-going through the crowds if we're invisible."

My friend's lips pop scarlet as she applies her lipstick. "Are you sure one of them will be here?"

"This is one of the largest nightclubs in London. Even if Jaida and Cari aren't here looking for food, there'll be someone who can lead us to them."

I stare at the club's entrance: a large ebony door set in a wall of worn, lamp-lit bricks. A queue of mortals winds down the sidewalk—the few faces at the front bathed in a wave of neon lights from behind the dark door.

Tucked away beneath all this flash and flare is an unmistakable flavor of magic. There's at least one huntress behind those black doors.

I start to step across the street when Breena's arm shoots out, clamps my shoulder.

"I'll take the lead," she says with all the decisiveness and authority of those extra one hundred years. "I don't want you doing anything rash."

My face must betray how I feel about her tone,

because Breena stares dead into my eyes. "I'm doing us both a favor, Emrys."

I wait until she's fully turned to release the brunt of my glare.

We cross the street, weave and thread through the crowd like swallows in flight. Thanks to Breena's tiny, almost unnoticeable spell, the club's bouncers are quick to let us in. The nausea hits immediately. I sway under the influence of the blinding lights and soul-rattling notes. Breena stumbles under the sudden wave of sickness, lurching into several well-dressed men in the process.

"Keep it together," I mutter to myself. The music's wasp-buzz bass is so loud it drowns out even the sounds in my head. I nearly retch under the intense blare of technology, but after this afternoon's purge there's nothing in my stomach. The sickness snakes through my limbs instead.

One of the men grabs Breena by the arm, steadies her. She stares, her eyes darting back and forth between the man's hand and his face.

"Easy there." He has to yell above the music.

Breena nods her thanks and edges away, like a beast eyeing some untested power.

"Are you okay?" I holler into her ear. She flinches at the extra volume, but doesn't move away from me.

How can the soul feeders stand this? The question leaps from her eyes into my thoughts.

I think back to the Darkroom, when Breena had been the picture of togetherness. Is this club really that much worse? Or have we Frithemaeg become that much weaker in such a short span of time?

"They must eat well. Save your magic," I warn her. "At this rate we'll need every ounce we can get."

Breena nods. Her face is pinched together in fierce determination. The sickness won't get the best of us. Not yet.

We push farther into the club, past the forest of elbows and whipping hair. Fleeting rainbows of neon dazzle our eyes and frenzied notes become everlasting inside our ears. I fight a path to the edge of the dance floor, where there are fewer chances of being thrashed in the face.

"This place is huge!" Breena's voice fights a losing battle against the dance track. "She could be anywhere!"

My closed lids don't do much to block the flashing lights, but they do make it slightly easier to concentrate. The taste of magic drips around us, honey thick, more viscous than it was in the doorway. I open my eyes, look to where it's strongest.

"This way." I point to the right, my finger forever disappearing and resurrecting beneath the throb of strobe lights.

We follow the wall, pushing past the dozens of beached dancers. The club goes on, rooms stretching into themselves, all packed with the silhouettes. We pass through three whole segments before the magic becomes unmistakable.

"Where are you?" I mutter, look over the dance floor.

It's as if all of young London is crowded in this series of flashing rooms. Even with my magical senses, the place is so crammed with the salt and sweat of humanity that picking out an immortal seems impossible.

Breena's fingers wrap cold around my arm. I look back to see her lips moving, forming words I can't hear, but understand. "Over there."

She's pointing deep into the shuddering shadows, by a curling wrought-iron staircase. It winds all the way up to a shallow balcony. There are no dancers up there, only loungers, taking advantage of the long row of leather chairs. A familiar twinge shoots through my nerves as I review the balcony's residents. Something's up there, watching the crowd. Waiting.

I lurch toward the stairs, but Breena's fingers don't release their grip.

I lead. Her eyes remind me.

The stairs are tricky to navigate. I clutch the iron railing so hard that it leaves a deep red line in my palm when I reach the top. The balcony unfolds—an entire room to itself—crowded with tired dancers collapsed on chairs, their half-drunk cocktails scattered over tiny black tables.

Breena steps in front of me, curls spilling gold into her dollish face. "In the corner," she mouths.

There, in the chair closest to the ledge, glowing drink in hand, lounges a Green Woman. The fiber-optic blonde of her hair reflects the neon chaos around her. Her face is lax, careless, as she looks out on the heaving crowd below. From the taste of her magic, it seems she's recently fed. She isn't here to hunt. She's here to relax.

I watch the lazing soul feeder, my mind scrambling for my next move. No magic. There are too many mortals around. Binding her is out of the question.

"Sit over there," I murmur in Breena's ear, and gently push her in the opposite direction. "I'm going to try and talk to her. If there's trouble, you can come help."

I move away before she has a chance to order me back. The Green Woman snaps her neck around, pale eyes trying their hardest not to widen as they watch me approach. Her drink shivers against tightening fingers.

"Good evening, sister. Mind if I have a seat?" As I yell I gesture to the empty seat next to her that no human has been brave or drunk enough to claim.

She watches me. Her look suggests she minds my company very much.

I let myself down into the chair, never tearing my stare away from her. Even a crowd of mortals isn't enough to guarantee my safety from this creature's magic. Laws of concealment mean much less to those who hunt humans.

"What are you doing here?" Her shout manages to sound like a normal irritated question. The gleam behind her eyes speaks of suspicion and barely contained magic.

"I was hoping you and I might have a little chat." My fingers drum against the leather armrest in constant half-time beat. "You see—I'm searching for someone—two people, actually. And I think you can help me find them."

Bony shoulders grow rigid beneath the gauze of

her dress. Even in the ever-changing light of the club, I can see that she's paled, lips pressed together in sheer nervousness.

No response.

"They go by the names of Jaida and Cari. I'm sure you've heard of them." I begin to grow slightly at ease. Although she is freshly replenished by her gruesome meal, the Green Woman across from me is younger. I sense the authority growing between us, all of it placed on my side.

"They don't come here." Her words are flash and fire. Like bullets. "You won't find them."

"Where are they?" I lean closer to the Green Woman, making sure she tastes my magic, what it can do.

She's silent but breaks her corpse-like stillness to sip her drink.

"I haven't even asked your name, sister," I remind her. "There's no way they'll know you helped me. Besides, they won't really care. All I want is to talk with them."

"I want something in return." The final dregs of her drink braid green down her glass, disappear into her throat. "A little bite of royalty perhaps? We're all dying to know what His Majesty tastes like."

She's toying with me, the way a house cat pricks claws

into its master's leg. I know this and still I can't keep the rage from rising, becoming phoenix and flame in my very core. The thought of her teeth in Richard's neck, tearing and mauling, is enough to make me want to kill her.

I swallow most of it back. Not for her sake, but because right now, she's my only answer.

The Green Woman, seeing what just passed behind my thin veneer of human eyes, begins to edge away. I lurch out of my chair and move closer, pinning her into the supple black leather.

"Now tell me, where can I find Jaida and Cari?" Every word leaves me through a fence of clenched teeth. My fingers dig hard into the Green Woman's skeletal shoulder, wanting to break her.

"Highgate," she spits out, her lower lip all atremble. "They've taken up residence at Highgate Cemetery."

"Do they ever leave?" I loom, an angel of death over her chair. It would be so easy to just let it all out, unmake her here and now.

"They don't come into the city. They have food brought to them."

"That's not what I asked." My hand tightens into her. Nails break through skin, creating five crimson moons. "Do they leave the cemetery?"

"Sometimes they go north. There's a magpie that brings messages—one of them leaves every time it arrives." A thin film of sweat has sprouted on the Green Woman's forehead. For all the pain in her shoulder, she hasn't cried out.

"And what happens when they return?" I ask.

But the Green Woman shakes her head lightly, begging me not to ask any more. Blood seeps down her arm, carving crooked trails through snowy skin. I pull my hand away, see the redness of her under my fingernails. This is all the information I'm getting from her tonight.

No magic, I tell myself. *Keep things simple. Walk away.*

I ease past the chair, keeping my stare on the Green Woman. Resentful slits of eyes glare back, betraying the withered ugliness beneath. Her killing face.

I turn and look for Breena in the darkness, searching through the line of pale, moonlike faces. A knife-sharp cry jolts every fine ginger hair on my body. Magic shreds the air around me with its sick electrical current. I whip around and crouch by the closest lounge chair.

The Green Woman looms in her corner, like a shadow drawn out by a spotlight, eyes blazing in her dead gray face. Her spell is white-hot lightning in the air between us, searing and tearing. There's no reservation in her curse. No mercy. This magic is meant to kill.

The countercharm is quick to my tongue, but not fast enough. The terrible force lances through the air like a fast-growing vine, intent on tearing the life out of me. And then it stops.

I blink, at first uncertain of my spared life. There'd been no other magic, no other shield to save my soul. Then I look down and know.

The girl's body lies close to my feet. Her dress of tangerine silk is only slightly rumpled over bent, milky limbs. Her eyes are open—but there's nothing behind them. She must've walked in front of me, caught the brunt of the blow meant to silence me.

In this moment of reflection passes another chance for me to be extinguished. Fortunately Breena is doing her job. My friend leaps from the crowd, arms outstretched with a spell much quicker and effective than mine. The Green Woman doesn't even have time to shriek before the flames envelope her. The balcony, so draped in shadows before, is now lit with terrible whiteness. Every corner is exposed. Every flaw on every stunned face jumps into sight. The dead girl glows like a broken angel at my feet.

And then it's dark again.

Breena glances at me, her eyes wide with nervous energy, and then faces the shocked, motionless crowd. *Forgietap* slides off her lips and into their minds. Fifty-two pairs of eyes blink at once as a new reality takes shape in their memories. The girl clutched her chest and fell. A young man gave her CPR, but her eyes glossed over, stripped of life before an ambulance could even be called. A freak accident. Heart failure.

"Come on." Breena's words are wavy with fear, or disgust, or both. "We've got to go."

The dead girl's hand reaches into the edge of my vision, its fingers curled like the petals of a withering flower.

"Let's go." Breena's dress flashes like a sterling signal fire as she pulls me toward the stairs. "Two death spells aren't going to go unnoticed. We have to get out of here now."

She's right. We have to leave before the scene starts swarming with Banshees, drawn by such a fresh passing of souls.

"We have to get to Highgate, before they're put on the alert," I call to Breena as we wind back down the iron staircase. With the death of a girl and a Green Woman on our heads, there's no other choice. We have to go to Highgate Cemetery and collect the information we need before it's gone forever.

My friend stops on the last step. I halt as well, nearly stumbling over her in the suddenness of our movements. Breena slowly turns and looks up at me.

"Is it worth it?" Her voice slices through the swell of the DJ's track.

"What?" I grip the railing extra hard.

"If we go to Highgate—it could be one of us that dies. Is it worth it to you? All of this just for a name?" Breena's gaze slips up to the balcony, where several screams have already erupted from the crowd.

"This could be it, Bree. We can root out the snake before it strikes. They know where the Old One is." Dread wells up in my throat. The stranger's death has changed things. The price is now too high for Breena to pay.

"Would you have done this for King Edward? Emrys, your emotions are blinding you! It's far safer to go back to the palace and barricade ourselves. Let Mab and her scouts do the dirty work."

"It's not safer for Richard!" I snap back. "There's already been one attack on his life. We can't afford to wait anymore."

Breena stares at me hard, the look behind her eyes as

immovable as a wall of granite. I return her glare. Another scream from upstairs cuts through our standoff, reminding us that exiting the club is in our best interests. My friend plows straight through the tangled crowd of dancers. I follow, breathing lightly for the reek of alcohol.

Air waves cool and fresh in our faces as we burst out of the club, back onto the street. I trail Breena down the block, out of the hearing of the long queue of mortals waiting to get inside.

"I won't stop you," she says as she comes to rest against a lamppost, "but I'm not coming with you. You're on your own."

I take a deep breath. "We promised to protect the crown—"

"This isn't protecting the crown! This is a witch hunt! If you want to protect Richard, go and be with him. No more innocent lives are going to be lost on my account."

Breeze lifts my hair away from my face, whips it back. Fiery strands wave into the night, flags of no surrender. Everything in Breena, her stance, her eyes, the crinkle of her mouth, tells me this—nothing I say will sway her. She's leaving.

"I can't just sit back and wait for the Old One's final move," I say.

"Why not?" It isn't really a question, but a gauntlet thrown on the ground between us to see if I'll rise to the challenge—tell her what I'm certain she already knows.

"I love him."

There's very little change in Breena's expression. Silence grips her as she takes in my words, ingesting their blunt truth.

"So you'll die for him either way," she says finally.

The wind turns, lashing my hair back into my face.

"So be it." She turns so I can only see the diving back of her glittering gown. "Good-bye, Emrys. I hope the Greater Spirit brings you back alive."

She drifts up into the night sky, not looking back even once before she disappears into the jagged row of rooftops.

Twenty-Five

Although it's still in the city's grip of cement and electricity, Highgate Cemetery is a territory unto itself, a jungle of gravestones and corpse-fed vines. There's a strange stillness in the air, as if the wind refuses to enter this sweltering forest of death.

At the edge of the cemetery, I kneel behind a cross-shaped grave marker and peer into the night. The moon is newborn in the sky, its whispering, watery light far too weak to rely on. But what mortal eyes won't see, my magic senses well enough. The spirits here in Highgate are powerful, their magic strengthened by such an overwhelming presence of death. I feel both Jaida and Cari—old and powerful enough to be queens in their own right. Maybe they were, before the Old One roped them in.

There are other soul feeders here as well. Sentinels, guards, messengers. Highgate is a fortress.

I stay still against the cross, gauging my options. Without Breena, this entire mission is much riskier.

One stupid mistake and I could get unmade.

I'll need a disguise. My aura is distinct, impossible to alter, but I can still change my appearance (something to afford me at least a few seconds of escape). My limbs shorten, peach hair and creamy skin spoil into a Black Dog's shadow-eaten fur. The paws feel heavy, webbed. I stumble even after a few practice steps—it's been years since my last shape-shift. The flame-haired girl has become like a favorite dress I hate to shed. Anything else just feels awkward, itchy.

I lope along the nearest row of gravestones. My run grows smoother, swifter, with each passing marker. I slink between headstones that slant and crumble like long-neglected teeth, relying almost as much on my new, keen sense of smell as I do on my magic.

Something about these graves unnerves me in a way it hasn't before. Death feels closer than it ever has.

You'll die for him either way. Breena's words are haunting, inescapable here. She must have thought I had made my choice. That I'd decided to leave her and so many other things behind for Richard's sake.

But that's what I'm doing. Isn't it? I'm here, slinking through weathered, lichen-stained stones, without Breena, ready to get exposed and unmade, all for him.

So it's not the death that terrifies me. It's the change, the unwinding into something I've never been. How can I live without magic?

There are no answers as I wedge my way deeper into the cemetery. Stones shift, take stranger shapes. There are crops of crosses. Angels and cherubs lounge in long, weeping grass, the curves of their faces worn away by hundreds of polluted rainfalls. Other faces, less heavenly, more skull-like and leering, gape under stony starlight. Each step past these markers pulls me farther into the sphere of the soul feeders' magic. Combined with the dark, eerie spell of the cemetery, it's almost intoxicating.

At last, I come to a place where I can go no farther. I huddle behind an unmarked grave and peer through overwhelming clusters of grass. Before me, in a clearing, is an entire crowd of soul feeders. Signs of a semipermanent camp litter the area, both visible and not: a smoldering clump of wood and charcoal by the foot of a larger gravestone, the unwinding structures of old spells, the pile of bones shoved into the far corner of a crypt.

I lay motionless, barely able to breathe as I watch the gathering. Real, massive Black Dogs tread a well-worn path around the camp. The grass under their paws is broken, wilted, exposing the dark, fertile soil of the cemetery's underbelly like wounds. Green Women and Banshees form a strange, almost unintentional circle around the ringleaders, as if they don't want to get close. The sight of them together, in peace, is unnerving. Like cats and dogs shoved together in a crate, keeping eerie harmony.

Jaida and Cari. It must be them. The two spirits, beautiful and regal in their borrowed bodies, rest on a hulking marble tomb at the center of everything, flecked by the fire's dying light. Not a word passes in the group. They sit, as silent and almost as still as the tombstones around them. It isn't a meeting I've stumbled on. It's a messaging center.

I study them, noting the numbers of their guard. There's no way I can slip unnoticed through that ring of restless spirits. I'd half expected Jaida and Cari to be holed up here on their own, waiting discreetly for words from the Old One. But this, the presence of so many soul feeders, shows me the truth. It's not a single death they want. It's a war. A war against the mortals and those protecting them.

A mournful, jarring cry calls my attention to the skies. For a fleeting moment, the white slice of moon is blocked out completely. I crouch close to the ground, praying that the bird doesn't see me. The animal flies on, unconcerned. It lands, a ruffle of white and black feathers, and struts proudly in a little circle. A magpie. The Old One's errand-bird.

The Banshee retrieves the scrolled message from the swaggering bird, her glare unyielding and calculating as she reads. It's the Green Woman, Jaida, who betrays her emotions. Her tongue runs along the edge of her berry-red lips, looping in a nervous repeat. Her eyes leave the paper, straying into the shadows beyond her guard. Something's changed. Her body seems stiffer. The midnight hackles of my back bristle as her stare passes over my broken grave. Her eyes are terrible, green searchlights, uprooting every vine and blade of grass in their path.

"I'll take care of it," Cari tells the Green Woman, her voice as emotionless as her face. "You should accompany the bird back north."

Jaida's eyes snap back out of the bushes. "I'll leave at once."

The Green Woman is flying straight where I need to go. All I have to do is follow. My body quivers, too full of excitement and fear.

Jaida stands; her spring-green dress falls flawlessly into place. Then, with the speed of a shooting star, she's off.

I force my paws into inching slowness, despite my urge to chase the soul feeder. It's only when several trees are between me and their camp that I launch into the sky, melting into its velvet canvas as a sleek raven. Like the Black Dog, the bird's form is jerky at first. My wings are tentlike and clumsy. Jaida and the magpie have a decent head start; their bobbing silhouettes are already fading into the far-off darkness. If I let them go too far, the trail will be lost.

I cast a spell: a tiny bit of magic to propel me forward. The words, the small spark of light, hurtle me through the star-spangled sky. I realize too late that this was a mistake. The spell wasn't as subtle as I thought, for on the ground, someone was watching.

Another's magic shoots under me, past me. It catches the tips of my feathers, singeing them into nothing. I try to move my wings, but they're lead. My flight becomes a sickening plummet; the heavy earth lurches forward to meet me.

A clump of vines breaks my fall. I blink through this

new hammock of leaves. Nothing seems hurt. Apart from the smoke wisping out of my wings, I'm fine.

"Track her!" Cari's command carries through the night, blanketed by heart-wrenching howls.

The Black Dogs are searching, seeking to root me out of my fragile hiding place. I struggle to sit up, but nothing happens. Not even a twitch of my dark raven legs. Then it hits me. The spell, Cari's magic, wasn't supposed to fry me. It was meant to freeze me, to rob my muscles of their will. I'm paralyzed, trapped.

There are distant snaps, howls, and sniffs—signs of approaching hunters. Time for me to produce a counter-spell is fading fast. I repeat spells frantically in my mind, feeling the force of the magic swell through numb limbs. None of them click.

"It's a woodling. I feel her. She's close. Keep searching!"

I want to close my eyes and stop my ears, to shut out the snarls of my hunters. Words, fragments of spells rush through my head with panic too extreme to control.

It's over, a despairing voice cries out in my thoughts. If, when, Cari catches me, she'll be sure to silence me. Unmake me.

Crack. Dry twigs break so close they sound like the snapping of bones.

No. I must live. For Richard.

His face rises up beyond my parched, glazing eyes. With it, in the last possible moment, comes the spell. *Áhredde. Áhredde. Áhredde.* A wingtip twitches. A clawed foot curls into itself. I shake free. Howls of my pursuers carry like wind, whipping against my ear. They aren't far—I have to move fast.

Flying is out. The Banshee's magic will only rip me out of the sky again. I need to be close to the ground, faster than the dogs. So I slip into the skin of a fox: fur of fire and nimble, dancing paws.

There's no time to grow comfortable in this new shape. I dash out of the underbrush, tearing free from the thin, scratchy vines. My feet carry me fast, making quick, instinctive turns to throw the snarling Black Dogs from my trail. Their breaths fall, hot and heaving against my tail, as I dart ahead. As hefty and large as northbound wolves, they can't slip through the same gaps my fox form can. I gain a few meters by ducking, leaping, and weaving through the labyrinth of Highgate.

My heart pounds, a frantic reminder of my preserved life. It isn't only the dogs giving chase. Banshees and Green Women blot the skies. I'm surrounded on all sides, except the path directly ahead, running for my life.

Finally the cemetery gate swims into my exhausted eyes. I push past exploding agonies in my muscles, run for it. The fox's slim frame fits perfectly through the bars. I'm on the other side, breathless, but I don't stop running. A simple gateway won't hold the angry soul feeders. I'll only truly be safe in Buckingham, under the protection of the Guard.

My legs won't last. The left one limps from an encounter with a gravestone. It won't be long until I collapse. Flying is my only choice; I must enter the skies so thick with hostile spirits. I can't even breathe right as I lope back into human skin. My body lifts off the ground in a rush of forced magic, shooting me down the street with the speed of a race car.

London whips by. Every blurred block saps a little more of my magic. At first, I treat the blocks of buildings like gravestones, slipping in and out of them to lose my pursuers. But the toll is too much.

Just before the river, my magic falters. I land softly on the street and pick myself up, wobbling on barely recovered feet. The old cramps return. I cry out in pain, but I can't stop. Stopping means death.

I hobble down the sidewalk, sticking close to the

many buildings I pass. After two blocks of this pain-lanced race, I begin to despair. There's no way I can keep this up all the way to Buckingham.

Then I see it. My blue-and-red savior: a sign for the Underground. My leg bones jar against each other as I push into a final, desperate run. I half slide, half tumble into the station entrance and collapse by a Cadbury vending machine, limp and without breath.

But at least I'm underground. My powers seep back through the once-white grout of the station's tiled walls. The only other people who trot down the steps are a slightly intoxicated, giggly couple and a gang of strangely dressed teenagers. I gather every ounce of energy that trickles back into me, until finally I have enough strength to make it to the trains. I push myself onto unsteady feet, shuffle through the turnstile, and trek down the remaining sets of stairs to the trains.

It's no secret that the Frithemaeg are stationed at Buckingham. I'd hoped, in my furious flight, to beat the soul feeders back, to reach the shelter of the gates and the Guard before they did. That chance died with my broken steps. In all likelihood, they've set an ambush around Buckingham, waiting for me. I can't go back there. Not yet. For now I'll stay on the train, making endless loops underneath London, saving my strength. I sit, rest my head against the window. The station falls behind in a streak of light as the train snakes off into the many wormholes of the Underground.

Twenty-Six

My joints are unhinged, cramped together only by muscles as tight as rubber bands when I walk down the platform, toward the station's exit. So many people rush past me, flooding the trains. It must be after dawn. The soul feeders are least likely to attack me in broad daylight. Now's my chance to return to Buckingham, to tell Breena what I've seen.

The Guard is bristling. Their faces are as pale as marsh lights, arms shake with uncast spells when I approach the palace. I halt several meters away, watch them with care.

"Your signature, sister," a chestnut-haired youngling calls out. I think her name is Lydia.

"Of course." I don't dare move as the sign slips from my fingers into the air. These Fae are too tightly wound, ready to explode.

My shimmering gold bird is enough to make them relax. I take in their row of expressions: tired, grim. "What's wrong?"

Lydia looks past me, into the lush tree line of Saint James's Park. "We were under siege last night. Banshees, Green Women, Black Dogs . . . all of them were out there. They left at sunrise. No doubt they'll be back."

So I was right not to return in the darkness. It only would've ignited the beginning of what I now know is an inevitable war.

"But the royals are safe?"

"Yes." Another youngling nods. "The king and the princess are both here."

Which means Breena is too. A shudder threads sickness through my bones. After not listening to her warnings and failing so miserably—how can I face her and admit I was wrong? I should have returned with her.

"Also there—" Lydia pauses, digs her slippered foot deeper into the chunks of gravel. "There was an attack. At least, we think there was."

An attack? I feel my blood slowing with my heart. "What happened?"

"G-Gwyn was unmade," the Fae says, unable to still the tremor in her voice. "There were traces of battle magic on the edge of the grounds. None of us felt the spells until it was too late. When we got there, Gwyn had already slipped away."

Lydia's pretty face has turned a peculiar shade of green. I look at the others, staring at me with wide, whitened eyes. Fear glosses over them, quick and catching.

"And the attacker?" I ask.

They shake their heads as one.

"No sign," Lydia offers. "It could still be in the palace."

My mouth is dry, resisting all attempts to swallow. "And no attack was made on the king?"

"None. He's safe. For now." There's defeat in the youngling's words. I can only imagine, after last night, the multitudes stretched out: dark, beautiful waves of monsters lapping at Buckingham's gate. How many hundreds of gruesome endings played out in the young Faes' minds as they waited for the attack?

But really, isn't there only a single ending? I close my eyes, try to blot out the images of shadowed hordes and gravestones. Right now we're alive. And it's my job to keep things that way.

The Guards step aside as I pass the palace's perimeter, their auras tingling and flaring against mine as

I pass. So fresh and untested. Now that I know what we're up against, I don't see how we can protect the crown as we are. We can't stay here, not with an assassin loose in Buckingham's halls, not with the city crushing, draining, squeezing any strength we have left.

The king's office windows yawn open to the warm gusts of morning breeze. I approach loudly, trying to make enough noise so Richard won't start at my appearance. Ferrin's head pops out from behind the curtain. Her curious expression morphs into a shock so gaping it causes me to look down.

"Lady Emrys, what happened to you?"

My dress is in black, lacy shreds, all intact fabric splayed in dirt. Heavy, red welts and bluish beginnings of bruises color my arms. A glance into the windowpanes shows my face a mess of scratches. My hair is irreconcilable, draped in knots and tangles over my shoulders.

"Rough night." My whisper is hoarse, like sandpaper. Either Richard doesn't hear it, or he's feigning ignorance as he hunches over his desk, fountain pen looping over creamy stationery. "I'd rather not talk about it."

I hover in the open window long after Ferrin and Helene leave for the perimeter. My body feels so mortal: aching and falling apart as it leans against the window jamb. I don't even know if I *can* move. All of me is so, so tired. Tired of running, of fighting, of having to choose.

Richard turns slowly. Rum-gold sunlight drips over his face. I have only a moment to admire it. So many curves and edges. In his jaw, nose, cheekbones, brow. The perfect balance of softness and strength.

But then he sees me, and the horror dawns. Eyes widen, taking in the signs of my narrow escape. His lips are pressed so tightly they turn white.

"It's okay, the others are gone," I tell him.

"Good God, Emrys! What the hell happened to you?" He jets from his chair, leaves it spinning as he comes over, hands outstretched. They hover just over my skin, too afraid to touch.

I'm stunned still by his reaction. My window reflection must have glossed things, made the wounds lesser than they are. Suddenly everything—the bystander's death, Breena's anger and abandonment, the run for my life—explodes in my chest. Warm, salty tears pour out.

"Are you all right?" Richard's hand steadies me. All the feelings, raging like a tempest set off by butterfly wings, fall still against his fingers. His touch is peace. Home.

The tears keep falling, despite the glassy stillness in

me. They drop thick and fast, rolling down my cheeks. There's so many of them that soon I cannot see.

Richard guides me to his desk chair and kneels next to it, hand looped fiercely into mine.

"What's wrong?" he asks, his thumb stroking the top of my hand.

"Just a rough night," I say, and wipe the heavy dew from my eyes.

He knows there's more I'm not telling him—the knowledge is scrawled all across his face. His mouth draws thin as he looks at my arms, the dozens of fine pink lines dug out by witch-claw thorns and vines.

"What happened? Who did this to you?" he asks, careful not to touch any of the raised scarlet scabs. Righteous anger traces his voice.

"I was being a Frithemaeg," I mumble. "I'd rather not talk about it."

Richard sighs, disappointed. I know it's because of my silence, but that's the one thing I can't break. It wouldn't do any good for him to know how much danger we're in, especially if he can't do anything about it.

"I'm sorry—" I begin, but Richard's head turns at a sudden sound. I look toward the window, my mouth falling into stunned stillness. There, on the crisp white ledge, perch three ravens, tar feathers glossing indigo under the sun. The birds seem smaller outside the walls of their Tower, but they're no less formidable. Black eyes gleam and their claws scrabble strange symbols in the ledge's paint.

I feel the tears swelling again, but this time they're fueled by panic. Never in the four centuries since their first arrival to the Tower of London have the ravens set claw or feather outside its boundaries. It's the worst of omens.

And I know, even before their large razor beaks open, that they've come to speak to me. Words of doom, inspired by their second sight.

"Listen well, sister, to what we have seen," the middle raven, the oldest of the bunch, croaks.

The bird on the right squawks. Its foot continues to scratch fragile lines into the wood. "The shadow is gathered. Her arm grows restless, her hand is moved. Two paths spring for Albion."

"When all the silver face shows, the angered one shall strike. Beware the crown! Beware the crown!" the last bird cries.

"The Lord of the Wood is waiting. Seek the power in the blood," the middle raven says as it flaps its wings.

The feathers are still meticulously clipped, to keep the animal from flying. The ravens must have used their own strange magic to make this journey.

"Do you understand what they're saying?" Richard whispers. Shock, white as the cliffs of Dover, washes out his face.

I squeeze his hand to quiet him, but the ravens have finished talking. They watch the king, a row of beady, unblinking eyes. Richard looks back, grows tense under their gaze.

"She is coming," the middle raven says. "She's coming for your crown and head."

Richard shudders, his hand an earthquake in mine.

"Have you seen her?" I ask the trio.

"She is only shadow. Old, dark shadow," the right raven shrieks.

"Beware the crown!" The left raven turns and hops off the window ledge. Its black wings flutter ineffectively—wind passing straight through its feathers.

"Have all of you left the Tower?" The question spills out, quick. The birds are getting ready to depart and the answer is one I can't afford to lose.

"We leave. Others stay. The road is divided. Farewell,

sister. We will not see you again."

The last raven bows and follows its brothers to the closest patch of grass. I watch from the open window as they gather into a small ring and stretch their wings. As soon as all their wing tips touch, the birds vanish from sight. My breath is sharp as I stare long at the space: green and bare. The ravens are gone. Really gone.

"So we're coming to the end." I speak across the emptiness of the lawn.

"Is it true?" Richard's voice drags me back to him. To his hand knotted tight in mine.

"Is what true?"

"The legend. Those were Tower ravens, yes?" He gestures toward the vacant window.

The prophecy of a failing crown and a fallen kingdom after the ravens' departure. The legend typed into tourist pamphlets and minded by every mortal Beefeater who keeps the birds' wings clipped. That's what Richard means.

"It is. But they didn't all leave. I think they still haven't seen the end. The ravens' sight only goes so far." I can't help shuddering. Even the fact that three chose to leave the Tower stirs fear in my blood.

"What did they tell you? I couldn't make anything of it. Sounded like squawking to me." Richard tries to laugh, but the sound is forced.

My fingers squeeze against his, offer him something firmer to cling to.

"They said that the Old One is coming for us on the next full moon. They want us to go to Windsor and seek Herne's protection. They haven't seen the outcome—only the two paths that this kingdom can take. One with you and one without." I fall silent, musing over the rest of the ravens' words, the ones that I don't fully understand. *Beware the crown. Seek the power in the blood.* Who am I supposed to be wary of? Richard? Anabelle? Both seem very unlikely. As for power in the blood . . .

"We'll go to Windsor then. I'll call Lawton and have him make all of the arrangements." Instead of moving to the phone, Richard steps closer to me. His hands rest on my hips, where they fit perfectly, and his forehead taps against mine. "We'll be fine. It'll all work out. You'll see."

I shut my eyes. His breath brushes warm past my eyelashes, rolls down my cheeks. I try to think of nothing, fighting off thoughts of last night, of the ravens' message. I try to feel only Richard, to be content in his arms. But it doesn't work. The thought of losing him is too heavy, strangling.

"There are five days until the full moon. I should go and warn Mab. She'll be able to send Frithemaeg to defend the edges of the city. And if we're in Windsor we can get the older Fae even closer. If we can convince Herne to protect us . . . we might even have a chance."

Richard's hands slide past my hips, dipping around to the small of my back and pulling me closer. "Do what you feel is best."

There's something he's not saying. I feel it in the tension of his fingers, his voice. "What's wrong?"

"Do you have to go to Mab? If we really only have five days left . . ." He takes a breath. "Emrys, I don't want to be without you. Stay. Please."

I'm tearing to halves in his arms.

It's my duty to go to Mab, to offer this vital information in the flesh, so it arrives safely. But in five days, when the Old One finally reaches us, it won't matter. It won't matter if my warning was spoken word or ink on paper. All I'll remember is this time with Richard, fitting so exactly against every divot and bend in his body. His arms holding me together, into him.

"Do you have a pen and paper?"

"Of course." Richard digs across the already cluttered surface of his desk and produces a sheaf of paper along with his elegant fountain pen.

I etch the ravens' words onto paper in blocky black script. They look so much more ominous and real when they're strung together as letters. Those two lines still stand out, taunting me with hidden meanings. After scrawling my name, I fold the paper into fourths, seal it with magic so it can only be opened with Mab's touch. When I feel it break I will know my message got through.

Richard watches me the entire time, his face washed blank. This quickly turns into a smile when he realizes I'm staring back. "I never thought my first few days as king would be so exciting," he says glibly.

"Nor did I." I don't have the energy to pretend that things will be okay.

It doesn't take long for the youngling to arrive after my summons. Our exchange is quick: she listens to my instructions with a never-ending nod and jets off into the hazy summer sky, soon swallowed by cotton-whipped cumulus clouds. They roll forward on furious wind, ready to cloak the city.

Twenty-Seven

The afternoon is perfect. A quilted sky, patched with aquamarine, sieves sunlight over Buckingham's gardens. Everything is warm, yellow, and happy. As if our world isn't about to crumble to pieces.

"We don't have to go if you're feeling too bad." Anxiety scores Richard's cheeks and squeezes his eyes with premature wrinkles, signs he's second-guessing the pre-scheduled lunch with his sister.

"No, no. I want to meet her." I pick at one of the larger knots in my hair, impossibly snarled and stubborn, and try not to think of how, very soon, I'll be facing Breena's dragon-fire contempt.

The picnic, complete with wicker chairs and a breezy linen tent, waits in one of the garden's larger clearings. I half expect to see a croquet set leaning up against the folding table or a group of petticoated ladies sipping tea. But no one is under the canopy—Richard and I are the first ones here.

"So Anabelle will be able to see you now?"

I double-check my veiling spell. "She should."

"Just a warning—she doesn't open up to new people easily. Not at first." Richard frowns. His eyes linger on the bloody reminders of last night on my arms, the bruises beneath them. "Is there anything you can do about those? Or should we come up with some excuse about a bad-tempered house cat?"

"Right. I forgot." My dress is still in utter ruins as well: frayed lace and black. The mending magic threads it back together, new within seconds.

I mutter a few more words and watch the spell unknot my hair, wash my skin clean. I stare at my arms long after the scabs are gone, studying the light dusting of freckles and pinkish skin, how clean and unscarred they are, even after all I've been through. If only magic could fix everything this way.

Richard's hand falls on my shoulder, fills me with shivers despite the warmth of the day.

"Are you all right?" he asks. "You don't feel sick, do you?"

"I had a fight with Breena. She's not going to like that I'm showing myself to Anabelle. Not at all." I swallow, thinking of how the sickness might even be preferable to what I'm about to face. The thought of Breena glaring at me throughout the entire picnic makes me want to curl up under the table.

"I'm sorry—" Richard's voice stops abruptly, replaced by the Morse code click of heels. "Belle!"

"Hey! Sorry I'm late." Anabelle slides her sunglasses down the bridge of her nose. Her chocolate-brown eyes spring out to study me. Her gaze holds the same steel as her father's did, as her brother's does now. "Who's this?"

My stomach drops at the sight of Breena, leaning in the doorway. Even several meters away her scowl is visible, loaded with condemnation. Her distance, her absence feels like I've lost a limb, not vital, but devastating.

Breena looks everywhere but at me, her nose slightly raised in the air.

"This is Emrys." Richard turns me so that I'm completely facing his sister. "My . . ."

The sounds of the garden swell up—hushed secrets of leaves and birds' untranslated ballads. I watch as Richard's face flushes pink. Anabelle's eyes dart between us.

"Girlfriend," I offer out of the tightness of my throat. "I'm his girlfriend."

Richard loosens next to me. Beyond us I hear Breena's indignant choke.

"Girlfriend?" Anabelle lets the word settle on her tongue. "I knew it! That's why you've been acting so off lately!" She shoots her brother a knowing look, then gives me a triumphant grin. "It's very nice to meet you."

"You too." I steal another glance at Breena's corner. She's unmoved, a cross-armed statue of disdain.

Richard gestures to our waiting meal. "Shall we?"

I want to hang back, force Breena into a confrontation, but Richard keeps an arm wrapped around my shoulder. We walk alongside his sister. The sight of Anabelle leaping in her heels, goatlike, through the lawn brings a real grin to my face. I catch that smile, preserve it. As distracted as I am by Breena and the whirlwind of events outside the palace, I need this meeting to go well. I don't need the other major female in my life to hate me too.

Breena doesn't join us under the tent. She lingers in patches of sunlight, standing outside of the canopy like the watchful Guard she is. I need to get her attention, tell her about the ravens. . . .

"So, where'd you guys meet?" Anabelle smoothes her salmon pencil skirt and settles into her chair.

Richard's right. She's stiff and reserved in front of me, like a television reporter reciting lines for an interview. The swearing princess who leaps feetfirst into pools is nowhere to be found.

My mouth is a drought-struck river, dusty and dry, as I scour for a convincing answer. Richard senses my panic, reaches across the table to lace his hand into mine.

"At a charity event," he says. His free hand begins sorting through the picnic basket. "She was one of the coordinators."

"Let the woman speak for herself." Anabelle tugs the basket away from her brother. Every action, every word between them oozes familiarity. "You're squishing the sandwiches. Let me do that."

"I often think she should have been the oldest," Richard mutters.

"Me too," his sister says, looking back at me over the basket. "Funny that you organize charities. It seems like I should have seen you before."

"It was my first one. I was rather nervous. I actually spilled champagne all over myself." I manage a light, wind-chime laugh. "Richard was the only one who noticed."

"Of course, that was a few months ago," Richard offers. "She's much less clumsy now."

"Why've you kept her a secret this long?"

"So you wouldn't torture her with Burberry catalogs and polo matches," Richard teases.

The siblings begin to banter, but I don't pay attention to their words. My focus returns to Breena's storm-cloud stare.

Bree, I need to talk to you.

She doesn't even flinch. I begin to wonder if the words got through to her.

What? she snaps back. *Is it about your hot date? Or are you ready to explain why every soul feeder in London was at Buckingham's door last night? Maybe you can tell me why Gwyn is dead.*

Her words are like a thousand tiny paper cuts, stinging me to pieces. I wince under them, let go of Richard's hand, and grip my chair's splintering wicker.

"Are you okay?" The princess's hand lands on my arm, jerking me back into the current, mortal conversation.

I'm clearly not going to get any effective communication with Breena here. But now's my only chance. I have to tell her while she's in my reach.

"I need to use the toilet," I tell Anabelle. "I'll only be a minute."

I scurry away from the tent, alter my veiling spell as soon as Anabelle's attention is elsewhere. Breena doesn't look at me when I approach. Her eyes lock solely on the royal pair. Everything else about her is void of emotion, like she's trying her best not to unleash.

"If it means anything now, I'm sorry," I begin. "I was trying to do what was right for the crown and I failed."

My friend remains a statue, looking only at the tent's chatting diners.

"Bree, talk to me. I'm sorry! I should've listened to you."

"But you didn't," she cuts in, syllables forged of cruel steel. "You let your love for Richard get in the way. Go and be with him. You're no longer fit to be a Fae."

"Maybe that's true. But you're going to need me. The ravens came this morning, gave me a message."

Breena's frozen state breaks enough to show me she's interested.

"There were three of them. From the Tower." I go on to repeat the ravens' prophecies, watching the horror thaw out Breena's pretty face.

"So you—we have forced the Old One's hand." Her voice fills with cracks. "Five days. That isn't much time."

"I've sent a message to Mab. I say we follow the ravens' advice. The palace has already been breached. Who knows if Gwyn's killer is still around. . . .

We need to get the royals to Windsor and ask for Herne's protection. It's what Mab wants us to do."

"Herne? What makes you think he'll offer us protection? All he cares about are his woods and his hunt." The words roll off Breena's tongue with distinct distaste. "As for Mab—she's been out of the city too long. She can't even go to Windsor herself! No. We should go north to Balmoral Castle, where Mab can protect us. Think of all the older Fae in the court. Their power will be enough to protect your precious king and the rest of the crown."

"North is where the Old One is. We can't go there. We have to follow the ravens' words. They've never misled us before," I say, firm. I feel the fight dawning between us, brace myself for it.

"They left, Emrys. They know what's coming. We have to go north. Those are my orders."

I feel the weight of her age, those extra years between us, pressing down, trying to force me into submission. Normally I would have to bow, let Breena have her way. But I have something stronger than age: Mab's blessing.

"I won't let you." The force of the queen's magic swells behind my words. Breena can challenge me all she wants, but she can't outrank me. Not in this.

"What do you mean you won't *let* me?" Breena's magic presses, probes me for weakness. "I just gave you an order."

I don't yield. "Mab gave me permission to ignore your orders if I thought they would hurt Richard. I don't have to obey you. Mab wants them to go to Windsor and so do I."

"Why would Mab do that?" Breena's nostrils flare and her eyes turn to cyan slits when she realizes I'm right. "Doesn't she trust me?"

I say nothing.

My friend buries her anger behind pursed lips and quick breaths. "You already have one death on your head. Are you prepared to handle the others?"

"It's what I'm trying to avoid." It's my turn to be ice. I see her eyes shift to the tent, to Richard. I see traces of her wild spirit behind that stare, and I realize how much I've hurt her.

Breena says nothing else. Her glare drills deep into the diners.

"So be it." I turn and walk back to the tent.

Anabelle is distracted with her shrimp salad sandwich as I approach.

"Oh! You're here!" The princess nearly drops her

sandwich when she spots me back against the wicker chair. "Richard and I were just talking about taking a trip to Windsor. I think it would be great if you could go with us. We'd get a chance to bond. What do you say?"

I force a smile, pry it wide across my cheeks. "I'd love to."

"Well, Windsor it is then." Richard holds up his sparkling water. "To Windsor!"

The glasses clink together. I swallow and try everything I can not to look back to where Breena is standing, staring.

"To Windsor," I echo.

Twenty-Eight

The spell jerks me out of my drowsy state. I sit up in the bed, careful not to disturb Richard's arm draped over my waist. He's asleep, lulled by the fat raindrops skating across the window. The sound is peaceful, soothing—almost enough to make me forget the trouble that comes with the storm.

The sealing spell on my letter has been opened, torn by Mab's hand. Cool air and relief flood my lungs. My messenger wasn't intercepted. The ravens' words got through. Now all I have to do is wait for the response. She'll send it to Windsor. That's where she'll expect us, now that London has been compromised.

I look down at Richard. With the windows' drapes drawn, he's barely visible. Only the accented lines of his face rise up from the whiteness of his pillow. Half of it's covered in lengthening hair. My fingers twitch, fighting the urge to brush it away. I must let him sleep while he can.

I lean back down and focus on the weight of his arm over my waist. This night has been a long one, filled with clamoring, avian prophecies and what I've done to Breena. My mind has been everywhere except with Richard, because I know what must be done. Time is running out for both of us.

There is no more middle ground. Only two separate paths.

The first is long and lonely, crowded with Fae, magic, and eternity. Sickness and slow decay. It stretches on and on. No end in sight.

The second path is much shorter. A single life. With Richard and all he's come to mean to me. Without the yawning emptiness. Without power. And a few leagues away there's a great blinding light, swallowing the path. The end.

After I made the choice to follow Mab, to look like one of them, I started on this road. I was always supposed to end up here, at this fork. For so many decades of queens, battles, and ballrooms, my humanness has been sprouting, pushing, and growing through so many tough, gravelly layers of Fae. Waiting for its exact moment to bloom.

I look at Richard, so peaceful and unaware of the

civil war inside me. The fears tangled with silent, nagging doubts. Will Richard always love me? What if he can't stay away from the bottle? Will this end as disastrous as the crumbling of Camelot?

No. Richard isn't Arthur, and I'm certainly not Guinevere. We're our own story.

But if he breaks my heart, breaks me . . .

This thought—full of dark debris—makes me shudder. Is the beauty worth the risk? Is the threat of brokenness worth the possibility of becoming whole?

Richard wriggles beside me and gives an unusually loud snore. Sleep has always been a thing of curiosity for immortals. That something could make the humans and the animals so powerless and unaware, but grant them visions and dreams of things to come, has always baffled us. Many Fae have even tried to dream—but the gift was never meant for us.

I stare back up into the blackness of the ceiling, watching the two roads in my mind's eye. My heart is torn no matter which way I choose. But in the end I have to take the step. I can't stay at these crossroads forever.

The air's different here. I feel it even through the car's thick glass windows. We're barely outside the city, not even free of the identical lines of row houses, but the change is obvious, lifting the sickness and charging newness through my veins. I feel like thrusting my head out the window and letting my hair flow like phoenix fire, wild and free. But I'm sitting next to Anabelle and very visible, so I just sit and watch the trees fly past in blurs of green.

The houses grow fewer and the trees herd into dark, lush groups as we get closer to Windsor. The castle straddles these two worlds. One side looks over the accordion rows of shops and houses in its namesake city. Another, broader side watches over the tamed foliage of the Great Park. Herne's territory. My eyes stay locked on the distant tree line as the car wheels up to the castle. Herne is here. I feel him.

He feels the royals' presence as well. Change seizes the air, though whether it's good or bad, I can't say.

Anabelle slides out of the car after me, and Breena follows, her face made of complete fury. I'm surprised she came and even more astonished that the entire Guard caravanned with us to Windsor. The other Fae gave me strange looks when they realized my veiling spell was completely gone, but none of them said anything. My rank is too high for any of them to reproach me as Breena did. My old friend doesn't speak a word. She uses Anabelle as an unwitting shield; every time I look at my friend I seem to be staring at the princess.

"Beautiful, isn't it?" Anabelle's arm sweeps out, presenting walls of weathered gray, their elegantly arched windows rimmed with yellow Bath stone. Beyond all this, the greenness of summer plays out in Herne's woods. "We should go riding around the Great Park. There's plenty of time before brunch."

"Sounds lovely." My stomach stirs, not with nausea, but from the thought of going into Herne's territory so soon. Getting permission to stay on his land is one thing. Pleading his help against an Old One is far more nerve-wracking.

The castle rooms are time capsules of crimson drapes, Jacobean furniture, and flourishing, gold-leafed ceilings. Impressive, but stifling. After such a fresh breath of air and trees, the last thing I want to do is sit behind four walls.

"We might run into Herne," I warn Richard as he changes into more casual jeans and a band T-shirt. "You won't be able to see him. But he'll want to talk to me. Or Breena," I add, unable to hide my wince. "Could you find some way to distract Anabelle?"

"That shouldn't be hard. What about Herne? Do you think he'll help us?"

"Herne—" I'm gnawing my lip, trying to think of how to contain such a massive spirit inside words. "Herne isn't bound by any rules, only the ones he makes for himself. He's only loyal to his forest. I can't say what his answer will be, but he's been willing to work with Mab before."

"Sounds like a wild card."

Richard smiles, and for a moment I forget all about the minutes ahead.

He reaches out, weaves his hand into mine, and nods at the door. "Shall we?"

Remnants of fear from my last encounter with Herne buzz through me, sapping the sunlight of our moment together. I try my hardest not to shudder. I can't let anyone know I'm afraid. Not Richard, not Breena, and especially not Herne.

At the stables, our horses are tacked and ready to go. I mount my ride quickly, without help from Richard or the surprised groom. Compared to Kelpies, the hefty black mare feels like a Shetland pony.

Anabelle rides up on a petite and delicate bay. She

smiles. It seems she's warming up to me, if only a little. "If we try, we might be able see most of the park today."

"And then what will you do for the rest of the week?" Richard asks, wheeling around us on his tightly wound roan. "You might want to save it. Besides, it's getting pretty hot."

His sister dismisses him with a laugh. "Listen to you talking all sensibly." Her horse ambles close to mine so that I can hear her whisper, "There was a time when he was real wanker. It wasn't that long ago, actually."

I try my hardest to act surprised. "Richard? No!"

Breena's snicker rises from behind us.

The princess continues to chat while we trot down the path, launching into several embarrassing childhood stories featuring Richard. I pretend to laugh and nod, but my eyes never leave the weaving tangle of trees. They're old, much older than the sidewalk sprouts of London, and they're moving. The stir isn't just in their leaves and smooth, windswept branches, but in their core. Where the Dryads live, awake, alert, and watching.

We ride for half an hour down the groomed trail, watched by countless silent trees. Breath abandons my lungs when we reach the end of the Long Walk and continue. Trees close in around us, pulling us into the heart of Herne's thick woods. The mare senses my great unease, her hooves grow jumpy, and crescent-white fear enters her eyes. The trees have stopped their slow, whispering movements. They're dead still. The reason is soon clear.

He stands on the path in front of us, his giant mount and his twin horns casting no shadow. I let my horse fall still with the others, too spooked to continue. Some deep, animal part of them knows that edgy, dangerous magic stands ahead.

"Come on, girl!" Anabelle digs her heels into her horse, but the bay keens, high and nail curling.

"Something's spooking the horses," Richard tells her with a quick glance at me. "Maybe we should choose another way."

Herne remains motionless. An untrained eye might mistake him for a grotesque cast-iron figure. He speaks. The words rumble across the space between us, their very sound exuding power. "So it's you, woodling. I never forget a pretty face."

I watch him, bound to silence by Anabelle's presence. The princess is entirely oblivious, distracted by her horse's breakdown.

"You've chosen to reveal yourself to the mortals?" Herne's head tilts, his lead-sharp horns skewering the empty space between leaves. "How odd."

My lips stay sealed as I glance at Richard. The king is staring at the path, his sight going straight past Herne's fearsome form. The powerful Lord of the Wood nudges his mount a step closer. The royals' horses back away nervously. Only my mare holds her ground.

"You have something to ask of me. I sense it. Tell me, what does your kind want now, youngling?" Herne's voice, closer and more terrible than before, causes my horse to shake and sweat beneath me. There's a bitter edge to it that makes my fingers coil.

We've come to ask for your protection.

Herne is silent. His eyes continue to burn into my skin like the bright orange end of a cigarette. I begin to wonder if he even heard my thought.

"You speak of what stirs in the north," he says finally.

Yes. It's coming for them. It wants to destroy the crown.

"What's wrong with you?!" Anabelle's face flushes bright as she digs her heels into equine muscles. Her hair has come unclipped, pouring gold like olive oil across her cheeks.

"And you wish me to protect them?" Herne finishes

my thoughts for me. "Your queen thinks she can use me like a mercenary? As a bodyguard for hire? I follow no one. Not even your precious Queen Mab. It wasn't enough for me to grant her the use of my land, she thinks she can demand my powers as well."

I stiffen, barely able to move. *What's Herne talking about?*

The confusion must be painted clearly on my face, since Herne's response is quick, aggravated. "Mab has already asked—no—*demanded* my aid. As if I were a hound suited to answer her horn."

I cringe, slouch closer to my horse's neck. Mab, out of desperation or some false sense of strength, had tried to command Herne. Rage rolls, full of sear and char, off the spirit's aura. Slowly, inevitably, I see our chances of survival slipping away. . . .

"Do you know why this is happening, little woodling? Why this force is rising? Perhaps you are too young to realize this, but the mortals have become too strong, too forgetful of the old ways. They've managed to destroy most of Albion with their machines. They are eating the land, killing our magic. Perhaps it's better that we stop them. I cannot say. But I will not raise my hand against them. They've done me no wrong." He nods toward Richard and his sister.

But the crown and the blood magic. It's what holds Albion together!

"I swore no oath to Pendragon. That was your precious queen." His voice rises, shaking the deepest marrow in my bones. "Now be gone. And bring no trouble to my woods!"

Herne's giant charcoal horse turns and vanishes in the wink of an eye. The faint green afterglow of the woodlord's shape stays in my vision. It gradually disappears as I blink, trying to process all of his words. The Old One is coming and there's nothing we can to do stop her.

I gasp as the air leaves my throat, leaving room for the settling shock.

Anabelle looks up at the sound, her face a mess of blonde and half-forgotten annoyance. "Emrys, are you all right?"

"I—I—" I struggle, fight for every new breath. It feels like my body simply doesn't want the air anymore. "I don't feel well. I think maybe I should go back to the castle and rest for a while."

Richard's face turns paler than the spots of sunlight falling on it. "I'll go with you."

"I'll come too. It's no fun riding alone."

Richard's mouth pulls tight. He's unhappy with his

sister's company. It's just as well. If I can't even process the truth myself, how am I supposed to tell him?

"You shouldn't have counted on Herne."

I jump at the voice, look down. Breena is close to my knee, keeping up with my horse's every stride. Her face is calm, collected—the exact opposite of my churning insides. There's no smugness in her blue gaze, just the solid knowledge that, in the end, she was right.

Why would Mab try to command Herne? She should've known he would get angry. . . .

"I'm sure she was only doing what she thought was best. There's still time to leave for Balmoral. We don't have to stay here."

The mare's jerky trot jars my backbone. I wish it would rattle my thoughts too. Then maybe I would be able to say something useful.

We'd be going in blind. There's no way of knowing how many soul feeders are between here and there. We should wait for Mab's response.

Breena's silence tells me I'm right.

I shut my eyes, trusting the mare to follow the other horses back to the stables. Not all's lost, I shouldn't think like it is. The Old One's strength is still untested and Mab's help should arrive soon. I manage to keep my face blank all the way back to the stables.

"We'll wait for Mab's response," Breena agrees once I slide out of the saddle, my skin zipping fast down polished leather. "It should be back by this evening, yes?"

Maybe sooner. Even my thoughts feel numb.

"I'll have the others start preparing the defenses. Four days isn't much time."

I'm dizzy, I realize as I walk away from the horse. Herne's denial was a bigger shock than I was ready for. I reach out for a stall door, try to steady myself against bars of unyielding iron. Instead, support comes from behind as Richard's hands wrap, warm and solid, around my shoulders.

"Are you okay?" he whispers into my ear, and guides me to the stable's bright, airy entrance.

I stare at the ground, at the scuffed edges of Richard's riding boots. What can I tell him? The one hope I had, my last resort, just rode away on his high black horse.

"What's wrong?" Anabelle is next to us, winding her hair up into a wispless ballet bun. Right now, if I could talk, I would tell her that it looks better down.

"She doesn't feel well. Stomachache," Richard says. "I think I'll take her to lie down."

"Anything I can do?" his sister offers.

"No need." Richard shakes his head. "We'll see you at dinner."

He guides me through the twists and turns of the castle. Windsor is the same as I've always remembered it, but I can only trail Richard's gentle steps like a reluctant child. My limbs have lost the power to move of their own will. I follow him, feet slow and dragging, into the bedroom.

"I'm fine."

"At least sit down. What happened? Did you see Herne?"

I have a seat on the bed, clutching the comforter's fabric in both hands. "He said no."

Richard's eyes don't move. I wait for the panic to creep into them, but it never appears. His stare stays steady.

"He doesn't want to help us," I go on. "He says spirits have a right to be upset because of all the machines the mortals have created and how the forests are being destroyed. He thinks your death might be a good thing, because it'll strengthen magic and help the Fae live on."

Anger simmers, burns slow in my veins as I speak. By the end, I'm shaking.

"And what do you think?" Richard's voice is stable, as unmoving as a monk in meditation. Compared to him, I'm an unraveled, childish mess.

I take a breath. The air leaks out of me slowly as I regain perspective and a tiny sliver of calmness. "He's a selfish arse, but he has a point. The Fae are unhappy with the world as it is. Some of us, like the Guard, have learned to adapt. But others, especially the older ones, can't stand to see magic falling apart. The Old One that's after you wants everything reversed. My guess is she wants Albion like it was long ago, before machines and mortals. The others want power too. They don't want to hide anymore."

Richard's quiet, buried in the depth of his thoughts.

"If you weren't bound by Mab's oath to protect the crown, what side would you choose?" he asks finally.

"It'd be nice not to be sick all the time," I mutter. "But that's hardly a reason to justify what they plan to do. Mortals and Fae coexisted happily long before the machines came along."

"So there's a happy medium."

"I don't know where or how—but yes. There has to be. It would change England forever in the eyes of the world. You would no longer have cars or lifts." I stop.

How silly to be arguing about machinery when our lives are at stake.

"But we would have magic." He stands from the bed. The mattress springs up, tossing me like a wave. "I want to talk to Herne."

"What?" I stare at him. He means what he says.

"Herne. I want to speak with him. Is that possible?"

"I don't—only if he wants to show himself to you. It won't do any good though."

Richard's arms fold over his chest. The veins in his forearms bulge, making crisscross formations beneath his skin. "I want to try. Can you take me to him?"

Visions of Herne in his primal wrath tear through my mind and, with them, panic. "You don't have to prove anything, Richard! We'll figure out something else. . . ."

He shakes his head. "I'm king now, Emrys. He might not listen to me, but he'll respect me. I have to try."

There's no telling *what* Herne might do, though I can see there's no changing Richard's mind. "We should wait a while. If we approach him again so soon, he'll just be irritated."

"After dinner, then?"

I nod, trying my hardest not to show how my insides are unraveling, looping apart with fear. Herne made it quite clear that he didn't want to be bothered again. And forces like Herne the Hunter shouldn't be dealt with lightly.

"We'll get through this, you know." Richard kneels down, touches his nose to mine. "Just have a little faith. Trust me."

My eyes close. I feel the time slipping over us, passing second by second. Grain by grain. Soon, very soon, we will run out, be smothered by the sand at the bottom of the hourglass.

I should tell him how I feel. But the moment is wrong, tainted by so much doom and darkness.

"I do," I whisper. "I do trust you. It's just that—"

He breaks off my words with a kiss, hands tangling through my hair. I let his lips take me away. Away from the worry. Away from the time we no longer have. I lose myself in him until the fire springs between us. Richard draws back, reluctant and slow, breath sharp like raining arrows.

"You've done so much to protect me. It's my turn now." He tucks a piece of hair behind my ear, his thumb ghosting across my cheek. "Let me do this for you. For us."

Everything about him speaks confidence. His touch, his voice, the hint of a smile on his lips. If only it were so easy for me.

Twenty-Nine

Dinner is a small, unremarkable event. I pick at my baked chicken—my stomach is turning too much even to think of putting food down there. I keep sipping at the tongue-twisting lemonade. It washes, the perfect combination of sour and sweet, down my throat.

"Mab's reply isn't here yet." Breena breaks our arbitrary silence. Her chilled words slide down the long glass-coated dining table. "That's not normal. Something went wrong."

As much as I hate to admit it, she's right. I sent my message over twenty-four hours ago. Any response, especially for a situation this urgent, should've arrived by now.

But Mab received the letter. I felt her open it.

"The message must have been intercepted on its way back." Breena frowns. Her stare drifts aimlessly around the gilded room, over tiger lilies and gold-plated utensils.

Even if that happened, Mab would know. She'd try a different way of getting the message to us.

"Maybe she's still trying."

But no matter how many times we move the pieces around a particular excuse, nothing fits the way it should.

Something isn't right, Breena. I feel it. Maybe Mab's court has been compromised.

Blood abandons Breena's face, leaving her vampire pale. "Then we're trapped here. Blind. Without protection."

"Can I get you anything, Emrys?"

"Oh, nothing." I straighten up, hoping Anabelle hasn't noticed my intense staring match with the vacant space next to her.

"I hope we aren't boring you," Anabelle says, her fingers winding delicately around the stem of her fork. "Things will be a little more lively tomorrow when the rest of the family gets here."

"The rest of the family?"

"I thought it would be nice to have the entire family here for a few days." Richard nudges me underneath the table.

It means more Frithemaeg, but also more people to protect. The Old One will come in here and wipe out the entire royal line like pieces from a chessboard.

"Oh, lovely," I say, my voice growing weak. "I've been wanting to meet them."

"What did the raven say?" Breena's nails tap against the table's sleek surface, regaining my attention. "Tell me the exact words."

I shut my eyes, struggle to remember the prophecies. All of this mental juggling is giving me a headache.

Something about a shadow. Her hand is moving. Two paths grow for Albion. When the full moon arrives, she will strike. The Lord of the Wood is waiting. Beware the crown! Seek the power in the blood. I falter at the last few sentences, suddenly facing those hidden meanings I couldn't wrap my mind around before.

"Beware the crown." Breena's lips tremble, a bruised, sickly shade of blue. "So Mab's court has been compromised."

Of course. The crown in the prophecy wasn't talking about Anabelle or Richard. The danger lurked in Mab's court, where I'd sent a youngling with all of our vital information. My only hope is that Mab managed to destroy the letter before it reached enemy eyes.

I'll bet it's Titania. She always was after Mab's power.

Breena's hands rise over her face, shielding her from everything. They stay there for ten long breaths. In, out. In, out. I mirror her lungfuls of air, try to fight the despair and hopelessness that creep up like the tide.

"There's no use speculating." My friend's hands fall

back to the tabletop. They stay flat and unmoving, like the depths of her eyes. "It could be any one of the courtiers. All that matters is there's no help coming. And no way of knowing where we should go."

How did we get into this mess?

"It's easy to see now. Whoever infiltrated Mab's courts must've had control over the scouting parties. It's no wonder they couldn't find anything. They were being led into dead ends the whole time!"

Something inside me breaks. It's myself, my spirit as it was before countless years of humanity's sugarcoating. From the years before Camelot, when I was a wild thing, tearing through the moors and mountains. Unbound. If I give in to it now, the room and everything in it, except Breena, will be destroyed.

Breena sees the breaking. "Save it," she says. "You'll need it for what's coming."

I close it up, stitch by painful stitch. The beast inside roars with protest, aching to be let out. My rational self silences it. Breena's right. I'll need it for what's ahead.

I pick up the polished fork and jab it into the closest piece of chicken. It doesn't matter that the food will upset my stomach. Not a lot matters now.

"Anabelle's afraid you don't like her," Richard tells

me later. "I tried to tell her you were just tired, but I don't think she bought it."

"I was busy talking with Breena." I'm blunt, in no mood for apologies.

But Richard doesn't ask for an apology. He doesn't even ask about my conversation with Breena. His mind is focused on one thing. "Will you take me to Herne now?"

I look through his bedroom window on to the fading scene of the Great Park. I feel him, roaming somewhere beneath those silver-etched trees. He won't be pleased to see us again.

But now the fear is gone. Herne's voice has already spoken. It said no. Let Richard have his turn. There's nothing left to lose.

"Yes," I speak into the panes. "I'll take you."

"Thank you." I feel him draw in close behind me, but he doesn't touch me. His reflection in the glass is all worry. It's the only anxiety I've seen on his face this whole time.

"Have you really given up already?"

I turn, meet him face-to-face. Deep-creased lines of concern around his eyes quickly blend into the rest of his skin.

"I'm sorry. It's just hard to see how it'll turn out any

other way. Mab's court has been compromised. There's no help coming. We're alone now." I try to keep my voice flat, like a windless lake, but there's too much roiling underneath. Some words break.

"Then we'll just have to convince Herne, won't we?" Our hands lock together. In this moment, his fingers twisted and curled into mine, the future isn't full of dark and burning.

"And if not," he continues, "we'll face what's coming together. I don't regret a moment I've spent with you, Embers. Even this."

Now. Tell him now. I realize I'm not afraid. Somewhere in these long weeks of emotions, I faced my sea serpent and jumped. I love Richard even more than I fear death. More than I fear losing my magic, my self. Because my magic *isn't* my self anymore.

It's not panic but a peace, released in my chest. This is it. The moment between moments—the time for me to give myself to him.

"Richard?"

He looks down, eyes full.

"There's something I want to tell you."

A question flutters behind the twitch of his mouth, but he waits, silent.

Another breath reins in the rapid gallop of my heart. I look. Really look at him. The night falling outside shines in his eyes. I see myself there, haloed by hazel and dusk.

"I love you."

Richard smiles, cups my face with his free hand, and brings our lips together. I feel his fingers move, sliding through my hair's copper depths as his kiss strengthens. I pull him close. My arms wreathe around his neck, anchor us together. The moment is enveloping. I want to stay in it.

A great sigh fills Richard when we fall away.

"I think—I think I've made my choice."

He stiffens. His eyes grow wider, letting in more of the dark.

"But," I continue, "before I do anything, I need to know that this is going to last. Is this forever?"

"I can't," he says.

All of the sudden I feel like an ax-bitten tree—hacked, hacked, and hacked until I fall dead against the ground. Rotting and devastated.

"I can't ask you to give everything up. Your magic. Your life . . ." He shakes his head. Relief washes over me, sinks in like raindrops meeting parched soil.

"I can't—I won't be the reason you die."

I blink, try to recover from the awfulness of his pause. "You didn't answer my question."

"Yes, Embers. You are my yes. You're the one I'll love until the day I die." Every word is sure, a stone mortared into place. They block up, brick by brick, filling me. And I know that, as long as I have him, my soul will feel whole. "But that doesn't mean you have to die too."

I rest my head against his chest and memorize the pulsing beat of his heart, how it murmurs its unsung ballad into my ear. He strokes my hair, his fingers threading through the long, smooth strands. But his fingers don't stop there. They continue down my back to the curving base of my spine.

"I can't keep living like this, Richard." I think about everywhere I've been, everywhere I'm going. "The sickness . . . being apart from you . . ."

"But your magic. Your future." Concern for me aches through his chest.

"That was my past. That world is falling apart," I tell him. "It's my choice. But I don't think it's going to matter. The way things are going . . ."

"We'll get through this. You'll see," he promises.

"I hope you're right." I look back out the window, at the milky white length of the Long Walk stretching far into velveteen darkness. "Let's go."

When we reach the line of thick, tangling trees I almost turn back. Leafy spirits stare through the darkness; their eyes rake over us, full of unwelcome. Richard walks forward with blithe, agile steps, unaware of the forest's hostile inhabitants.

"It's better if you stay behind me." My voice fills the empty spaces between the trees and I fall silent, feeling as though I've breached something sacred.

Richard wheels around, backtracks to the patch of earth behind me. "Is he close?"

I pause. Herne's presence is everywhere. It's impossible to tell how close or far he is in a place like this. His magic soaks the soil, rolls in the air. It's only when I see him with my own eyes that I'll know for sure where he is.

"I don't know. But he knows we're here." The Dryads' whispers travel fast. I'm sure they've reached his part of the woods by now. "He should come." Out of blatant irritation or curiosity if nothing else.

We're stopped by the base of a sprawling, many-limbed

oak. It stretches over us like a squid, its reach tangled and endless. "I think we should wait here."

Richard starts to lean against the worn, grooved trunk.

"Don't touch anything." I reach out and stop him. "Herne's very protective of his trees."

Richard grunts but stands straight again.

We don't wait long. The low thunder of Herne's horse rises into the air. The thick hedge of trees leans aside to let the commanding rider through. In the darkness, all I can see of Herne are his coal-glow eyes. They burn through the evening—twisted, throbbing stars.

"I've already answered your request. What more do you want of me, young woodling?"

"King Richard wishes to speak with you." As I say this, Richard stiffens and looks into the same empty spot of trees. "Will you show yourself to him?"

The request catches Herne off guard. His piercing eyes roll from me over to Richard. Their orange depths flicker, as if seeing the mortal for the first time. "The king? What words does he have for me?"

"I don't know," I answer truthfully. "You'll have to speak with him yourself."

For a terrible moment, I think Herne will turn away,

but the Lord of the Wood is too curious. He stares at Richard, studying every facet of the mortal's face. Something about the king seems to satisfy him.

Beside me, Richard jumps, focusing on the patch of darkness as it shapes into the horse and its fearsome rider. Richard's fingers twitch, but his expression is set, unmoved by the rider's spiral horns and furnace eyes.

"It's nice to meet you," he says, making a tiny half bow.

All of the muscles in my body grow tight. Was this a mistake? I thought that bringing Richard here couldn't have done any more harm than good. Maybe I was wrong. The slightest insult could send Herne over the edge.

Windsor's spirit returns the bow, bending close to the towering neck of his horse. I feel like I can breathe again.

"What is it you want, O king?" Herne's voice booms a strange mix of disregard and respect. Despite all of his earlier statements, it seems Herne still holds the mortals' crown in special consideration.

"I've come to ask you to reconsider your decision," Richard says.

"Is that so?" Herne grunts. "Well, I'm sure your Frithemaeg has told you of my reasons. What have you to offer instead?"

Richard begins to pace. Dead leaves kick up under

his feet as he walks the same line, as though he's patrolling a courtroom. "Is the destruction of England's humanity really the answer to your problem? For years, the mortal and immortal have existed, side by side— but then your kind chose to plunge us into ignorance. Faeries and other spirits vanished. They forced humans to push them into the realm of myths and legends. And now you're angry for what we've created instead. We can't know that we've damaged magic if we aren't even aware of its existence."

Herne moves. I almost throw myself in front of Richard, but there's no need. The old spirit is only dismounting his horse.

"Go on," he says.

Richard doesn't flinch as the towering being draws closer. Even off his steed, Herne is nearly as tall and solid as the trunk of the nearby oak.

"Since I've met Emrys, I've begun to understand that spirits and humans weren't meant to live apart. We're supposed to work together, side by side. That's what made Pendragon's kingdom so legendary. That's what brought England to its golden age. We can have that again. We can create a new alliance." Richard pounds his fist into his hand to emphasize his point.

"And how would this benefit me?" Herne interrupts. "This is all well and good, but how is it not easier just to let you be killed?"

My heart drops, like a starling struck dead in the sky. Herne—like so many other spirits—is truly a neutral force, indifferent to the lives and deaths of all around him.

Richard jumps into his argument without skipping a beat. "Even if the Old One takes my crown, the mortals will put up a fight. There'll be chaos, pandemonium. People will run into the woods to hide. I'm sure many trees would get destroyed in the process. If we face the Old One together we can avoid that destruction."

Herne is frozen, almost impossible to pick apart from the sentinel-still trunks of the woods. Richard has found the spirit's one weak spot: his love for his forest.

The king goes on, "I promise you that once the alliance between mortals and spirits is cemented, I'll focus on rebuilding the forests. Your forest will be wild—and I mean truly wild—again. You have my word."

"And what assurance do I have that you'll keep this word of yours?" Herne growls after a moment's hesitation.

"It's my life." Richard spreads out his hands in surrender.

My heart beats faster, like a rabbit startled into flight. For the first time in days, a real tangible hope sits in front of me. Herne hasn't said no or ridden off into the bushes. He simply stands there.

"You." His eyes flick back to me, burn twin holes into my gut. "What does your queen have to say about all of this?"

"I—I don't know," I manage. "We've lost all communication with Mab's court. We believe it's been compromised."

"Treason? Mab's grip got too tight, did it? Or maybe it wasn't tight enough," the woodlord adds grimly.

I bite my tongue and wonder if I should resort to begging. But Richard speaks again before I can open my mouth.

"So that's your choice. You can help us establish a kingdom of mortals and spirits and allow your woods to prosper. Or you can stand back and let anarchy destroy what little wilderness you have left." He faces the forest spirit, arms crossed. Gone is the young man who refused to face his future. Somewhere, in the past few days, a monarch has risen from the ashes of his fear.

Richard is a king now.

The lofty air has vanished from Herne's aura—

replaced by a keen sense of wariness. He's studying Richard. His glowing eyes scour the king's face.

An owl's call breaks the silence, low and lonely. None of us move.

"I like you," Herne says finally. "You have backbone. But I need more than your word that my trees will survive."

He's talking about his price. A spirit with no loyalties must be bought.

"My magic." My offer spills out before Richard substitutes something dangerous or equally irretrievable. "If we survive the battle, you can have my magic."

All of Herne's energies focus in on me, digging a shudder out of my body. The spirit glides forward, horns twisting so far above me they seem to spear the light of the stars.

"You are the Lady Emrys, are you not?" he rumbles. "Mab holds you in high esteem. She says you're gifted for one so young. . . . Your power isn't something to be given lightly. Tell me, why would you sacrifice it?"

"It—" I glance over at where Richard stands, straight and rigid like a toy soldier. "It doesn't matter. It's my choice."

"For him?" Herne's voice rises with surprise.

"But only after the battle," I tell him again when he takes another step forward. "I have to be able to defend myself." *And Richard.*

"Certainly. If only I might have your word." The spirit extends a dark-gloved hand.

I take a deep breath, knowing what will happen when I lock fingers with him. There will be no going back. No second chances. But the choice was already made, long before this moment. My hand stretches out, out.

"Emrys, no." Richard steps in front of me. My fingers crumple against the center of his chest. "We'll find something else. There has to be another way."

I shake my head. His heart slams hard; I feel every beat beneath my nails.

"It's okay, Richard." I swallow and try not to think of everything I'm about to give up. I focus on what's in front of me. What I'm touching. "Death . . . it doesn't matter. Because being with you is worth all of that."

"Are you sure?" Richard's hands reach around mine, hold me to him. I look at him and wonder how he can doubt, how he doesn't know that he's worth all of this.

"Yes, Richard." I smile and repeat those words he offered only minutes before. "You are my yes."

Richard still holds my hand, looks at its nails and

creases like they're some sort of treasure. After a long, lingering moment he steps aside and lets go.

There's a sound like the cracking of thunder, Herne clearing his throat. "Does your offer still stand, Lady Emrys?"

"It does," I tell him, and step forward.

My hand slides into Herne's and I feel the magic beginning to work. It fuses us together, weaving the words of my mouth into an unbreakable contract, cementing and binding them. My future is sealed now. Either way the battle turns, I'll meet death.

"You have my sword then," Herne says once he releases me. Even though our hands fall apart, I still feel the harsh tug of my promise to him. "When do you expect the Old One to arrive?"

"The ravens said it would be at the full moon," I tell him.

"Four days." The spirit glides back to his horse. "Barely enough time to get the Hunt together."

So he's gathering the Hunt. The idea should reassure me, but all I feel is a nervous rumbling in my innards.

"I'm going to round up my followers." Herne mounts his horse and it whinnies, haunches rippling and ready.

"When I return, we will meet to decide battle tactics."

With that he's off, the earthy rumble of hooves ruling the night air. I stand still, eyeing the broken underbrush the darker-than-night animal just plowed through.

"So it's done." Richard stares too, eyes wide, at the empty space the woodlord left.

"It's done." I nod, watching as the woods creep back to reclaim the path Herne carved. The gaping darkness soon fills with bark and leaves. "He agreed. How did you know what to say to him?"

"I was improvising." Richard's lips turn sheepish with a grin. "Reading him. You have to do that a lot when you're dealing with politicians. Dad taught me how to do it."

"Well, it worked. And Herne really does seem to admire you."

Wind breaks through the stillness of the trees. Moonlight leaks and swells through cracks in their branches.

"Emrys?"

I look over. His face is so sharp, so beautiful under the moon. It's almost Fae-like.

"Thank you." He wraps his arm around me, drawing me close.

Few words can contain what it feels like, his shoulder curling over mine. Full, complete. No more hole. No more gaping.

And I know, no matter how many days I have left, that my choice was the right one.

Thirty

The mortals are on edge, though none of them know exactly why. Arguments break out, exploding through archaic, tapestry-cloaked rooms like artillery shells. One leaves a duchess's daughter in tears. Of all the inhabitants of Windsor Castle, both visible and unseen, only Richard seems completely unaffected.

"You're not nervous at all?" I whisper to him during a particularly raucous family dinner. It's the first night of the full moon. I feel the battle rolling closer, cracking like thunder on the edges of my mind.

"Why should I be?"

"We should tell Anabelle. Maybe even the others. It would be better that way. Some of them might even be able to help," I mutter.

"Tell me what?" Apparently the princess has the hearing abilities of a wolf. She leans in from Richard's opposite side, eyes fiery with curiosity.

"Nothing we can talk about at the dinner table," Richard shoots back.

A thin, dramatic gasp escapes Anabelle's lips. "She's not pregnant, is she? Ooh, Mum will have a fit when she gets here."

Richard reaches over for his sister's half-filled wine-glass. "No, Emrys isn't pregnant. But I think you've had a bit too much Riesling."

At that moment, the massive set of dining room doors is thrown open. I almost jump out of my skin at the crash. The mortals hear it too. A few glasses are spilled and several utensils clatter rudely back onto china. The long row of heads turns to the end of the table, where the doors stand.

There, on the floor, in a state of filth and rags, is Duchess Titania. Her bun is undone, silver hair spilling across the floor like a river of mercury. Her face is dark, from dirt or deep, sinister bruises. I'm too far away to tell which. I start to run to the weakened Fae's side, but Richard's hand closes firmly around my wrist.

"Don't worry, Emrys. The butler will get the door."

I blink. None of them can see the woman crumpled against the crimson carpet. Nor can they feel the mass exodus of Fae flooding to her side. All they see is me, clutching the thin gold frame of my chair, my face painted with horror.

So many Frithemaeg cluster around Titania's limp form that I can't even see the duchess anymore. I look back down at Richard. The tightness in his lips tells me he senses what's really going on. He's trying his best to maintain the mortals' façade.

"I need to go to the toilet." I pry my arm from his fingers and walk slowly, deliberately, past the frantic Fae. As soon as I round the doors, I make the necessary adjustments to the veiling spell.

Titania is sitting up by the time I return. She's in a bad state, eyes barely open and chest buckled as she slouches against a shell-shocked youngling. When I kneel in front of her, she begins coughing. Flecks of blood fall wet on the carpet, blending perfectly into its red fibers. Everything around us, the metal and machines, is eating her from the inside.

"We need to get her into the woods," I say, and wipe a large speck of her blood off of my arm. "I'm sure some of it's the sickness."

Breena points to two stunned Fae. "You, grab her

arms and legs. Lady Emrys is right. We need to get her closer to the trees."

"No!" Titania jolts to life. Her fingertips sink like claws into the hems of my skirts, dragging me closer. "There's no time!

"She's coming." The duchess gasps and begins coughing again. The rattle in her lungs brings up more awful, clumped blood. Her lips are the worst shade of red. "For the castle. There's no time."

"Who's coming?" I press, but Titania grows limp in the arms of her helpers.

"Get her out of here," Breena barks at the hesitant younglings. "Can't you see this place is killing her? Get her into the trees!"

The Fae jerk to life, hoisting Titania's frail body off the carpet. They vanish quickly through the doors.

"Herne isn't back yet," I whisper at Breena, although every Frithemaeg around knows what I'm saying.

"Then we'll just have to fight without him." My friend's words are grave. "We should get the mortals somewhere easily defensible, like the cellars."

The cellars. A dark place beneath the earth with only one way out.

"We'll be blind there," I argue, "and more cornered than we already are."

"*We* will be on the perimeter," she replies coolly. "If we need to retreat, we'll end up in the cellars with the royals."

Being apart from Richard. The idea makes me sick, cramps up all of my muscles so they feel spiked with steel. I look back to where he's sitting, slicing through the pink middle of his beef Wellington. I see the empty chair next to him, my chair, and wish I could just go sit back down.

"It's the best way," Breena goes on, "and you know it."

She's right. Deep inside I feel the wild thing stir, testing the strength of my willful stitches. If, when, I have to let it out, Richard can't be anywhere close to me. I can't risk it. "I'll tell Richard."

Breena glances over at the princess. "I think it's time we all unveil."

"Yes," another Fae pipes in. "They need to know so they won't wander off and get themselves killed. We could always wipe their memories later."

I shake my head, still staring at the long row of royals, so proper and laughing as they spear pieces of the third course from their plates. "If we survive, the divide won't be necessary anymore. Our worlds are merging."

Helene, Ferrin, and a few of the other younglings nod. Others just stare, blank. Most of them came into existence after the great taboo was set. They've never talked to a human or even thought it a possibility.

I turn back to Breena. "Just let me talk to Richard first so he can warn them. We don't want to set them off into a panic."

Her silence is my confirmation. I shed a layer of invisibility and walk over to Richard.

I keep my whisper soft, not wanting to startle him. "None of the others can see me. Just keep eating."

He obeys, taking a long draw of his lemon-rimmed water.

"A Fae from Mab's court just arrived. She's in bad shape, but she says the Old One is coming. Soon. We need to get all of the royals down into the cellars, now."

One of his eyebrows lifts in an unvoiced question: *How?*

"We've decided to reveal ourselves. But first we need you to prepare them for our appearance. Can you do that?"

The room plunges into darkness. The black only lasts for a second as the electric lights flicker back to life. My skin tingles. Somewhere beyond the gilded castle walls is a storm laced with vengeful, angry magic.

The lights of Windsor won't hold out for long.

"We need to hurry," I urge him.

Richard stands and raises his glass high into the air, where it catches the unsteady, rainbow-tinged light of the chandeliers.

"I have a toast," he begins. "Well, it's more of an announcement really."

The royals' murmurs and exclamations fall silent, their faces turn to him. They're all so different—wrinkled, smooth, scarred, and beautiful—yet so alike in their curious ignorance.

"Our world isn't always as it seems. We sometimes think it's so simple: living, driving our fancy cars, drinking our champagne, and giving to the less fortunate."

He has their attention. Out of the corner of my eye I watch the other Fae flit close to the table, like so many moths drawn to a single light.

"But there's another reality, and it's taking place around us every day. That reality is magic."

"The papers are right! He's finally cracked," one of the older, drunker dukes whispers loudly to his wife, who turns pink and stifles his mouth with a well-manicured hand.

"Magic—the force that shows up in so many of our

legends and folktales—is real. It's all around us. A few months ago I never would have believed it. But then came proof—living, breathing proof that magic exists, and it's in our everyday lives whether we know it or not. That proof is Emrys."

"Oh God, I *am* drunk." Anabelle lays her forehead on the table.

Richard ignores his sister and the rapidly growing glances of skepticism from across the table. "Emrys, the lovely redhead you've acquainted yourselves with over the past few days, is my guardian Faery. We all have one.

"I'm telling you this because our lives are in danger. There are spirits out there who've decided they don't like the way we've run things. They think our deaths will be an answer to their problems. Our Faery guardians want to keep us safe, but they need our help to do so."

The faces are stunned, outraged, uncomprehending, and any number of emotions. But all of them are silent. Now's the time to unveil.

One by one we appear. When my veiling spell drops, Anabelle screams and shrinks back in her seat. Her wineglass tips, shatters against the glossy tabletop. But her reaction is mild compared to the others. Duchesses scream and leap from chairs, then scream more when they see the other Fae ringed around the table. One of the oldest—Richard's great-aunt—slumps over the side of her chair in a sloppy faint. Some of the men clutch at knives and forks, anything they might use as a weapon. One even lunges for the heavy metallic vase at the center of the table, spraying a chaos of food and broken glasses into the laps of his relatives. The older, drunker duke simply curses and throws back the remainder of his wine.

The younglings don't move. They watch the chaos, puzzled and separate, like demigods.

"It's all right! They're not going to hurt you!" Richard is shouting next to me, but his words are lost to the impressive, combined lung power of the royal line.

"*Stillaþ.*" With a single word from Breena the room stops. The mortals are stretched, suspended in motion. Only their eyes can move, spinning crazy with terror.

I frown at my friend's magic, but I don't undo it. This is the only way they will listen. "It's all right. We're here to help you."

All eyes that can, shift to me. Blue, brown, green—most shine bright with manic fears. Only Richard's stay steel-edged and straight.

"There's a Faery, a very old force of magic, who's on

a mission to destroy the crown and spill your blood. We're your Frithemaeg, your guardians, and we've sworn never to let that happen. We want you to see us because we can't protect you without your cooperation. The Old One is coming very soon, and we'll need to place you in the most defensible area. We'd like to ask all of you to move into the cellars now."

The scene stays frozen, like some elaborate tableau. I start to speak again, but my words are sliced short by a second power surge. This time, the earth shakes. Forgotten dust lodged in crevices showers over heads and half-eaten food. The crowd's agonized faces look twice as pale under the failing lights.

"We don't have much time," I say when the lights return to a steady, weakened state. I grab Richard's shoulder. "Help me get them downstairs. Please."

Breena releases her spell, and the scene turns into chaos again.

The king waves his arms, howling alpha shouts into every freed ear. "Didn't you hear what she just said? Everyone needs to get to the cellars. Now!"

The stampede of humanity somehow grows organized, a swell of frizzing hair and pastel skirts rushing toward the doors. Staff and royals alike. Chairs tumble onto the lush carpet. Passersby skip over them with panicked energy. Younglings struggle to keep up with their wards.

"Go straight into the cellars," I roar above the crowd. "Don't try to grab your jewels or valuables. There's no time!"

Richard stays by my side, watching his stunned relatives fight and pour through the dining room doors.

"You have to go with them, Richard." I'm clutching his arm and pushing him away at the same time, wanting two irreconcilable things.

His feet are planted firm in the scarlet carpet. My shove does nothing more than sway him. "I want to stay here with you. I want to fight."

"There's nothing you can do. . . . These spirits that are coming, they're powerful. They'll eat you alive. You have to hide." My voice wilts into a plea. I'm not beyond spelling him into obedience if I have to. His life is worth it.

"I want to help." There it is. That flash of defiance in his eyes. I might have to spell him.

Or not. An idea pops into my head. "Are there weapons here?"

Richard frowns and scans the walls—nothing but mirrors and aged art. "Kitchen knives. I think there are some ornamental swords in the Lower Ward. Oh, and lots of bows and arrows. Dad loved archery."

"Perfect. See if you can gather all of them. I might be able to try and spell them so that you're not completely defenseless."

"I'll help." Anabelle springs out of my peripheral vision. Her face is sharp and serious, showing none of the panic that threw her against the back of her chair. The Faes' appearance seems to have sobered her up.

"No, Belle." Richard looks at the door. The dining room is mostly empty now, a wake of chipped plates and disemboweled flower arrangements. "You go with the others."

"Like hell I am," she huffs. "You don't just get to tell me I have a flipping Faery godmother and that we're being attacked by some old thing and then go traipsing off into God-knows-where. I'm coming with you."

"She can go," I say. "It's easier for us if you stick together."

"Will you go with them? Or should I?" Breena steps around an overturned chair toward us.

"I'm going outside to get a feel for our situation."

I swallow hard, steal a glance at Richard. Though I trust Breena beyond anything, it's hard to leave him, especially now. "It'll only take a few minutes."

"We'll meet you at the cellars then." Breena herds her new protégés together. "Come on, let's go."

"Wait in the cellars," I tell Richard. "I'll come for you."

"I'll see you soon." He pulls me close for a quick tease of a kiss. The mark lingers— soft on my lips— long after he's gone: a reminder that, whether in life or death, we'll soon be together again.

Thirty-One

I've seen many storms in my life, but none quite as menacing as this. The northern sky is black with night, the light of its stars leeched dry by some powerful, unyielding force. A magic different from Herne's squalling tang rises in the air. It's old, and in many ways familiar, like some irritably snatched memory. At some point in my existence, I met this magic, experienced it in the flesh. But the details of this encounter, the Old One's name and face, don't appear to me. I nearly bite my lip through trying to think of it. Was she one of the ancients I tried to hunt and exterminate after London's electric lights first whirred to life? Or was she some force I whisked past when I myself was bodiless, unaware?

Wherever she is, she's close. Accents of lesser magic punctuate my senses as her followers ring in. There are hundreds, maybe even thousands. It's hard to tell in a sky so clouded with danger and dark.

These obsidian heavens stir, break open with the smallest movement. A bird—a magpie—wings its way to the castle walls, its few white feathers spearing through the unseeable. I hold out my arm and wait. The bird circles and finally lands, its claws digging without mercy into my forearm. I ignore the sparks of pain, dislodge the paper from its leg.

The Old One offers terms of surrender. First, all mortals of royal blood must be handed over to her. Second, all those participating in the Guard must go into exile on the Isle of Man. If these terms are met, the Old One promises to let you live.

"And the mortals, what will happen to them?" I grit my teeth, trying to keep a good grip on my bucking anger. I know the answer. It's the same one I gave Richard in his drawing room the night we first officially met. The family would be sacrificed, all of them slaughtered like lambs for the magic in their veins.

The magpie cocks its head against the question. I toss the bird back into the air. It squawks, angry, and wings back over the wall.

I glance down at my arm and wipe away the six pinpricks of blood left by the bird's talons. The piece of paper in my hand crumples under my grip. I look back at the southern sky, where the stars still fight against the inky black, and the moon's fullness conjures shadows from every corner.

"Come on, Herne." I try feeling for the woodlord's magic, but the Old One's aura is too overwhelming, taunting me with its familiarity. "Don't fail us."

"Lady Emrys?"

My gaze falls back down to earth to find Helene, hovering a few paces away. She's a portrait of starkness; her dark hair melts into the air around us, edging sharp against creamy skin. The only grayness is under her eyes. I can tell that, despite the proximity of the woods, she's tired. We all are.

"Yes?"

"We've set up the defenses along the perimeters, and the mortals are all safely in the cellar."

I look skyward again, but this time my eyes don't drift over the horizon. They scan the rooftops instead, picking out the tall black shapes of tense sentinels. They line the untouched battlements like archers, peeking through gaps in the stone. Night air shivers, grows tense as they ready their young, supple magic.

It isn't enough.

"Good. It's good," I say, trying to smooth the

shakiness out of my voice. "Any word on Titania?"

"They're still in the woods. That's all I know."

A terrible sound, like steel screaming apart, murders the sky. My mouth drops open, hands fly to stop up my ears. In the edges of my vision, I see Helene doubling over. It's their war cry.

As soon as the noise dies, I glide up to the battlements. My sisters stand there, faces strangely blank. I feel the fear shredding through each and every one of them.

"Prepare your countermagic," I call down the line, and gaze out into the darkness.

Treetops and shingled houses shudder in the strengthening wind. I feel the Old One, hanging just beyond the fringes of town. She must be fighting the sickness. It won't hold her back for long. If a spirit wants something bad enough, the sickness becomes secondary. Herne's presence in his wood and our long days in London are proof of that.

The second spell—a scathing white light—rushes in, consumes the castle whole. I throw together several defensive spells before it reaches me. Other Fae do the same, but a few aren't quick enough. The rest of us watch, helpless behind our curtains of magic as the unshielded Frithemaeg thrash. Their movements grow sluggish; soon they stop moving altogether. The light vanishes, leaves us blinking wide against the dark. I stare at the nearest fallen youngling. She's sprawled on the battlement stones, eyes open. Nothing enters or leaves their glazed surface.

"They're using dark magic!" Helene hisses beside me. She too is studying the strange, living corpse. "She's gone."

Is she? I fight the temptation to reach out and feel the Fae's aura. It could be a trap. I've never seen this spell before—whatever it is, the Old One means business.

"Set up a shield around the entire castle," I shout to the survivors. "We can't let them keep picking us off like this!"

Threads of defensive magic twist up from every Frithe-maeg. These streams of light meet over our heads, weaving into one giant blanket of a spell. It stretches like liquid, dripping over battlements and coating Windsor's walls of stone. Like the other defenses, this spell is patchy, but it's strong enough to carry us through at least one more major assault.

We wait. First they're like shadows flickering in the corner of my eye: there one moment, gone the next. Then, through the glow of our magic, I see them. Some are flying, leering carrion circling until there are enough bones to pick. Others race across the ground, leaping over houses and trees in their race to the castle.

The Black Dogs are the first to reach our shield. Their leader rushes headfirst into the overwhelming light, giving a terrible howl before it bursts into flame. Its followers slow to a halt, their noses almost touching their defensive spell. Their new leader, a dog much larger than the rest, paces along the light's edge. His nose twitches as he sits on his haunches. The other dogs do the same.

They howl. The leader's notes rise above the rest, his magic like a saw's edge. Alone the dog's rough music wouldn't worry me. But the pack's collective power makes our shield waver. Sweat sprouts on my hairline, pours down my face in beads. The strain of holding our defense shows on the other Fae as well. Faces flush, hands tremble.

Then I see the next wave, racing fast in shades of emerald and night toward our flaming shield. We won't be able to hold back the Banshees and Green Women.

"Drop the shield!" I scream my sudden decision. "Focus on beating them back! Unmake everyone you can! Show no mercy!"

The Frithemaeg pull back their energies and the light above us vanishes, breaks open to hostile skies. I waste no time, showering spells over our attackers. The dogs keep howling and howling; my head throbs with their subtle magic. The beautiful heralds of death draw closer.

Magic hurtles by. The spell brushes so close it singes the ends of my hair. I duck closer to the battlement and peer through the gaps in the stone. The Green Women and Banshees are fast, riding the air like ragged witches. My spells whistle through the sky like tightly strung arrows. One strikes a Green Woman straight in the chest, knocking her to the ground several meters below. Three more soul feeders fill the space she emptied.

I pick them off, one by one, but my spells aren't enough to hold them back. They fall from the sky, a swarm of vengeful locusts. I stop trying to aim my spells. My magic goes left and right, striking any creature unfortunate enough to stray into my path.

I feel the beast inside me tugging, begging for release. The battle's heat and blood excites it, causes it to push harder. I look around at the unfolding destruction—at the awful, leering gray of the Green Women; the icy, still beauty of the Banshees as they pour over the battlements in numbers too overwhelming to count. And the Black Dogs, shadow-licked and howling, eroding us from below. I don't have much of a choice.

If we want to survive, I have to let go.

Letting go is dangerous. It's something we're taught at a very early age not to do. As soon as Mab binds us in these bodies we learn not to go back to the essence. Our undiluted spirit form. Letting go means losing yourself, your memories. It means unleashing a power you can't control, with no guarantee you'll piece back together again. That's why, even in the most desperate circumstances, the Frithemaeg hesitate to tap into the full extent of their power. You might not be able to return from it.

But I have everything to lose if this battle doesn't turn.

Threads snap. I feel my body dissolving, blowing away piece by piece like a windswept dune. I become pure spirit, leaking into the air around me, feeling every spell cast in the breezy night. Freed from that frail, bipedal body, I could float into the stars or dig down into the deepest parts of the earth. I'm free.

I'm still wandering, slightly bewildered with this aged, yet new way of existence, when a Green Woman's curse breaks into my territory. I start as the magic reacts with mine. The counterspell flows out of me: reflexive, natural. I look around. I see a battle, but my thoughts struggle to wrap around it. Was there a reason for the fight? I can't even remember coming up to this tower. Strange, blurred fragments of memories bounce around in my head. None of it makes sense.

Another curse rushes past me, dragging my consciousness back into the present. While the first spell might have been a mistake, the second definitely wasn't. The Green Women and the Banshees are trying to extinguish the others. Me.

I rush for the nearest Green Woman, the one who cursed me. Sick, jaundiced eyes grow wide when I coil around her and squeeze. Her spirit slides out like seeds from a squished grape. I watch it flicker, fluttering like a fledgling before it goes out altogether.

But this single, silent death does nothing to calm my rage. My next victim is a spindly, screaming Banshee. She puts up more of a fight; her high, piercing yell is hot needles against my nonexistent skin. I absorb her, engulf her entire body. I feel the fragile length of her bones, so easy to snap.

The trail of bodies grows as I go down the wall. It takes twenty deaths before the other soul feeders focus their efforts on me. The Frithemaeg stand back, fear tainting their auras, their eyes. They see me for what I am, impartial and unstable, ready to destroy anything.

Spells surround me, many and ruthless. I'm a cornered tiger, thrashing, letting fury feed my strength. But it isn't enough. Their magic is too overwhelming. I fall under the weight of it onto cold, hard stones. Curses cram me back into my human skin. Fine grains of sand—lodged in the battlement's cracks and grooves— press into my palms. My attackers circle in, hovering like gargoyles in my dark, smudged vision. Ready to devour me to the bone.

I curl into myself, bracing for the deathblow. I think of Richard. I think of the Greater Spirit. I shut my eyes.

But it doesn't come. A single, commanding sound fills the air. It's a note: low but high at the same time, rising from the south. Every spirit, including my attackers, falls still. I push myself up from the stones, heart racing. I know the call of that ram's horn. It's the arrival of Herne the Hunter, the beginning of the Wild Hunt.

The southern stars have disappeared, blotted out by Herne and his fellow riders. They gallop at the head of heavy thunderclouds, their horses' hooves wreathed in lightning and rain. Herne has gathered spirits from all across Britain—guardians of forests and woods long forgotten. Behind them, in full force, are the Dryads—thin, waiflike women, without clothes or color. They look strange outside their trees, as if they're walking around without some essential limb. The sight stirs a sick kind of fear in me.

Herne's horn sounds again, and the Hunt surges forward with the storm. The air quakes. My lungs rattle, my bones hum. The maelstrom swallows the castle whole, shaking its stones to their very foundations.

Herne rides in the front, eyes burning with a red ferocity that would haunt any mortal's dreams. He's a storm unto himself, his horse treading the damp air with fixed determination. Every spirit beneath their shadow cringes, but the Lord of the Wood passes over Windsor without touching down. He rides into the other horizon, to the heart of the attack.

The rest of the Hunt hurtles to earth. Herne's hounds leap for Black Dogs' throats. Yelps and barks of pain puncture the air as the animals tangle together. The wind burns like sulfur from the clash of their magic.

The Dryads sweep down, vengeful phantoms. Their eyes burn almost as violently as Herne's. The strength of the trees is surprising. Many of us forget, because they stay so silent and still. But their roots go deep in the earth, giving them secrets and spells the rest of us don't remember.

At first the Banshees and Green Women fight, but the Dryads rain down like propeller seeds, whirling and endless. The battle thickens and turns with the Hunt's arrival. The Old One's followers begin a slow, steady retreat.

My mind, still fuzzy from transformation, soon finds its way back to the most important thing. Richard. I have to see if he's all right. I have to protect him.

I claw my way through the string of vicious duels. Spells color the sky like fireworks, shedding just enough light for me to see by. The moon has long since disappeared behind storm clouds, and with the electricity gone, the world is completely black.

I slip off the battlements to find a way into the castle. I nearly run into a door before I slow down enough to cast a Faery light. It drifts just over my head, illuminating the castle's eerie, empty halls. Screams from the battle outside echo through the cavernous rooms, a reminder that things aren't as deserted as they seem.

I make it safely to the cellar door, approaching it like a stalking cat, unsure of what waits beyond. There's nothing, no one behind it. I let my light dim to the strength of a firefly, just enough to see the steps in front of me.

When I reach the bottom, all I see are rows and rows of wine bottles. Their green glass catches the Faery light, giving the room a peculiar, undersea feel. I pause at the final step.

There's a ragged yell. One of the room's inhabitants jumps out from a stack of wine. It's the old, drunk duke. His collar is flipped and his vein-lined hands clutch the jagged remains of a bottle.

I hold up my palms in a symbol of friendship, hoping he's sober enough to register it. He takes a few wavering steps forward before he lowers the shattered bottle, hands shaking.

"You're Richard's girl," he says rather loudly.

I nod, peering into the room's long, endless dark. Richard's aura is undeniably absent. "Where is he? Have you seen him?"

The duke shakes his head. "I haven't seen him. We haven't seen anyone new since we got down here. What's going on?"

Richard isn't here. Fear bubbles up, like explosive lava. "Are any Fae down here?"

He shrugs. "How'd I know? You all look like us."

Two younglings peek out from rows of wine bottles. My panic leaves them no time to speak. "Why aren't you at the door? Where's Breena?"

"Lady Breena hasn't been here. It's just us," the Fae to my right offers, timid. "We didn't want to get too close to the door in case one of the soul feeders sensed us."

Numbness falls over me, killing every limb and layer as I center in on the terrible truth. It was Breena. It was Breena all along. Mab tried to warn me out of my centuries of trust, but I ignored her. The temptation to let go returns, riling the magic in my veins. The younglings sense it too; both take a step back.

I turn and lunge back up the stairs. I can't be too late. I just can't.

Please let him be alive, I beg the hidden stars as I blast out of Windsor's hollow halls into the night. *I'll do anything.*

I pause on the veranda that looks out on to the Long Walk. Rain pounds everywhere, soaking my hair, my face, blurring everything. My breaths are short and spasmodic as I reach out for Breena's aura. As always, it's familiar, easy to find. She must've forgotten how effortlessly I could track her. I pray that's not the only mistake she's made.

Thirty-Two

The forest. She took them to the forest.

My magic is a wolf on a leash. I try my best to rein it in. I can't lose control if Richard and Anabelle are still alive. But if they aren't . . . I pause by a tree, try to regain my grip. Just thinking about Richard's death is enough to push me into madness.

The forest is empty. Its trees are somber, dead without their spirits, just sticks wedged into the ground. I weave past their roots and trunks, hardly paying attention to where I'm going. Breena's aura calls me, tugs me forward with invisible string.

They're nearly a kilometer deep from the tree line, huddled in a small glade. The sight of Richard and Anabelle squatting beneath branches to get shelter from the rainfall, alive and well, saps the anger out of me. Breena stands at the clearing's edge, rigid and alert.

I let my magic settle back. It's clear I was wrong. Breena hasn't betrayed us.

"Emrys?" Her call is soft, owl-like. "I know you're here."

I break through the snarled hedges, into the open. "What are you doing out here? Why aren't you in the cellar?" A glance at Richard and his sister tells me they made it to the archery equipment.

"The way back was cut off, so I brought them here. I tried to find Titania and the other two, but they've just vanished."

"It's a big forest," I say.

Richard stands, trots across the mulchy earth. His shirt, a white button-up, clings like paint to his sodden chest. Water drips down his hair, sheeting his cheeks and falling down to me as he pulls me close.

"You're alive," he breathes into my ear.

"You sound surprised." I wrap my arms around him, cling to his shaking self as hard as I can. It seems I can't keep him close enough, even with our bodies pressed so fully together. I want to melt into him, to make sure I'll never lose him again.

"It just looks so crazy over there, I wasn't sure. . . ."

Something inside me seizes up, like a turtle scared into its shell. I pull Richard behind me. Something else is in these woods. Something close and powerful.

Breena feels it too. She curses and jumps in front of the princess, movements made of rainfall and gold.

We stand, silent and still, staring steady at the trees. I begin to feel like a deer under a hunter's crosshairs, waiting for the trigger to hammer down.

Richard's fingers rest on the small of my back, shooting me full of shivers. I want to turn around, kiss him. But the danger of the woods looms, clawing through crystal walls of rain. Instead I relish this connection between us, trying not to think of how it's probably our last.

The bushes shudder, violent and hushed. My magic coils back, ready to strike at any moment. There's no point in hiding anymore.

A lone figure pushes out of the underbrush and pauses. I squint through the downpour. Something about the creature's aura is familiar but untraceable.

"Mab," Breena whispers.

And then I realize my friend is right. It's our queen standing at the edge of the glade, an albino vision through blurring rain. Magic hums, shimmers around her like a quaking star. Something's wrong. I should be breathing a sigh of relief, but instead my insides collapse.

"It's you." Breena's voice trembles. "It's been you all along."

Mab's spell leaps without warning. Sick white light slices through the storm, bursts apart the rain. Its lightning claws into Breena's chest, ripping through her like wind tunneling through broken glass. Her spirit leaks out. It clings desperately to the edges of her body, but Mab's spell is too strong. Breena's essence spirals high, snags crooked branches, slips through them, leaving me.

There's her body, bent, empty, and pelted by rain. She's gone. Dead. I know this, but I can't make myself believe it.

I can't move. I can't think of any spells to protect us. I only look at Mab and notice that, for once, her eyes have snagged a single color: cutting red, deep as murder. Her pale lips open to speak another spell of destruction.

It's Anabelle who saves us. Her arrow flies, plowing into our huntress's bony shoulder. The Faery queen shrieks, a sound so unearthly and deep it wakes me from my trance.

"*Blodes geweald!*" I spread my arms, forming a circle of protection around the royals and myself. The shield is hasty, but steady.

The queen is bleeding. Maroon stains her silver bodice, looking almost black in the lack of light. Her howling dies and she reaches down, plucks the arrow out of her muscles. Breena's spell swims faint over the bloody arrowhead. Mab's wound will fester with it, unable to heal for a time.

She throws the arrow onto the ground, grinds it beneath her bare heel.

"What are you doing, Mab?" I find my voice again. "What have you done?"

My queen's face looks as it always has, a profile etched in marble. Only her eyes sputter, wavering between the humans and me. "It's over, Emrys. For centuries we've been bound to them, protecting them. And what have they done to thank us for it? They've forgotten the old ways and created this poison."

I see it, just behind those crimson eyes. That unsteady flicker that rose in the faces of every Old One we had to put down—the sickness. Somehow, despite all the Fae in her court, the sickness took Mab without anyone seeing. It crept through her veins, slipped through the cracks of her mind. . . . She's lost to it now. Her magic is warped, tainted by insanity. No wonder I didn't recognize it.

"But you swore an oath to Arthur," I remind her. "All of us did. We can't break it. You know that."

She spits at the ground. Blood. I pretend not to notice the bright red spattered on long-dead leaves. Despite her immense age and power, Mab is weakening, unraveling so close to the city. If I can keep her talking long enough . . .

"My oath to Arthur was in a different age. . . . We were vanguards once. Now we're only slaves. I knew I couldn't break the oath without consequences. But there are loopholes. Oh yes, there are always loopholes." The vicious, lusty glint steals through her eyes again. "If the crown were destroyed—if Arthur's line and lineage was completely decimated—then we would be free of our bonds. But it wasn't just about freedom. The problem still remained. How could we survive without the blood magic? There were ways that power could be harnessed, ways we didn't dare try to take back in the golden age, when mortals held magic of their own. Still, they existed. Merlin never told us much about Arthur's magic, yet I knew that death transferred power, just as birth did. It was only when I remembered this that I decided to kill Edward."

Keep her talking. Let time do its work. I take a deep breath. "But how? How did you get to Edward without anyone seeing? I was with you the day he died. . . ."

A smile, crazed and satisfied, slips across the queen's face. "It was no easy task, trying to assassinate a monarch without the court catching wind of it. I knew they would try to stop me. They're still too blind, too loyal to the promise we so carelessly gave those centuries ago. But the soul feeders were more than willing. They even decided to play nice with one another once I offered them a place in the new kingdom, the Albion without mortals. So I stayed in the Highlands, keeping court while the Banshees and Green Women did their work. It wasn't until the Banshee killed Muriel and King Edward that I realized that only the monarch's killer can partake in the blood magic—another thing Merlin refused to tell us. The Banshee took it all for herself, but I was still more powerful. I killed her and started again, from scratch. It was Richard's blood I needed— and I knew this time I had to slay him by my own hand.

"But how to get to Richard? I sent a Green Woman, protected by layers of my own magic, to fetch him— but you proved too strong. I realized that if I wanted to get to Richard, I would have to distract you. So I tried turning your suspicions toward others of the Guard. I knew that if you were looking for a traitor, you wouldn't see what was happening right under your nose."

I watch, hard-eyed as her blood blooms, staining the beaded lengths of her sleeves and bodice. Mab played me. She played me well.

"Yet you seemed to be so determined on keeping Richard in the city, where I couldn't reach him. I had to set the stage: create the illusion of a safe haven. Windsor was the perfect place. All I had to do was procure Herne's permission to use the land . . . to let as many immortals in as I pleased, be they Frithemaeg or soul feeders. I knew too that if I demanded Herne help you, he would rebel. I counted too much on his pride perhaps . . . for I see you've found a way around that. No matter.

"Once Jaida and Cari found you spying, I knew I had to move. The soul feeders did their best to crowd you out. It worked."

"So you're going to kill them? All of them?" My voice shakes, a horrible mix of anger and fear. How could Mab, the queen I gave myself to, served so loyally for years, be capable of this? The madness must reach even deeper than I imagined.

It's in this moment that an irredeemable knowledge settles on me, crushes with its weight. We're dead. Any hope, any thought I had of reasoning with Mab, wilts under the insanity in her eyes. And the queen, with centuries upon centuries of power, could destroy me in a heartbeat. My magic won't be enough to save us.

But I must be strong, for Richard. For Anabelle. I cannot let them die afraid.

"The mortals will keep taking until nothing is left, Emrys. Their short existence is tainted with misery and mire. What could you ever want to do with one?"

Her words are bitter wormwood, impossibly harsh to bear.

"There's beauty in them too," I say, though I know none of my words will change her mind. Time is the only thing we have left now—I'm stretching, grasping for every granule I can get.

"So it's love, is it?" Mab sneers. All at once I see her ugliness, lurking in the wrinkle of her nose, the leer of perfect, white teeth. "And you, of all Fae. I had the most faith in you. You had a gift—a talent for magic! Everything would have been much easier if you'd listened to me."

"There are other ways to do this. We can come out of hiding. Richard wants our worlds to merge. We can be together again." I raise my hands, a small, hopeless offering.

"They'll drive us out. Their technology will spread. It won't stop until it covers everything. Our strength is a thing of the old days. But the blood magic will bring it back." The red of her irises comes alight, flaming with twisted desires. Behind them, I see visions of death. "Oh yes. Their blood will make us powerful again, Emrys. We can wipe out the plague that's infested our lands. Albion will be whole again."

I edge closer to the border of my shield. Always I'm aware of Richard and Anabelle behind me, breathing hot on my ears.

No matter what happens, stay behind me. I'll hold off her spells. For as long as I can.

Richard jerks. He's received my warning.

"I won't let you kill them. I can't."

Her laugh slides like a serpent through the raindrops, cruel and cold. "And what, little youngling, do you think you can do to me? Your magic is paltry. Nothing." Mab spits the words.

I try not to think of how right she is as I brace myself.

"If only you'd had a chance to grow. Such a pity. You had real promise."

Mab's first whispered curse lashes out like a bullwhip. The light of my shield shatters, pours down to the ground in a thousand useless pieces. I feel Anabelle cringe behind me, trying to grow smaller. I steal a glance at Richard. His hazel eyes are set, his jaw locked, determined. He clutches something at his side. I can't get a clear look at it.

As soon as the shield fails, I cast a counterspell. Mab swats it aside with ease, growling at the pain of her still-bleeding shoulder. Another curse hisses out of her, poisons the air of the glade. I face the spell full on. It stops, just barely, under my resistance.

"Lie down and I promise I'll give you an easy death," she mocks.

I'd counted on the sickness to gut her away from the inside, but it's not working fast enough. Mab is still stronger and she knows it. Until now she's been playing, a cat batting about a scrabbling, defiant mouse. As soon as she wants to get serious, we're all dead.

I know what I have to do: go for the cat's throat.

As soon as I jump forward, you and Anabelle have to run. Understand? I tense, fill myself with everlasting breath. *I love you, Richard. Never forget that.*

Mab is preparing another spell when I lunge, throwing myself at the side opposite her wounded shoulder. She has no time to raise her gimpy arm. We fall into the withered leaves, her spell unfinished. Somewhere through the drumming rain and sizzling of magic,

I hear the royals' footsteps, slogging and frantic. I have to hold Mab off long enough—give them time to escape.

Although Mab's stunned, she's quick to react. Magic lights her skin, making it acidic to touch. I push through the blinding pain, dig my blazing fingers into her wounded shoulder. Even with Breena's spell, the arrow's hole has almost closed. I shove through the clotting blood.

Her shriek is worse than a Banshee's. Something bursts inside my left ear, but I keep ripping, digging, tearing. Desecrating the human body Mab loves too much to leave. The beauty she clings to, the physicality she forced on us, is my last weapon. My only, final hope is to damage this vessel so severely that the royals will be far off when she kills me.

"We've had our turn, Mab." My scream rises above hers, climbs endlessly through this cathedral of trees and rain. "We've drunk so deeply of life that we've forgotten what it means. Death is inevitable."

Mab's good arm swings up. Flaring, chalky skin torches my face, making my world white with anguish. For a moment, I wonder if death has finally struck, but then I feel the blood and tendons beneath my fingers.

My work isn't done.

She screams, strikes me again. This blow is harder,

filled with sinister magic. I land face-first in the moldy foliage. My vision is still blurry—a hazy, unfinished puzzle. I scramble through mud and leaves, sliding toward the closest tree.

Somewhere behind me, Mab growls against the pain. The earth wrinkles with sounds as she picks herself up and crawls toward me.

I wrap my arms around the tree, skin digging hard into its scaly bark. There's no Dryad here to comfort me, only rough wood and emptiness. I try to think of Richard instead of the terror rising up, pure and paralyzing.

"How could you love him?" Mab rasps. She knows she's winning or she wouldn't have wasted her words.

I let go of the tree and turn. The queen stands, a mess of silver, white, and blood against my poor sight. She's a fallen star in the wood's womb-like dark. Alien bright.

"You wouldn't understand."

"Don't patronize me." Mab shuffles closer, her features sharpening beneath my gaze. Years of suppressed emotions mottle her face, rot her like the Green Women. "I've seen it all before. The loss of reason, the stupid sacrifice of magic, the heartache. Just like Guinevere and the others . . . Loving a mortal only brings suffering. Even if you did end up with His Highness and get everything you wanted, what did you think would happen? What's your ending?"

My throat catches. Something about the forest behind Mab isn't right. We aren't alone.

"I can't live without him," I say, pushing through the thickness in my throat. Breena's broken body lies in the edges of my clearing vision. The sight of it brings pain, searing and deep. Mab killed one of the only things that might have made me stay.

"Then you won't live." Mab's high, hysterical voice plummets into icebound malice.

Something flashes in the darkness—not a spell, but Mab's own pallid light reflected back on her. The long, narrow mirror of a blade comes down, bursts through the Faery queen's stomach. Blood, bright and fresh, cracks like a spiderweb across her bodice. The queen gasps when it pulls out of her. Her spell, half spun, runs back through the sword.

Richard falls with a silence far more horrible than any scream. His hair blends into the ground's mush of mud and decay, his mouth gaping wide from Mab's caustic magic.

"No!" *No! Not him. Not him.*

I dive into the leaves next to Richard, press against his

warmth. The blue of cold and shock creeps over his face; his lips lined with red that should be on the inside. But the spell didn't tear all life away. There's a flutter deep within him, fainter than the beat of a butterfly's wing.

"Live!" I wrap an arm around his chest, trying to feel the extent of the damage.

He gasps at my word—a wretched sound, filled with pain. I can tell, just by this one noise, that I'm losing him.

"Just hold on, Richard. I'll fix you!" I sit up and look around, frantic, for anything that might help. All I see is Mab, shuddering a few meters away. The sword has only damaged her, its wound already healing. It will take a strong spell to break a spirit as old as her, magic that's beyond my strength.

"Embers." Richard's rasp brings me back. His eyelids flicker. He's struggling to stay with me.

I push the hair out of his face. Raindrops mixed with his sweat slick down my palm. "You have to stay with me. I can't lose you now."

"I'm not going anywhere." He tries to smile, but it's too much. The curl of his lips withers, like it was never even there.

I lean even closer to him. Our lips touch. His are

motionless. I press gently into them, grabbing desperately for any signs of life. His pulse quivers beneath paper-thin skin. Beat by beat, it's slowing.

Then I taste the blood, sanguine and hot, reaching into me with a slow, salty burn. My lips, my mouth, everything is on fire. Magic. Magic that isn't mine or Mab's. An old force, rusty but powerful, now inside me.

I pull away from him, wiping my wrist against my lips. It comes away, smeared with a thin film of Richard's blood. Mab got what she wanted. I tremble, let my hands fall. With all the crown's magic before me, I can do nothing but cry.

Something moves. My heart jerks, certain that it's one of Richard's limbs calling me back to him. Instead my eyes lock onto Mab. Her stomach wound has healed enough for her to crawl across the forest floor. Inch by inch, she's heading toward Richard. I arch over his body like a rabid animal. The queen sees the wildness in my stare and blinks.

"Give it up, Emrys. He's gone. At least make his death worth something. Let me take his blood. . . ." She reaches out, her hand gnarled and wanting.

Anger and something much more profound surges

through me. Power that isn't mine—Richard's blood right—mixes with my magic. It shoots through my veins like a special fire, waiting to be lit for centuries.

"I won't let you kill the others too." I seize control of my shaky limbs and start composing the spell.

Mab sees the curse weaving together, piece by piece. She sees her own doom rising before her.

"Think of all the years I loved and protected you," she grovels, eyes desperate with horror. They're clear now, blue as Breena's were. "I was the one who taught you, who made you what you are."

I say nothing, all of my attention trapped inside this spell. It's unlike anything I've ever created before, with a hundred more intricacies than the one that destroyed the Banshee. I knit it together, looping all of the stitches into place.

"Those days are clearly over," I say, all emotion drained out of my voice. Finally the spell is ready. I hold it between two palms—a horrible, beautiful thing, flames glinting with the transience of opals.

"Mercy . . ." The word comes out in a pitiful whimper.

"Sometimes justice *is* mercy."

I look straight into her stare and let the spell fall. It peels at the Faery queen, like a knife paring an apple down to its core. I refuse to look away, even when the strips of flesh fall from her bones. Her eyes stay on me, phasing through every color, constant in their hatred and pain. I stare back until they're gone, swept away with everything else. Nothing is left. Not even dust.

The curse's light dies, plunging the clearing into darkness. I bend close to the ground feeling for Richard's arm. My fingers find his. They're strangely cool, unwelcoming. He's beyond my magic now.

I find his side and fit myself against it. There's no light heaving of his chest, no warmth or softness to press against. I lay there, staring past shadows and raindrops into the space beyond. Death is overwhelming in this clearing. It pins me down against the leaves, holds me hostage. With all my heart I want to join it, but I can't even find the strength to move.

Thirty-Three

I've never woken up before. It's one of the simple facts of a spirit's existence. We don't sleep. We don't need to: magic gives us all the energy we need.

But when I stared so blankly into the darkness, I left myself. I can't say how. Maybe it was the grief or the shock of the blood magic. Whatever it was, I was gone, lost for hours.

Something, someone, is shaking me. Light forces through the cracks in my eyes. My body feels stiff, old, as if all of the years I've lived have finally passed through it. I sit up from the damp leaves and look around, my neck robotic and slow.

Morning—the clearing is bright and blue with it. The ground oozes wet with last night's storm. Gashes of movement scar the drying mud, leaves splay everywhere.

"Emrys!" The princess is next to me, her hair mussed

and golden like a lion's mane. Bright, angry pink lines her eyes, framed by the old smear of coal-black makeup. "Emrys, wake up!"

Breena's body is haunting in its closeness. I can't not look at it, angled and sprawled like a broken marionette. The sight makes my insides hollow, drained like a cracked egg.

"What happened? Where's Richard? Is he hurt?" Anabelle looks as unstrung and desperate as I feel. "I lost him when I was running through the woods and I thought he might come back here. . . ."

Something explodes, sharp and hot, inside my chest as memories of the night before rush back. Heartbreak all over again. I look away from Breena's broken corpse and steel myself for what's beside me. My hand goes out to touch him, but it falls into slimy ground.

Richard is gone. Stolen. There's a slight imprint in the earth where he lay next to me, so rigid, so cold. Mab's cronies must have arrived during my trance and taken it.

"No. No, no, no," I sob, bringing my fist down into the rotting leaves. After all this, they still got Richard. They wrenched away our last moment together.

Anabelle stares into the mess of mud and mulch beside me. Her face is crypt white—tattooed with fear. "What happened?"

I look around the clearing, scanning for anything that can get me back to him. Last night's footprints are everywhere, littered and preserved in claylike ground.

Anabelle's hands snag my shoulders, firm and determined. I find myself looking into her eyes. They're the color of earth. "Emrys, where's my brother?"

My head buzzes with truth I can't make myself speak. *Dead. Richard is dead. I failed. I lost him.*

"So, you're both alive." The sudden, gruff voice makes my body jerk.

Herne slips out of the trees, composed of shade and gloom even under glaring daylight. He looks smaller after the battle, all of his terrible energy released on some poor souls.

"It was her all along then?" His citrine eyes pick out the spot where Mab fell. He's reading the spells, piecing together everything that happened. "Wouldn't have guessed it. That's why I tend to stay out of these affairs. Never know who to trust."

"Have—have you seen the king's body?" I manage.

"It's gone. I'm afraid it's been stolen."

Anabelle's cry is desolate, filled with terrible knowledge and loss. It shatters what's left of my heart.

"Body?" Herne steps closer and studies Richard's shallow casting in the leaves. "The king is dead?"

I nod, fighting hard against the sobs that try to claw their way out of me. I can't even bear to look over at Anabelle. "Mab's magic tore him inside out. No mortal could survive that."

Herne kneels down to touch the earth. One by one, leaves fall back, tattered and brown, through his gloved fingers. "Tell me. How did you manage to kill the Old One? You're far too young to manage such a thing on your own."

"Richard stabbed her and I finished her off." I don't want to think back on those last moments. Not now. Spare the princess those last, terrible details. Her crying is mewling and awful. It scratches at my back like a pitifully angered kitten.

"There was something else. Something old," Herne says, and brushes the last of the vegetation off his hands.

"Something happened—" My throat collapses. I can't find the will to get past the choking.

Herne walks over to Mab's other victim. The body they left.

From here I can see Breena's fragile sketch of a face. Even in death she clings to her beauty. Her hair springs around porcelain skin like a crown; eyes glazed in a mysterious, knowing way. There's no fear in them, no terror at the emptiness. Only peace.

Peace that's beyond me now.

"Let's take her back to the castle. It will do us no good to linger here," Herne growls; his ember eyes flicker meaningfully toward the princess.

With her shoulders slumped and her hair inextricably knotted, Anabelle reminds me of a lost young girl. But when her eyes meet mine, they harden and all thoughts of weepy children are lost to me.

"You promised you would protect him! He's dead because of you!" she yells, her stare pinning me like gravity. Her accusations are only lighter echoes of the condemnations ringing through my mind.

I don't speak. I don't move. I just stare back into the devastation.

Anabelle keeps screaming words she doesn't mean. Words she has to say.

It's Herne who finally intervenes. He approaches the princess and touches her on the shoulder with surprising gentleness. There's magic in his fingers—a soothing, merciful spell that causes Anabelle to crumple into his arms, fast asleep. Golden hair spills over the woodlord's leather gloves as he gathers her to his chest.

"Come, Lady Emrys." He steps toward the edge of the clearing. "I'll see to it that the Dryads bring Lady Breena after us."

There's no will in me. No reason to fight. I follow the wild spirit through his woods, my thoughts buzzing with Anabelle's words of blame. Not once do I look back.

There are many dead. More than I thought possible. Corpses drape Windsor's turrets and walls—macabre garlands. Limp bodies of Black Dogs and Green Women lie tangled with the hollow forms of Fae. I recognize some of them as we separate the bodies, burning the soul feeders and setting the Frithemaeg aside for a final good-bye. Others, like Titania and her attendants, have vanished altogether, unmade by more brutal spells.

I feel useless without Richard, floundering in the middle of this desolate sea. His body isn't among the others. Not that I expected it to be. It's far from us now, in the clutches of some Banshee or Green Woman scavenging it for blood magic. They'll find nothing. It isn't Richard anymore. Just a carved-out shell.

It's evening when we begin the funeral rites. It isn't often that Fae must say good-bye to their own. Some of the younglings have never even been to such a ceremony. I stand by Breena's body.

Tears blot my eyes as I arrange the leafy tiara perfectly against her head. Breena had been there even in my earliest days. Her words were the ones I followed. Her counsel and confidence had been as vital as water.

And now, like Richard, she's gone.

I stroke her hair. Each brush of my finger brings back a separate memory. Of how, in the early days, we flew along coasts without tiring, grazing cliffs and skimming the iron-gray waves of the North Sea. Of the battles we fought with magic and steel, of the ballads that sprang from them. Of the gowns and gavottes, the cellos and long, candlelit dances drenched with wine. Of her pouch of birdseed and those dirty, adoring pigeons.

There are well over a hundred bodies laid out on Windsor's emerald lawns. Like Breena, the dead are dressed in white, crowned with garlands the Dryads fashioned for us. Every surviving spirit and even some of the mortals are here, gathered around the fallen with closed, solemn faces. My breath grows weak at the sight of so much death and, for a moment, I'm not sure I can stand.

"Lady Emrys?"

It's Helene, now next to me. Several younglings fan out behind her, their mouths drawn tight. I stare at them, keeping my precious words to myself for a moment longer. My throat hasn't released me since that hour in the clearing.

The Fae is undeterred by my silence. "We were wondering if you might conduct the ceremony."

A quick scan at the ranks of the living confirms what I suspected. In light of Breena's death and Titania's disappearance, I'm the oldest here. It's my duty to perform the funeral rites, to cast the farewell spell.

"Will you do it?" Helene nudges after another silent moment.

"Yes," I say because I must.

Satisfied with my answer, the younglings return to the group of observers. I feel eyes on me. The gazes of both the dead and the living, waiting for me to speak.

"Friends and Fae," I begin. My voice wavers as it breaks its dormancy. "It's easy for us to forget that this life comes at a price. In the end we all must pay it, whether it be a score of years or millennia from now. These noble sisters of ours have willingly accepted that debt so that others might live.

"We do not know what lies beyond this plane. We can't imagine where our sisters might be now—yet we know they aren't gone. Not really. We must not let their sacrifices be in vain. We must continue to defend what they died for and live in the acceptance that sooner or later there's an end. One day, when the dark glass between lives is lifted, we'll all be together again." The choke returns, trapping what other words I might speak in the lump of my throat.

I wrap my hand around Breena's rigid grasp. Her fingers are like stone, pale and unyielding.

"Thank you, friend, for standing by me all these years," I whisper into her wintry ear. "I'll see you again, soon enough. *Hæl abide.*"

At my farewell spell, the dead Frithemaegs' bodies begin disintegrating. A light, great and gold, wells up from inside each departed Fae. Every secret of Breena's alabaster skin is illuminated with the brightness. Pieces of her begin to dissolve, fly apart like dandelion seeds blown straight into the sun. I hold on as tightly as I can, until it's only my own palm my nails dig into and Breena is gone.

I stand here as the others disperse, disappearing back into the castle. The sun is just slipping out of sight.

Its rays wash over everything: my bare arms, my blood-stained skirts, the empty grass. Every detail is redeemed in this dying light.

But not everyone is gone. I see his shadow first, long and terrifying. The sharp edges of his boots creep into my sight.

"We had an agreement, Lady Emrys. Lest you forget." The evening trembles against Herne's cold words. With them comes the night.

"I know."

The spirit holds out his hand, ready and waiting. I stare at the smooth, eternal leather of his glove. Even with Richard gone, I have no desire to cling to my immortality. Death is something I've already embraced, a much-needed end.

"There's something I must do first. I need one more night," I tell him.

The woodlord grunts. His coal-glow eyes pierce through the gathering darkness. "I'll give you until dawn, woodling. Then I'll take what's rightfully mine."

He turns and flows back to his woods, where his trees and hounds are waiting. And I stand alone, aching for everything that will not return.

* * *

I spend the night on the battlements, gazing into the black space that holds the stars. Constellations are strung tight and unwavering, telling the same stories they always have for those who take the time to listen. Everything is so quiet, so bright after the battle. I stare on and on, trying to keep the pain from eating me alive.

And I know now that the emptiness will always be there, yawning wide until the end. Because some cruel twist of fate decided that Richard's sacrifice was better. Because I lived and he did not.

It's still dark when I enter Anabelle's bedroom. The princess is curled on top of the comforter, in the exact same spot Herne placed her almost an entire day before. His spell was a powerful one—staving off her grief and hysterics with heavy, dreamless sleep.

Her eyelids flutter as I draw close, but she doesn't open her eyes. I'd never noticed before how much she looks like Richard. The same high cheekbones, the light splash of freckles coaxed out by the sun. Their resemblance is so strong that I can't bear to look at her long. Instead I stare out the window, where the moonlight tangles with the tops of Herne's trees.

The memory spell builds; I weave it slowly, deliberately. It has to be just the right strength—potent enough to make her forget everything that happened in the woods that night. Strong enough to stanch some of the princess's agony. If I could I would erase everything, give Anabelle a fresh start, a childhood without Richard. But the world, and the order of things, won't allow that.

Once the magic is finally ready I look back down. Anabelle's face is serene, despite her mass of tangled hair and the smudges of dirt. I can't make myself speak the word that will release her from her past. She needs the pain and memories as much as I do. She needs to know that her brother died well. Who am I to take that from her?

My hands drop to my side, and the magic slips away, unused.

It's almost, but not quite, dawn. Herne will be waiting for me. I've already stalled as much as I dare.

"I'm sorry, Anabelle. I'm sorry I failed." There are so many other things I could tell her, but none of them seem fitting. In the depths of her slumber she won't hear them anyway. "Good-bye."

I turn and go.

Mist gathers at the edge of the woods, wreathing in and out of ghoulish trees. I expect Herne to rise out of its embrace at any moment, but everything remains still. I draw closer to his woods with hesitant steps, feeling for his magic.

"Herne?" My call is little more than a whisper. The stillness of this night's end seems holy, something I shouldn't break.

The answer I receive is not from the woodlord, but his trees. The Dryads have returned to their leafy abodes. They stir the branches without any wind to guide them, their leaves brushing together hushed words.

Farther in. He's waiting.

I follow their subtle movements, leaving a trail of scattered dewdrops in the mossy, morning earth. Here, in the dark woods, it's impossible not to think about Richard. Just a few nights ago we were walking this very path together to see Herne, to bargain for our lives.

I don't realize where I am until it's too late. The clearing seems larger than normal. The impression of the king's body still scars its center. The trees have retreated from it.

I collapse to my knees, press my fingers into the chewed, rotting leaves. Birdsong, the hymn of nightingales, bursts into the glade. Their notes punch into the silence like a drum, trilling and hopeful. What was once—what is—beautiful, only causes my fists and teeth to clench.

"Shut up!" I scream into the branches. All I want is silence. I want to drown in it.

"Yelling at birds, are we?"

I shudder at the voice behind me, but I don't turn. The gloom of Herne's presence is obvious enough.

"Why did you bring me here?"

The woodlord steps around into my sight, eyes burning fast into mine. "Bring you here? What are you talking about?"

"Your trees, they guided me to this place." I look past the wild spirit's gaze into the surrounding woods. The darkness beyond them gives way to the sun. The morning light is soft, casting pale greens and yellows through the tree branches.

"The ways of Dryads are strange." Herne shrugs. "I have little to do with them. Are you ready to give me your magic?"

A sound apart from the birdsong emerges from the woods before I can reply. It's the noise of dead branches breaking, snapping under the weight of unseen feet.

Both Herne and I look up to the same edge of clearing. Duchess Titania stands under the arch of two young saplings. Her platinum hair is loose and luminous in the dawn's growing gold. Her face is just as severe and composed as I remember, worlds beyond the dying Fae in the castle.

"You're alive?" I manage in my shock. Like everyone else, I assumed that Titania's disappearance meant her undoing. She'd only been waiting, deep in the wood's embrace, until her sickness retreated.

"Yes, and it seems that I'm not the only one." Titania glances back over her shoulder, waves to someone hidden in the trees. "We found him just a short while ago. He wandered into our camp, as if he was sleepwalking."

I barely hear her words as a new face breaks out of the foliage. Everything I've grown to love is still there: the clean slant of his jaw, his almond eyes, the light laugh lines that will only deepen with age, his smile, clear and bright. But there's something more now, something just beneath the skin that causes him to glow.

I sit still, stunned. The man I saw two nights ago, blue and caked with blood, could never become the one that stands here now.

"We thought the art of magic was lost to the mortals,

that the crown was simply a carrier of the power and not a wielder. We were wrong." Titania shakes her head. "Something woke it up in him."

Richard finishes the distance between us in three strides. When he reaches me he falls to his knees, brings his eyes down to mine. Two strong, steady arms pull me into him. Our chests press together, breathing in unison, and all doubt vanishes. This is my Richard.

"You're alive." My words are made of laughter and a great, joyous gasp—they don't feel like mine. "Greater Spirit. You're alive!"

He hugs me tighter, gentle fingers tugging through my hair. His breath curls over my neck, taking in my scent. My skin rejoices under it.

"How?" I pull back and the sight of him is new all over again. New and glorious. "I saw you dying."

"I don't know." He shakes his head. "I felt myself die. Or, I think I died. I don't know. But then I woke up and I was wandering through the forest. They found me."

I leave Richard's eyes and reenter the glade. Herne stands with his arms crossed. Titania and her company stare at us—utterly beautiful sculptures—both surprised and unreadable.

"Something woke up the blood magic," the duchess

offers. "It healed him. There are traces of it all over him. And even some on you," she adds, her eyebrow quirked.

The blood magic. Just what the ravens predicted. But what woke it? The kiss? We'd kissed before. What made that night so different?

"Tell me, has there ever been something between you two? A connection?" Titania looks between us, as if trying to read our short history together.

"The first time we met . . ." I pause. "There was something like electricity. I don't know. It wasn't magic necessarily."

"It's called a soul-tie. It's rare, uncommon, but it does happen. Your souls tied together. It also meant your magics connected. When Richard gave himself up for you, your magic responded. It sparked his to life."

I breathe in, the dawn air dewy and deep in my lungs. "So our—our connection saved him?"

"It takes true love to die for someone." The older Fae stares at Richard. Admiration, bare but bright, gilds her face as she takes him in. "That love, that bond you both share, saved him."

"What happened at the court?" I ask.

Titania's expression hardens. "There was no warning. There were too many soul feeders, hundreds upon hundreds. A whole swarm of them. In the end though, it was Mab who trapped us. She lured us into the throne room. It was then I saw the sickness in her eyes. I ran. The other court members held the way long enough for me to escape. I knew of the gathering at Windsor—I was there when Mab received your letter. I knew I had to come warn you, before her army came."

"This is all well and good, but I have yet to receive my payment," Herne interrupts. In all of his sulking silence I'd forgotten he was there.

I turn to face our growling ally, pulling myself to my full height. "My magic is yours. I don't want it anymore. I want to be with Richard, to be mortal."

Slight, silvery gasps from the other Faeries fill the clearing. Titania's expression goes sour then sharp, as if she wants very badly to say something. Richard is the only one smiling.

"So be it," Herne says in his typical brusque fashion.

My eyes squeeze shut and my whole body grows rigid as I brace myself. I don't know what to expect: pain, emptiness, or at least a little discomfort from the separation.

"Your Majesty, may I?"

Richard's hand slips out of mine to be replaced by Herne's rough gloves. My skin prickles like ant bites as he probes beneath it, seeking a good grasp on my magic. In the end, my power finds him. It flows toward Herne like a magnet. For a moment I feel like a ship off ballast, all heavy on one end. Then it leaves.

It isn't what I thought it would be. Not a draining but a weight shedding off of my chest. Weakness takes over. I feel cemented to the earth, a wizened old oak that's lost the desire even to sway. I open my eyes, find Richard. He stands close; his smile gives me something to cling to. It fills the strange absence of my magic.

Herne pulls away, all suddenness and jerk. Not all of my magic is gone. I feel the last dregs of it stirring in me. I look up at the woodlord, eyes narrowed.

"I've left you some," he explains.

"I want all of it gone!" My hand goes out again. "Please."

He shakes his head, the twin spiral of his horns dig into the deepening sapphire of the sky. "You should never forget what you were. Don't worry. It's not enough to stave off death. It's not even enough to do anything more than a minor spell."

He's right. There's hardly any magic left. It coats my insides like a thin film of oil. All of it gathered together is enough for a mending spell or something equally small. I blink and pass a few fingers over my stomach. The nausea is gone. All of it. It's been so long since I haven't felt the sickness.

"It worked?" Richard's question is soft, barely there.

I throw my arms around his neck and kiss him. This kiss is different from all of the others. It's pure, unhinged. There's no danger between our lips. I don't have to worry about breaking him like a doll. It's just him and me, together.

It's like I'm diving into him, swimming down, down and never coming up for air. And I never want to. His tongue grazes mine, inviting me deeper. To places I could never go in the presence of so many watchers. Still, these waters are full of sunlight and joy.

"Yes," I whisper back between breathless kisses. "I'm one of you now."

I don't let Richard out of my sight. Not when he returns to the castle to wake up his stunned sister. Not when the other Fae cluster around him in amazement. Not when we go to visit Breena's final resting place. I keep my hand always wrapped in his, afraid that if I let him go, I won't be able to get him back. That this will all prove a dream.

It's Titania who finally breaks us, drawing up beside us as we stand over my friend's grave. "Your Majesty, do you mind if I speak with Emrys alone?"

Richard doesn't reply; he only squeezes my shoulder and looks down at me.

"It's okay," I whisper, even though my insides are frantic to stay close.

I know he feels the same. There's reluctance in the way his arm slides from me.

"I won't be long," Titania promises.

Goose bumps plague my skin as soon as Richard pulls away. I shiver when a breeze whips past and cross my arms over my chest. I've never felt so bare before, stripped of magic and without Richard. It's a strange feeling, being so exposed and raw. But I won't trade it. Not if it means being with him. Being whole.

Titania waits until the king is beyond hearing. We're alone in the yard.

"You did well, Emrys."

I look at Titania. Her face is like Mab's used to be—unreadable and without cracks—encasing secrets. I turn her words over in my head. *Well. You did well.* That statement feels so far from the truth, now that I'm standing by Breena's grave.

"You protected the crown. You did what needed to be done. The Guard will be sad to lose your services." Titania pauses. "You're sure you won't reconsider? I have some sway with Herne. I can get him to return your magic."

How can I explain to her that none of this was for the Guard or the crown? That it was all for Richard? For a life and a future with him? "I—I can't."

Silence holds the duchess for a moment. The wind wreathes through her hair, sparking off brilliant glints of light. "Mab was in love once, you know."

Mab? I think back to the rabid creature in the woods, the one that scorned my love for Richard. "What?"

"She loved the Pendragon. It's one of the reasons she bound all of us to him. She wanted to keep him safe from Mordred and all the soul feeders that were out for his blood."

"Mab loved Arthur?" I can barely believe the words I'm saying. They sound absurd coming from my lips.

"She never told anyone. Not even him. I only knew because I plied the truth out of her. I thought an alliance with the mortals wouldn't be in our best interests and I told her so. It soon became clear that she'd let emotions interfere with politics." Titania sighs, a sound full of years and loss. "When Guinevere left to become the Pendragon's queen, it crushed Mab's heart. I thought it might be the end of her—but she was stronger than that."

Memories of Mab's wrath after Guinevere's choice return. I see them in a new light, from the other side of the looking glass. It wasn't Guinevere's loss that our queen was mourning, but her chance at King Arthur's heart.

"I suppose though, she always held a seed of resentment against the crown after that. As deeply as she buried it, she couldn't protect it from the madness. When it started stealing her reason, she took all that anger against the crown and started wreaking her revenge. As twisted as it was . . ." The duchess's words fade, eyes hazy with memory.

For some reason the betrayal seems easier to accept, now that there's some pain, some emotion behind Mab's actions.

"I'm staying with Richard," I tell her. "It's what I need to do."

"It's your choice." The way Titania says this makes me think she wished it wasn't.

A cough, brutal and filled with pain, racks Titania's body. I hear the blood rattling just behind her lungs.

Despite the closeness of Herne's woods, the Fae is too old to be here.

"You're going back north?" I ask, my question pointed. It would only do harm for her to stay, inviting the madness.

"It seems I must," she admits between coughs. "There will be much to tend to in light of Mab's unmaking. Herne has told me of the accord he struck with King Richard."

"Yes . . . the world will be very different now. For the better, I think."

"Such hope. Such youth." Hair like water-strung comets pours over Titania's shoulders as she laughs. The sound rings like a church bell, full of sorrow. "The world has always been spinning forward, evolving. . . . Only time will tell us what difference this will make. But I hope, youngling, I hope for all our sakes that you are right."

It's strange, looking at her and knowing our worlds are now severed. I won't be in the court when the new queen rises from the swell of courtiers. I will not watch as the strongest, most ruthless of the Fae first rests on Mab's earthy throne. But there's little doubt in me which Frithemaeg it will be. Titania's sway in the court is already strong. Not many will challenge her.

"Peace be with you, sister," I say.

She nods. "And with you."

Those words mark the end of my life as I know it. The end of Fae and the Guard. The end of spells and soul feeders. The end of forever.

There's a light on in Richard's window, clear and dazzling despite the late morning sun. I run to it.

Thirty-Four

Mortality is a sweet, terrible cup. I've learned to drink it slowly, day by day. The weeks seem longer than before, filled with complicated duties. Introducing magic into the mortal's world is no easy task, but it's one Richard has accepted wholeheartedly. They laughed at him, Parliament, the press, all of them. Then the Fae began appearing. The mortals were terrified at first. But after several silver-tongued speeches, Richard put most of their fears and misgivings to rest.

I've become an ambassador of sorts: the go-between for magic and mortal. My days are filled with reports from the surviving Fae and interviews with the clamoring press. It's hard without Breena. I miss her every day, and that ache refuses to go away.

Even in the middle of all this chaos, we still find time together: stolen, candlelit dinners, strolls down the river in the last long draws of autumn light. Some evenings we're too exhausted to talk much. We just enjoy each other's company: strokes of the arm, the brief, tingling meeting of lips.

This evening, walking along the Thames beneath the amber sunset, Richard's face looks especially agitated. I hook my arm into his, walking nimbly over the pattern of gray-brown stones.

"What's wrong?" I catch glimpses of shadows behind us, Richard's human security, following at a distance. And somewhere, on the other side of the river, the youngling Ferrin keeps watch.

"Long day." He shrugs, rakes his stray hairs back with his fingers. "We talked about the concept of magically infused technology in Parliament."

"Oh? How'd they take it?"

"There were lots of questions, of course. You'll have to go talk to them. They want to know about all of the different properties of magic: its reliability and safety. Things like that. I don't even know where to begin with that stuff."

"You? The most magical of us both?" I tease him with a jab between the ribs.

He jerks back, bumping into the river barrier. "Hey, now! I might have to hex you or something."

"I'd like to see you try." I smirk. Richard's magic,

though powerful, was never like mine. It works on its own terms. He hasn't quite gotten a handle on it.

"Will you see them?" he asks after our playful banter dies.

"If that would make it easier for you. But I'm going north to meet with Titania tomorrow to talk about the redistribution of the Guard and policing London for soul feeders. She's just been appointed the new queen." News I greeted with relief. Despite my past differences with Titania, her blunt ruthlessness is what it takes to run a kingdom of Fae.

"How did they decide that?"

"It's mostly an age thing. . . . But I think most of the older ones didn't want the job—it's a lot of responsibility."

"You don't have to tell me," he laughs.

"It's good it's not one of the older ones," I go on. "We don't want a repeat of what happened with Mab."

"Well, I'm glad it's Titania. I like her." Richard wraps his arm around me, steers me in his own direction.

"Where are we going?" I forget Titania and all of the meetings.

"I want to show you something."

We cross a street thick with traffic and walk along

the bridge over the river. It's soon obvious where we're going. Straight ahead is a structure of such power and elegance that all of London revolves around it: Parliament's clock tower.

We climb the limestone steps all the way to the tower's iconic clock face. Fire-flared, tangerine sun-rays fill the glass around the lacing black iron. I stand, admiring the web of light.

"My father used to bring me up here when I was a boy. He loved clocks. Loved the gears, all of it." Richard lets out a little laugh. There's only a hint of the old sadness in his eyes. "Of course, you probably remember that."

"I wasn't with you then," I whisper, entranced by the show of color. The light ebbs, fading into pale rose before the glass returns to frost white.

"That was just a sideshow," Richard tells me, and walks back to the stairs. "The real view is up here."

We climb a few floors above the cloudy clock face.

My heart aches at the height. I hold my breath and look out on the blooming night lights of London. One by one they flicker on, like harmonic, long-lived lightning bugs. The view is bittersweet: a breathtaking reminder that I'll never fly again.

"You showed me my kingdom once," Richard says, coming up behind me. He wraps his arms around my waist and gazes out onto the glowing landscape. "You showed me what I could be. You showed me how much you loved me and believed in me."

I clasp his hands tighter to me. Being up so high, without the reassurance of magic, has made me a bit dizzy.

He hugs me closer. "None of this would have happened without you, Emrys. It's just as much your kingdom as it is mine."

London's lights form patterns—an electric cosmos riddled with constellations. I squint my eyes and they become a blur. A single, blinding brightness.

"Do you remember what you asked me at Windsor? The night you made your choice?" Richard moves to my side. The wind bites my back where he once stood. "You made me promise that this—us—would be forever."

I turn from the smearing lights and stare at Richard. He's looking down at me, eyes smoky and intense.

"It's you and me now, Embers. And one day, someday, we'll tell the whole world that. But for now all I can offer you is this." His hand slips into the pocket of his trousers and pulls out a small velvet box. "It's a symbol of my promise."

The ring inside is jade and silver filigree. I gaze into the band, studying how its sterling curls over a base of minty, sea green. Deep in the fullness of my soul, I know Richard is right. No matter when that final end comes, we are forever.

"It reminded me of your eyes," he says after a moment.

"It's beautiful!" It truly is. Somewhere in the world a jeweler sleeps well, knowing his masterpiece has found a home. "It's enough. You're enough."

Richard closes the last few inches between us and kisses me. I bask in the taste of him—purely him. No panic, no worry. Just Richard. His sun spices and sea salt. The unyielding muscles of his arms under my palm. The warmth and love of his breath on my face.

His lips against mine are passionate, yet not frantic. There's no fear of discovery, no rogue magic behind the intimate brush of skin. It's simply us together: a sea of red hair swirling with his lion's mane. Milky skin on gold, freckles dancing everywhere. The night bathed with hushed whispers and secret smiles as we become closer to one.

In a brief break of passion, I catch sight of the stars and their luminance. They are few, scattered at this hour, twinkling and dancing to music those of us on earth can't hear. I think of Breena. Of all the others who've slipped up into the heavens. One day, in a few short decades, I'll join them.

Richard's fingers tighten around mine, tugging my thoughts back down to the clock tower. I smile and kiss him again. Big Ben chimes the hour, shaking the stones beneath our feet. The time is here and now. It is ours.

Acknowledgments

There are many, many people who helped this story bloom into a novel. Those who were there at its birth: my sister-in-law, Cara, who oh-so-innocently gave me an encyclopedia of faeries for Christmas; my dear friends, Helen MacMillan and Ferrin Gersbach, who read chapter two in its short-story form and demanded more.

Many more loved it through all of its awkward growth spurts: my amazing critique partner, Kate Armstrong, who rescued the second draft from a jerky prince and moist kisses; my college professor, Trish Ward, who answered my small mountain of emails asking for Old English translations; my agent, Alyssa Henkin, who dug this manuscript from the bottom of the slush and took a chance on it; my editor, Alyson Day, who took the diamond I'd already pulled from the rough and polished it even more; Wendy Higgins, who sustained me through revisions with lots of advice and digital chocolate.

There are also many, many people who helped me

grow from a writer into an author. Those who were there at my birth: my mom and dad, who taught me the power of faith and chasing my dreams, and who didn't freak out when I chose to spend their money on a creative writing degree.

Many more loved me through all of my awkward growth spurts: my writing teachers—Rene Miles, Marjory Wentworth, and Bret Lott—who showed me the strength of words and how to wield them; my friends and family all over the world, who challenge me to new heights every day; my brothers, Jacob and Adam, who accompanied me on imaginary adventures and let me kill them off with sword-sticks in the backyard; my husband, David, who goes on real-life adventures with me. Who shares my soul-tie.

And over it all: God, the giver of stories and life, who has blessed me with so much of both. Soli Deo Gloria.